BETRAYING SEASON

Marissa Doyle

SQUARE
FISH

HENRY HOLT AND COMPANY

New York

SQUARE
FISH

An Imprint of Macmillan

Library of Congress Cataloging-in-Publication Data
Doyle, Marissa.
Betraying season / Marissa Doyle.
p.   cm.
Summary: In 1838, Penelope Leland goes to Ireland to study magic and prove to
herself that she is as good a witch as her twin sister Persy, but when Niall Keating
begins to pay her court, she cannot help being distracted.
ISBN: 978-0-312-62916-8
[1. Witches—Fiction.   2. Magic—Fiction.   3. Courtship—Fiction.
4. Ireland—History—1837–1901—Fiction.   5. Great Britain—History—
Victoria, 1837–1901—Fiction.]   I. Title.
PZ7.D7758Bet 2009
[Fic]—dc22
2008040593

Originally published in the United States by Henry Holt and Company
Square Fish logo designed by Filomena Tuosto
First Square Fish Edition: 2010
www.squarefishbooks.com
10 9 8 7 6 5 4 3 2 1

LEXILE 820L

For Kate and Robin, and for Véronique, Jennifer, Tim, Sean, and everyone at Henry Holt Books for Young Readers, with my deepest thanks for your insight, guidance, talent, tact, and, most of all, your unswerving enthusiasm and support: How did I get so lucky?

For N and K and C, the most splendiferously, awesomely wonderful young adults on the planet

And always, for Scott

"Saints preserve us!"

The shocked cry and a wild jangle of harness yanked Pen Leland from her reverie. She gasped and looked up . . . and up. Two handsome gray carriage horses loomed, snorting and jerking as they stopped bare inches from her in the center of the cobbled street. One rolled its eyes and whinnied directly in her left ear.

She squeaked in alarm and leapt backward . . . into a puddle that immediately saturated her new blue kid boots.

"I'm *so* sorry. I should pay more attention when crossing the street, shouldn't I?" she panted to the driver of the gleaming maroon closed carriage when he had soothed his horses into silence. Poor man, he looked as shocked as she felt.

"Jesus, Mary, and Joseph, I'll say ye should!" The silver-haired coachman crossed himself as he spoke, then pulled a red handkerchief from his coat and mopped his brow with it. "What were ye thinkin' there, you shatter-witted—oh, pardon me." Pen saw his expression change as he took in the fashionable cut and material of her cloak and bonnet. "Are ye all right then, miss? I didn't mean—"

"No, it was my fault," Pen apologized again as she gingerly stepped out of the puddle. Something felt unpleasantly wet and heavy around her ankles. Had the hem of her mantle gotten soaked as well as her boots? Drat! Ally would be cross if she'd ruined them already.

Pen's former governess hadn't liked the thought of her running out to the apothecary without escort, but she herself was in no condition to stir from her bed. And besides, it wasn't as if this were London, where well-born young ladies did not go out unattended. But still, getting herself run down by a carriage her first week in Ireland wasn't good form. Ally might decide she couldn't go out alone here too, which would be simply horripilatious.

"Are your horses all right?" she continued.

A small knot of passersby had gathered on the pavement behind her, necks craning. When they saw that there was no dying victim or bloody corpse, they dispersed, looking mildly disappointed.

"Padraic, what was that? Why have we stopped?" called a woman's voice, sharp and imperious, from the carriage's open shutter.

"I'm sorry, yer ladyship. 'Twas a bit of a near thing with this young lady, but no harm's done." The coachman still looked white and scared, but Pen's concern for his horses seemed to have calmed his anger.

"Who?" The carriage door opened and a woman looked out. "Padraic, you must be more careful!"

"It wasn't his fault, ma'am. I stepped out into the street without looking." Pen bowed slightly to the woman and got an impression of quiet opulence from her maroon shot-silk mantle, which matched the color of the coach itself so exactly that Pen found herself wondering if she had given paint samples to her modiste. Her hat, in the new smaller, rounder shape, was as fashionable as Pen's.

"By Danu's veil! I don't care if you want to destroy yourself, girl, but you might have chosen someone else's carriage to throw yourself und—" The woman stopped abruptly as she met Pen's eyes.

Pen had plastered her face with a contrite smile, the one she'd always used on Ally back in the schoolroom when she hadn't finished her lessons for the day. But she felt it fade under the woman's fierce scrutiny.

Her slanting eyes were a piercing pale green, like sea ice, arresting but so cold that Pen felt goose bumps rise on the back of her neck. The rest of her face was striking too, with aristocratic features that skated the slender line between elegance and boniness. Only fine creases at the corners of her mouth and eyes indicated age in her otherwise flawless complexion. It was a beautiful face, and a forbidding one. Pen took an involuntary step backward—into the puddle again, unfortunately—as a cloud of perfume wafted over her like a breeze, musky, with hints of clove and spice.

"I do beg your pardon—" she tried to say through a suddenly dry mouth. But as soon as she spoke, the woman's face changed. All at once the frosty eyes glowed warm and the thin lips curved into a kindly smile.

"Why, you poor child! I'm grateful you weren't injured. Are you sure you're all right?" The woman actually climbed out of the carriage and, taking Pen's hand, surveyed her carefully.

"No, really, I'm fine. I'm sorry to have bothered you." Pen stood still in surprise as the woman reached out to adjust her bonnet. It was an unexpectedly intimate gesture from a stranger, especially one who had, seconds before, been looking at her as if she were a toad swimming in her teacup.

"You're white as a ghost. Please, let me drive you home. What if you should grow faint from your shock?" She tugged gently on Pen's hand.

"Oh, you don't have to do that. . . ." Pen trailed off. The woman's gaze pinned her, making her feel like a gaffed salmon waiting for the fisherman's net.

"No, I insist. I am sure it will rain again any minute now." The woman gestured to the small, heavily freckled boy who rode with the coachman and who had watched the proceedings with open mouth. He leapt down from his perch and held the door open, staring expectantly at Pen.

"Where can I take you, my dear?" the woman asked.

Pen gave herself a mental shake. Though a brisk walk to clear her head would have been nice right now, not to mention giving her skirts and boots a chance to drip dry, she couldn't refuse the legendary Irish kindness to strangers without being rude. Netted fish? Her imagination had been far too active lately. "To the Reverend Doctor Carrighar's house in Upper Ogham Street, thank you."

"Yes, of course." The woman nodded as if she had known what address Pen would give and gestured her into the carriage. "Padraic?"

"Yes, mum. Upper Ogham."

Pen started to settle on the back-facing seat, but the woman motioned her to sit facing front, then seated herself opposite.

"Here I am, carrying you off in my carriage without introducing myself. I am Lady Keating, my dear. And you must be a visitor to

Cork." She leaned toward Pen and gave her a gracious, toothy smile. Only her teeth belied the perfection of the rest of her; they were unpleasantly large and yellow in that delicate face.

"I'm Penelope Leland, ma'am. I'm visiting Ireland with my former governess." Pen wasn't sure whether she cared for Lady Keating's scent, overwhelming in the closed carriage; it was complex and exotic, and somehow disturbing. "She is married to Dr. Carrighar's son."

"How interesting. Yes, I am acquainted with the Carrighars. Which son?"

"The younger son. Michael." Pen was surprised for a moment. Were the Carrighars that well known in Cork?

"I see." Lady Keating's fine brows drew down in thought. "Leland . . . ," she murmured.

Pen answered her unspoken question. "My father is Viscount Atherston. We live at Mage's Tutterow, in Hampshire."

Lady Keating's smile flashed. "What a charming name! I have not been in Hampshire for many years. In fact, I've not been to England since my son left Oxford. Too busy here at home, alas. Are you enjoying your stay?"

Pen hesitated. How should she answer? Yes, because the country and the city alike were achingly beautiful and the people a delight? Or no, because her twin sister, Persy—Persephone, really—was back at home, happily married after her first season, and not here to giggle and talk and share everything with?

"It is quite—" she began, but Lady Keating stopped her.

"I am detecting a bit of homesickness, aren't I? Well, we must find some new friends to distract you. Come and take tea with me tomorrow, my dear. You shall tell me about your home and what you are learning here with your governess. Are you still in the schoolroom? I should have thought that a handsome young lady like yourself was past lessons."

"I had my first season in London last spring, ma'am. But I wanted to continue my studies, and my family agreed that I should accompany my former governess to Ireland for a visit."

"In London?" Lady Keating sat up straighter. "When were you presented?"

"In April, to Queen Adelaide. And again in July, at Vic—at *Queen Victoria's* first Drawing Room." Pen couldn't keep the warmth from her voice. But it wouldn't do to boast of their friendship. The order the queen had created, DASH—Dames at Service to Her Majesty—to reward Pen and Persy for saving her from an evil enchantment, was a secret. And besides, Persy was the one who had really saved Victoria. Pen still felt she didn't deserve to wear the little jeweled figure of a spaniel with a star at the end of its tail that they had designed as DASH's emblem, now tucked away in her handkerchief box.

"So you've seen her, then. How very interesting." For a fleeting moment, Lady Keating's face resumed that icy expression. It melted into a smile once more. "In that case, you must come and visit us tomorrow, and tell us all about it. Doireann and Niall—my daughter and son, of course—will be fascinated to hear your stories."

The carriage slowed and drew to a halt, and Pen saw the blue-painted front door of the Carrighars' house outside the window. But Lady Keating held her back.

"I shall send Padraic and the carriage for you. Will three o'clock do?"

Her voice was warm and pleasant. But Pen could hear the note of command underlying it and thought about pleading a prior engagement. Why was this rather alarming woman being so friendly to her, a total stranger who had badly spooked her horses?

"Dr. Carrighar is an old acquaintance and highly esteemed in this city. It would give me great pleasure to make his guest feel welcome here," Lady Keating continued, with a wistful smile.

Ah, so that was it. Having Dr. Carrighar's guest to tea would be a social coup. Well, why shouldn't she go? Lady Keating was probably just eager for London gossip. And it would be diverting to socialize a little, since Ally's condition was, of late, rather more miserable than "interesting." She would probably just spend tomorrow lying on the couch in the parlor again, a basin nearby in case her meager lunch of tea and toast made an unfortunate reappearance. Not surprisingly, her symptoms had kept them from undertaking any social engagements since their arrival.

"Thank you, Lady Keating. I should love to come."

"Wonderful! We shall see you at three, then." She glanced out the carriage window. "There, I told you it would rain again. Well, that's an Irish spring for you." She rapped on the shutter. "Sean! The umbrella for Miss Leland!"

Pen managed to climb the steps of the Carrighars' house without having her eye put out by the umbrella inexpertly wielded by the freckled boy, and paused to wave at the carriage. Just as the maid opened the door, she saw Lady Keating staring through the carriage window at her. There was a peculiar hint of satisfaction in her smile.

Niall Keating was reading by the drawing room fire when he heard his mother return from her round of visits. He slipped a ribbon into his place, then let the book carelessly drop to the floor as he yawned and stretched. The light was really too dim in here to read by, especially anything as long-winded (and in such small print) as a monograph on the effects of the new railroads on political stability in the German principalities. An interesting topic, though Niall cynically wondered if the author held stock in any rail companies. But what else did he have to do but read, stuck here in town under his mother's thumb? If she wouldn't listen to him, he'd have to take matters into his own—

"Niall! Doireann! I want you!" Mother called from the front hall.

Niall shrugged to himself and rose. He could picture her discarding her cloak, gloves, and bonnet like a python shedding its skin, knowing without a backward glance that one of the maids would be there to gather them up and take care of them. Niall could never decide whether to be amused or disturbed by his mother's feudal behavior.

She breezed into the drawing room and stopped short when she saw him. Her eyes sparkled like polished peridots set in the carved ivory of her face. *"Mo mhac,"* she cried, holding her hands out to him. "My son! Where is your wretched sister? I've news, important news! This might finally be the opportunity we've waited for!"

"His wretched sister is right here, *dear* Mother." Doireann stood with her back to the closed drawing room doors, wearing a malicious smirk. Niall knew she took great delight in her ability to move noiselessly through the house, terrorizing new housemaids.

Lady Keating ignored her sarcastic emphasis. "Ring for tea, Niall, darling, and come sit down. I think I've found a way out of the difficulties your sister has placed us in."

Niall was about to ask what difficulties, when he looked up at Doireann and saw her glare with cold green eyes nearly identical to their mother's. Relations between the two women had been worse than usual lately. His mother and sister were coldly polite to each other most of the time, but they reminded him of boxers, constantly circling each other, looking for an opening. Mostly their bouts were private. Niall was grateful for that fact.

Mother ignored Doireann. "We are expecting a guest for tea tomorrow. A young lady who seems to possess all the qualifications your sister once had. As soon as I saw her I knew—"

"Qualifications!" spat Doireann, as if it were a rude word. "Is that what I am? A set of attributes for your use?"

A knock stopped her. One of the downstairs maids, her face carefully blank, came in with a tea tray that she set down on the table by the sofa. Niall murmured his thanks to her, but she had already turned toward the door.

Mother and Doireann didn't even seem to notice her entrance; they sat rigid in their seats, eyes locked as if they still carried on their argument in words inaudible to others.

"Aren't you one to talk about being used, Mother?" Doireann continued after the door had closed behind the maid. She smiled a soft, dangerous smile.

Mother grew very white and still. "How dare you!"

"Besides, I'm stronger than I was before." Doireann tossed her black side curls proudly. "Is that what's bothering you, Mother dear? Having someone in the family who is as powerful as you?"

Unexpectedly, Lady Keating laughed. "As powerful as I? I am a *Banmhaor Bande,* and I doubt you'll ever be my equal, even if you are my heir." She stared at the teapot. It lifted itself and poured a thin brown stream of tea into a cup. The milk pitcher followed suit, and then the cup and its saucer drifted into her hand. The ancient ring that she wore, silver and green, seemed to glow faintly in the firelight.

Niall glanced at the door, but it was safely closed. Why did Mother have to do things like that, especially here at the town house? It was one thing for her to be so careless at her own house at Bandry Court; all the servants there were used to demonstrations of their mistress's unusual abilities, having worked there all their lives. How many times had he asked her to think before she did things like pouring tea without touching the pot? It would hardly do for a servant to drop dead of shock. But with the mood she was in, Mother would probably not be willing to listen to him.

He concealed his irritation as he usually did, though it was getting harder and harder to do. "What exactly is so important about this guest?" he asked as he poured a cup of tea by more usual means and passed it to Doireann, who was glaring at the teapot so hard that it should have shattered.

Mother's brow smoothed, and a smile Niall didn't like crept across her face. "Yes, our guest."

"Thank you, Norah," Pen said as the maid took her damp cloak and hat. Despite the boy and his umbrella, she had gotten soaked in the dash from Lady Keating's carriage to the door. Why did Irish rain seem wetter than the rain at home? "How is Mrs. Carrighar?" she asked.

"Well, her lunch left not long after you did, if you take my meanin', miss," the maid whispered with a grimace. "Cook's hopin' she'll take a little sago puddin' for her tea. She's in the parlor, a-layin' on the sofer. Mrs. Carrighar that is, not Cook."

Pen chuckled and crossed to the closed drawing room doors. She paused on the threshold to check the state of her skirts. Still damp around the hem from the puddle, but maybe Ally wouldn't notice. She opened the doors a crack and peeked in.

Ally—Melusine Allardyce Carrighar, really, but Ally for as long as Pen could remember—lay on the green brocade sofa, her pale face borrowing something of its color. Her dark hair was loose on her shoulders, and a woolen throw covered her dressing-gown-clad figure. Seeing her with her hair down and still in her nightclothes in the middle of the day—Ally the indefatigable, the energetic—was disconcerting. If this was what childbearing did to women . . . Pen shook her head.

As Pen watched her, Ally stirred and, without opening her eyes, said, "Good afternoon, Pen. Please inform Cook that I loathe sago."

"You said that about dry toast and weak tea, too." Pen slipped through the doors, shutting them behind her. "How are you feeling?"

Ally opened one eye and stared at her balefully. "How do you think I feel?" She paused and sniffed. "Are you wearing perfume?"

"Does it bother you? A lady offered me a ride home in her carriage and she'd rather bathed in it, I think. Is it so bad? Shall I go change my gown?"

"No, it's not that bad. It's just . . . strange." Ally shivered and drew her robe closer around her throat.

Pen pointed at a straight chair near one of the windows. It scuttled obediently across the room and settled itself next to Ally's couch.

"The apothecary said he didn't have anything for queasiness that you hadn't already tried. Isn't there *anything* the Carrighars can do to help you?" She seated herself and took Ally's limp hand.

"I set Michael to reading through my grimoires to see if there weren't any charms we could try, and Dr. Carrighar tried two spells this afternoon that only made things worse. Fortunately, their effects were temporary." Ally shut her eyes again, as if to block out an unpleasant memory. "His strength is theoretical magic, anyway, but I don't have the heart to remind him of that fact."

"Really?" Pen smothered a grin. "What did he do to you?"

"You sounded distinctly like your brother when you said that. Unlike young boys, true ladies do not take a prurient interest in unpleasant bodily functions, Penelope." Ally opened both eyes that time and raised one eyebrow at Pen. "You just wait until it's your turn to start a family."

"As I'm not married nor even acquainted with many eligible gentlemen right now, I think children are hardly a concern for me," Pen said with a small sigh. "One does require a husband first, so I understand. And I'm not here to find a husband. I'm here to do what I should have done before and learn magic."

"You should have stayed with your sister at Galiswood and studied with her," Ally reminded her gently. "Then you could have gone into London right at the start of the season and accomplished both."

"I know I could have. Persy wrote that Lochinvar was coming along well with his magic lessons. But I—I didn't want to. Three's a crowd, you know." Pen looked down at her hands, folded in her lap.

Her sister had been wandering around in a veritable pink-tinged cloud ever since her marriage to their neighbor back at home, Lochinvar, Viscount Seton. While visiting them last November, Pen had more than once come upon them entwined in an embrace that made her blush and back away on tiptoe. She was thrilled that Lochinvar and Persy were so obviously in love, especially after the rocky start to their courtship. But it wasn't always comfortable to be around two people so engrossed in each other.

Ally was right, though. Persy could have tutored her very well. Since their magical escapades in London last May saving Princess

Victoria, Persy had realized that she was, indeed, a powerful witch, as powerful as Ally was.

Well, she'd studied and practiced enough all these years. If Pen had worked half as hard at her magic, she might have been of some help in saving the princess. Instead, Persy had been forced to rescue *her*, too.

"You've come a long way with your studies here. I saw you summon that chair just now." Ally's voice broke into her thoughts. "It took very little effort, didn't it? This time last year, you would have twisted your face and turned red before the chair even twitched."

"Oh, pooh." Pen made a mock-indignant face.

"And I know how hard it was for you to accept Michael as your teacher since I've been ill," Ally added, reaching out and taking Pen's hand.

"Well . . . I've gotten over it, I think." It *had* been hard at first. Michael Carrighar had been in on the plot to bewitch Princess Victoria. Switching from viewing him as an enemy to accepting him as her beloved Ally's husband had taken time. But she had learned to because Michael's devotion to Ally was as evident as Lochinvar's to Persy.

"I know you have, and we're both grateful," Ally murmured.

"Grateful for what?" Michael himself poked his head around the door just then and grinned at them.

"That human gestation is not as long as equine." Ally made a face at him as he came into the room, followed by Norah with the tea tray.

Pen smiled and gave up her seat by Ally to him.

"How's my dearest wife? Oh, look, Norah's brought us an excellent tea," he said, nodding his thanks to Pen as he sat. His odd eyes—one blue, one brown—twinkled at her.

Ally peered up at him. "I'm perfectly dreadful, thank you. And do not think that you are going to convince me with your appalling cheerfulness to eat anything right now."

"Would I do that to you?" He pulled a hurt face and smoothed her hair back from her forehead.

"In a moment, and you know it." But Ally turned and softly kissed his hand.

Pen sat back in one of the armchairs by the fire and listened to them banter. It must be wonderful to feel cherished and loved and so part of each other. Michael was actually talking Ally into sitting up and taking a few sips of sugared ginger tea. No one else could have done that, not even her.

Were all happily married couples like this, finishing each other's sentences half the time? She felt a pang of—not jealousy, but of exclusion. Three was a crowd here, too, just as it had been at Galiswood.

"You shall be doubtless pleased to hear," proclaimed a voice from the doorway, "that I have at least discovered the reason for your debilitation, my dear."

Dr. Carrighar, Michael's father, nodded solemnly at them as he came in and took a seat by the fire opposite Pen.

"I think we already knew the cause," Michael muttered to Ally.

"Shhh," Ally murmured back, but a faint pink stole into her cheeks.

Pen rose and went to the table to pour a cup of tea for the doctor. He thanked her as he took it and stretched his legs, clad in their old-fashioned hose and breeches, toward the fire. The silver buckles on his shoes gleamed in the firelight.

There was a great deal of the old-fashioned about the Reverend

Doctor Seamus Aloysius O'Donnell Carrighar. Pen often wondered why he didn't still powder his hair, for much else about him seemed to be fixed in the last century. Once she had gotten used to those eccentricities, though, Pen realized that Dr. Carrighar was extraordinary in other ways as well. For one thing, his magical knowledge exceeded Ally's as much as Ally's exceeded hers. Ally's statement that his practical magic lagged behind his theoretical had more to do with her nausea-induced peevishness than reality.

"I suppose I should be glad. But right now I'm more interested in hearing what can be done about it," Ally said in a louder voice, with a hint of her former crispness.

"Well, my dear, it would seem that the offspring of magic-using persons who will themselves, *post utero*, be potent witches—or wizards, as the case might be—frequently cause maternal distress and discomfort whilst *in utero*. Something to do with the latent powers of the child engendering an antagonistic effect on those of the mother, with maternal indisposition being the result. In other words, you're ill because your babe will follow in her parental, and grandparental, footsteps, and be a cracking good witch. Isn't that splendid?" Dr. Carrighar beamed.

Pen smiled behind her teacup. Dr. Carrighar's way of speaking had taken some getting used to.

"Just marvelous," Ally agreed, with less enthusiasm. "And in the meantime?"

Dr. Carrighar's smile dimmed. "In the meantime you might, er, try some of Cook's sago pudding."

Ally groaned and fell back against her pillow.

"Or the ginger tea. Ginger is excellent for stomach ailments. . . ." Dr. Carrighar trailed into silence at a look from Michael.

It seemed a good time to change the subject. "Speaking of tea," Pen said brightly, "I've been invited to tea tomorrow. By an acquaintance of yours, sir," she added, turning to Dr. Carrighar. "After I frightened her horses this afternoon, she decided to take a liking to me."

"She? What she is this?"

"A Lady Keating. She seemed quite interested to hear that I was your guest. I got the impression she asked me more out of respect to you than anything else."

"Nuala Keating?" Dr. Carrighar frowned and glanced at Michael. "How did you meet her, Penelope?"

Pen explained about the near-accident that afternoon. She watched Dr. Carrighar stare at the buckles of his shoes as he listened.

"And what did you think of her?" he asked when she had finished.

"I don't know. She was a little strange—very cold at first, then very friendly. She seemed quite interested in hearing any gossip from London. Said she hadn't been there since her son was at university."

"No, she wouldn't have. That would have been about when Lord Keating fell ill. Lady K. has been running the estate ever since. Hmmph." Dr. Carrighar continued to study his shoes, brows drawn.

"Is there anything wrong with her?" Ally asked. "Would it be proper for Pen to visit her? Society is less formal and constrained here, I understand, or I wouldn't allow her out on her own. But still—"

"No, no, she's perfectly respectable. Her family's quite ancient. She has a title that predates Christianity in Ireland, though it has no real meaning in these modern times. And no scandals, not of recent vintage, anyway. It's just . . . oh, nothing. Penelope is a mostly grown woman now. She should be able to choose her own friends and acquaintances."

"No *recent* scandals?" Pen sat up straighter in her chair. "So there are some?"

"Good heavens! The statute of limitations on gossip never runs out, does it?" Dr. Carrighar shook his head and pursed his lips primly, but Pen caught the twinkle in his eye.

"Not when you drop tantalizing hints, it doesn't." She grinned at him over her teacup. "Come on, sir, you can't stop now."

"Oh, it's nothing particularly interesting." The older man shrugged. "Just the usual chatter about a child who looks nothing like his reputed father."

"You mean Niall Keating," Michael said. "Yes, I remember hearing about that."

"Hearing about what?" Even Ally, who had often warned Pen about the evils of gossip, looked interested now.

Dr. Carrighar gave her a roguish glance. "Thou too, Melusine? Very well. Lady Keating's husband was—is, I suppose I should properly say, as he's more or less alive—"

"More or less?" interrupted Pen.

"He was stricken some years ago and lost use of his legs," Michael replied. "He's been confined to a chair ever since."

Dr. Carrighar harrumphed loudly. "As I was saying . . . Lord Keating was a third son and, as such, was sent into the army. His father purchased him a commission as a staff officer in the Fifteenth Dragoons, the Duke of Cumberland's regiment."

"The wicked duke," Ally murmured.

"So it is said, if you give any credence to the rumors that he murdered his valet over a woman and that he's plotting to kill his niece Queen Victoria before she marries and has an heir so that he can inherit the crown. But I doubt he's any more wicked than the rest of old King George's sons. I've always thought people feared him because he has more brains and ability than the rest of his brothers and actually takes an interest in politics rather than in mistresses and racehorses. Well, he knew he'd inherit the throne of Hanover after King William's death, since Victoria could not, being female. Remember, intelligence is what makes people dangerous, my dear." He waggled one eyebrow at Pen.

"Anyway, it's rumored that the duke took an especial interest in his officer's beautiful young wife. The affair ended only when Keating was called back to Ireland after both his elder brothers' unexpected deaths, making him heir to the title. Her son was born six months after their return, and as he grew up, there were plenty to comment on his striking height and handsome, er, Hanoverian features, rather different from his short, dark father's."

"My goodness, how romantic!" said Pen. If the doctor's story was true, that would make Lady Keating's son—Niall, was it?—first cousin to the queen. She would have to pay attention tomorrow and see if there was a resemblance between them.

Dr. Carrighar snorted. "Romantic, my foot. But everything is romantic to young ladies these days, isn't it?"

Pen put out her tongue at him.

He chuckled. "That's better. I prefer you acerbic to gushing, child. And speaking of acerbic, perhaps you might find time after tea to enumerate the main points of the chapters of John Scotus Eriugena I asked you to read."

"Yes, sir," Pen agreed meekly. Dr. Carrighar had lately begun to take over her tutoring from Michael, so that Michael could devote more time to reestablishing his interrupted university career. Good thing that she'd read the chapters. It didn't do to neglect Dr. Carrighar's assignments.

"Well . . . ," Ally said slowly. "Since it's just a rumor of scandal, and an old one at that, I suppose you may go tomorrow. It was kind of her to send a carriage for you. What will you wear? Your brown cashmere with the embroidered chemisette?"

"Perhaps," Pen replied, and for a moment felt guiltily glad that Ally was, for now, a semi-invalid. She was going to wear something far more stylish than that demure brown dress. She'd have to, to not be completely eclipsed by Lady Keating.

Pen ignored the rest of the tea conversation and brooded. She'd enjoyed the parties and balls of her season last year. But so much of her time at them had been taken up by being Lochinvar's confidant as he pined after Persy that she'd not been able to pay much attention to other young men. It would be diverting to have a social life once again and perhaps meet some.

You're just going for an afternoon call, goose, she reminded herself. *Don't build it up into something it isn't.*

But she couldn't help being a little excited. Living with the Carrighars was undoubtedly stimulating to the mind, but not entirely satisfactory in other ways. Lady Keating had been right—she *was* lonely. Meeting new people tomorrow would be fun. Especially since one of them was reputed to be a tall, handsome young man.

2

Niall Keating pulled the collar of his coat higher around his neck. It was sunny today but brisk, more January than March, and the wind off the river Lee penetrated even the thickest wool as if it were a gauze shawl. Damn Mother anyway for sending him out for a walk, just so that he could make a grand entrance for her guest's benefit. And damn himself, for agreeing to go and then forgetting to wear a hat in a wind like this.

But it would serve Mother right if he came back with a red nose and chapped cheeks. Then they would see how impressed this girl was with Lady Keating's fair-haired son.

The childish crankiness of his thoughts made him even more irritable. Somehow all his recent interactions with his mother left him feeling this way. He found a sheltered shop doorway and consulted his watch. Another half hour. Did he dare slip into a pub, just to kill the time? Anything would be better than freezing his arse off out here.

He ducked into the next pub he came to—so dark and low-ceilinged that he had to keep his head bowed as he entered—and asked the landlord for tea. Mother would have his guts for garters if he came home with whiskey on his breath, and he loathed beer. A year of studying in Germany had seen to that.

Niall sat down in a quiet corner away from the other patrons, where he could be alone with his thoughts. The aproned landlord arrived a moment later with a steaming mug.

"Care for a bit o' something to flavor that, m'lord?" he asked with an ingratiating smile and a keen look at Niall's polished boots and well-tailored coat.

"No, thank you," Niall returned politely, and handed him a coin. "And I'm not a lord."

"Hmmph," said the man, and dug in his apron for change. "You're not one o' Father Mathew's converts, are ye, who're swearing off the drink? Thirty breweries an' ten distilleries in this city are providin' bread for the tables of their workers, an' he wants everyone to stop having a pint now an' again. Temperance, he calls it. Trying to put honest publicans out o' business is what *I* call it."

"No. I just need to keep a clear head."

"Aye, well, sometimes a nip of the whiskey can aid in clearing the head something marvelous." The landlord winked broadly.

Niall smiled and shook his head. "Thank you anyway. Keep the change."

"Thank *you*, sir!" He patted his pocket and scuttled back behind his counter before Niall could change his mind. Which was just what Niall had intended. He was in no mood for chitchat just now.

He leaned his head against the settle's high back and stared across the room at the peat turves glowing on the hearth. Why shouldn't he overpay for weak tea from a not-too-clean cup? What else could he do with the pocket money Mother gave him? He sighed and curved his fingers around the earthenware mug to warm them.

What was Mother up to this time? What could yesterday's chance meeting with an unknown young Englishwoman have to do with her schemes to unite him with his real father?

It was on his fourteenth birthday that Mother had told him the truth of his birth. She'd called him into her boudoir and showed him the portrait that went everywhere with her, from house to house, packed with the greatest of care. It was of a handsome, martial-looking man with large side-whiskers and a chest full of ribbons and decorations.

It had made Niall giddy at first to think that his real father was a royal duke, and that his grandfather had been the king of England. Mother had played on that reaction, filling him with stories of the glorious future that awaited him when he was grown and could take his place at his true father's side. He had gone back to Harrow and studied hard, had gone on to Oxford and studied harder. He'd learned to fence and to shoot and spent a year studying military sciences with a retired drill sergeant from the duke's own regiment, who'd wept like a sentimental old woman at times because of Niall's resemblance to his former colonel.

But an Oxford degree hadn't been enough. With the ink barely dry on his diploma, Mother had summoned him to the duke's portrait once more and told him he was going to have a grand tour. For three long years, he'd toured Europe, ending up in Hanover for a course of study at the University of Göttingen. By the time he was through, though, he had changed. Or maybe being away from Mother for so long had made a difference.

"I don't care how much I look like the duke," he'd tried to argue with her on his return. "What use will he have for a son he can never claim? I have a home and an inheritance in Ireland. I should be learning how to live my life here, not chasing a dream."

Mother had refused to listen, however. "His only other son is a blind invalid. When the duke sees you, how he'll rejoice! With your education and experience of foreign life, you will be invaluable to him one day." She'd smiled at him through sudden tears. "His very image! So tall and straight and fair. . . . Be patient a little longer, *mo mhuirnin*. Now that you are a man, I must write to the duke. We shall go to England later this summer and bring you to him."

But no summons to London had ever arrived. Mother's face grew closed and stony when Niall asked her about it. A quiet desperation slowly grew in his mind as they waited through summer and into autumn and, with it, anger.

Niall frowned, shifting in his hard seat, and took another gulp of tea. Was he going to wait forever for his life to begin? He was twenty-four now. No matter what happened with the duke, he would still inherit the ancient title of Baron Keating of Loughglass from Papa, as well as the nameless but more-ancient-still lordship of his mother's lands at Bandry Court.

Sometimes he thought about going back to Loughglass, where Papa lived his invalid's life, being wheeled around the gardens and conservatory by stolid male attendants. But that wouldn't help. What would he say to him? *Papa, I'm not really your son, but it's time I started acting like I was?* Niall didn't think so. Besides, when had Papa ever had any control over Mother? Even if he once had, what could he do now?

It was time Niall embraced his Irish heritage. And more than time he slipped out from under his mother's thumb.

But how? Mother had brought him up to be something other than a provincial, if wealthy, Anglo-Irish baron. Brought him up, hell—had *drilled* into him that one day he would take his place at the side of a royal father he'd never known. She held the purse strings and the power in their family. Niall knew she wanted what she thought was the best for him, and he had done as she had asked, studying and improving himself while other young men of his age and class wasted their time and money with drinking, gambling, and wenching. And he couldn't help being at least a little intrigued at the thought of meeting his dynamic, powerful father.

So what should he do? Listen to his mother and hope her plans for him came to fruition, or go back to Loughglass and the man he called Papa, and take over the running of the estate?

There was, however, one more point to consider. One did not cross Nuala Keating lightly. Pouring tea without touching the teapot was the least of her powers. He knew she loved him deeply and completely, but if he were to deny her. . . . He shrugged his shoulders uncomfortably. Restlessness and rebellion thrashed and simmered beneath his always-polite exterior, like a dozing volcano slowly rumbling awake. The only difference between him and his sister Doireann was that she let her frustration with Mother out, while he kept his bottled in.

But maybe all this was about to change.

Niall took a gulp of tea and looked at his watch again. Ten minutes. He'd better start back for home before their guest got too alarmed by Doireann. He rose, nodded to the landlord, and stalked back out into the March wind.

Mother hadn't given him many hints about who this girl was, only that it was important for him to make a good impression on her and, if possible, to pique her interest. It was a far cry from her usual admonishments whenever he took an interest in a pretty girl.

"You must save yourself for someone worthy of you," she would whisper fiercely to him if he danced more than once with the same girl at a ball. Hmmm. Could this girl have something to do with the duke? A court connection, perhaps? Someone who might be used to introduce him to his true father?

He bloody well hoped so, before he did something desperate.

"There ye are, sir."

Niall was brought up short. Back already. Padraic the coachman was loitering on the pavement outside the house, communing with his horses still hitched to the carriage. He touched his cap respectfully as he spoke to Niall. "Her ladyship's opened the curtains o' the drawin' room. That means she'll be wantin' you in there whenever you're ready, sir. She told me to tell you as much."

"Thank you, Padraic," Niall replied, and turned toward the front steps. Mother hadn't said whether this girl was pretty or not. He hoped she was. It would help him sound at least nominally sincere when he did his best, on Mother's orders, to beguile Miss Penelope Leland.

Pen sat stiffly in her chair in Lady Keating's green and gold drawing room. It wasn't easy paying calls on her own. Last year she and Persy had always made formal calls with Mama, and if it was sometimes difficult not to be swamped in her formidable wake, it was also possible to let Mama do all the talking and fade into the wallpaper if she felt like it.

But she couldn't get away with that today. As the only guest, she was the focus of two pairs of very green eyes as she sipped

Lady Keating's black china tea from a delicate porcelain cup and answered questions about her London season.

At least Lady Keating was being entirely charming today, so much so that Pen had begun to wonder if she had imagined her initial coldness yesterday afternoon. Lady Keating had greeted her with a kiss when she arrived and slipped an arm about her waist to guide her into the drawing room.

"You will have to excuse Niall. I told him to be on time, but he's late, the rogue," she laughed after presenting Doireann. "If there's not any tea left for him by the time he returns, he'll have to go without."

"I rather doubt that," Doireann murmured, gazing at nothing in particular. "Niall is not accustomed to stinting his appetites."

Goodness! What a thing to say about one's own brother! Pen murmured something noncommittal and saw Lady Keating shoot her daughter a dark look.

After twenty minutes of conversation, Pen still hadn't been able to figure Doireann Keating out. She was a shorter, more fey version of her mother, with her green eyes and dark hair, but lacked Lady Keating's self-assurance. And though Doireann's manner was pleasant, if reserved, Pen could sense something underlying her civility. She reminded Pen of the lions in the Zoological Gardens in London, placidly dozing in the sun but always with one eye cracked open, waiting.

"And your twin sister was married at the end of her first season?" Doireann was saying now. "How very efficient of her."

Pen couldn't help laughing, though Doireann's word choice was ever-so-slightly barbed. "Believe me, it wasn't her plan at all. She would rather have stayed home with her books and studies. I was far more eager than she to go to London."

"Her husband-to-be must have been very persuasive, then." Lady Keating smiled.

"No, not particularly. He was nearly as shy as she was. I spent weeks trying to convince him to talk to her." Pen smiled too, but a little sigh escaped her.

Lady Keating leaned forward and patted her hand. "At the sacrifice of your own pleasure, perhaps? Surely you weren't so busy playing matchmaker for your sister that you had no chance to find a handsome young man to lose your own heart to?"

"Well, er. . . ." Blushing, Pen took refuge in a sip of tea. Was she that obvious? And that selfish?

Persy hadn't been selfish. She'd concealed her search for the kidnapped Ally from Pen last year, so as not to get Pen in trouble and hurt *her* matrimonial chances with Lochinvar, who she thought admired Pen. But their comedy of errors had been resolved, and Pen was sincerely glad for Persy and Lochinvar. She was only eighteen, after all—well, nineteen, come May. There would be plenty of time to meet eligible young men next season, after she'd studied—

The drawing room doors flew open just then, banging back against the wall as if blown by a gust of wind. Startled, Pen turned in her chair.

A tall man strode across the room, hatless but still wearing his greatcoat. He carried a scent of fresh, cold air and peat smoke with him, and his fair hair was tousled and windblown above strong, regular features.

"Sorry I'm late, Mother. My watch needs to go to the clockmaker's shop for a cleaning, I think." His voice was low and musical, with a faint hint of Irish lilt underlying it.

Lady Keating shook her head in remonstrance, but her face was lit by a warm smile. "Naughty boy. Come and meet my guest. Miss Leland, this is my son, Niall Keating."

Pen looked up into deep blue eyes set under straight brows. The eyes widened as they met hers, then crinkled in a slow smile that made her heart skip a beat.

"Miss Leland," he said, bowing and clicking his heels. "Do forgive my lateness. Though I'm not sure I forgive myself, now that I see what I've been missing."

"Yes, Mother did order a spectacular tea today, didn't she?" Doireann delicately brushed a crumb of cream cake off her sleeve.

Niall Keating shrugged off his coat, took the empty chair next to Pen, and accepted a cup of tea from his mother. Neither he nor Lady Keating seemed to notice that Doireann had spoken.

Pen tried not to as well, but she couldn't help feeling stung. Why was Doireann being so . . . so unfriendly to a stranger? Niall's apology had been charming and gallant, delivered in a caressing tone that made her insides do a quick happy flutter. But his sister's reply had made the sweetness suddenly seem overdone, like too-ripe fruit.

She stole a glance at Niall. The corners of his mouth quirked the faintest bit as he caught her looking at him. With a shrug, he rolled his eyes upward, then gave her a small, conspiratorial smile.

Pen stifled the urge to giggle. Niall Keating resembled his sister in neither looks nor temperament, it seemed.

"Are you fond of walking, Mr. Keating?" she asked politely.

"I am when it isn't raining," he replied. "Which isn't often in Ireland, as you might have noticed, so I must take my walks when I can. Have you been in town long?"

Pen let him draw her into polite conversation about her visit and about her home in England. It was all such familiar territory, this courteous tea-table talk, that she was able to make the required responses with just half her attention, which allowed her to focus the rest on examining this splendid young man.

She could well believe the rumors Dr. Carrighar had mentioned concerning his paternity. She had seen portraits of the various sons and daughters of George III in Princess Sophia's apartments in Kensington Palace last year and remembered the princes as being handsome, if fleshy, with fair hair and sleepy-lidded, come-hither blue eyes. Niall Keating would not have looked out of place among them. But his mother's elegance of feature had refined the hearty Hanoverian in him—if the rumors were true, that is—and made him more attractive still. Pen hoped she wasn't staring, but she couldn't help it. He would have set the feminine hearts of London ablaze just by strolling through a ballroom and smiling that lazy white smile.

"Miss Leland is here to further her studies, Niall," Lady Keating interjected. "She is staying with her former governess, who has married Dr. Carrighar's son."

Niall's eyebrows rose. "You're a scholar? How interesting. But London's loss is our gain. Dr. Carrighar has a fearsome reputation as St. Kilda's most carnivorous tutor. I hope he doesn't chew you up as well."

"He hasn't yet, though I have noticed the occasional smear of blood in his study after a tutorial. But only one or two of his scholars have required medical assistance while I've been there," Pen said, and felt faintly dizzy when Niall flashed a grin at her.

"Perhaps he draws his teeth for bouts with you, Miss Leland, lest the battle be too unequal," Doireann said with a sugary smile.

Pen pretended to consider this. "No, I don't think so. Though petticoats might provide some protection, I like to think that it is my own bite that has kept me unscathed so far."

"I might venture to guess that you can give as good as you get, Miss Leland," Niall added, a note of laughter in his voice.

"Within the bounds of maidenly propriety, of course," she replied. Oh, this was fun! She hadn't been able to dance verbally with anyone like this since she'd left Persy behind at home. And the admiration she saw in Niall's eyes made it even sweeter.

But she was suddenly aware of a shift around the table, as if the air had somehow changed. She looked up and saw Doireann glance at her mother with a sardonic lift to her eyebrows. Lady Keating frowned at her daughter, then bent forward and placed her hand on the teapot.

"Please ring for the maid, Doireann," she commanded. "The tea has gone cold."

Niall leaned a little closer to Pen. "That's not all that has," he murmured out the corner of his mouth as he reached past her for a cake.

"Shh," she whispered back, but it was hard not to laugh at his conspiratorial wink.

"What was that?" Doireann asked sharply, half risen from her chair.

"I was just commenting to Miss Leland that we seem to have gone back to winter with this cold wind," he said blandly, straightening and biting into a pastry.

"It did seem to go right through my cloak today," Pen agreed, matching his tone. She tried not to meet his eyes, lest she giggle.

"It's an oceanic wind here, Miss Leland," Lady Keating explained.

"London modistes don't know how to defeat it. I must bring you to mine so that you can order an Irish cloak. We can't have you freeze."

Doireann returned to her seat. "Miss Leland would look quite handsome in one," she observed. Pen remembered the lions, amiable one minute and snarling the next.

Then the maid came in, bringing a fresh pot of hot tea, and conversation returned once more to conventional lines. Except now Pen was even more aware of Niall Keating next to her, as if he had bound her to him with that quick wink and their shared humor. She felt his eyes on her through the rest of that visit, his regard almost as tangible as the Irish cloaks Lady Keating had spoken of; she was warmed, rather than alarmed, by his attention. When she stole glances at him, he was sitting back in his chair, stroking his curling sidewhiskers absentmindedly as he watched her, the way one would pet a cat. It was an endearing gesture.

Perhaps too endearing. This was *not* why she had come to Ireland. She needed to keep her mind off handsome Irish men and on Irish magic.

But it wasn't just his looks. It was the expression in his eyes that made her feel as if they already knew each other very well. She got the feeling that if they were to sit there without speaking, even their silence would be companionable.

A friend. She missed Persy and her chuckleheaded brother, and she was looking for friends. She had rather hoped Doireann could become a friend. Now that she'd met her, though, Pen wasn't at all sure she cared to spend more time than was necessary with her. But Doireann's brother . . .

When the maid came to announce that the coach was ready to

bring Pen home at the hour she'd specified, Lady Keating rose and took Pen's hands. "Must you go so soon?"

"I don't like to leave Ally—I mean, Mrs. Carrighar—alone too long while she's feeling unwell," Pen explained. Lady Keating's hands were warm on hers. She wore a curious ring on her right hand, made of heavy silver wire elaborately braided around a cloudy, pale green stone.

Lady Keating tsked in sympathy. "Such a pity she's ill. Is it our climate?"

"No. That is, I expect she'll be over it in a few months," Pen replied without thinking, then winced inwardly. Had that been too bald a reference to Ally's condition in front of strangers? She withdrew her hands from Lady Keating's and pulled her gloves on. Then Niall unobtrusively helped her on with her mantle, and she forgot her embarrassment in awareness of his proximity and warm, clean scent.

Lady Keating nodded. "Of course. Then it is all set. I shall pick you up at two on Thursday and bring you to my dressmaker so we can order you a proper cloak, and bring you back here for tea again so that Mrs. Carrighar can have her rest."

Pen blinked. When had that been decided? But now Niall Keating was bowing to her again, his eyes sparkling.

"It sounds good to me, Mother," he said cheerfully. "May I see you out to the carriage, Miss Leland?"

When Niall came back into the drawing room, Lady Keating was pacing the room, her face aglow. "You were perfect, my love! Simply perfect!" she cried, taking his hands and squeezing them. "Miss Leland could not help but be smitten with you."

"It didn't seem to be too wearing a task for the poor boy, Mother." Doireann rolled her eyes.

"No, it was rather a pleasant one," Niall said easily. Sometimes agreeing with Doireann was the best way to shut her up. "Now that it's done, may I ask again why I was supposed to be so charming to her?"

"It's not done yet, my dear one. It's only just started. I didn't know that her governess was ill. That will make it even easier." Mother looked at him, and her smile faded into sternness. "I want Miss Leland so in love with you by May that she'll do anything for you."

"What? In love?" Niall suddenly felt wary. "Why? What will she need to do for me?"

"*Mo mhac ionuin.*" Mother pulled him across the room and pushed him into the sofa. "My dear, *dear* son. Please, trust me. We need Miss Leland's help. What better way to get it than to make her love us?"

"Her help in what? Mother, what is going on?" He started to rise, frowning, but she pushed him back down again with just a glance.

"Shhh. All in good time, darling. All in good time. Just keep going on as you have begun, and all will be well."

Doireann stretched and yawned. "Oh, for God's sake, Mother. Why don't you just put an attraction spell on the chit and save the poor boy the trouble of being charming?"

"Don't be an idiot." Mother's eyes narrowed dangerously. "You know very well why that wouldn't work. I need her to come to us of her own free will, not under influence of a spell."

Niall took a deep breath. "I'm not sure I like the sound of this. It's one thing to befriend her. It's another matter entirely to set out to entrap her."

"Niall, Niall! Miss Leland is a grown woman with a season's worth of experience in matters of flirtations and love affairs. She's not made of glass. She won't break if she's eventually disappointed in love." Mother bent and dropped a kiss on his head, then swept from the room.

Doireann rose from her seat. "Just go on as you have begun," she mimicked. "Poor girl. She'll be putty in your hands. Dare we trust you with her?"

Niall closed his eyes for a moment and pinched the bridge of his nose. "I should like to discuss this some other time, Doireann. Perhaps in the next century?"

"Oh, does Mummy's little diddums have an achy-wakey head? Poor iddle mannikins." Doireann's voice twisted in a parody of sympathy. "Just do what Mummy tells you, and evvyting will go better again, Mummy promises. . . . Good God, it makes me want to puke, the way she fawns over you just because that bloody duke got you on her."

"I didn't ask to be the duke's son." He and Doireann seemed to have this conversation at least twice a year. Well, it was March, after all. They were probably due for it about now.

"I know. And you don't have to be so damned nice about it to me all the time. That makes it worse, somehow." Doireann pirouetted around the couch and leaned over his shoulder, laughing. Her quicksilver moods left him dizzy sometimes.

"Poor Niall, to have to deal with both Mother and me," she whispered in his ear. "Between us we're probably enough to sour you on women forever. Well, iddle mannikins, take your sister's—pardon me, *half* sister's—advice."

He sighed. "Yes?"

"Watch yourself while you lure sweet little Miss Leland into falling in love with you. Make sure that she doesn't make you the biter bit." She laughed and kissed his cheek, then tugged a lock of his hair hard enough to hurt.

Niall sat staring into the fire long after she had danced, chortling, from the room. It didn't feel right, setting out to intentionally trifle with a girl's affections like this. It would be nice if Mother would stop being so mysterious about her plans, but he knew from long experience that she would tell him when she was ready to and not before. There wasn't much he could do but play along until then. In the meanwhile, flirting with a beautiful young woman certainly beat brooding about his life and reading about German railroads.

3

"Don't worry, my dear. It will be all right."

Pen looked up from her book into Dr. Carrighar's face. "Who said I was worrying?"

"That was the third sigh you have fetched up from somewhere near your toes. Unless you find it too close in here, I must assume that you are worried, or nervous, or otherwise perturbed. Don't be. After the initial shock, they'll get over it. You are as advanced as they are in your studies—you won't be a drag on them. In fact, you might give some of them a run for their money." Dr. Carrighar leaned back in his chair and gave her an encouraging smile.

Dr. Carrighar had long since retired from his positions as chancellor and professor of metaphysics at St. Kilda's University. But he had retained a position as tutor to a handpicked group of scholars, chosen by him to be tutored in magic, as well as the more conventional subjects offered at the university. Today would be the first day that Pen would join in a tutorial session, and despite her brave words, she *was* worried. Females did not attend university. Would Dr. Carrighar's scholars mind sharing their tutorial with a girl?

Dr. Carrighar knew she could keep up with his regular students—at least he kept saying so. Pen herself was reserving judgment until after she had met them.

Footsteps and a murmur of voices in the hallway outside the study told her that her wait was over. She sat straighter in her chair, at the far edge of the semicircle drawn around Dr. Carrighar's writing table, and clasped her hands tightly in her lap as the doctor replied, "Come in!" to the knock on his door.

Norah came in first, bobbing a curtsey. "The students, sir," she announced, and shot Pen a fierce look that was probably meant to be encouraging, though on Norah's homely face one could never be sure. Pen assumed the best and smiled her thanks back at the maid.

Four young men shambled into the room, scuffling their feet and flapping hats to rid them of the worst of the latest rain. The first stopped dead when he saw Pen and nearly caused a pileup of his three cohorts as a result. After that first shocked look, he bobbed his head and quickly claimed the seat farthest from her. It was almost comical, and Pen might have giggled if she weren't so very apprehensive.

The other three students shot her looks of varying surprise and uneasiness as they too filed in, and there was a minor scuffle to see who could get the next farthest seat. The ultimate loser, a tall, red-headed young man, took the chair by her with ill-concealed irritation and pulled it as far from her as he could while twitching aside the folds of his academic gown, as if casual contact with her would taint them.

Dr. Carrighar made the vague, rumbling sound that usually preceded his speeches. But right now it was accompanied by twinkling eyes, and Pen realized that he was muffling a laugh.

"Miss Leland," he finally began, "these are the messieurs Doherty,

Sheehan, Quigley, and O'Byrne, my students of magic. Gentlemen, I am pleased to announce that we have been joined by my house-guest, Miss Penelope Leland, who is visiting from England."

There was a silence. Pen pretended to examine one of the botanical prints hanging on the wall with great interest so that she wouldn't accidentally meet anyone's eyes. Then one of the students, the small, dark-haired one who had entered first, squeaked, "Er, just for today you mean, of course."

"Just for today, Mr. O'Byrne, and just for as long as her visit lasts. She has come here expressly to study, and I thought that both you and she would benefit from each other's knowledge."

One of the students—she couldn't tell which—smothered something that sounded suspiciously like a snort.

"Yes, Mr. Quigley?" Dr. Carrighar inquired mildly.

"Nothing, sir." It was the second youth from the end, the one with sandy brown hair and a long nose. "Just a cough, sir."

"*I* have something to say, if Fergus isn't brave enough," said the student closest to Pen. Just now his face matched his spectacularly red hair. He shot Quigley a quick, contemptuous look, then turned to Dr. Carrighar. "We're here to learn, sir, not play nursemaid to a visiting English who has the fancy to play bluestocking for a week or two. I object to her being here."

Dr. Carrighar appeared to consider this. "On what grounds do you base your objections, Mr. Doherty?"

"Why, on what I just said," Doherty replied, scowling.

"I see." Dr. Carrighar made a steeple of his hands and tapped them against the end of his nose. "Miss Leland may choose whether or not to consider herself a bluestocking, but she may claim the title of serious scholar with all due truth and honor. She is indubitably from England, but I can and do emphatically vouch for her right to be here. It is my tutorial, after all, and you are here because you have been invited. I have invited her as well. If you do not feel comfortable in her presence, you are certainly welcome to leave."

Doherty blinked. "But, sir. She's a woman."

Pen tried to maintain a gracious expression, but inwardly she seethed. *He has spoken the word* woman *in the same tone he might have used to say* smallpox.

"Yes, I am aware of that fact."

"None of the great magic wielders—at least, not the *real* ones—have been women. Only men were chosen to be Druids. Women aren't capable of doing more than curing warts and concocting love charms for the incredulous. Hedge-witch nonsense. I thought we were here to study *serious* magic, and we can't with a woman among us."

Dr. Carrighar's face was bland and smooth. "You think so, do you?" he asked gently.

Pen glanced at Doherty. Couldn't he sense the mounting annoyance in Dr. Carrighar's tone?

The young man in the third seat—Pen deduced that it must be the one named Sheehan—shifted uncomfortably in his chair. "Maybe we ought to give her a chance, Eamon. We don't know what she might be capable of."

Eamon Doherty shook his head. "Dr. Carrighar, you should know that only men can wield true magic."

Pen felt herself flush with anger. What about Ally? What about Persy, who had bested Dr. Carrighar's own son last year in a magical duel? This Doherty probably couldn't hold a candle to either of them. She opened her mouth to start to refute him, but caught Dr. Carrighar's faint shake of his head.

"I am sorry you labor under that misapprehension, Mr. Doherty," he said. "Perhaps I have been remiss in allowing your personal preferences to indicate the course of our studies thus far. It was, I see now, an error. Let us discuss what reading you have done since our last meeting, and then I think we will explore a new topic."

Doherty glowered. The one called Quigley tried to do his best to copy Doherty's expression, and O'Byrne and Sheehan looked cautious but agreeable. Pen remained silent, but pulled out the notes she had made on Eriugena.

She did not volunteer any comments during the discussion that followed, but answered the questions Dr. Carrighar put to her as quickly and concisely as she could while ignoring Doherty's barely concealed sighs and impatient shifting in his chair. Even so, the atmosphere remained strained. Pen was grateful when after two hours Dr. Carrighar put down the old-fashioned goose-quill pen he had toyed with through the tutorial.

"I think that will do for today," he announced. "For our next meeting on Saturday, I should like you to begin researching the role of the Triple Goddess, also called Danu or Dana, in Irish myth and magic. Come back and tell me what you find, and we shall construct our investigations accordingly."

Eamon Doherty slammed his book shut, stuffed it with his notes into his leather haversack, and left the room without speaking after shooting Pen a burning look.

"'The Maiden, the Mother, and the Crone, three goddesses and one,'" recited Patrick Sheehan as he wound his muffler around his neck. "My gran could have told us about the Triple Goddess."

"Which one? The Maiden or the Mother? No, it must have been

the Crone," said Quigley contemptuously. "Did they get together for cozy chats over tea?"

"Go easy, Fergus," muttered O'Byrne as Sheehan turned a dull red.

"Gran got milk from her cows and eggs from her hens all winter when she asked the Goddess's blessing on them at midsummer," he said to Quigley. "When your husband is dead and you've got six mouths to feed, there's not much better magic than that."

"None better, indeed," Dr. Carrighar echoed. "Good afternoon, gentlemen."

Quigley left, his nose in the air. O'Byrne nodded briefly to Pen and followed him out. Sheehan finally finished with his muffler and turned to Pen. "*Failte,*" he said to her, then ducked his head and left.

Pen turned to Dr. Carrighar.

"It means 'welcome,'" he said. "Well, one and a half out of four is not bad, for the first day. Sheehan is a good-hearted lad, and O'Byrne was mostly civil. I think they will all come around, eventually."

"I hope so." Pen sighed and slumped in her chair. Those two hours had felt more like six.

"Excuse me, sir, miss." Norah stuck her head around the door. She looked excited. "There's callers, if you please."

"Callers?" Dr. Carrighar raised one eyebrow. "At the front door or the back?"

Norah opened her mouth and closed it, and held a small silver tray out to him. He leaned forward in his chair and took the cards it held.

"Lady Keating and Mr. Niall Keating," he read aloud. "Front door, I assume, then."

Pen looked down at her dress in dismay. She had worn her plainest, most severe gown of gray merino without even a touch of lace or ribbon, hoping that such a sober costume would make Dr. Carrighar's students take her a little more seriously. Did she have time to run upstairs and change her dress, or at least fix her hair more becomingly? Or maybe a quick summoning spell to bring down a ribbon or her lace cuffs—

"Shall I bring in tea or such, sir?" Norah asked eagerly. "Mrs. Carrighar was in the parlor, so I took 'em in there to her."

"The parlor?" Poor Ally was, as usual, resting by the fire in the drawing room, which had a coal heater in it. The scent of peat smoke from the other fireplaces in the house worsened her nausea. Pen knew she would be mortified to receive guests in her night robe. She shook out her petticoats and hurried down the hall to the front of the house. She'd have to see them as she was, looking most definitely like a bluestocking.

Lady Keating's distinctive perfume announced her presence, even with the drawing room doors closed. Pen hoped Ally wasn't finding it too overwhelming. It would kill her if she were to throw up in front of visitors.

"Ah, Miss Leland!" Lady Keating rose as she entered. "Since I am carrying you off to go shopping tomorrow, I thought that I ought to reassure your guardians that you will be well protected while under my care." She turned her smile on Ally. "It is delightful to meet Mrs. Carrighar, though I am sorry to find her indisposed."

"A passing infirmity, Lady Keating," Ally murmured from her sofa. She seemed no paler than usual, and in her quilted satin dressing gown she reminded Pen of a medieval queen, receiving visitors from her bed. "Won't you ask Norah to send in refreshments?"

"She's on her way." Taking a breath, Pen turned and curtsied to Niall Keating, who had stood silently during their conversation. "Mr. Keating."

"Miss Leland." He bowed, then gave her a long look. Pen remembered again her plain gown and scraped-back hair and wished she could hide behind Ally's sofa. But his expression was clearly admiring.

"Penelope has just had her first tutorial with Dr. Carrighar's students," said Ally, nodding her into a chair near Niall's. "A little unconventional for a young girl, I know, but it would be foolish not to take advantage of such an opportunity for learning."

"Ah. We couldn't help wondering who the young men were." Lady Keating relaxed into her chair. Pen saw her exchange a glance with her son. "Did it go well, my dear?"

"As well as could be expected. They didn't quite throw me out of the room, though it seemed a near thing at first. I am not sure if they were more put off by my being female or English," Pen answered. An image of Doherty's sneer rose in her mind's eye.

"This is a very conservative country, I think you will find. And there are still strong feelings about the presence of the English on Irish soil. Old wounds—and some not so old—that have never fully healed." Lady Keating sighed. "It is, however, to Dr. Carrighar's credit that he recognizes your intellectual abilities. What are you studying with them?"

"Oh, er—" Pen floundered. "Dr. Carrighar was going to give me some readings, since I cannot go to the university library to study. Some aspects of ancient history . . . um, and metaphysical trends of thought—"

To her relief, Dr. Carrighar came in just then, followed by a harassed-looking Norah bearing a tray of small wineglasses and biscuits. "My heather wine," he said with a gracious smile. "It came out rather well last year, I thought, but you must be the judge. How are you, Lady Keating?"

Pen gratefully let him take over the conversation. She would have to concoct a believable cover story for her magical studies. And the sooner, the better, if she was going to start meeting people outside the household.

"Sitting through that tutorial can't have been an easy thing to do," Niall Keating said to her under Dr. Carrighar's cheerful rumbling. "The greater number of my classmates at Oxford and Göttingen would never have admitted that most women would be as intelligent as they were, given the same education. It doesn't sound as if students here are any different."

"They weren't. It bothers me that most of them weren't even willing to give me a chance, though I really can't have expected otherwise. I tried to look unfrivolous and academic, to make them feel more comfortable." She gestured at her plain gray dress.

He gave her an appraising look. "That was sensible of you, but I'll wager it didn't work."

"I beg your pardon?"

"Your plan backfired. True loveliness is at its best when unadorned. Only inferior jewels require showy settings."

"Oh!" Pen nearly gasped at this blatant compliment. Did he really think her beautiful? But his tone was matter-of-fact, as if he were simply stating the obvious.

She must have reddened, for he suddenly looked contrite. "That was a little blunt, wasn't it? Forgive me if I've embarrassed you,

Miss Leland. I've spent too much time in universities and not enough in drawing rooms."

"No, it's—" All at once, Pen couldn't help laughing. "Now I can't agree or disagree with you without sounding either vain or coy. I suppose a plain thank you won't get me in too much trouble."

He smiled with her. "Probably not. Unless I open my mouth and plant my foot in it sideways again. Hopefully you'd be kind enough to help me draw it back out without my losing too many toes. After a London season, I must be an interesting change."

"Niall, my dear, we must let Mrs. Carrighar get back to her rest."

Lady Keating's voice startled Pen. She looked up and saw that Lady Keating stood by her, smiling.

"It was a pleasure to see you, ma'am," said Dr. Carrighar as he rose.

"And you, sir. Mrs. Carrighar, perhaps you might permit me to send over a little herbal elixir I brew with my housekeeper's help. It is a sovereign remedy for certain discomforts associated with . . ." She let her voice trail delicately. "A teaspoon mixed with water taken twice daily might prove soothing."

"Thank you, Lady Keating. That is most kind of you. Penelope?" Ally nodded toward the door, then leaned back against the couch, looking vaguely greenish again.

Pen led them into the front hall. "I'm sorry you must leave so soon."

"I am too, dear, but I think we wearied poor Mrs. Carrighar enough for one day. We shall see you tomorrow, don't forget." Lady Keating kissed her cheek, and a fresh wave of her scent wafted over Pen as Norah, stationed by the door, opened it.

"Good day, Miss Leland," Niall said as she turned to him.

She looked up into his direct blue gaze and paused. "An interesting change after London, yes. And perhaps, one for the better," she said, trying to keep her voice steady.

The brows over those blue eyes drew down for a moment as he considered her words. Then he laughed. "I'll do my best to earn that opinion." He clicked his heels, bowed again, and left.

Norah shut the door behind them and peered out one of the curtained sidelights. "Sure, and that's a handsome man, miss," she said, tucking a twig of hair back under her cap.

"Yes, he is, Norah." Pen sighed and leaned against the wall. Had she been too forward, saying that to him?

"Though her ladyship's a handful, I'm guessin'," Norah continued, still peering out the window.

"You haven't met *my* mother," Pen murmured.

"No, that I haven't. But I'm sure she's a lady through an' through." Norah turned away from the door and looked at Pen. Her homely face took on the anxious expression Pen had noted before when she brought in the wine.

"I was wonderin', miss, if I could ask your help with somethin' that I don't care to trouble the doctor with," she said, twisting her hands in her apron. "You bein' a *bean draoi,* an' all."

Ban dree? Then Pen remembered one of Dr. Carrighar's lessons right after she had arrived and begun to study with him. *Bean draoi* was Gaelic for "magic woman."

"Um, I'm happy to try," she said cautiously. "What is it?"

Norah glanced past Pen toward the closed drawing room doors. "'Tis the clurichaun, miss. It's troublin' me somethin' dreadful," she whispered.

For a moment, Pen thought she was asking for medical advice. "The . . . ?"

"The clurichaun. In the cellar, miss. Just now when I was after gettin' the heather wine, I thought it would frighten me into m' own grave afore it's dug. The doctor tells me to ignore the heathen creature, but when it leaps out at me with that ugly face leerin' under its red hat, it's more than I can do not to yell the house down." Norah looked half ashamed, half terrified as she spoke.

One of the Little People! Pen had caught glimpses of fairy folk back home at Mage's Tutterow, but Ally did not approve of them. "They don't think as we do, and dealing with them can be difficult and even dangerous, if you don't know how," she'd always said. "I don't recommend that you try to interact with them until you're older. If ever."

In Ireland they were said to be nearly everywhere. What had the doctor called them? "One of the *Sidhe*," she said.

"That it is, miss. I don't like to drive it away, for that's said to be mortal bad luck for the household, and the doctor's taken a fancy to the creature for some reason. But I shake in my boots whenever I'm asked to go down to the cellar. My gran always said that the *Sidhe* respect witch-women. I hoped as maybe you could go down an'—" She shrugged eloquently.

"And ask him not to trouble you anymore?"

"I would truly appreciate that, miss." Norah looked relieved. "I've a lamp here all ready." She hurried over to the small table that stood by the staircase down to the cellars, lit the lamp that stood on it, and handed it to Pen. "You'll be wantin' this too, just in case," she added, and pulled a fork from her apron pocket.

"Do you want me to poke it?" Pen took the fork and examined it dubiously.

"It's steel, miss," Norah explained. "The *Sidhe* don't care for the cold iron, see. If it gets to threatenin' you, just show it this."

"Oh." Pen pocketed the fork as Norah opened the cellar door for her. Privately she might have preferred an iron knife, but perhaps a fork would be sufficient if wielded in a properly threatening manner.

"I'll be standin' right here if you need me." Norah looked a little embarrassed as she spoke. "But I'm sure you'll put the nasty creature to rights."

"I hope I can do something helpful, Norah." Pen turned up the flame on the lamp and started down the steep stairs, clutching the rope banister. This had been quite a day—first the tutorial, then the Keatings, and now an errant fairy in the wine cellar. She would have to start a letter to Persy tonight.

The stone walls of the cellar were cool and dry. No musty or damp odors were evident, and the floors were well swept and tidy. It was the least eerie cellar she'd ever seen, hardly an appropriate haunt for a supernatural creature. But she was grateful not to have to face cobwebs and spiders as well as a clurichaun.

At the bottom of the stairs was a small chamber, with doors leading forward and back. "Which way, Norah?" Pen called up to the square of light at the cellar door.

"Back behind, miss. That's where the wine and beer are kept. Have at the wicked thing for me!" Norah's voice sounded much braver now.

"What do you want me to do? Truss it up like a turkey?" Pen muttered to herself. She turned, set the lamp down on a stair, and called a protective circle around her. If it wouldn't stop much, it might at least give her warning if an enraged fairy were about to attack her. Then, straightening her shoulders, she picked up the lamp once again and opened the heavy wooden door that led to the wine cellar.

Wooden racks of bottles and a few casks on stands, as well as a small table and chair, met her eyes as she peered into the dark space. She pushed into the room, hardly breathing, feeling around her with her mind as she walked to the table and set her lamp down on it. But there was no presence anywhere that she could sense, apart from a fruity, wheaty smell left from years of wine and beer being stored here. Was Norah letting her imagination get away with her?

Pen approached one wide rack of bottles. Dr. Carrighar was rather a connoisseur of port and Madeira, and these bottles were the right size and shape for those wines. She pulled one gently from its rack and saw "1819" written neatly on a paper label affixed to it. The year she and Persy had been born. She pushed it back into place with a smile and pulled out another, labeled "1797." Though the label was brown and spotted, the cork was smooth and intact, and there was not a speck of dust on it. Or anywhere else in the cellar, for that matter.

"Of course there isn't. What do you think I'm here for? Be careful with that bottle, missy. It's one o' *Draiodoir* Carrighar's finest. He's saving it for when his granddaughter is born, come the seventh of October," said a creaky, slightly slurred voice from somewhere near her knees.

Pen managed not to scream and drop the bottle, though it was a near thing. She did let out a squeak.

The voice chuckled. "There, I nearly made you drop it anyway. 'Twould have been a shame, for 'tis a grand one. I've drunk its counterpart in *An Saol Eile* often enough, haven't I?"

Pen took a deep breath and turned toward the voice. There was nothing there.

"And why should I be showing meself to ye, if you're not showing yerself to me?" the voice asked reasonably.

What? Pen remembered the protective circle she'd cast around her. It must make her invisible to fairy folk. "Then how do you know I'm here?" she asked, not moving.

"Well, it's not every day lamps come floating into me cellar on their own. Even if I can't see you, I know you're there, *bean draoi*. You would have noticed me too, if ye were after knowing how to look."

"How do you know I'm a witch?"

"Oh, for Dagda's sake, who else would be casting circles o' guard round themselves? Are ye daft, *cailín*? Now that the formalities are over, maybe you'd like to be telling me what I might do for ye?"

Pen decided to take a chance. She gripped the fork in her pocket and said, "It's disconcerting to talk to a disembodied voice. If I put off my circle, will you show yourself to me?"

"Hmmm," said the voice. "How do I know you're not a hideous hag, come to frighten me to death in me own cellar, the only home I've got in me declining years?"

But Pen caught the note of jesting. "You don't sound like you're in any danger of imminent demise," she replied. Imminent hangover was another issue. "Nor do you know if I'm the queen of witches, fair as the dawn, come to ask you to grace my court with your wit and wisdom."

"Ho ho!" the voice chortled. "Is that how it is? Very well, Your Majesty. I'm ready an' waiting."

"No," Pen replied firmly. "We both have to reveal ourselves at the same time."

The voice was silent for a moment. "All right, then," it finally said. "On the count of three. Then you'll have to tell me what you want."

"Done." Pen gathered the circle around her like a cloak and prepared to toss it aside.

"*A haon, a do, a tri,*" counted the voice, "now!"

Pen threw off her protective spell and looked down to where she had heard the voice. There was nothing there.

"That's not fair—" she protested, when suddenly there was a loud *pop!*

Standing next to her, his head about level with her kneecaps, was a tiny figure. Bright eyes twinkled in a swarthy face that was seamed and wrinkled like a very old man's. When he saw her indignant expression, he chortled again and leapt into the air, twirling and giggling, though his landing was a little precarious.

"Hee hee! You should see your face! Well, I had to make sure you weren't something you oughtn't to be, come to persecute a poor old clurichaun." He swept the red hat off his head and executed a courtly bow, holding his hand over his heart—or where his heart would have been, were he human—and nearly brushing the ground with his long red nose. As he rose again, he staggered and grabbed hold of Pen's skirt to steady himself.

"Whoops!" he cried. "That wasn't a good idea, me mannikin. Best keep yer head up where it ought to be." He jammed his hat tightly back on his head, as if to keep it from rolling off, and then dusted off the sleeve of his old-fashioned long coat, which fastened with shiny brass buttons barely half an inch across. Maybe Dr. Carrighar liked him because they had a similar fashion sense.

"I was just after sampling the clarets over there, to make sure they hadn't gone," he explained, swaying slightly. "It's hard an' thirsty work, being a clurichaun is. When ye've got rebonspilisity—rebonsipility—re*spon*sibility for a cellar as fine as this one, it keeps a body busy. Dusting an' sweeping and turning the bottles so the corks don't perish o' the dry rot—ye've no idea. And that clod-footed, snaggletoothed maid up there's no help at all to a poor, hardworking elf." He fetched a deep sigh.

Pen smiled. "What's your name?" she asked him.

A crafty expression crept across the little man's face. "Oh, no ye don't, missy. Ye won't have my name out o' me anytime in a month of Sundays. Next thing you'll be telling it to that turnip-faced harridan up there, an' she'll be after me poor hide to make her bootlaces with."

Pen remembered that to have a fairy's true name could give power over that creature. "I mean, what shall I call you?" she amended.

"Now, that's more like. Let's see . . . hmmm. Corkwobble would do, to be going on." He peered sideways at her from narrowed eyes.

To her surprise, Pen kept a straight face. "Corkwobble would do very well, I should think. And Norah's not turnip-faced, nor a harridan. You just frightened her badly, that's all."

"Well, she was after moithering me something awful, too. It works both ways, ye know," the clurichaun said with an air of wounded dignity that didn't seem completely feigned.

"Do you think it would be possible to call a truce between you? I'm sure she appreciates how nice you keep it down here," Pen wheedled.

Corkwobble snorted. "Hmmph. Be nice if she'd show her appreciation in some other way than frightening a body half senseless, lurching about and praying at the top of her voice just to find a bottle o' heather wine. A dish o' new milk or a bit o' toasted bread with honey mightn't go down too badly now and again," he said, then looked down at the large buckles on his shoes as he scuffed his toes on the ground. "'Specially if you was to bring it. You're some easier on the eyes than she is. And I misdoubt you'd be hail-Marying all over the place, neither."

Pen laughed, but she couldn't help feeling touched. "I'd be happy to, Corkwobble, so long as you behave yourself."

"Oh, I will all of that, ma'am," he said, his creased face sober. "It doesn't do for the likes o' me to be trifling with a *bean draoi*. I could get away with it on Mistress Lard-bucket up there, but not with you."

"Miss Leland? Are ye all right?" called Norah's voice from the top of the stairs.

"*A anail bo!*" cried Corkwobble, and vanished.

Pen blinked and waited a few seconds, but he didn't reappear. "That didn't sound very complimentary to poor Norah," she said to the air.

"It weren't meant to be," Corkwobble's creaky voice said, from somewhere behind an ale cask, "'less ye consider 'cow breath' a dainty bit o' flattery."

"Miss Leland!"

"I'm fine, Norah!" Pen called back. "I'll bring you some milk this evening," she said softly into the room. "And I'll come back for a visit in a day or two and bring you your bread and honey."

She picked up her lamp and left the wine chamber. As she was about to set foot on the first step, a small voice wafted from the door behind her.

"*Lots* o' honey on the bread, if ye please."

4

Pen stood in the front hall of the Carrighar house, buttoning her gloves and peering out one of the narrow windows that flanked the front door. Lady Keating had said she would come at three, and it was only twenty minutes till. But Pen had an idea that Lady Keating would not cheerfully tolerate lateness, unless it were her own.

Behind her the drawing room door opened. Pen turned and saw Dr. Carrighar peering out at her.

"Ah, good. You've not gone yet. Might we have a quick word?" he asked.

Pen glanced again at the door and hesitated. But surely she'd hear if Lady Keating's carriage pulled up to the house. "Certainly," she said.

Ally lay on her couch. She looked up at Pen and motioned her to a nearby chair.

"Is everything all right?" Pen asked. Ally's face was haggard, and her fine brows were drawn in an expression of concern. "Is there something I can get you while I'm out?"

"Aside from a new stomach?" Ally smiled for a moment, but her troubled expression returned, and she sighed. Pen caught the sharp, sour note on her breath that the doctor said was due to her not being able to keep down enough fluids, as were her sunken eyes and papery skin. A pang of guilt lanced through her; here she was, off to shop and socialize, while poor Ally lay here feeling wretched.

"I am not entirely comfortable with this sudden friendship of Lady Keating's," Ally said, without preamble.

"Oh." Pen blinked. This was not what she had expected. "Why not? I thought Dr. Carrighar said she was respectable enough? She certainly seems to be well-off, too."

"I thought I taught you better than to take wealth as a sign of virtue," Ally chided, sounding a little more like her old self. "But I am not concerned about her respectability. Oh, why couldn't this . . . this *process* be easier, so that I could take better care of you?" She gestured down at her body with a fretful, impatient wave.

"Um, then what bothers you about Lady Keating?" Pen asked. Ally couldn't be jealous that she was becoming friendly with another woman, could she?

Ally and Dr. Carrighar exchanged uneasy looks, and Pen guessed they had been talking at length on this topic.

"I can't say anything specific," Dr. Carrighar said, removing his spectacles and polishing them on his scratchy tweed vest. No wonder they looked as if they were made of frosted glass. "But Nuala Keating is not known for her general sociability or friendliness, even with people she supposedly knows well. It seems somewhat strange to me that she should have taken such a liking to you for no particular reason. . . . Or rather, I worry that there *is* some particular reason that she is pursuing this acquaintance with you."

A fleeting picture of Niall Keating flew through Pen's mind. "What if there is?"

"All we ask is that you be on your guard with her," Ally said earnestly. "You don't have to go shopping with her today, you know. We could say you are indisposed when she arrives."

Pen stood up and went to look out the window, to hide the irritation she knew must show on her face. What were they talking about? Yes, Lady Keating was an unusual woman, confident and strong-willed, perhaps a little quick-tempered. But did that make her dangerous to know? Did it make her son somehow unsuitable?

"Telling her I'm ill would not be honest," she managed to say mildly enough, knowing that the comment would find its mark.

Behind her, Ally sighed. "You are being willfully scrupulous, Pen. Small fictions like that are frequently used in society, and you know it."

Pen took a steadying breath. "All right. You've asked me to be careful of Lady Keating, and I will be. I would have anyway, because we are such new acquaintances, and if she does or says anything that is objectionable, I won't accept any more invitations from her. But I've been in this city for two weeks now, and I would like to be able to get out and meet people. I can't study magic every minute of the day."

Ally opened her mouth to speak, but Dr. Carrighar raised one hand. "Indeed you can't, Penelope. We understand your feelings. Go and have a good time with Lady Keating."

Ally opened her mouth once more, but Dr. Carrighar shook his head at her once again. She leaned back into her pillow, and her worried expression deepened.

Pen looked from one to the other of them. There was something else they weren't telling her. Ally was about to, but Dr. Carrighar stopped her. Why?

A clatter of wheels on the cobbled street below broke into her thoughts. Pen flew to the window, then rushed back and kissed Ally's forehead. "I'll be fine," she whispered, and hurried out to Lady Keating's elegant carriage.

Later that evening, Pen wrapped herself in a quilt over her nightclothes, lit an extra candle, and settled at the desk in her bedchamber.

Dear Persy,

I am now (or will be in a few days) ready to brave the frequent and horripilatious (Where did Charles find that word? I can't stop using it now!) Irish rains and tempests, courtesy of the new cloak I ordered today from my new friend Lady Keating's modiste.

Yes, I have at last started to mix the littlest bit in society here. Lady Keating nearly ran me down with her coach while I was out walking (it was my fault) and then decided to befriend me. There's some delicious gossip about her romantic entanglement years ago with none other than the Duke of Cumberland—I suppose I must call him the king of Hanover now, since he inherited the throne there—but Dr. Carrighar says she is quite respectable. Of course, if you saw her son, Niall, you might think it more than gossip. Remember those family portraits we saw in Princess Sophia's rooms at Kensington? I shall let you draw your own conclusions. Just think, that would make him the queen's cousin, wouldn't it?

Both Lady Keating and her son are quite charming; I have had tea twice at their house, and they have visited here as well. Lady K. has told me that she intends to have a dinner party so that I might meet more of Cork's polite society before they all go to London for the season. I can't help being the smallest bit jealous of them heading off to London, but my studies are going well, I think.

But back to my shopping trip. Lady Keating directed her driver to go very slowly, so that she could point out the houses of her acquaintances (usually with devastating character sketches that made me giggle most indecorously). She was not what Ally would call charitable, but it was so amusing, and of course I would never repeat a word of what she said. I think perhaps I found it all the funnier just because I have been so serious lately, so immersed in my studying that I was like a naughty schoolgirl, playing truant. Really, I haven't had such fun since I left you.

Pen tapped her nose with the end of her pen and stared at the words she had just written. Her last sentence was a bit of a white lie—Persy had been fun during their time together at Galiswood, but her being married couldn't help changing things between them, no matter how subtly. Even when they were alone together, Pen could sense Lochinvar's presence in Persy's thoughts.

Lady Keating's modiste was refreshingly un-French (oh, shall I ever forget Madame Gendreau "mon Dieu!"-ing all over the place during our many fittings last year?) and promised my cloak, of a very fine dark blue wool lined with heavy lighter-blue satin, would be ready next week. And as a treat to myself for being so studious of late, I ordered another in green shot silk, lined with black, for warmer weather. They are quite handsome and distinctive, being fuller than the cloaks at home, with graceful pleats set into a broad collar and with a large hood as well. If you would like, I shall have one made for you too as a birthday present.

After that we returned to Lady Keating's house for a long and cozy tea. Doireann Keating, Lady K.'s daughter, was in bed with a feverish cold and did not come down, but Niall Keating was there. I wish you could meet him and tell me what you think of him. He does not precisely flirt with me, but says outrageously complimentary things in a very matter-of-fact way, as if he were discussing the cycles of the moon or some other incontrovertible fact. I do not quite know what to make of it, but cannot say that I dislike it. Lady Keating said that he was quite put out the other day when they paid us a visit just as Dr. Carrighar's scholars were leaving, and examined them keenly in order to size up "the field." Utter nonsense, of course, as the doctor's students are

*barely willing to even acknowledge my presence in the
room, much less vie for my attentions. True, Lady
Keating might have made up the whole scene. But that
would mean that she—oh, never mind. I'm making
mountains out of molehills, I'm sure. But I couldn't
help feeling a little bucked up by this episode, real or not.
    Poor Ally continues under the weather—*

Again, Pen stopped writing and stared up at the cheerful yellow curtains at the window before her desk. In all likelihood, Persy was going to find herself expecting a baby soon, if she wasn't already. Would it be kind to tell her horror stories of Ally's morning sickness?

*—but we hope her symptoms will ease soon. Lady
Keating very kindly gave me an herbal concoction for
Ally to try, and it did seem to offer some relief.*

Was relief the right word? Oblivion might be closer to the truth. Ally had had a particularly bad day today. She was barely able to keep down half a slice of toast at midday. When Pen brought the little flask of yellowish green syrup after she returned from tea and shopping, Ally had shuddered at the unpleasant color. But the elixir's scent had been sweet and refreshing. Pen mixed the teaspoon Lady Keating had directed in cool water, and after a first tentative sip, Ally had drained the tumbler. When Pen looked in on her after going upstairs to wash, she was fast asleep, and a faint color had returned to her pale lips. She did not show any signs of waking at dinnertime, so Michael had carried her upstairs and put her to bed. Well, perhaps some sleep untroubled by nausea would help her.

Well, dearest sister, I must start on the essay Dr.
Carrighar has set me, lest I disgrace myself before his
students and prove to them that females are not worthy
students of magic. Please write soon and forward any of
Charles's letters, since the dear Chucklehead can't
seem to find it in him to manage letters to both of his
sisters. My humble duties to Mama and Papa and
Lord Northgalis and love to Lochinvar and yourself—
with the most of it to yourself, of course.

Your devoted sister,
Pen

Pen sanded her letter and set it to one side of the desk. She paused to picture Persy in her cozy blue-painted morning room at Galiswood in a week or two, reading it. Would she laugh and shake her head at the passages about Niall Keating? A pity he had gone to Oxford, or Lochinvar might know him.

Enough thinking about Niall. She squared a fresh piece of paper on her blotter. Rain began to spatter against the window as she picked up her pen once more.

The Maiden, the Mother, and the Crone are the
three aspects of the Great Goddess, her three
incarnations, worshipped throughout Europe in the
distant past. She symbolizes the wheel of the year, from
spring awakening to summer bounty to winter fading, and
also the moon that goes from waxing to fullness to

waning. Both are eternal cycles, without beginning and end, and the Triple Goddess also has no beginning or end. Here in Ireland, she is given the names Dana for the Maiden, Brigid for the Mother, and Badb for the Crone, though the names Dana or Danu and Brigid also are used for her collectively. Remember that this is not a strict scientific classification, and names and functions of the gods vary across distance and time.

 Each aspect has its own attributes. The Maiden represents rebirth, the vigor of spring, the freshly awakened energy of new growth, and any other beginning. Her color is white. The Mother is fullness, bounty, fruition, birth, and the giving of life. Her color is the red of blood shed in women's cycles and childbirth. The Crone signifies endings and completions—not just the inevitability of death, but also the wisdom and knowledge gained with age and, eventually, rebirth as the Maiden. The Crone is generally regarded as the most powerful of the Three, because of her acquired wisdom, though each aspect has her own strengths related to her nature.

 As a female figure, the Triple Goddess is the mother of magic. Her cauldron, round like the moon, is—

Her hand was cramping. She set down her pen and stretched her aching fingers while rereading what she had written. Would Dr. Carrighar's students be able to endure references to such delicate female subjects as menstruation? So much for men being the stronger of the sexes. She'd love to see that self-righteous Eamon Doherty have to put up with the pain and mess of monthly courses, something that women everywhere endured silently and without complaint.

Not to mention childbearing. Persy had told her about the talk Mama had with her before her wedding, and Pen was happy that she didn't have to worry about such matters quite yet. Funny to think that this time last year she was the one who looked forward to being married. Then again, she hadn't found her own Lochinvar the way Persy had.

"I'll follow the Maiden's path for now, thank you very much," she said aloud as she covered her inkwell, the hideous orange glass one that Charles had given her for Christmas last year. The Maiden, goddess of new beginnings. Wasn't that what she was doing, here in Ireland? Finally beginning to take up her magical heritage?

With a yawn, she snuffed her candles and climbed into bed, stretching her feet down toward the flannel-wrapped hot brick Norah's cousin Maire, who was "obliging" for both Pen and Ally, had tucked under the covers a little while ago. Pen rather regretted that Ally's sister Lorrie had stayed on with Persy as her lady's maid. Lorrie had far more flair for clothes than Maire, who was scandalized by Pen's passion for embroidered fancywork stockings.

But socks aside, there was nothing cozier than snuggling into a warm bed and listening to rain falling outside. Pen closed her eyes and let sleep take her.

Rain still hissed down beyond the entrance of the cave, but within, it was surprisingly warm and dry. Pen held her candle before her as she picked her way downward, deeper into the earth, following the voices that whispered her name.

"Where are you?" she called.

"Heeeerrrre." The soft liquid vowel seemed to touch her face like a breeze. "Dooowwn heeere. Cooooome."

"I'm coming," she replied, peering into the dark beyond the little circle of light cast by her candle. "But it's hard to see where I'm going."

"Huurrryyyyyy." The word floated insistently up to her. And as if the voices *had* been a wind, her candle abruptly went out.

Pen gasped out loud and stopped dead. The gray light from outside the cave had long since faded, and there was not a particle of light anywhere. The darkness of the cave surrounded her like a tangible object, wrapping her up in itself like a pall of black velvet, swallowing her whole the way a python did its prey. She began to shiver, though the cave was still warm.

"Come," the voices said again, quiet but authoritative.

"I can't," Pen forced out from her dry mouth. "I can't see where to go."

"You don't need to see to find us. Come."

At first her feet would not respond.

"Do not fear us. Know us."

She took one jerky, hesitant step forward, and another.

"Yes." It was a soft sound in her head. "Yessss."

Another step and another. Pen held her hands out before her, trying to feel, but there was nothing to feel.

"Knowledge, not fear, is where the power is. Power. Strength. Life." The words washed over her, through her. Pen took another step, then two more. She dropped her hands and walked faster, then broke into a run.

Light bloomed around her, like warm golden lightning. It came from the three candles being held by two women who were suddenly there in front of her, bouncing and reflecting off the thousands of tiny golden crystals that lined the cave.

One of the women was tall and robust, with shining reddish brown hair and a wide, happy smile on her handsome face. She wore a robe of red silk that clung to her full breasts and ample hips, and she had something white draped over one arm and held a red candle in her other hand.

The other woman had once been as tall as the first, but a slight hunch to her shoulders made her appear shorter. Her white hair glittered in the light of the candles, her lined face was calm and dignified, and she wore a black woolen robe. In her hands she held two candles, one black, one white.

"We have been waiting for you," the first woman said, her voice deep and resonant.

"I knew you would arrive," said the second, in a thinner, more silvery voice, like a bell. "You followed the path. Now you know us."

"Here," the first woman said, and offered the white object she held out to Pen. It was a shift made of white linen. Pen obediently slipped it over her head.

The second woman nodded her approval. "Take this, child, and we will be complete." She held out the white candle.

Pen stretched her hand out to take it. As her fingertips touched its smooth whiteness, she felt a sense of fulfillment, of wholeness.

"Remember," said the silver-haired woman to her. "Always remember who you are, and who you will be, and who you were. Changing and unchanging. Different and the same. Knowledge, not fear."

The cave, and the women in it, faded, and Pen drifted into a deeper, dreamless sleep.

Before she went in to breakfast, Pen peeked into the drawing room. She had heard Michael helping Ally down the stairs with murmured words of encouragement, heard Ally's clipped, monosyllabic replies. Her heart sank a little. Evidently Lady Keating's elixir hadn't helped after all.

"'Scuse me, miss," said Norah from behind her. She carried a tray with a small covered china basin and a pot of tea on it.

Pen sidled in after her as Norah set the tray down on the low table by Ally's couch. Michael Carrighar looked up at her from where he knelt on the carpet, holding Ally's hand. A patch of morning sunlight from the front windows made his odd bicolored eyes even more obvious.

"'Tis a grand milk puddin' Cook's made," Norah coaxed. "Won't ye but sample it, Mrs. Carrighar?"

"If you won't try it, I might," Michael said. He lifted the lid off the pudding basin and sniffed. "I used to look forward to getting a quinsy in the throat when I was small so Cook would make me one of these. They go down very easily."

"Do they come back up as easily?" Ally asked, sounding peevish.

"Did you sleep well, Ally?" Pen thought it would be a good time to interrupt.

"Good morning, Penelope. Yes, I did, thank you." Ally smiled faintly. "I don't know what was in Lady Keating's concoction, but I slept all through the night without feeling ill."

"That's wonderful! In that case, why don't you try eating a little and having more of her remedy? Maybe it will help you keep it down," Pen suggested.

Michael glanced up at her again with a grateful smile.

"You go have your own breakfast," Pen said to him. "I know you need to get to the university. I'll have some tea with Ally while she tries a little of Cook's masterpiece, and then we'll see if Lady Keating's remedy helps again."

Michael had been forced by Sir John Conroy to give up his teaching position at St. Kilda's last year and go to London to try to enchant Princess Victoria. Now queen, Victoria had very kindly gotten the prime minister, Lord Melbourne, to pull strings at St. Kilda's to have Michael reinstated there. Pen knew he was anxious to appear conscientious and deserving to the deans, which meant long hours and extra duties within his department. Michael nodded his thanks, kissed Ally, and followed Norah to the dining room.

To Pen's surprise, Ally ate almost half of the pudding before setting down her spoon. "Was Michael right? Is Cook's milk pudding worth becoming ill for?" she asked, taking Ally's tray.

"If you like that sort of thing." Ally shuddered delicately. "And I'm not convinced it was wise to eat that much of it."

Pen hastened to the side table where Norah had left a pitcher of water and the little bottle of elixir. "Then let's get some of this into you before anything untoward happens," she said, mixing a glassful and bringing it to Ally, who drank it straight down.

"Mmmmm," she sighed, and smiled again as she handed the glass back to Pen. "Thank you, dear. I had the loveliest rest last night. If it was Lady Keating's medicine that did it, I hope it works again."

"I do too," said Pen. She picked up the tray. "I'll just go bring this to the kitchen and be right back."

"That's fine." Ally sank back against her pillows and closed her eyes.

When Pen peeked in just a minute later, Ally was asleep. That seemed a little strange. Hadn't she just gotten up an hour earlier, after a good night's rest? But she hadn't been sleeping well for weeks because of the nausea. She probably had a lot of catching up to do. And she looked so comfortable, a small smile just showing at the corners of her mouth and a definite, if faint, flush on her thin cheeks. Pen shut the door again and tiptoed down the hall to the dining room for her own belated breakfast.

"Good morning, Penelope." Dr. Carrighar somehow managed a courtly bow without rising from his chair or ceasing to ladle oatmeal into his bowl from a tureen. "How is our dear little Melusine this morning?"

Pen concealed a slight grin as she seated herself at the long table and reached for the coffeepot. She'd never thought of using the adjectives *dear* and *little* in connection with her formidable former governess. "Asleep again, but she ate half a bowl of Cook's pudding for breakfast."

"Ah, so that was the cause of the crowing I heard from the kitchen. Asleep again, you say? Hmm. Well, a few days of that won't do her any harm." He stirred an enormous dollop of cream into his oatmeal. "Which leaves us free to have a practical exercise today for your lesson."

"Really?" Pen nearly overfilled her cup. She hastily set down the pot. "With your other scholars?"

Dr. Carrighar shook his head as Norah brought in plates of coddled eggs and sausage and grilled tomatoes. "They were, er, not receptive to the idea of combining our practical as well as textual lessons."

That was hardly a surprise. "All of them?" Pen asked, thinking of big Patrick Sheehan and his shy smile.

"Not all of them. But mastering new magic in a hostile environment is not what I would have you experience, even though"—he raised a hand to stem her protest—"even though I know that you would be entirely capable of learning under any circumstances. I'm just not sure my digestion could handle it. And I am not certain that those lads could learn while you were there. So much for the stronger sex, eh?" He smiled at her.

Pen was quiet for a moment, buttering toast. "Very well, then," she said, trying to sound gracious. "When shall we have our lesson?"

"Why not right now?" He chased an errant blob of oatmeal around his bowl and spooned it up, frowning meditatively. Then he looked up at Pen, grinned impishly, and vanished.

Pen was just able to keep from exclaiming out loud. She waited a few seconds, considering, and said, "That did not feel like a movement spell, so I must assume you are invisible."

"Very good, my dear." Dr. Carrighar reappeared, beaming.

"But my sister taught me that last year." Pen thought for a moment, then cast the cloaking spell that Persy had used on herself and Charles when they sneaked into Kensington Palace.

But Dr. Carrighar shook his head. "That spell does not make you invisible. It just makes you harder to see. A subtle difference, true. The cloaking spell works well enough when you merely wish to go about unnoticed. As soon as someone intentionally looks for you, it no longer conceals. Do you see the difference? Its benefit is that it takes less energy to cast and to maintain. But for true imperceptibility, even to those who seek you, the invisibility spell is what is required. I should know; I have experimented extensively with both over a long career of avoiding tiresome colleagues at the university. Now eat your victuals while I explain the theory."

Pen ate as quickly as she could without being uncouth. "The problem with invisibility," lectured Dr. Carrighar, "is not the spell itself, but how you conduct yourself whilst you are invisible. Are you finished? Good. Now, you try it."

She took a deep breath. *Concentrate. Know your intent and make it happen.* "Ambition and volition are the keys to spells and witchin'," her brother Charles had declaimed as they all practiced together one hot afternoon last summer, and Persy had pretended to throw up into his Eton hat. But his schoolboy doggerel was essentially correct, and Pen had found herself using it as a sort of incantation on its own, to focus her mind. It made her grin as she worked any magic, though, which tended in turn to make Ally sigh and roll her eyes during lessons.

"Very good," exclaimed the doctor. "But recall, invisibility spells are for being hidden. You are indeed hidden, but imperfectly. Your napkin is still on your lap, mind, and very odd it looks, floating above your chair like that. And your chair itself is still drawn up to the table. You could not leave the room or even move without giving yourself away. And that is what makes invisibility so difficult— not the spell itself, but thinking it through, so that it *truly* conceals."

Norah bustled into the room, carrying a tray. "Shall I be clearin', sir, or would ye like more coffee—now, where is Miss Pen? I've a note here that just came for—saints, miss, don't do that to me!" She staggered backward, dropping her tray with a loud clatter as Pen reappeared in her seat, grinning. The note fluttered to the ground.

"Well, it worked well enough that time, didn't it?" she said to Dr. Carrighar. "I'm sorry, Norah. That was not fair."

Norah bent to retrieve the tray and the note. Her freckles stood out in her white face as she handed the note to Pen. "I should be used to it by now, workin' in this household. You're as bad as that clurichaun, miss, frightenin' me half to death. If ye don' mind, I'll just go have a sit-down for a minute or two." She whisked back out of the room.

"Mischievous twig." Dr. Carrighar chuckled.

"That wasn't at all nice, was it? I'll go apologize to her again after I read this." Pen unsealed the note and read.

My dear Penelope,

I hope you can be spared Wednesday evening for dinner at my house, to meet a few dear friends whom you really ought to know if you're to stay any length of time in this city. I should be honored if Dr. Carrighar and Mr. and Mrs. Carrighar could accompany you, but at any rate you must come. I'll send the boy around later to collect your reply. It shall be such fun—do say you'll be there.

Fondly,
Nuala Keating

"How nice of her," Pen said, and gave the note to Dr. Carrighar. A suggestion of Lady Keating's musky perfume drifted past her nose as she did. "She really does seem determined to make me feel welcome here."

"Yes," Dr. Carrighar murmured, scanning the slip of paper with a slight frown. "I wonder why?"

"Thank you," Pen said stiffly.

"My dear nitwit." Dr. Carrighar dropped the note and shook his head at her. "I am not implying that you're not deserving of the most cordial of welcomes here. It's their source that concerns me. I doubt Melusine will be able to go out yet, but I think that I shall escort you to this party myself, if you don't mind. I want a chance to see if Nuala is up to anything."

Pen knew that Dr. Carrighar did not care to venture much into society. "Thank you, sir. I would be most happy if you came," she said. "And I hope you'll see how nice Lady Keating is."

"I hope so too." Dr. Carrighar rose from his seat. "Lessons at half-past nine, don't forget. Let's see what my scholars have made of the reading I set 'em on the Triple Goddess." He grinned at Pen, bowed in his old-fashioned way, and left the room.

Pen poured the leftover cream from the pitcher onto a square of jam-covered toast, sprinkled the mess with a liberal amount of sugar, and headed for the basement.

"Corkwobble?" she called as she pushed the wine-cellar door open with her toe. "I've brought you a treat."

There was a small *pop!* as the little man appeared, perched on the edge of the table. "That's bad form, it is, *bean draoi*. Ye're not supposed to tell a *sidhe* that ye're gifting him something. We're proud, mind you, and don't care to acknowledge such things. In point o' fact, we usually leave a house where the big people start making a fuss o'er their gifts." He leaned toward Pen and sniffed appreciatively at the saucer she carried.

"You old fraud." Pen laughed as she set it down on the table.

"Just thought I'd tell ye, so you're knowing the etiquette next time. In the meanwhile, 'twould be a shame to let any o' this go to waste." He waved one tiny hand in the air and a golden fork appeared in it. "See, it's been a useful rule. Gives us what we wants and keeps the human folk from sniffing about us and interfering with our ways. We just make it generally known as we appreciate a bit o' a snack now and again, without any fanfare an' fussing. We have our cake and eat it, too."

"Literally."

Corkwobble grinned around an enormous mouthful of toast. "'Tis truth you speak, *bean draoi*."

Pen set her candle down and sat at the table to watch Corkwobble. He polished off his plate of cream toast, belched comfortably, and snapped his fingers. A small silver goblet appeared on the table in front of Pen.

"Go on, *bean draoi,* have a drop. It won't poison you." He nodded at it.

"What is it?" Pen picked it up and sniffed cautiously. It had an elusive scent, like sunlight on distant green fields and ancient oak forests.

"The *Draiodoir* Carrighar's best *uisce beatha.* Whiskey to you Saxon heathens," Corkwobble said with a grin. "Or it sort of is. It's from the *Draiodoir's* barrel as it is in *An Saol Eile*—the fairy world, you'd call it."

"Fairy whiskey? It sounds deadly." Pen eyed the tiny goblet.

"Not to you it won't be, missy. It's just a ghost of itself, here. 'Tis how I keep watch on everything in the cellar here—by sampling it there. Wouldn't be much left, otherwise." He grinned sheepishly. "Try it. Ye've been kind to me, an' I want to thank ye."

"There's a catch somewhere, isn't there? If I drink it you'll be able to keep me in your cellar indefinitely, like Persephone and the pomegranate seeds."

Corkwobble chortled and shook his head. "Oh, ho, *bean draoi.*

Think ye're so clever, do ye? But no, it's not like that. This is the *Draiodoir*'s house, isn't it? An' his whiskey as well, in spirit—heh heh, *spirit*." He chuckled at his joke. "Go on—it'll put the heart into you before ye go back up to face those narling gloits that call themselves scholars."

Pen groaned. "How do you know about them?"

"D'ye think I don't know what goes on here? Many a day I've ground me teeth listening to those nits go on about magic being one o' the 'high sciences' till I want to do my dinger."

"Pardon me?"

"Till I go stark, staring mad. Ooh, one o' these days I'm going to catch 'em in the hallway an' give 'em what for. High sciences, indeed!"

Pen sighed. "Yes, well, they don't want me in their class because women supposedly aren't capable of true magic."

Corkwobble snorted. "Ye could show 'em a thing or three, *bean draoi*. Take yer drink, then. You'll need it."

Pen sniffed at the goblet again. "Will it make me drunk?"

"It can't. It isn't a part o' this world, mind ye. Drink too much of it and all it'll do is send ye into a sleep with dreams the like o' which ye've never had."

"That sounds lovely, but another time, Corkwobble. I want my wits about me when I deal with the—what did you call them? Gloits? It sounds suitably derogatory, whatever it means. Anyway, I thank you for your courtesy." Pen took a quick glance at her watch and exclaimed under her breath. "I'm sorry, my friend, but I'm late to class. I'll bring you a bit of Cook's milk pudding tomorrow. Ally liked it." She rose.

Corkwobble stood too and bowed low, then picked up the goblet and let a few drops fall on the table in front of Pen before he drained it dry. "An' I thank ye for yours, ma'am. Ah, that hit the spot. Come back soon, and talk wi' old Corkwobble again."

Pen wasn't sure if the thunderous expression on Eamon Doherty's face was caused by her lateness to class or something else. He rose when the others did at her entrance into Dr. Carrighar's study, but with such a sneer of disdain at her murmured apology that she nearly turned on her heel and left. At least Patrick Sheehan's polite greeting seemed sincere. Pen took the empty seat next to him with a smile and a nod.

But to her surprise, it was he who spoke first when Dr. Carrighar leaned back in his chair and said, "Well? How went your initial investigation of our new topic?"

There was an eloquent silence. Next to Pen, Sheehan shifted his big frame in his seat, as if it were uncomfortable. He cleared his throat and spoke.

"I'm sorry, sir."

Dr. Carrighar raised one shaggy eyebrow. "Sorry for what, Mr. Sheehan? Did you not do your work, and are seeking absolution?"

"Oh, I did it, sir. It's just—" He glanced at Pen and cleared his throat again. "It's just that I don't think discussion of the Triple Goddess's, er, attributes are suitable for discussion in a group such as this."

Pen's heart sank.

Dr. Carrighar appeared perplexed. "In what way?"

Sheehan gave him an agonized look.

"He means," drawled Doherty, "that it's all utter bollocks, sir."

Sheehan grew red in the face. "No, that's not what I meant, if you please, Eamon. And don't talk that way in front of Miss Leland."

"Why not? If she's good enough to work with us, then she has to get used to our ways. I'm not going to change how I speak just because she's here."

"Uh, excuse me." Pen rather surprised herself by speaking.

"That's the problem with you, Eamon. Everything always revolves around you, doesn't it—"

"Excuse me," Pen spoke a little louder.

"No, it doesn't. I'm just tired of the damned English coming over here and thinking they can—"

"Excuse me!" Pen stood up and nearly shouted. "Mr. Sheehan, I thank you for your concern for my feminine sensibilities. But I shall promise not to be embarrassed by any speech or subject matter in these tutorials if you will do the same. Please just forget my sex and regard me as a scholar. Mr. Doherty, I can't change my nationality any more than I can change my sex. But can you temporarily suspend your own dislikes while we are here, for the sake of learning?"

Everyone—the four students and Dr. Carrighar—stared at her as she stood there, breathing hard. Fergus Quigley let out a soft, nervous giggle.

Doherty narrowed his eyes. "Very well, Miss Leland. For, as you say, the sake of learning. Then I'll repeat my previous statement. This reading on the Triple Goddess was utter tripe. Ignorant peasant superstition. Three goddesses in one—it's nonsense."

"Mmm-hmm." Dr. Carrighar leaned back in his chair and stared up at the ceiling with a meditative air. "Now, what major religion have I heard of that is based on a similar doctrine?"

Doherty flushed. "It's not the same thing! And furthermore, it has no relevance to magic. It's how the biddies kept their families in line, invoking some dread crone if they didn't do as they were told. What does it have to do with the ancient bardic knowledge and rituals of the Druids that are the true magic? Which was, I might add, the exclusive province of men."

"Reverence for the Goddess predates the Druids," O'Byrne commented thoughtfully. "Before them, there was the Great Mother—this Triple Goddess—and her horned consort, the Lord of the Greenwood. Why do you suppose—"

Doherty interrupted him with a rude noise. "Yes, and sprites and pixies in every mud puddle and blade of grass. It was superstition and nature worship. Not the basis of real magic."

"Mr. Doherty." Dr. Carrighar sat up very straight in his armchair, a bad sign. "I was not aware that personal opinion and belief had come to take the place of intellectual discussion in my tutorials. Perhaps I ought to invite Father Kelley from the rectory and let him debate the existence of magic with you. Miss Leland, I feel I must apologize for my class today. I had expected better of them."

Pen shriveled in her seat. Oh, why had he addressed such a comment to her? All it did was separate her from the others. "It's not—that is, I don't want—" she began.

"There, see? We've upset her." Sheehan leaned toward her with an apologetic, hangdog expression. "I hope you're proud of yourself, Eamon."

"Stop it, all of you!" Without thinking, Pen leapt out of her seat again and fled upstairs to her room.

This wasn't going to work. She threw herself onto her bed and stared up at the ceiling. Dr. Carrighar's students would never be able to accept her among them. Studying with her sister under Ally had shielded her from the reality of masculine attitudes toward female learning, from Doherty's outright contempt to Sheehan's well-meaning but misguided urge to censor in the name of protecting her "feminine sensibilities." In the end, both attitudes were equally repugnant. Would she have to go back to studying alone with Dr. Carrighar? Would he have time to tutor her alone, or would he even want to?

Oh, why did Ally have to be so ill and wretched? But Pen couldn't burden her with her upset over today's scene. She rolled over, clutched her pillow, and let out the tears that burned the back of her throat.

"Now, child. Crying about it won't help," a quiet, creaky voice chided gently.

Pen stiffened. Who'd said that? She hastily rolled over and pushed herself up on one hand.

A very small, very dainty old lady stood next to her bed, watching her with a faintly disapproving frown. She wore an old-fashioned white mobcap on her wispy gray curls and a white fichu collar over an equally old-fashioned sprig-print beige gown. Above a small pair of spectacles perched on her nose, her eyes twinkled with quiet sympathy and humor. They were also odd—the right one blue, the other brown. Pen blinked. They were just like Michael Carrighar's eyes.

"I'm sorry. I didn't hear you come in," she said, scrambling off the bed and smoothing down her dress.

"I know you didn't. It's all right, girl. As I said, crying won't help, but sometimes it just feels better when you do." The little lady nodded and perched herself on the edge of Pen's bed. She patted the counterpane next to her. "Sit and tell me what happened."

Pen sat, but couldn't help asking, "Er . . . may I ask . . . I don't recall meeting you before, ma'am. . . ."

"No, I generally keep to myself. Too much fuss with people makes me bad-tempered." The odd eyes twinkled again. "I'm Mary

Margaret Carrighar, and you're Penelope Leland. It's my grandson who's been teaching you, hasn't he?"

Her grandson . . . that had to be Michael, of course. Good heavens, that made her Dr. Carrighar's mother! Somehow it was hard to picture Dr. Carrighar as being someone who had once been young. How odd that neither Dr. Carrighar nor Michael had mentioned that she lived here too. Why, she must be well into her eighties, if not older. If she never came downstairs—and she hadn't in the almost two weeks Pen had been there—she wouldn't know that Dr. Carrighar had taken over her tutoring from Michael. Well, this was a large house, and Pen hadn't thought it polite to poke about uninvited. Good thing she hadn't. This elder Mrs. Carrighar had more than a touch of vinegar about her, and probably wouldn't have taken kindly to intrusion. Not that it had stopped her from walking into the room just now—

"You needed someone to talk to, 'tis plain as plain. Otherwise I wouldn't have bothered you. Now, why such tears? Come on, out with it." The lady whisked out a tiny handkerchief tucked into a loop at her waist and handed it to Pen. A whiff of camphor and gillyflower rose from it, old-fashioned scents that matched its owner perfectly. Pen smiled and dabbed at the already-drying tears on her cheeks.

"It's nothing, really. I don't want to trouble you, ma'am—"

"No, it isn't nothing, and I want to be troubled, and you will please to address me as Mary Margaret. It is appropriate for equals, and equals we are—or shortly will be, Goddess willing. With a little more work, I can see that you'll be a fine witch someday, if you don't get distracted." She nodded solemnly.

Pen blinked. "You're a . . . ?"

Mary Margaret drew herself up. "And what else would I be?"

"I'm sorry. I've just been so used to being secretive about magic all my life. I ought to have known that you were a witch." What else would Michael's grandmother be? "And I'm trying my best to learn and study, but the other students don't want me to share their studies because I'm English and female."

"Now, the English part—you can't blame them, in light of history—but I'm sure it's more to do with your sex." She sighed. "In my day, magic was mostly the province of women. We followed the Goddess, bless her name. Only men with a very strong calling to it followed the old path. Most of the others with just a little of the magic in them set it aside in their hearts and joined the church instead. It was a more sure way of getting ahead in the world."

"Well, that would explain the speeches I've been hearing about men taking back magic from the hedge-witches and grannies—"

Mary Margaret snorted. "Not that Druid nonsense again? Child, don't listen to them. They fear the Goddess and the power we women magic users wield, and would take it for their own. So they've created a false past to justify their actions. Don't let them stop you."

"I won't, but it's frightfully hard to concentrate when you can feel their anger hovering over you like a storm cloud. . . . And if they're not angry, they're convinced that my sensibilities are too delicate to study the . . . er, earthier aspects of magic."

The dainty old lady snorted again, in a most undainty fashion. "Why doesn't *that* surprise me in the least? If that lot could see what went on in the tall grass at a good old-fashioned Beltane celebration, their squinty little eyes would fall right out of their heads. When I was a girl, we didn't wrap ourselves in false modesty and call it—" She peered into Pen's face, which felt as if it were fourteen different shades of crimson. "Well," she went on in quieter tones, "times have changed, I suppose. Still, they would do well to remember that magic is male and female, just as all of the earth is. For all that we served the Goddess, we honored her consort too. But never forget that it is the female side that bears fruit. And speaking of bearing fruit," she sniffed slightly, "I wish we could find you a female teacher now that Michael's wife is ill with her megrims."

"Oh, it's not a sham illness. Poor Ally couldn't even keep a glass of water down," Pen protested. "And I won't let the other students keep me from learning."

"There are matters in magic that are best passed from female to female. Especially when you're talking about the Triple Goddess." Mary Margaret stood up and straightened her fichu. "I shall have to think about this. And you should have a rest, I think. Women are the stronger sex, but it doesn't do to overtax oneself. Come along, lie down."

She looked so accustomed to being obeyed that Pen didn't protest that she wasn't tired, but stretched out on her bed. The lady nodded her approval.

"Very good. I shall come visit you again soon," she murmured, gliding to the door.

It wasn't until a gentle knock awoke her that Pen realized she'd dozed off. "Yes?" she called, her voice hoarse.

"Yer lunch, miss. The doctor thought as how ye might like it up here." Norah came backing into the room with a tray, followed by Maire with two jugs of water for washing.

"One hot an' one cold, as ye like it." Norah set the tray down on her desk and bent to peer into her face. "Ye might try a cold towel on the eyes fer a minute or two. 'Twould make ye feel better." She nodded at Maire, who wet a linen towel with water from one of the jugs and brought it to Pen.

"Thank you, both of you." Pen took the cold cloth and pressed it to her eyelids. "Oh, that feels good. Why do some men have to be such—such—"

"Imbeciles?" Maire supplied brightly.

Norah snorted. "That's bein' kind. Don't let the doctor's half-baked scholars get ye down, miss. They're not worth the powder to blast 'em all to hell."

"Norah!" Maire nearly dropped the jug of water.

"'Tis true! Ah, now, see? She's smiling again. A wash and lunch, and you'll be fine, Miss Pen. Come on, Maire, and don't be such an old lady before yer time." Norah gave Pen a conspiratorial wink and propelled Maire toward the door.

"What if Father Kelley should hear ye usin' such language?" Maire protested as the door closed behind them.

"He won't unless he's told, will he?"

"But 'tis yer immortal soul I'm worried about!"

"Aye, and if the good lord can't countenance a bit o' plain speakin' about the sillier half o' his creation, then I don't . . ." Norah's words faded as the two women descended the stairs.

Still smiling, Pen took Norah's advice and washed her face. An enticing, savory smell drew her attention back to the tray Norah had left her, but as she crossed the room, a small, crumpled object on the floor caught her notice. She bent to retrieve it and smoothed out the slightly yellowed square of linen, edged with lace like enchanted cobwebs. Mary Margaret Carrighar's handkerchief. She'd meant to ask Norah about Mary Margaret. Well, she'd do it later.

Pen had finished her lunch and was reading one of Dr. Carrighar's books when Norah knocked once more, then entered, looking pleased.

"Miss, there's a caller for you." She held out a card.

Pen took it and saw THE HON. NIALL KEATING engraved on it. A little curl of pleasure rose in her throat. "Thank you, Norah. Where is he?"

"I offered to show him to the parlor, but he said he'd wait in the hall. Said he didn't want to disturb Mrs. Carrighar."

"How is she, anyway?"

"Still sleepin' when I peeked in at one. Dr. Carrighar said we should let her be, if sleepin' meant she'd suffer less."

"I see." This would be the first time she and Niall would be alone together, without Lady Keating or anyone else interrupting their conversation. So tempting . . . but it would hardly be proper to invite him to stay and take tea without a chaperone.

"I could show him into the library," Norah suggested eagerly. "Or Mr. Michael's study. Or even the dining room, if ye'd like. Table's been cleared an' all. Cook could have tea ready in a minute."

Pen hid a smile. Norah wasn't going to let a possible suitor for her get away if she could help it. "It's all right, Norah." She hurried downstairs, wishing she'd taken a moment to check that her eyes were clear.

Niall Keating stood at the bottom of the stairs, hat in hand, grinning up at her as she descended. His cheeks were pink and his hair tousled; evidently he had walked there.

"Good afternoon, Miss Leland," he said with a bow. "I believe in her note of invitation my mother said she'd send a boy around this afternoon for your answer."

"And you're the boy?" Pen paused on the last step and smiled back at his impish expression.

"I volunteered for the job," he explained. "Little Sean has a cold, and I thought to spare him going out. And after all, I am a boy, am I not?"

"*Are* you, Mr. Keating?" Pen asked demurely.

"Don't tell anyone, but I feel like one just now. Won't you come and play truant with me, Miss Leland? It's a beautiful sunny day, and we don't always have many of those this time of year. Can you pry yourself away from your Greek or whatever it is you're studying and come for a walk?"

Pen didn't let herself stop to think. "I'd love to, if you'll give me a moment to get ready."

"I'll be generous and give you two, but no more than that or I'll start to pine." He pulled a long face.

Pen resisted the urge to reach down and ruffle his hair. "Yes, Master Boy." She sketched a curtsey and turned to hurry back up the stairs.

She took five, but Niall was in no mood to complain. When she did appear in her new cloak, which made her eyes even more intensely blue, and slipped a gloved hand over the arm he offered her, all his banter fled, and he felt like a tongue-tied boy of sixteen.

Mother's directives notwithstanding, this Penelope Leland intrigued him. How was it, in three years of travel in the most cosmopolitan countries on earth, that he'd never met anyone like her?

Most of the pretty girls he'd met were as empty-headed as they were attractive—or at least their interest in European politics was severely circumscribed. He supposed he couldn't blame them—sometimes his interest in it was severely circumscribed as well. But just imagine, this Miss Leland was voluntarily missing the London season in favor of studying. He wondered what it was she was studying so diligently.

She was a heady mix of straightforward enthusiasm and girlish reticence and intellectual gravity, all rolled into one charming package. And yes, she was quite charming. But Niall could see that she had yet to reach her full beauty; she was like a fruit that needed a touch of frost to fully ripen. When she was thirty-five, she would be magnificent. How he would love to see her then.

He wrenched his mind away from that train of thought. "Shall we walk along the river? The wind is on holiday today, and you won't be blown to Blarney."

"Ah, but if it does blow, I'm prepared." She spread a fold of her new cloak and waved it at him. "And anyway, that might not be such a bad thing. Isn't kissing the stone at Blarney supposed to confer eloquence of speech? I could have used some of that in my tutorial this morning."

"Bad day?" But he scarcely needed to ask. Her irritation with Dr. Carrighar's students was obvious in the sudden stiffness of her back and features. Mother needn't have worried that they'd interfere with his wooing of her. If anything, they'd show him up in a better light. He'd have to reassure her on that point.

"Did you have a disagreement?" he continued. "Sometimes intellectual battles are even more virulent than personal ones."

"I suppose so. But when they're both intellectual and personal, they reach a whole new level of unpleasantness. Doherty spent class today staring at me as if he hoped I'd suddenly burst into flame and disappear. It was positively horripilatious."

"Excuse me?"

"Oh." She colored prettily. "Horripilatious. My little brother says that all the time, and it's infected the rest of the family as well."

"You're close to your family."

"It's hard not to be when you've got a twin. But yes, we are all close. I miss them a great deal," she said softly.

He resisted the impulse to squeeze her arm. "What topic has Dr. Carrighar set you that's roused such fervor?"

"It's . . . it's a little hard to explain. Oh, is that spire over there St. Anne's Shandon? It seems as though it's been shrouded in mist ever since I got here. How nice to actually be able to see it."

Niall could hear the forced enthusiasm in her voice as she peered up at the cathedral's tower, with its distinctive red and white stone faces. This was the second time she'd evaded discussing her studies, which seemed odd. Surely academics would be a safe, easy topic of conversation. Perhaps she was afraid of appearing to be too much the bluestocking.

"It's a pity Dr. Carrighar's scholars haven't been more welcoming than they might have," he said quietly. "Half of a university experience is the talk, among students as well as from the masters. But if they're too busy resenting you because you're female, or English, or some other silly reason, it can't be very pleasant for you."

She bowed her head so that he couldn't see her face set back in the frame of her bonnet. "It's lonely. I've always had my sister to study with. But now—"

That time he did squeeze her arm, very gently.

"You don't know how grateful I am to Lady Keating for being so very civil to me," she said in a rush. "I enjoy Dr. Carrighar's conversation very much, but he's not Persy. And with Ally ill and wrapped up in—in her condition . . ." She peeked at him sideways, blushing. "With Ally ill, I don't have anybody. It's so kind of your mother to make the effort to befriend me."

"It's no effort at all. And Mother doesn't do anything that she doesn't want to." Niall smiled wryly to himself. That was bloody well true. "She wants to be your friend. We all do." He let his voice drop and soften till it sounded like a caress. "*I* do."

He heard her sudden soft intake of breath and felt her hand tighten involuntarily on his arm. A twinge of guilt lanced through him. Had he gone too far? Could Mother be mistaken about her experience?

But devil take it, he was just following orders. If he ever wanted to get anywhere, he would have to go along with Mother's plans for this girl, whatever they were. If he was supposed to make her fall for him, then he might as well get down to business.

"That is . . . most kind of her," Miss Leland said, sounding a little breathless. "I—I value her friendship highly. Isn't it remarkable how one can feel so drawn to new friends after just a short acquaintance, Mr. Keating?"

He smiled down at her averted face. Was she flirting back? "I had noticed that very same thing, Miss Leland," he said. "Quite drawn."

"Oh!" she breathed, so quietly that he barely heard it.

It made him smile again, but with less pleasure. If she had been flirting with him, she should have given him a sidelong look and a faint smile just then, not that half-shocked, half-pleased monosyllable.

Mother was wrong. This girl may have had a London season, but she was no experienced coquette. Blast. She was going to get hurt if he kept going down this path. A mental picture of her beautiful blue eyes, raised to his in pain and anguish, struck him so forcibly that he nearly stopped dead in the street.

"Are you all right?" Miss Leland looked at him as he stumbled slightly.

"I'm fine. Stone in my shoe, that's all." He patted her hand, smiled, and tried to ignore the small voice in the back of his mind jeering "Liar!"

5

For dining at the Keatings', Dr. Carrighar made a concession to fashion and wore clothes of more modern cut than his usual long, loose coat and breeches. Tonight, Pen thought with amusement as she surveyed him seated across from her in the gig, he at least looked nineteenth century. Beau Brummel or the Prince Regent might have worn a similar coat once.

She smiled down at her hands, encased in delicate lace mitts. Persy had sent them to her, along with a length of pale gold organdy for a gown and an enthusiastic request that Pen indeed send her an Irish cloak. Pen would be glad to; it would give her an excuse for another outing with Lady Keating to her modiste, and perhaps time with Niall. . . .

There she went again. How many times did she need to be reminded to keep her mind where it belonged—on her studies?

But even Pen's interior scold was starting to sound halfhearted, at least on the subject of Niall Keating. Snippets of his conversation on their walk last Saturday kept sounding in her mind—not so much his words as the tone and timbre of his voice. It made her feel slightly warm and breathless, as if her corset were too tight.

It also left her hungry for more. She hadn't seen him since that day, though she had gone driving once with Lady Keating. Would he have more to say to her tonight?

"I am sorry Melusine did not feel up to coming with us." Dr. Carrighar's baritone rumble broke into her thoughts. "It would have been a good opportunity for her to get to know more of Cork society."

Pen shushed Niall's voice in her mind. "At least she's feeling better than she was." She then asked, "Do you think it's proper for her to be sleeping so much? I mean, is it healthy?"

Over the last few days, Ally had spent twenty out of each twenty-four hours asleep. She was actually eating now—toast and soft-boiled eggs or Cook's milk puddings, mostly—and keeping down what she ate. As soon as she finished breakfast, she eagerly drank a glass of water with Lady Keating's elixir and drifted off to sleep until late afternoon. Then, after a light supper, another dose sent her back to sleep until morning. Her color was better and her face less wasted, but still . . . it seemed strange to see the energetic Ally so indolent.

Dr. Carrighar sighed. "I don't know, Penelope. This stage of gestation is a prodigious labor for women, and most tend to be somnolent. And at least when she is asleep she's not uncomfortable. The one day we tried to go without Lady Keating's remedy, poor Melusine reverted to her old distressed state. I don't see that the sleep is harmful, but I understand your unease. It's not like her, is it? Remind me this evening to ask Lady Keating what is in her elixir, won't you? I am sure it is entirely harmless, whatever it is. Yet . . ."

"Yes, sir. Thank you." It would be easier for Dr. Carrighar to ask such a question than for her. Pen didn't want to offend Lady Keating, after all her kindness. Or jeopardize seeing Niall.

Idiot girl. Did all her thoughts have to come back to him? She laughed inwardly at herself.

The Keating house was ablaze with light, though evening was not yet fully fallen. As soon as their carriage drew to a stop, the front door opened to reveal Lady Keating herself, in deep blue silk and a turban, smiling and nodding as Pen and Dr. Carrighar ascended the stairs and entered the house.

"My dear Doctor! This is indeed a great honor." She curtseyed slightly as she held out her hand to him. "And our sweet Penelope. Welcome!"

Lady Keating's musky perfume seemed to reach out and surround Pen in a cloud of scent. Or was it simply the force of her personality, somehow made physical? But Pen had begun to rather like her distinctive fragrance, now that she was used to it. She inhaled it appreciatively as Lady Keating enveloped her in a warm embrace, then held her at arm's length and looked at her.

"How perfectly lovely you are, *cinealta* Penelope. That warm rose color suits you so well." She slipped an arm around Pen's waist. "Doctor, I can't imagine your scholars get much work done when Penelope is part of the class."

"It can be a struggle for them," Dr. Carrighar replied with a straight face. Pen just managed to keep herself from sticking her tongue out at him.

"I should think so. Niall, dear, our guests are arriving," Lady Keating called. "Where are you?"

"Here, Mother." Niall appeared on the staircase landing, exquisite in a dark green coat and green-and-gold-striped waistcoat. The lamplight glinted on his carefully combed hair and cast his strong features into dramatic, sculpted relief.

Pen watched him as he descended the broad stair and crossed the hall toward them. There was an unusual grace and strength about his movements that she loved. So many of the young men she'd observed last year in London had walked like animated lumber, stiff and unbending, as if their leg joints didn't work correctly. Others plodded flatfooted, like well-dressed ducks. Niall moved with an ease that was nearly feline. He would probably be a wonderful dancer, too. Would she ever have the chance to dance with him?

As she met his eyes, he broke into a slow smile that made her knees weak. Virtuous thoughts about the reading she had to do after tonight's dinner fled; she knew she'd be too busy replaying in her mind how he'd looked tonight, admiring each perfect detail. Couldn't they just skip dinner and let her sit and stare at Niall all evening instead? Especially if they could have another conversation like their last one. . . .

"Niall, why don't you take Dr. Carrighar into the library for a few moments, until the rest of our guests arrive?" suggested Lady Keating. "I'd love for him to see that folio of artists' reconstructions of the palace at Newgrange. Don't worry, you can monopolize Miss Leland afterwards."

"I'll hold you to that promise, Mother." Niall's grin flashed at them. "This way, sir. It's an interesting volume, and only a few dozen printed, by subscription."

Dr. Carrighar good-naturedly followed Niall across the broad hall and back up the stairs, while Pen swallowed her disappointment and let Lady Keating lead her into the drawing room. She would have liked to see whatever book it was, too, if only to have kept close to Niall.

Doireann was bent, poker in hand, over a crackling, snapping fire in the drawing room's large, black marble fireplace. She straightened when they entered, and gave Pen a radiant smile as she set the poker on the chimneypiece and shook out the folds of her pale green gown. Evidently she was in a good mood tonight.

"Pen, you're here! I say, you look just splendid in that dress," she called cheerfully. "Come see these pinecones my old nanny sent, won't you? They wash up on the beaches in Aran. When you put them on the fire they make it burn purple and green. Fun, isn't it? I've been tossing them in for the last hour, just to watch the colors."

Good heavens. Doireann actually sounded glad to see her. "How curious! I've never seen anything like that before." Pen slipped from Lady Keating's arm and approached Doireann cautiously. "Is it the salt from the ocean that makes the colors?"

Doireann shrugged. "Probably. Nanny would have said they were from pines that grew in the Summerlands, but your explanation is a little more likely. Here, you do one." She held out a pinecone to Pen with a grin surprisingly like Niall's.

Pen felt herself warm toward her under the influence of that smile. Was Doireann finally starting to like her? Maybe they could be friends after all. "What fun! Thank you," she said, crossing the last few feet between them and reaching out to take the knobby lump.

A small grating sound made her stop and glance up. Among the other ornaments there, a pair of large alabaster vases stood sentinel on either end of the high chimneypiece. One of them was slowly tipping over.

Pen froze, watching the heavy vase tip as if time had slowed, directly above Doireann's glossy black curls. In a scant second it would strike the vulnerable back of her head, quite likely killing her.

"Ponere!" she gasped, sweeping her hand as if to knock the vase aside. The vase jerked as if it were on a wire and crashed to the ground several feet behind Doireann, shattering in an explosion of white shards on the polished parquet floor.

"Wha—" Doireann gasped too and whirled around, staring at the broken remains of the vase.

"The vase, it started to fall. . . ." Pen wished she could sit down. Her heart pounded so hard in her breast that she could practically hear it. "Are—are you all r-right?" she stuttered. Doireann's face was as white as the pieces of alabaster scattered around them.

"The vase—good heavens above! My dear Penelope, you just saved Doireann's life! How providential that you saw it fall and warned her to jump out of the way." Lady Keating threw her arms around Pen's neck and embraced her, then drew back to look at her with sparkling gemstone eyes. "You dear, clever girl!" There was an odd, thrumming note of excitement in her voice.

"Are you all right, Doireann?" Pen asked again as her mind raced. Thank goodness Lady Keating had taken her translocation spell for a shout of warning. Hopefully Doireann would be so shocked at her narrow escape that she would too. But how had the vase fallen? Had Doireann knocked it with her poker somehow? And why was Lady Keating here fussing over her? She should be at Doireann's side, making sure that her daughter was all right, comforting *her*.

"Providential?" Doireann still stared around her at the fragments on the floor. When she finally looked up at Lady Keating, her face was still and strained, as if she were holding some vast emotion back lest it choke her. *"Providential?"* she repeated through clenched teeth.

"Indeed it was." Lady Keating embraced Pen once more before letting her go. "We are most fortunate to have found Penelope, aren't we?"

There was a discreet cough from the doorway. Pen glanced up and saw Lady Keating's butler trying not to look alarmed as he surveyed the remains of the vase.

Lady Keating did not turn around. "Healy, one of the vases fell off the chimneypiece."

"Yes, my lady," said the butler. "Right away." He vanished.

Pen tried one more time. "Doireann," she began, holding out her hand.

Doireann ignored it. "I'm fine," she snapped. "Just fine. Excuse me for a few minutes, won't you?" She swept past them and out of the room.

Pen was almost sure that she deliberately stepped on as many pieces of vase as she could, grinding them into the polished wood floor. Why did she seem so angry? "Lady Keating, I—"

Lady Keating put a comforting arm around her once more. "You must excuse her, my dear. Doireann does not care to be coddled and fussed over a great deal. Even when she was a little girl, she could not endure it. Why, poor child, you're trembling! It was frightening, wasn't it? I'm feeling quite faint myself. Shall we leave the servants to clear this up and join Niall and the doctor in the library? Healy!" she called to the butler, who returned with a footman and two broom-carrying housemaids. "Please bring a glass of sherry for Miss Leland to the library. Come, my dear. I'll help you up the stairs."

Pen sank gratefully into a chair by the library fireplace while

Lady Keating gave Niall and Dr. Carrighar a dramatic retelling of the episode of the falling vase. Dr. Carrighar looked sharply at Pen, but Niall bowed, and taking her hand, kissed it.

"Thank you for rescuing my sister," he murmured, then grinned. "Even though she probably didn't deserve it. She can be pretty horripilatious at times."

Pen was startled into a laugh. "I hope my brother doesn't talk about me that way. She was actually being quite affable when I—when it happened."

Healy came in, followed by a footman bearing a tray of glasses. "Sir John and Lady Whelan are here, my lady."

Lady Keating herself took a glass of sherry from the footman's tray and handed it to Pen. "There you are, dear child. Show them up here, Healy, and tell me when the drawing room is cleared."

Pen sipped her sherry and shivered slightly. Reaction was setting in, and she felt cold and shaky. Again in her mind's eye she saw the vase slowly falling toward Doireann's unprotected head. Doireann could have been badly injured, or maybe even killed, if she hadn't used her power to save her. But using magic in public . . . she hadn't been too obvious, had she? At least Lady Keating seemed to have taken her spell for a warning shout. Thank heavens people could observe an action and rewrite it to fit their own view of events.

What about Doireann, though? Anyone else would have been shocked at such a narrow escape, not to mention grateful to her rescuer. Doireann had been shocked, true. But it had been fury and resentment, not gratitude, that had blazed in her pale green eyes. Pen shivered again and drank the rest of her sherry in a gulp. Some of Corkwobble's otherworldly whiskey would have been welcome about now.

Niall took her glass and unobtrusively replaced it with a full one from the tray the footman had left on a table. "Are you all right?" he asked quietly, pulling a chair next to her.

"I—it's . . . just a little shaky, that's all." Niall's eyes were so very blue, and so very sincere. Pen suddenly wished she could lean over and rest her head on his broad shoulder and have a good cry. This evening wasn't turning out as she'd hoped it would.

"Here. You didn't see this." Niall rose and brought her the large folio he had been showing to Dr. Carrighar. Seating himself again, he took her hand under the folio's cover and squeezed it gently.

Pen nearly did cry, then, undone by his quiet sympathy. She gripped his hand tightly in return and did not let go, even when he relaxed his hand to give her opportunity to do so. His hand felt so strong and warm over hers, and so very comforting.

Sir John Whelan and his wife came in. They were a red-faced, hearty couple totally given over to conversation about horses and their racing stud, but they greeted her very kindly and seemed to be somewhat in awe of Dr. Carrighar, to her secret delight. The rest of the guests arrived quickly after that: a tall, pale viscount, his equally attenuated wife and son, and his unexpectedly buxom and pretty daughter. They were followed by an elegant, elderly baronet who greeted Dr. Carrighar with unfeigned delight.

"Good lord, it's Seamus Aloysius Carrighar. I'd heard you couldn't get out of your house anymore. Haven't the books covered every portal by now?" he cried, clapping him on the back.

"Ah, Percival Gorman, you forgot about the chimneys." Dr. Carrighar beamed. "How are you, old friend? And what are you doing out of doors? I'd heard Mary no longer let you out in public lest you frighten young children with that ugly phiz of yours."

Lady Keating sidled over to Pen. "Ah, I was right," she whispered, watching Dr. Carrighar and the man trade affectionate insults. "I recalled Sir Percival mentioning that he and Dr. Carrighar had been to school together but that they hadn't met in years. I do so want you both to enjoy yourselves tonight."

"I'll do my part toward that end, Mother," Niall chimed in dutifully. Under the folio, he squeezed Pen's hand again and raised one eyebrow very slightly at her.

The last of Pen's upset over the vase incident melted away like April snow under his warm regard. She knew she really ought to withdraw her hand before they were caught. It was a most improper thing for anyone not engaged to be doing.

Instead she smiled at him and squeezed back, wishing she could slip off her mitts and feel his skin against hers. The shocking thought made her feel unaccountably giddy. Would Niall think her a shameless coquette, holding hands with him like this? Or was he the one being a dreadful flirt? But he had said he was not versed in society's ways. Surely he was just being kind, and did not understand the effect he was having on her. . . .

Until, with great delicacy, he rubbed his thumb against her palm in a slow, deliberate circle. The pressure of his finger seemed to propagate up her arm and into her very core. Her breath caught in her throat, and she felt a telltale warmth spread up her throat and into her face as she looked up at him.

He returned her look steadily, not smiling this time. A dark, smoldering intensity darkened the blue of his eyes.

He knew, then, exactly what he was doing, and it went far beyond what usually passed for lighthearted flirtation. Should she snatch her hand away and shriek in indignation, or just be done with the whole thing and kiss him on the spot?

Before she could do either, Healy reappeared in the doorway. "Dinner, my lady."

With a final, lingering stroke across her palm, Niall released her hand, closed the concealing folio, and rose. Pen wished she could down one more sherry, to calm her beating heart. She rose too and accepted the arm Niall offered but could not look at him. How was she supposed to act as if nothing had just happened between them? She'd gone from one kind of upheaval to another. Surely something of her agitation must show in her face?

Something must have, for Lady Keating stopped her as they were about to pass through the door. "Poor child, you're still overset about that unpleasant little episode downstairs. Please don't let it ruin your evening. I'm so grateful to you. Doireann . . ." Lady Keating's green eyes were suddenly bright. She leaned forward and kissed Pen's cheek, then smiled and gestured them onward.

Something about Lady Keating's tremulous smile made Pen forget a little of her own unrest. "Where *is* Doireann?" she murmured to Niall in as steady a voice as she could manage. "I'd hoped to talk to her about . . . about what happened."

He shrugged. "She makes her own rules. She'll be back when she's ready, or maybe not at all."

But a silent, tight-lipped Doireann joined them as they were all descending the stairs to the dining room. Pen saw her dart down the stairs ahead of them, ignoring the surprised greetings of the rest of the guests, and then seat herself between Sir John and Dr. Carrighar at table, too far for conversation. Pen tried to catch her eye, but

Doireann wouldn't even look at her over Lady Keating's gleaming silver-set table.

That annoyed Pen. Doireann was acting as if *she* had caused the wretched vase to fall on her, for goodness' sake. And she'd been so friendly before it happened.

"Don't let her bother you. That's just how she is. I'm used to it by now, but I know it's hard," Niall murmured in her ear.

He had taken the seat next to her at table, after staring down Viscount Enniskean's pale son who'd been about to claim the chair. Pen looked at Niall and saw his expression was resigned as he looked at Doireann.

"Why? I want to be her friend, but—"

"Don't lose any sleep over it. I'm her brother, and *I* don't know where I stand with her most of the time. She's like the weather— there's nothing you can do about it, except seek shelter when it's stormy." He lifted his shoulders in a helpless gesture.

"But why is she this way? *You* aren't moody and inconstant," Pen said.

He shifted in his seat and frowned down at his napkin in his lap. "It's a little hard to explain why she is the way she is." Then he looked up at her with a crooked half smile. "Moody I'm not. But how do you know I'm not inconstant?"

Pen knew she was supposed to laugh and blush and play the flirtation game. With anyone else, maybe she could have. But not with Niall. Not now. Not after what had just passed between them upstairs . . . unless that had just been a game too.

"I hope you are not," she said, carefully emphasizing her words. "I had rather taken you for someone with a reasonably well-developed sense of chivalry."

"'Reasonably well-developed'?" He laughed, and Pen thought she detected a hint of unease.

"Am I wrong?"

"Might I have advance warning of questions like that in the future?" he asked.

"It wasn't a question."

"No, just a highly leading statement. Are you studying the law with Dr. Carrighar, Miss Leland? You could argue before the bench as well as any barrister."

Pen waited while the footman served their soup, grateful for the pause. What was going on here? This conversation was starting to feel as perilous as a walk on thin ice.

"I define a chivalrous man as one who is always aware of the probable feelings of those around him and who acts accordingly," she finally continued. "You were kind to me upstairs when I was overset at your sister's near-accident. Therefore I assume you possess a sense of chivalry."

Niall picked up his spoon and gazed down into his pale green watercress bisque. He was biting his lower lip. Pen watched him, waiting for his reply.

What was it that made her look up then and catch Lady Keating's gaze upon her? Beside her she felt Niall move. When she glanced at him, he too was looking at his mother at the other end of the table.

"An admirable barrister," he repeated. "Perhaps it was kindness or, as you called it, chivalry. But might it not have been something else, too?" His tone had gone from wary to caressing.

"Such as?"

"Such as . . . pleasure?"

"You are a dangerous man, Mr. Keating." Pen ignored the fluttering sensation that danced in her middle at the way the word *pleasure* had slipped from his lips. There was no doubt; now he *was* flirting with her.

What was Niall? Was he the grinning boy who had asked her to go walking last week and who had apologized for his lack of social polish, or the worldly man whose dinner conversation was making her feel warm and breathless? And which one of them had been holding her hand in the library? She half wished they would stop so she could think about it all . . . and at the same time, she wanted to see how far it would go.

"Why?" He leaned toward her slightly as he spoke. "What is wrong with combining concern for others with one's own enjoyment? Must one's motives be purely selfless? Was it wrong of me to take pleasure from giving you the reassurance you needed? Surely there would be more kindness in the world if both the donors and receivers of kind actions received equal gratification."

"A good deed is its own reward."

"You make good deeds sound like castor oil—good for you, but not necessarily palatable."

"I did not say that, Mr. Keating. You did," she returned, and then felt . . . tired. Perhaps she wasn't cut out to be a flirt. It took far too much energy to maintain a conversation on multiple levels. "I am grateful for your kindness upstairs and must confess that I, too, found it . . . pleasurable as well as comforting. I must leave it up to you to decide what your feelings on the topic are and what they mean." She turned her attention to her soup.

"I am sorry, Miss Leland. I see that I have . . . have . . ."

She looked up. The bantering edge to his voice had slipped, and when she met his eyes they were narrowed ever so slightly, as if he were uncomfortable. There it was again—was he merely pretending to be forward? Did he find keeping up this two-edged conversation as tiring as she did?

"Offended me?" she finished for him.

"Have I?"

She sighed and reached for her wineglass. "No. Confused me, perhaps, but not offended."

"Then I apologize again. Barristers do not like to be confused, I know." Niall smiled and, lifting his wineglass, held it up in a salute to her before drinking.

She hesitated, then sipped from her own. Turn and turn again. Would their entire evening be like this?

But he was quiet after that, and remained quiet through the remaining dinner courses until it was time for the ladies to leave the men to their after-dinner port.

Over tea and coffee in the now-tidied drawing room, Lady Keating, Lady Whelan, and Lady Enniskean were talkative enough that all Pen had to do was answer their questions politely and smile a great deal, which seemed to satisfy them. Pen was grateful; the last thing she felt like doing just now was chatting. Fortunately, the Enniskeans' daughter, Charlotte, seemed as disinclined to conversation as Pen was, and Doireann had somehow vanished en route from the dining room.

Pen took her cup of coffee in Lady Keating's exquisite china and thought about casting a mild cloaking spell over herself, just to keep from being drawn back into the group of ladies on the sofa. But Ally had always disapproved of using magic in social situations apart from emergencies, so instead she wandered over to examine a display cabinet of curios. It had the added benefit of being as far from the chimneypiece as it was possible to be. She rather doubted she'd ever be able to sit in Lady Keating's drawing room again without remembering the sick feeling in the pit of her stomach at the sight of the heavy urn falling toward Doireann's bare, unprotected head.

What should she feel about Niall Keating now? More to the point, what did he feel about her? Was she overdramatizing everything that had passed between them? And if she was, what did that mean about how she felt? Could her train of thought grow any more circular? She managed a smile at her silliness, but it was a small one.

She could not help liking him a great deal. Nobody could help liking him—she had noticed Charlotte Enniskean glance at him frequently during dinner with a small, simpering smile on her pretty face, hoping to catch his eye. She hadn't, which pleased Pen in a most uncharitable way. Which, in turn, made her feel slightly cross with herself. After all, it wasn't as if she cared if he noticed Miss Enniskean . . . did she?

It was time, as her younger brother, Charles, had once said, provoking a storm of hilarity, to take the bull by the tail and face the situation. She was falling in . . . in, well, in *something* with Niall Keating. How could she not, when he was as fascinating and as obviously interested in her as he seemed to be? The question was, where would it lead?

If he was just looking for a flirtation to while away his time, then he could look somewhere else. She had a job to do while she was in Ireland, and it didn't involve amusing bored young men. But what if there was something else behind his charm? Something that might, with nurturing, grow into a deeper, truer emotion?

And how, *how* was she supposed to tell the difference? Could she dedicate the time and attention her studies required and still be able to explore this friendship with Niall? What if she became too distracted by him, only to discover that his feelings were all on the surface? On the other hand, what if she stuck to the straight and narrow path and ended up missing the love of her life?

Voices in the hall distracted her. The gentlemen had cut short their time over port and cigars and were returning to the ladies. Charlotte Enniskean hurried over to a pair of Louis XV bergères set tête-à-tête in a corner and settled herself on one. It didn't take much work to guess who she hoped would join her.

Feeling slightly defiant, Pen kept her back to the door and pretended to be absorbed in examining the porcelain figurines in the cabinet as the men came in, followed by Healy and a footman with more coffee. It was not good manners, and Mama would have been scandalized, but Mama was not here. Besides, there was no one she particularly cared to—

"May I get you more coffee, Miss Leland?" Niall murmured behind her.

Mama's training won out. She turned away from the cabinet and bowed slightly. "No thank you, Mr. Keating." There, that would do. She would be perfectly correct, but it would be up to him to set the tenor of their conversation.

After several minutes, it did not appear that there would be any conversation. Niall stood beside her, hands behind his back, smiling and bowing whenever anyone caught his eye, neither speaking nor showing any inclination to stir from her side. From the corner of her eye, Pen saw a pouting Charlotte Enniskean watching them. On the other hand, Lady Keating only smiled at them whenever she glanced their way. It was very odd, and increasingly awkward.

After several more minutes, Pen couldn't stand it anymore. "Don't let me keep you from playing host, Mr. Keating," she murmured.

"You're not," he replied. "Aren't you a guest?"

She wanted to pour the remainder of her coffee over his shoes in exasperation. "Yes, but . . ."

He reached up and rubbed his head, tousling the thick blond locks into boyish disarray. "You are gently pointing out to me that I should be circulating among my mother's guests making amusing conversation, but I can't. I can't even say what I want to say to you right now, so I'm forced to stand here staring at you and make the both of us uncomfortable with my silence."

Was this more of his banter? She swallowed and asked, "What did you want to say to me, sir? I beg you, please do not say anything unless it is for a reason. Even barristers tire of words after a while, if they're empty ones."

The chill little "sir" she couldn't resist adding seemed to pain him. "You're not making it any easier, you know," he almost growled, under his breath.

"Making *what* easier? Mr. Keating, I don't know—"

"My dear Penelope." Dr. Carrighar suddenly appeared beside them. "I've just asked for the gig to be brought round. Might you be ready to leave shortly?"

She glanced up at Niall and saw his brows draw down in an expression half pleading, half relieved, and wondered if her own face mirrored it. Why couldn't Dr. Carrighar have waited just two more minutes, so she could have finished this enigmatic conversation? "Yes, of course. Will you excuse me, Mr. Keating?"

Pen saw Miss Enniskean's face light up when Healy brought their wraps. Good luck to her if she hoped to extract any lively conversation from Niall.

Lady Keating accompanied them to the door, protesting that it was far too early for them to leave. Dr. Carrighar demurred. "I'm an old man and not used to socializing."

"Well, you must get used to it, sir," Lady Whelan boomed gaily from the drawing room doorway. "I've decided to have a dance in a week or two, and Miss Leland must surely be there."

"And I had hoped you would attend our party as well," Lady Enniskean added from over her shoulder, glancing at her son and then at Pen with a meaningful smile.

Dr. Carrighar stiffened, but his tone remained gallant. "All the more reason for me to rest up now. Good night, Lady Keating."

Pen embraced Lady Keating and bowed to Doireann, who had reappeared as unexpectedly as she had vanished. Niall stepped forward and bowed over her hand. But he did not give it a clandestine squeeze, as she half expected him to. Instead he met her eyes steadily for three or four seconds, then looked away.

In the gig Dr. Carrighar leaned his head back and sighed. "No wonder I do not usually go out in society. It's deuced hard work, having to be polite for such an extended period. I am more accustomed to verbally abusing my scholars than making parlor conversation."

Pen smiled at him. "You're a fraud, sir. You're never anything but courteous at all times."

"Ah, but you don't know what I am thinking while I'm being courteous, do you? And verbal abuse is much more effective, not to mention amusing, when done politely. Well, I suppose I feel a little better about Nuala Keating after tonight."

"A little better?"

"Yes, a little. I still think she bears watching. There are wheels, there, turning, but I don't think you're in any immediate peril from the Keatings."

Oh, yes she was. At least from one Keating. Botheration, what had he wanted to say to her? She put that thought aside. "From their household ornaments, perhaps. It was me that made sure Doireann Keating wasn't brained by that vase, you know. I was worried she or Lady Keating had noticed that I pushed it aside with magic, but I don't think they did."

"So that's why you had a guilty look on your face when you came into the library. No, they wouldn't notice. No one ever does, so I hope you weren't expecting gratitude from Miss Keating." He closed his eyes and sighed again. "I've earned my rest tonight."

Pen stared out the window at the dark waters of the river Lee's North Channel as the coachman—Norah's brother James, who took care of Dr. Carrighar's horse and gig when he wasn't packing butter at the Exchange—drove them across Griffith Bridge. No, she supposed she hadn't been expecting thanks from Doireann. But it might have been nice.

She pictured Doireann smiling broadly, poker in hand, when Lady Keating had brought her into the drawing room, and gave herself a little shake. Doireann would probably never talk to her again, because she'd—

The poker. In the dark carriage Pen's eyes widened. Doireann had set her poker down on the chimneypiece when she'd come in, hadn't she?

So how had the vase managed to fall, without knocking the poker off, too?

6

Niall was relieved when the Whelans, who never seemed to know when a party was over, finally left. He ushered them to the front hall and exchanged a wry glance with Healy as the door closed behind their backs. Too bad it hadn't been Miss Leland who'd lingered so late instead. He'd desperately wanted to drag her back to the library and hold her hand again and tell her . . . tell her what? He shook his head at himself and turned toward the stairs as Healy locked the front door.

What had possessed him to behave the way he had tonight? At first it had been instinct: Miss Leland had been visibly shaken by the falling vase incident, and he simply wanted to comfort her. Then it had seemed like a good opportunity to forward Mother's plan. And then . . .

Then it had turned into something else entirely. All at once Niall had wished everyone in the room would go away so that he could crush Miss Leland . . . Pen . . . to his breast and kiss her till he had no breath left. At dinner he'd said the first things to come into his head—outrageous things, he knew—both because Mother was watching him and because he couldn't help himself. And finally in the drawing room he'd been seized by remorse for his waywardness at dinner and wanted to kneel at her feet and confess. Was Doire- ann right? Was he starting to take his wooing of Pen seriously?

Healy cleared his throat, and Niall realized he'd been standing on the bottom step, one hand on the banister, for the last several seconds. "I'm sorry, Healy. Woolgathering. Was there something you wanted?"

"Sir. Lady Keating requests that you join her in the drawing room before you retire, if you please."

Niall suppressed a groan. All he wanted to do right now was go to bed so he could contemplate the memory of the soft curve of Pen's cheek when she smiled. It had fixed his attention more than once during dinner and was far more comfortable to think about than their conversation . . . and far safer to dwell on than the feeling of her hand in his and the way she'd blushed when he'd stroked it. "Thank you, Healy. Could you bring me a brandy first?"

"Right away, sir." He glided to the dining room.

Niall sat on a step and glared at the drawing room door. Now what? Did Mother want a progress report? Could he bring himself to tell her about holding hands with Pen under the folio in the library? That would buck her up for the evening for sure, and maybe she'd let him escape to his room without a further grilling. Niall rose and took a few agitated paces.

However, he couldn't, just couldn't, tell her about their later con- versation.

"Your brandy, sir." Healy appeared at his elbow. "Will there be anything else?"

Niall put on his polite face. "Not from me, thank you."

He waited until Healy had disappeared through the door to the kitchens, then took a large gulp of his brandy. The sooner he got this over with, the sooner he could go upstairs and figure out what the hell he was going to do about Miss Leland. He squared his shoulders and opened the drawing room door.

Mother was pacing the length of the Aubusson carpet, her turban abandoned, black hair hanging over her shoulders like ravens' wings. She paused to smile at him as he entered. Doireann was curled in a chair, still glowering.

Niall's eyes went immediately to the fireplace, with its missing vase, and he took another sip of brandy before saying, "Yes, Mother? Dinner went well, I thought."

"Sit down, darling. Yes, quite well," she replied. "Quite well, indeed."

Doireann made a small noise, almost but not quite a whimper.

Mother ignored her. "You seemed to have a pleasant time with Miss Leland. I saw you conversing at dinner."

"Yes." Of course she had. He could practically feel her willing him to be outrageous to her. He chose a chair where he could watch both women.

"And was progress made?" Her voice cut across him like a whip.

"Well, I suppose. . . ." He swirled the brandy in his glass and breathed in its fumes, hot and dry and smoky, contemplating Mother over the rim of his glass. It would be now or never. He set down the brandy and leaned forward in his chair.

"Damn it, Mother, why? When are you going to let me in on what's going on? How in blazes is Miss Leland supposed to help us with getting to the duke?"

Doireann spoke up. "You haven't told him yet?" There was an edge of amusement in her voice.

Mother didn't look at her but instead kicked at the rug's fringe. "Quiet, girl. You hardly have any right to speak, given that this is all your fault."

Doireann snorted.

Mother stopped pacing and came to kneel at his feet in a graceful movement. "Very well, darling. I suppose it is time for you to know. You know how I tried writing to your father last summer and received no reply. I have tried many times since then, without a single word of response. I don't know what has kept him from answering, but I intend to remove whatever obstacle it is that stands between you, using whatever means I have at my disposal."

She waved a slender hand, and an image of Miss Leland shimmered in the air before them. Niall wanted to reach out and touch it, but before he could act on the impulse, the image smiled at him and faded into nothingness.

"What has my making Miss Leland fall in love with me have to do with that?" he asked. He remembered her hand holding his fiercely under the folio in the library and the expression in her eyes during their murmured conversation at dinner, and suddenly he wanted to turn on his heels and leave Mother and Doireann and take his memories of the tall, honey-haired girl away from them, to be cherished in private.

"It occurred to me that I could remove the barrier separating you from the duke with a gentle application of my powers," Mother replied. "So I prepared a magical, ah—*procedure* to remove the barrier, one that required assistance from two others, equally though differently endowed in magic. Great-aunt Nessa was prepared to come down from Belfast to help, though at her age such a long carriage journey would be difficult. Your sister was the other—"

"His half sister, Mother dear. Don't you think we need to be precise, since we're on the subject?" Doireann inserted.

"Shortly before I was ready, your halfwitted half sister did something untoward to make it impossible for her to be a part of it, just when I needed her help." Mother rose, pointedly looking away from her daughter.

But Doireann just laughed quietly. "You're so genteel all of a sudden. 'Something untoward'? I stopped being a virgin, little brother. It was boring, so I went to bed with someone. Shocking, isn't it? Can your delicate ears stand it? Poor Mother needed a Maiden and a Crone to play second fiddle to her magic, and I ruined it all. What I would like to know is why it's all right for a man to do as he will with his body, but not a woman."

"Idiot!" Mother spat the word. "You know very well why in this case. Any man can rut like an animal. It doesn't matter for them. But to waste your maidenhood just because—what did you say?—because you were *bored* with being a virgin? I thought I had trained you far better than that. Throwing away your power—" Her hands clenched into fists.

"I did not throw away my power. I went from Maiden to Mother and exchanged one sort of power for another. If anything, I've increased it," Doireann shot back.

"Oh, yes, *increased*," Mother mimicked. "You did this knowing full well that it was your power as a Maiden that we need right now. With Nessa and you and me performing the spell, we had not only the power of the Three, but the power of family as well."

"I'm not sure that I want to hear any more about this, Mother." Niall walked to the fireplace and stared down into the dancing flames. So this was the cause of the increased acrimony between them over the last months. His head had begun to spin, and it wasn't the brandy's fault.

"Is it too much for the diddums's pure little ears?" Doireann lisped. "Is the big, bad world too naughty to hear about? Well, Saint Niall, we don't all choose to live as monks just because Mother says to."

Niall willed his fists not to clench. "Doireann, please."

"Without your sister, we could not perform the . . . procedure," Mother continued as if she had never been interrupted. "I had to find someone else to help us. Finding a young woman with our ability who was also a maiden was difficult enough. But I had lost the added power of her being a part of our family, power that we needed if my plans were to work. With the power of the Three, bound by family ties, I can do what needs to be done to bring you and your father together."

"But what does Miss Leland—"

"Miss Leland is a witch," Mother interrupted him calmly. "I saw it at once when I met her. She practically reeks of magic. Her connection with the Carrighars only confirms it. You know Dr. Carrighar is one of the most powerful wizards in Ireland. And after what happened tonight, I am sure."

"What?" Niall's jaw dropped. Penelope Leland . . . a *witch*? Like Mother and Doireann? It couldn't be. Not her. He shook his head, as if to clear it. "What happened that makes you so sure?"

"Just Mother dear up to her usual tricks," Doireann said with cheerful malevolence. But her face had gone white and pinched. "That alarming little incident with the vase?" she continued nonchalantly. "Mother made it start to fall on my head, to see if Miss Leland would stop it with magic. I say, darling Mother, just out of curiosity, what if you'd been wrong and she hadn't been a witch?"

Niall stared at her. "So that was what . . . good lord! Mother, surely you could have found some other way to test her without . . . are you all right?" No wonder she had glowered so this evening.

Doireann rolled her eyes. "If I weren't, we wouldn't be having this cozy chat, would we? You'd have been mopping up my brains and pretending to mourn instead of flirting with that English *bean draoi*."

"Niall, do you really think I would have let any harm come to your sister?" Mother looked annoyed.

"Well, no, but—"

"At least not too much," Doireann added sweetly. "What harm is a smashed skull?"

Mother clapped her hands. "Enough, both of you! This is important. Not only is she a witch, but she is also a gently brought up young lady, which almost certainly means that she is a virgin as well. Listen to me, Niall. If she can be encouraged to love you, then she'll want to help you. You will have to ask her to marry you so that she will be bound to us by a family tie. But that is easily taken care of, and then we can proceed with the important part and bring you and your father together at last."

"Although that means *you'll* have to take the role of the Crone, Mother dear," Doireann purred. "But as you say, the cycle of life is inevitable. One does become a crone with time." She shrugged. "Of course, there is compensation for becoming old and ugly. The Crone is supposed to have the most power, isn't she?" Doireann's expression indicated her opinion of that trade-off.

Mother turned a dull red. "Old and ugly?"

Niall rose abruptly and stood between them, trying to make sense of this all. "So in order to get Miss Leland's help so that I can have some chance at the future you've chosen for me, I must make her love me and accept my proposal?"

There was an odd rushing noise in his head and the room seemed to recede around him. Ask her to marry him. He would have to take her in his arms, and kiss her, and gaze down into those endless blue eyes, and tell her he loved her—

"Which of course you won't have to go through with, darling. Don't worry." Mother glided over and took his arm.

Words tumbled out of his mouth before he could stop them. "What if I wanted to?"

Her green eyes narrowed and her grip on his arm tightened. "Nonsense, dear. Once your father has accepted you, you shall have a duke's daughter to wife at the very least. You won't need to throw yourself away on some member of the lesser nobility. We just need you and Miss Leland engaged when my spell is performed. You will break it off afterward—the very next day, if you like."

"Her grandfather is the Duke of Revesby. That's hardly lesser nobility," Niall countered.

Doireann laughed suddenly. "Ha! Didn't I warn you, baby brother? Getting too fond of our dear Miss Leland, aren't you?"

Niall gritted his teeth. Blast Doireann anyhow. "It's not that. It's— I just can't go around proposing to granddaughters of important peers without intending to keep my word. It's breach of promise."

Mother turned him to face her. "Nonsense, Niall. It will all work out in the end. Trust me, darling. To make an omelet, one must break eggs. Miss Leland will recover from her jilting. She's an attractive enough girl and will find someone quite easily next season if her marriage portion is as handsome as I suspect it is."

"Lucky girl," Doireann said to the room. There was an odd note in her voice that Niall didn't understand, but Mother had fixed him with her green eyes.

"Listen carefully. Now that we know she's what we need, it's time to move in for the kill. No, don't turn away from me like that. I'm speaking metaphorically, you softhearted boy. You must increase your efforts with the girl. I want you calling on her at least every other day. Make it clear you're utterly fascinated by her. In a month's time, she'll be putty in our hands. Do you understand?" She reached up and patted his cheek. "You are tired, my dearest one. Go to bed."

At last, a chance to escape. Niall bent dutifully and kissed her cheek, then turned to Doireann. "I'm glad that you're safe, whether you believe that or not," he said.

His sister draped herself across the sofa and smirked up at him. "Of course I believe it. You're too damned nice to think anything else." She gave a sarcastic little laugh.

Niall kept his impassive face and straight posture until he was safely in his room with the door locked. Then he leaned against it and closed his eyes.

A witch! Penelope Leland, a witch!

It would explain many things—her puzzling mix of youth and wisdom. And why she didn't want to talk about her studies. Not if she was studying magic with Dr. Carrighar. That must mean that her governess was a witch as well. And the married sister back in England. Penelope had said that she missed studying with her sister.

But a witch? Niall tried to picture her pouring tea without touching the teapot, as Mother did. She wouldn't do anything quite so— so showy, he guessed. Magic was not a convenience for her, a way to smooth life over and make it easier. From the way she talked about studying, it was more a sacred duty.

But those candid blue eyes. That smile. The girlish pleasure in her new cloak. How could she be all those things and a witch too?

Niall wrestled his coat off and began to untie his cravat before it strangled him. It was time to engage a valet, if he could find one who could learn to live peaceably in the same house with his mother and sister. The one he'd hired to accompany him on his continental trip had lasted only two months after returning to Ireland with him. He paced restlessly up and down his room as he fumbled with the linen.

His picture of Pen Leland was shifting, changing. It was as if he'd only seen her through a filmy curtain before, and now the curtain had been withdrawn. Beneath the charming, hesitant young girl exterior was a disciplined, strong woman. There had to be. No one could wield magic and not be those things.

And he was supposed to try to work his own sorcery on her, and enchant her with honeyed words and meaningful glances into using her power for him? Good God, if his cravat didn't choke him first, the irony would. Surely she would see through him at once, see how he was trying to manipulate her, use her.

Only a fool trifled with a witch. And here he was, trifling with one in about as enormous a way as was possible.

If she's a witch, she should be able to protect herself, said a small, dubious voice in his head.

Could she? Could anyone, where their emotions were involved? Love was blind, and lovers blinder. Even witch lovers. Look at Mother and her duke.

Pen saw him as genuine and sincere, and was responding to his deceitful flirtation with honest emotion. Damn it all, the last thing he wanted was to make her fall in love with him, then find him out as a lying scoundrel.

What could he say to Mother? Nothing that she'd accept. To her, Penelope was a tool. Unimportant, except as a means to get to the duke. She'd already said as much. His sudden attack of conscience wouldn't hold any water with her.

Niall threw himself on his bed, staring morosely at the plaster knotwork on the ceiling. If he was lucky, his blasted cravat would throttle him before he had to deal with any of them.

A soft scratching at the door made him sit up. "Yes?" he called.

The door opened, and Doireann came in. She shut the door and leaned against it. "Still awake, little boy?" she asked. Her color was high and her green eyes hard and bright. Evidently she and Mother had had words after he left.

Niall rose. "Are you all right, Doir?"

She shrugged and gestured with one hand, and his cravat untangled from his neck, snapped itself smartly against his cheek, then flew into a corner and collapsed in a limp heap.

"Thank you." Niall did not allow himself to rub his cheek where the fabric had stung him. Doireann was incapable of doing him even a small act of kindness without adding some little edge to it. It had always been that way from the time they were both small, when he had tagged everywhere after her, trying to keep up with his fierce, fearless big sister.

"You're welcome." Doireann straightened and grinned at him. "So what did you think of Mother's exhortation? Are you ready to move in for the kill? Miss Leland will make a charming corpse, undoubtedly."

Don't react. Don't let her see. "It will be interesting, I suppose.

Doir, about you . . . I don't want to pry, but you and . . . it was Brian Lenehan, wasn't it? Sir Dominic's son?"

"Why, Niall, what a question to ask a lady!" She pressed a hand to her cheek, pretending to be shocked, then laughed and tossed her head. "What about it? What if it was? I wanted him. He wanted me. It was an equal exchange, unlike most relations between men and women these days. Come on, dance with me." She curtsied to him and grabbed his hands, digging her nails into them.

It was easier to humor her than to argue. Niall waltzed her around the room in careful arcs, skirting the furniture. "Do you love him?"

Doireann froze in midstep, a black scowl on her face. Then she laughed again and resumed their dance, taking over the lead from him. "Insofar as I love anyone—for what they can give me. Brian gave me pleasure, not to mention the joy of tweaking Mother's nose. It was worth it for that alone, almost. Why?"

"Because though you may not choose to believe it, I'd like to see you happy. I expect Father would give his consent to your marrying Brian even if he isn't the oldest son. He's an honest, well-meaning sort, and there's a substantial estate and all, so you'd always be comfortable. . . ."

To Niall's surprise, Doireann neither laughed nor scowled as he trailed off. Instead her face was thoughtful.

"Good God, Niall. After all the years I spent making your toys vanish and putting your stupid dog up on the roof of the stables when we were small, you still seem to care about me. Why? Our Christian upbringing at Mother's knee?" She gave a short bark of laughter. "The unimpeachable code of honor you imbibed at Harrow?"

"Or the fact that you're my sister, no matter what, and I care about you? God knows why," he added, to forestall her derision.

"Ah! So even half blood is thicker than water, eh?" She led them into a tight turn, then another. "Brian *is* a fine boy. He worships the ground I tread upon, which is even better. I could do worse, no matter what Mother promises after we've done her little deed."

"Just what *is* Mother planning?"

She laughed again, but he could sense that she was not amused. "You don't really want to know. Take my word for it. But it will all work out for the best. I promise you that, little brother. This has been an interesting talk." After another series of turns, she came to rest at the door, dropped his hands, and curtsied to him.

"Very interesting indeed," she repeated. With another grin, she slipped around the door.

7

The day after the party at the Keatings', Ally did not come downstairs to take her usual place on the sofa in the drawing room. At breakfast Michael put a matter-of-fact face on it, saying that she had decided it would be easier for everyone if she just stayed in her room. But Pen sensed the anxiety in his too-cheerful manner and excused herself after a few hasty mouthfuls of bacon and toast to check on Ally herself.

Ally lay propped in bed, languidly sipping a glass of water tinged a faint yellowish green. In her white nightgown and plaited hair, she looked uncharacteristically girlish and vulnerable.

"Oh, good morning, Pen," she said. "I thought that sounded like your knock. How are you today?"

Pen inspected Ally's breakfast tray and noted that she had eaten her toast and eggs. "I'm fine. What's more important is, how are you?"

Ally smiled a slow, heavy-eyed smile. "Not bad, really. Two eggs this morning. Aren't you proud of me? So long as I have my medicine as soon as I eat, I'm fine. No nausea or discomfort." She held up her glass to the morning light and contemplated it with an air of drowsy satisfaction.

Pen studied her. "You look better. Your face is filling out again."

"Is it? I hadn't noticed." Ally yawned and took another sip. "I suppose that's a good thing, though."

"Of course it is! You can't grow a healthy baby if you're not healthy, and that means getting enough to eat and keeping it down."

"Mmm. That's true." Ally finished the contents of her glass, carefully set it on her bedside table, and settled back onto her pillows.

Something about her air of lazy contentment bothered Pen. It was so un-Ally. "Michael said you'd decided not to come downstairs today. Don't you feel well enough, now that you're stronger?"

"Oh, I don't know." Ally shrugged. "I'm so sleepy all the time that it seemed silly to come downstairs and nap on the sofa. Why not just stay here and keep out of everyone's way? Michael's gone all day, and you're busy with everything." She gestured vaguely. "And it's more comfortable up here. More peaceful."

Pen nearly goggled. Was this the same brisk, energetic Ally who had seemed to be everywhere when she was their governess?

"Well, I suppose it's important that you get your rest." She took Ally's unresisting hand. "But this just doesn't seem like you. You've always been so busy and in charge, and it feels very odd not to have you . . . well, being *you*. I miss you horripilatiously. Sometimes it's as if you're not even here, lately."

Ally closed her eyes. "I've not gone anywhere. You're being fanciful, Pen. And please stop using that silly word of Charles's."

That sounded a little more like Ally. "Well, it feels that way. Sometimes you feel as far away as Mother and Persy back in Hampshire, and I don't know who to talk to about some things."

A faint frown appeared between Ally's brows, and Pen could have bitten her tongue. Poor Ally was just starting to be able to keep down the mildest of foods, and here she was, whining to her like a six-year-old.

"I don't want to burden you. You've got enough to worry you right now," she added quickly.

Ally gave a small sigh. "No, it's all right. What do you need to talk about?"

What didn't she need to talk about? *No, keep it simple.* "Oh, I don't know. Little things, really. Like last night at Lady Keating's dinner party. It was, well, it was alarming in a lot of ways, and I don't know what to do or think about it all."

Ally didn't open her eyes. "'M listening," she mumbled.

Pen held Ally's hand more tightly and tried to choose her words carefully. "I had to do magic there, to keep a vase from falling on Doireann Keating's head. I don't know if anyone noticed. And I don't know how the vase could have fallen in the first place, because there was something in front of it. Nothing all that momentous, really, but I'm—I don't know. Something feels not right about it."

"Mmm-hmmm."

Should she continue? It was such a relief to be talking to someone who understood. "And Niall Keating. He's becoming very friendly, but I don't know if it's just a flirtation to him or something else. It's not as if this were London and I could judge his intentions by how he behaved to other girls."

Words began to fall out of her. "He's—I can't help liking him a great deal. He's handsome and intelligent and charming and eligible, and I'm sure Mama and Papa would love him. And Lady Keating seems to like me, too. But it's all happening so fast, so neatly, as if it were planned. I'm afraid, almost—afraid I'll neglect my studies and make a fool of myself over him. What if it is just a game to him? He seems so restless under all that charm. I thought his sister was like the lions at the Zoological Garden, napping in the sun. But he's like the cheetah, pacing his cage. What if he's just amusing himself with me?"

Her throat burned slightly as she blinked back tears. "Oh, Ally," she whispered, "what should I do?"

Her only answer was a soft snore.

Pen opened her mouth, then shut it. To wake Ally would be unforgivably selfish. She had been so uncomfortable and miserable before Lady Keating gave her the elixir. If it made her sleepy as well as relieving her discomfort, then that was just something Pen would have to put up with. Surely Ally would wake up later. They could talk then.

Pen sat by Ally's bedside for another few minutes, watching her. Ally wore a faint half smile, as if she were having pleasant dreams. Well, there wasn't anything wrong with that, was there? She deserved some relief.

But part of Pen's mind couldn't be silenced. For Ally, the person who cared most about her in the world after Mama and Persy, to fall asleep in the middle of a conversation, especially one like that, just didn't feel right. Lady Keating had said it was harmless, but still . . . was a medicine as powerful as that good for an expectant woman?

Pen picked up Ally's glass and sniffed the dregs of the medicine. It had a fresh, green scent that reminded Pen of newly mown grass, but with an underlying bitter note. It also reminded her of something she'd smelled recently, but she couldn't remember what. Something herbal with tincture of poppy added, perhaps? That might explain the sleepiness. Surely it could not be good to have much of that. But Dr. Carrighar hadn't been able to find anything wrong with it.

Well, perhaps it was for the best. Would Ally be able to understand her questions about Niall? She had avoided all her suitors before becoming their governess, and her courtship with Michael while he had held her captive at Kensington Palace last year had been anything but usual.

A nearly empty bottle of Lady Keating's tonic stood next to the glass. She'd sent two more home with them last night, but she might like this empty one back. Pen slipped it into her pocket and left Ally to her slumber, wishing she could stop feeling so uneasy.

Pen planned to devote all her free time that day to the readings Dr. Carrighar set her, mostly seventeenth-century translations of earlier Irish treatises on magic and the Triple Goddess. Not surprisingly, the quaint, antique language made uphill work. For the first dozen pages or so, she was properly attentive. But then some chance word or some stray thought, or sometimes nothing at all, would make her start thinking about other things, like Niall . . . the feeling of his hand on hers last night, or the sound of his voice when he'd half whispered the word *pleasure,* or the way he'd looked at her last night when she'd been called away by Dr. Carrighar.

When that happened, she would give herself a firm mental shake and get on again with another dozen pages until something else tipped her back into daydreams. Finally, after a few hours of feeling like a shuttlecock, she closed her book and stared moodily out the window at the dripping street. Rain again, of course. She would have to pay a call on Lady Keating that afternoon to thank her for the dinner—it was what one did after being entertained at someone's house. And she'd have to do it in the rain. How lovely. Would Niall be there too, to see her in all her damp glory? What should she say to him if he were there?

Even though Ally had fallen asleep before they could discuss them, speaking her worries and doubts aloud had helped focus her thoughts. Last year in London she'd rather enjoyed watching the posturing and maneuvering that took place between the sexes at balls and parties: the sidelong glances full of meaning, the dropped handkerchiefs, the giggles and pouts.

But she'd been sitting on the sidelines then. It was different now that it was her. Different now that she'd seen what marriage could mean to two people. Like Ally and Michael. Or Persy and Lochinvar. She wanted the kind of marriages they had. She wanted to find true love.

Had Niall merely been flirting with her? A little shiver ran through her at the memory of the feeling of his hand on hers last night. It had gone far beyond flirtatious words or glances. Surely she should find it alarming.

And yet she could not believe he was what Mama would have referred to as a "rogue," someone who viewed a young girl's virtue as a challenge. He'd felt so comfortable, so sympathetic, so like a friend in their first interactions. She shifted irritably in her chair. Thoughts of him were making it impossible to get any studying done.

"I didn't come here to fall in love," she muttered aloud. There, she'd said it. The fact was, she was falling for Niall Keating, whether she wanted to or not. He was charming and handsome and educated and heir to a barony, no matter who his father really was. Papa and Mama would surely approve of him.

With a shake, she opened her book again. Something would have to be done, and soon.

That afternoon Niall was seated next to Charlotte Enniskean in the drawing room, hiding his boredom behind a veneer of languid agreeableness. It was a façade he'd learned to cultivate on his travels on the Continent, where the young ladies either seemed to be extremely shy and retiring or extremely predatory. It seemed to be nonalarming to the former and discouraging to the latter, and permitted him to navigate many a social event with a minimum of bother.

Unfortunately, Miss Enniskean seemed to be regarding it as a challenge. She'd never been quite this persistent when they were both children, but young women could change from sparrows to eagles overnight when in search of husbands. The amused looks the also-present Sir Percival Gorman kept casting in their direction weren't helping, either. For the fifth time, Niall wished he'd found some pressing bit of business to take care of this afternoon, so that he could have avoided these courtesy calls from Mother's dinner guests.

The reason he hadn't was made clear shortly after, when Healy appeared in the doorway and announced, "Lady Keating, Miss Leland is here."

Next to him, Miss Enniskean made a small sound that distinctly resembled an indignant hiss.

Mother rose and glided toward Pen. "Naughty girl," she scolded. "You walked here, didn't you? I should have sent Padraic with the carriage for you." She softened her words, however, with an affectionate kiss.

"I enjoyed the walk. It's turned into a lovely day," Pen demurred as she returned the kiss and curtsied to Lady Enniskean and Sir Percival.

Niall saw her glance involuntarily toward the fireplace. He had told Healy to remove the alabaster vase that was mate to the smashed one, because he didn't want to see it any more than she probably did. Damn it, Mother had gone too far that time. No wonder Doireann had still been glowering at breakfast this morning.

"Miss Leland." Niall unfolded his frame from the sofa and came to bow over her hand. She colored slightly. Was she remembering how he'd held her hand last night?

Just as he'd relived it over and over, till he'd finally fallen asleep as dawn broke?

"I say, Miss Leland," Edward Enniskean said eagerly. "We should be happy to drive you home again."

"I daresay you would," Mother replied before Pen could open her mouth. "Miss Leland's just arrived, and you are about to leave, I'm sure, and I shall require her presence for a while yet." She gave Lady Enniskean a bland smile. "Most kind of you to call today. Dinner was delightful last night, was it not? We must coax Dr. Carrighar into society more often, along with his charming guest."

She spoke with such a tone of finality that Lady Enniskean was drawn to her feet and to the drawing room door before she quite knew it. Niall saw her look of bafflement as she and Mother bumped cheeks in farewell. It was classic Mother: If she'd been a man, she would surely have gone into politics or some other field where her talent for managing others could have been fully realized.

"Good day, Mr. Keating." Charlotte managed to squirm past the embracing ladies and hold her hand out for Niall to bow over. "Now don't forget, you must take tea with us very soon. Edward's quite keen to show you his botanical collection. Aren't you, Edward?"

Niall looked over at Pen, who still wore a polite smile. But a faint glimmer of devilment in her eyes indicated that her thoughts were probably less polite. "Er . . . thank you, Miss Enniskean," he replied. "I am . . . um . . . always delighted to spend time in the company of . . . er . . . beautiful flowers."

As soon as the words left his mouth, he immediately wished them back. Pen's brows had lifted ever so slightly, and the corners of her mouth quirked in . . . distaste? Damnation, why had he said something so stupidly flirtatious when Pen would dislike it and Charlotte would take it all too much to heart? He cringed as Charlotte laughed and shot a triumphant smirk at Pen.

"Then we'll have to have Miss Leland as well," Edward put in quickly.

Was that a snort from Doireann? Niall glanced at her, but her head was bent over an embroidery frame.

"Charming." Mother swept back toward Pen and herded her and Niall to the sofa as Healy bowed the Enniskeans out of the room. She gave him a meaningful look as she settled next to Sir Percival.

Niall seated himself on the sofa by Pen. Should he apologize for making such a stupid remark, or would that make him look even more foolish? Devil take it, he was a grown man, and here he was, acting like a tongue-tied boy of sixteen. "Miss Leland," he began.

She leaned forward as if she hadn't heard him. "Sir Percival, I am quite convinced that you must be a font of stories about Dr. Carrighar's youth. I would be most obliged if you would tell us a few of the most unflattering ones that I might store away for use as ammunition at some point."

Sir Percival laughed. "How could I refuse so irresistible a request? But I fear I will incriminate myself in the process."

"We will grant you a witness's immunity from prosecution in return for your cooperation, will we not, Lady Keating?" Pen smiled at Mother.

She managed to keep Sir Percival chatting for the next thirty minutes, much to Niall's annoyance. When she rose to leave, scant minutes after Sir Percival left, Mother stepped in.

"I know you won't let me call the carriage, but you must allow Niall to accompany you home. No, no protests! It's totally selfish of me—I couldn't live with myself if something unpleasant should happen to you when walking alone. And I had hoped you might accompany us to a concert on Wednesday night. It's at the home of a dear friend I should like you to meet."

Pen stiffened slightly, then seemed to take herself in hand. "Thank you, ma'am, for both offers." She cast a cool look at him. "And thank you, Mr. Keating."

Clouds had begun to gather once again as they set out, but a soft, watery sunshine still brightened the streets. Niall noticed that Pen had tied her bonnet loosely, so that she could tip it back a little. As they set off down the street, he saw her peek around the edge of it. Up close, her eyes looked tired. Had she sat up as late as he had?

"Mr. Keating," she said abruptly, after a few moments of silence.

Here it came. "Yes, Miss Leland?"

"Last night before we parted, I was under the impression that you wished to say something to me."

He kept walking, staring straight ahead. Now that the chance had come for them to talk, really talk, his mind was void of anything but his awareness of her slim gloved hand on his arm and her nearness. "Um . . . did I?"

"I thought you did—oh!"

A sudden impact cut off her words and sent her crashing into him. He staggered but managed to hold on to Pen's arm and keep her from falling.

A young man, tall and redheaded, had evidently tried to hurry past her and misjudged his footing, bumping hard into her left shoulder. He too staggered, trying to regain his own balance, and his hat tumbled off and landed at their feet.

"Sorry," he muttered, bending to retrieve it. "In a rush." Then he rose. "Good God, it's you!" he blurted, staring at Pen. His face turned an alarming shade of crimson that clashed horribly with his hair.

"Er, good afternoon, Mr. Doherty. Is your hat all right?" Niall heard her struggle to make her voice sound cordial as she rubbed her shoulder.

He stared at her for the space of several breaths, then seemed to recall himself. "What? Oh, it's fine." He glanced at Niall and scowled. Jamming his hat back on, he turned on his heel and hurried ahead of them without another word. In another few yards, he paused, glanced back at them, and scowled again, then ducked into a doorway and vanished.

"Are you all right?"

She was still rubbing her shoulder and staring after the young man. "Oh, um, yes, I'm fine. Thank you."

"An acquaintance of yours?" He held his arm out again and they resumed walking.

"I suppose you might say so. He's one of Dr. Carrighar's students with whom I'm supposed to be studying, but he usually either ignores me or disagrees with whatever I say."

They drew abreast of the door the young man had entered, and he saw a small, discreetly lettered sign above it that read YOUNG CORK READING ROOM—MEMBERS ONLY. Ah, that would explain a great deal. "It would appear your friend Mr. Doherty is politically minded," he said to her.

"Friend?" Pen shook her head. "Hardly. And what makes you say he's political?"

"Most of the radical Catholic anti-Unionists have gone underground since the Emancipation Act gave them the vote. Just because they can vote and stand in Parliament doesn't mean they're happy being joined to England. For now they gather in 'clubs' or 'reading rooms' like that one and discuss how to rid Ireland of outside rule."

"Oh." Pen glanced back at the innocuous-seeming door. "I can't say I'm surprised. I'm not sure if Eamon Doherty hates me more for being English or for being female."

Niall gave a short laugh. "If he does hate you, I'd have to say it's the former. The look he gave you just now wasn't one you give someone you find loathsome." It hadn't been. Niall had felt the man's shock and resentment, but it had been directed at him, not her. The look he'd given Pen, though—

She almost stopped walking. "It pleases you to jest. *Loathsome* is probably the word he would use. I'm trying not to let his resentment interfere too much with my studies."

"I do not joke, Miss Leland. It was me he scowled at, not you. If he does bear you any resentment, it's probably because he can't keep his mind on his studies when you're there."

That time Pen did halt. "Stop it, Mr. Keating. If this is more of your . . . your banter like last night, stop it at once. I had thought we would be friends, and I . . . I was pleased, because I'm"—she swallowed—"because I'm lonely. I don't want to play games, or flirt, or whatever you choose to call it. I have serious work to do while I'm here and don't want to waste my time or my . . . my heart on empty flirtation. If that is what you wish our acquaintance to consist of, then it might be best if we cease our . . . attentions to one another."

Damn, damn! She was going to confront him now. Penelope Leland was not going to let him get off easily, was she? Why couldn't she have turned out to be silly and empty-headed like Charlotte Enniskean, so that he could make her fall in love with him and not worry about hurting her? Why did she have to be challenging and spirited and so damned attractive that he felt like a moth fluttering around a candle?

Because then she wouldn't have been herself. Would he want her to be any other way?

He swallowed and stared down at his boots. "Miss Leland, I don't quite know what to say."

She resumed walking, but her step had lost its spring. "I see."

"No, you don't. I've never—that is, I don't—is this the new fashion in London?" he challenged, glancing sideways at her. "For the sexes to be open and forthright with each other?"

She was silent for a moment, and he thought he saw her jaw tighten, as if she were struggling to contain some strong emotion. "I apologize, Mr. Keating," she finally said. "But I saw enough posturing and hiding behind words in London last season to last me a lifetime. An inability to talk forthrightly nearly kept my sister . . . that is, made her life miserable. It may run counter to how the rest of the world works, but I choose not to be that way. I take my studies very seriously, and if I am going to be distracted from them, it won't be merely to play a game with you. Do I make myself clear?"

Their eyes met for a swift second before he turned his head. This was it. He could no longer put her off with banter, nor could he lie. She would know.

A strange emotion—part defiance, part exhilaration—swept through him so that he felt almost dizzy for a moment. Mother be damned. He would go along with her plan and encourage Pen Leland to fall in love with him.

But he was going to do it honestly. If he had to take her heart, he'd give her his in return. Who knew? When it had all worked out and he'd achieved what Mother wanted for him, maybe he'd be in a position to choose his own wife.

Pen began to speak again, in a high, uncomfortable voice. "I believe that making small talk would be an appropriate thing to do just now. Are you politically minded, Mr. Keating? What precisely do these reading clubs of Mr. Doherty's hope to accomplish?"

"Penelope." Even in his own ears his voice sounded desperate.

"I beg your pardon?" She sounded surprised at his sudden use of her given name.

"I was never very good at games. They quite despaired of me at school because of it."

"Mr. Keating, that's not what I meant—"

"I know," he interrupted. "I'm just trying to find some way to tell you that as far as I'm concerned, if you're going to be distracted, it won't be for the sake of a game. My . . . my intentions are serious."

He tightened his arm so that her hand resting on it was trapped against him. Very carefully, he reached with his other hand and covered hers, glancing down at her as he did. She walked looking straight ahead, but that beautiful rosy flush of hers had crept up her cheeks. More important, she had not removed her hand from his.

"I—thank you, Mr. Keating. It makes me feel . . . I mean, thank you."

The remainder of their walk to the Carrighars' was silent. At the door, he bowed and declined her polite invitation to come in; from the relief on her face, he guessed she needed some quiet time alone to think as much as he did. He left her with a quick squeeze of her fingers, and she blushed again but did not look displeased.

On his brisk walk home, Niall smiled and nodded to all passersby. The handsome houses lining the South Mall had never looked so elegant, and even the thickening clouds threatening rain by dusk looked beautiful. He'd done the right thing, the proper thing, and Mother would just have to accept it eventually. In the meanwhile, he would court Pen honestly, as she deserved.

8

On Wednesday night, Pen attended the concert, a small wind ensemble playing at a private home, with the Keatings. Two days later, Lady Keating took Pen with her to call on friends, and the day after that to go shopping. By the day of the shopping expedition, Pen didn't even ask Ally's permission. Her conscience troubled her at first but soon lapsed into silence. Why bother Ally when she would never miss her? Lady Keating's elixir continued to keep her comfortable, for which they were all grateful. It also kept her unconscious nearly all day. Still, she had finally begun to gain weight, much to Cook's and Norah's approval—though Pen couldn't help wondering how two childless women had come to regard themselves as experts on the subject of pregnancy.

But their wise noddings and oracular declarations gave Pen the excuse to spend as much time as she liked with the Keatings. It was like having two homes.

She'd even left her embroidery bag at their house rather than carry it back and forth, and Lady Keating had presented her with a pair of velvet house-slippers with her initials on them that fit her perfectly. The small blue upholstered armchair by the window in the library had become "hers," and either Doireann or Niall was usually in its mate next to her.

Since that walk home the other day, Niall had been . . . well, she wasn't sure. At least his conversation never again took on that suggestive, flirtatious tone it had the night of the dinner party, for which she was grateful. Was his declaration that he would not trifle with her feelings part of why she had come to feel so at home here?

Now Niall talked to her about his reading and correspondence with some of the people he'd met on his European tour—intelligent, serious discussion about the politics and economies of the many little German principalities. She could see how deep his knowledge and understanding of the area were compared to the young men whom she'd met last year during her season.

"You should go to London and work for the foreign ministry," she said to him the following week as they sat in the library one rainy afternoon. "I'm sure they'd snap you up in an instant."

"With Lord Palmerston as foreign minister, being chewed up and spat out would be the more likely outcome." Niall smiled up at her from where he knelt at her feet, holding a map of the tiny kingdom of Hanover, which he'd been describing to her.

The Duke of Cumberland had inherited the throne of Hanover when his elder brother William, king of both England and Hanover, died, because Queen Victoria's sex barred her from inheriting the crown. Pen looked down at Niall's gold hair, shining even in the dull gray light from the window, and restrained the urge to run her fingers through it. Did he know that his probable father was now Hanover's king? Was that why he had spent nearly a year there?

On the sofa near the fireplace, Lady Keating laughed her silvery laugh. "Goodness, I should hope not. Perhaps you will see Niall in London someday, my dear. But for now I am glad that he's here."

"I'm glad I'm here, too." Niall surreptitiously rubbed the toe of one of her slippers where it peeped out from the hem of her dress.

Pen smiled and shook her head at him for taking liberties. It was odd how he never did that sort of thing when they were alone, but only when they were with Doireann or Lady Keating. It had been her experience that young men usually waited until their mothers and sisters were elsewhere to indulge in such demonstrations—the little squeezes of hands, the fleeting touches—but Niall seemed to run contrary to this rule.

Not that Lady Keating ever seemed to notice, apart from the occasional indulgent smile. Pen could only assume she approved of Niall's attentions to her. And she was glad to not have to fend off too-amorous gestures on the few occasions when they were alone. That would have been worse than the verbal flirting. Though more and more she'd wondered what she would do if he tried to kiss her. Would she mind?

Probably not. At least, not if the dream she'd had about him last night was any indication.

She squirmed slightly, hoping he wouldn't notice the warmth she could feel in her cheeks. Mary Margaret's earthy description of Beltane rites must have been stuck in her mind when she went to sleep last night. Maybe that would account for it. What was happening to her? A few days ago, she'd objected to his flirting with her, and now she was thinking about how his lips would feel on hers. . . . She shifted again in her chair.

Niall glanced up at her. "May I get you anything?"

"N-no. I was just thinking that I ought to go back to the Carrighars' and do some reading," she improvised.

"Do you have to?" He slid a finger under her skirt and tapped her toe again.

"Beastly boy," she murmured to him.

"Tell me to stop and I will," he whispered back.

"Double beast."

Unfortunately it was true; she really ought to go back and study. There were several chapters that she hadn't got to yet, and class was tomorrow. But it was so much more pleasant here, with Niall being quietly outrageous and Lady Keating so welcoming—

There was a knock on the door, and one of the maids entered the room, bearing a large tray. "Cook's baked some tarts, mum," she announced, setting the tray on the table and leaving.

"You must stay and have tea before you go, Pen dear. I won't let you walk home in this rain, and it will take Padraic some time to get the carriage ready." Lady Keating leaned over the tray. "Mmm, are those lemon curd tarts?"

Pen stayed.

"The poor thing's only eighteen. Must she marry now? She's barely had a chance to breathe, let alone enjoy herself for five minutes. Why can't she have another year or two to herself?" Pen asked, as she and Niall strolled down St. Patrick Street a few days later.

A dense fog had drifted in from the harbor, and the atmosphere was heavy with moisture. Pen tried to ignore the tendrils of hair at her forehead that were curling riotously in the damp air. It was fun to go walking in the fog like this because it was different from a London fog—clean and sea-tinged, not yellow and choking. The passersby were fewer than usual, and the fog muffled the sounds of the city around them. It was as if they were in their own little world.

"Because she's the queen, not a flighty debutante." Niall frowned down at her, then laughed. "Unlike some people I know."

"Flighty? Ha! I'd like to show you flighty." She could, too. Perhaps a quick trip to hang by his coattails from the spire of St. Anne's. Honestly!

But to debate like this with Niall, what with his knowledge of the political situation and her knowledge of the queen, was most stimulating. "All I'm saying," she continued, "is that perhaps she should be allowed another year or two to learn her own mind, so that she chooses the right man to marry. Don't you think it of great import to the nation that she marry the right man?"

"Oh, that's easy. It will be either Albert of Coburg or a prince of Orange, though I've heard she didn't like them when they met. Of course, there's Grand Duke Alexander of Russia, but I somehow don't see the queen marrying a Russian. My money's on Albert. It's what everyone's expecting in Germany."

Niall would know, after all the time he'd spent abroad. But still. "Well, I don't know why she couldn't marry an Englishman, if she so desired. Must she take a husband from a different country?"

He shook his head. "If she marries in England, it'll have to be to one of her Cambridge cousins, and I don't think Parliament or her mother favor the match. And anyway, what's wrong with marrying a man from a different land? Are you saying it's necessarily a bad thing? Would you refuse on principle to marry a man from, oh, say, Germany?"

"As my German is not as good as it should be, our courtship might be problematical."

"Well, if not a totally foreign land, then what about a slightly foreign one? Would you, say, consider marrying an Irishman?"

That was somewhat surprising; Niall usually saved remarks like that for when they weren't alone. But by now she was better able to respond to them. "Good heavens!" she cried, as if in shock. "Why, I've never even considered such a thing! Marry an Irishman?" She peeked up at him from the edge of her bonnet.

He grinned back at her. "Not even considered it? Not in your wildest, most horripilatious fancies?"

"Well. . . ." She pretended to consider the question. "I don't know. It's rather a far-fetched notion. Are there any Irishmen you think might be suitable for me to—"

A sharp, shrill sound made her break off midsentence. It rose and fell, and then seemed to split in two.

"Did you hear that?" She pushed her bonnet back and turned her head a bit. "It sounded like a constable's whistle. Or was it the fog playing tricks?"

"No, you're right," Niall replied, pausing. "Sounds like several constables' whistles. Oh lord, not again." He sounded disgusted.

"What? What is it?"

"Some anti-Union agitators kicking up their heels, I'll wager. Hotheaded idiots. They'd get a lot more accomplished going to school and becoming politicians, not fighting them."

"What are they doing?"

"Who knows? It might have been a public speech that got a little too inflammatory. It's happened before. Some young lad gets carried away by the rhetoric he hears and starts a bit of trouble with a constable. I don't know why they can't do their speechifying in their clubs, rather than in public. At least innocent bystanders can't get hurt that way." His voice grew grim. "Padraic's youngest daughter was blinded in one eye by a rock about ten years ago when she happened to be in the wrong place at the wrong time. And that was a quiet year for the agitators."

Pen stared into the mist, their flirtatious conversation nearly forgotten. Now shouts could be heard from somewhere ahead of them, but the fog made it difficult to see where they came from. It was eerie, knowing that somewhere nearby there might be fighting and mayhem. "The clubs, you said? As in the reading club that we passed once?" Like the one they'd seen Eamon Doherty enter?

"Yes, that's—" Niall broke off at the sound of rapidly approaching footsteps. He pulled Pen back against the wall of a building just as a pair of young men came flying out of the mist, closely pursued by a police constable waving his stick. He blew his whistle, but the pair ahead of him never slowed.

"Good heavens!" she breathed as they passed, close enough to touch, and disappeared up the street.

"I think we should go back to the house and have Padraic drive you home a little later," Niall said above the growing clamor. His face was grim as he held his arm out to her.

A woman leading a small girl and boy hurried past them, looking terrified, and a one-horse gig did an abrupt turn in the street and trotted smartly away. Other pedestrians, farther away in the fog, could be heard hurrying away from the site of the strife.

There was a shout nearby and a sharp, unpleasant *crack!* as if something had been struck. Pen remembered the constable's stick and felt ill. "Yes, I think you're right." She took his arm, and they turned away.

Another figure materialized suddenly out of the fog behind

them as they walked. Pen heard whoever it was moaning as he breathed heavily, trying to run, and looked over her shoulder.

A tall, thin youth, hatless and with his coat trailing from one arm, half staggered, half ran behind them. Blood as bright as his red hair streamed down his face and over the hand he held clapped to his head.

She froze. Though the man was bent almost in half at the waist, she knew immediately who he was.

"What?" Niall turned as well.

"'Scuse me," Eamon Doherty mumbled, trying to hurry past them. "Gotta go. Can't let them find me, not this time. . . ." He stumbled against Pen, then straightened and lurched forward.

Without thinking, she reached out and grabbed his arm. "Mr. Doherty," she murmured urgently.

"M' name's not Doherty," he said, head still down as he tried to pull away. "You've got the wrong man, lady. Lemme go."

"Eamon!" she said, more forcefully. He looked up then. Gore ran down his face from a gash on his forehead and from his nose, and one of his eyes was almost squeezed shut by a bruise that seemed to darken even as she looked at it, but it was definitely he. As their eyes met, a look of horrified recognition covered his face. "Jesus!" he cried, and tried again to yank his arm from her grasp.

"Hold still, you idiot!" she hissed. "You're hurt."

"I'll be hurt worse if you don't let me go. The damned constables are after me, and I'll be sent down from the university if they catch me! Not to mention tossed in gaol for the next year or more." He succeeded in breaking her grip and nearly fell sideways. Niall caught him.

"You should have thought of that before you started joining political groups." Pen wanted to poke him in the chest as she would have her little brother if he were misbehaving, but she didn't. "Right now you're hurt. You'll never get away from them."

"I know I won't, if you don't let me g—" Another burst of whistles and shouts sounded behind them. Doherty's face paled where it wasn't covered in blood. Pen looked from him to the mist beyond them and made a quick decision.

"Niall, give me your hat." The tone of command in her voice surprised even her.

He looked at her, then handed the tall beaver hat to her.

"Christ, Miss Leland, what are you doing?" Doherty groped for his handkerchief and blotted the blood that dripped into his eyes.

"Saving your neck. Now be quiet while I do this." Could she do a spell in the middle of a foggy street, on the edges of a riot? And which one should she use? Not concealment, surely—she could do that for herself, but not for another person. She held Niall's hat in both hands and stared into it. Ah, that might do. But how? She'd have to improvise and hope for the best.

"*Dona speciem tui domini . . . er . . . cuiquam gerat te,*" she whispered, narrowing her attention on the silk band inside the crown, where Niall's initials had been embroidered. The anxiety of the moment receded for a few seconds, and she felt the hat shift in her hands, as if it had altered its shape slightly. The brushed felt surface dulled and grew subtly paler.

"There," she said after a moment, and shoved the hat at Doherty. "Niall, will you please walk ahead of us and catch the first hackney home you can find? This won't work if you're here. I'm going to take Mr. Doherty back to the Carrighars'."

Niall frowned. "I can't let you do that."

Pen didn't bother keeping the impatience out of her voice. "Yes, you can. I won't be alone, and Mr. Doherty is known to me. And besides, I can take care of myself."

"But—"

She looked at him very hard. *"Please."*

He opened his mouth, then closed it. "All right," he finally growled. "But I'll be calling at the Carrighars' in exactly thirty minutes to make sure you've made it there safely. Do you understand? Thirty minutes." He glared at her, then at Doherty, and stalked off.

Relieved, Pen turned back to Doherty, still swaying beside her. "Put that hat on, quickly."

"I will not," he said, trying to draw himself up and look indignant. She reached up and jammed it on his head. He gasped and tried to twist away.

"Look, do you want the constables to catch you? I put a temporary enchantment on the hat so that you'll take Mr. Keating's appearance while you're wearing it. It should last long enough to get us back to the Carrighars', maybe longer if we're lucky. Now are you coming with me, or do I have to walk home alone? The least you can damned well do, after nearly mowing me down, is accompany me back to my house."

"Miss Leland!" Good; her unladylike language had shaken him out of his indignation, just as she'd hoped it would.

"Will you please come?" she asked, in quieter tones. "I assure you, you are quite changed."

He looked down at her, then at himself, with Niall's blue eyes widened in shock. She doubted the real Niall had ever worn such a comically affronted expression.

"I'll take that as a yes." She took his arm and began to propel him up the street. "We can walk quickly without being noticed, just like everyone else is. If a constable stops us, just shake your head and look concerned and let me do the talking. I don't think this spell will disguise your voice as well. Now, come on."

He didn't offer any further protest. Pen set as quick a pace as she thought he could manage and kept an iron grip on his arm, lest he stumble. They met a pair of constables on the street who hurried by them with hardly a glance. Her spell had worked.

"How is your head?" she asked softly, after a few minutes.

"It's bleeding a lot. I can feel it running over me." He slowed, reaching his free hand to touch his face, then stared at his clean fingers. "But I can't see it. What the hell kind of spell did you put on this hat?"

"I don't know. I just made it up. Come on. Let's get you safe before you lose too much blood. I don't want to risk you fainting and having the hat fall off." She tugged impatiently on his arm.

"Why aren't you fainting, then? I thought gentle-born young ladies always did at the sight of blood."

Pen ignored him, but began to walk faster.

"All right, that was uncalled-for. I'm sorry. But why are you helping me, anyway?" He scowled at her, then winced.

"I don't know. Does it matter? Come *on*. Just a few more blocks."

At the Carrighars' house she didn't ring and wait for Norah to let her in, but opened the door herself. "Downstairs," she mouthed at him, pushing him toward the door to the cellars.

Halfway down the stairs, she created a bubble of cool flame and tossed it into the air above them to light their way. Doherty paused and blinked up at it as it bobbed along ahead of them but said nothing. She led him into Corkwobble's room and pulled the door shut.

"There aren't any chairs, so you'll have to sit on the table." She gestured toward it, then turned away. "Corkwobble? Are you there?"

An annoyed sniff came from behind the ale casks. "And since when are ye bringing strangers unannounced down to me home, me only sanctuary in this cold, cruel—"

"What the—" Doherty exclaimed, jumping and knocking the table over the stone floor.

Pen tsked and bent to right it. "Sit down," she commanded. "And don't be so jumpy. It's just the Carrighars' clurichaun."

"Pardon me, *bean draoi,* but I'm just me own clurichaun, if ye please." Corkwobble sounded even more annoyed.

"I know you are, Corkwobble, and I'm sorry to disturb you, but I needed to bring Mr. Doherty somewhere." Pen pushed Doherty back down on the table and took Niall's hat off. Instantly he was himself again, bloodstained and disarrayed.

"Mr. Doherty, is it?" Corkwobble appeared next to her and cackled. "Oh, ho ho! One of *Draiodoir* Carrighar's students, then? Not a pretty sight, I'm thinking. So did ye finally get tired of him sneering at ye and give him what he deserved, *cailin?* Ye must have a mean right arm on ye."

"Could you find me some wine or brandy to give Mr. Doherty while I figure out what to do for him?" Pen tried not to laugh at the mental picture Corkwobble's words had drawn.

"Ho, could I!" Corkwobble chuckled evilly.

"*Human* spirits, if you please. Not any of that fairy stuff you once offered me. I don't want him asleep in the cellar for the next twelve hours."

"Ye've no sense of humor," said the little clurichaun, looking disappointed.

"Yes, well, it would be your cellar he'd be snoring in." Pen gestured the ball of light into place above Eamon's head and began to examine his injuries. "You choose."

"Ah." Corkwobble put a finger next to his nose and nodded. "When ye put it that way . . . I'll be right back." He vanished in a small *pop!* of displaced air.

"Th-th—" Doherty swallowed hard. "That was a clurichaun."

"Yes, I know it was." Pen took his chin in her hand. "Hold still. I want to see if I can heal this on my own."

"B-but you were talking to him . . . and he . . . he was real . . . I saw him."

"Jolly good, yes. You saw him. Well done." Why wouldn't he stop babbling and let her think? It would be so much easier to just close his cuts and sneak him out of the house than to bring Dr. Carrighar or anyone else into this. First thing was to get rid of the blood and see how badly he was hurt.

"*Purgare,*" she murmured, and the blood vanished. The wound that had produced it all was above his left eyebrow, a gash that trailed into a shallow cut. It still oozed, though not as profusely as it had before. Blood seeped from his nose as well—it must have been broken—and now it was obvious that both his eyes had been blackened.

"Aye, I was right. A pretty sight indeed, isn't he?" Corkwobble reappeared next to her, holding a bottle. "Give him a swig o' that. It'll take his mind off whatever ye're going to do to him next."

Doherty flinched.

Pen thought about stepping on Corkwobble's toes but didn't. "Thank you," she said instead, taking the bottle from him and uncorking it. Plain brandy, good. Nothing from the fairy world. "Drink." She shoved it into Doherty's hand.

"Miss Leland—"

She sighed. "Yes?"

"What are you . . . why are you doing all this? I've . . ." He stared at her, the pupils of his eyes slightly dilated.

Had he been hit over the head and concussed? Ally had given them a course of practical training in medical emergencies two years ago and had discussed head injuries. "I saw no reason for you to be tossed into jail and prosecuted, or worse, just because you're a hotheaded idiot," she replied tartly. "Dr. Carrighar might have been dragged into it, which I did not want to have happen."

His pupils contracted again as his eyes narrowed in anger that blazed up briefly, then died. Good. Probably not concussed, then. She wasn't sure she could do anything for a concussion without help.

"I'm not an idiot, I'm a patriot," he said automatically. "And why are you helping me, after the way I've treated you in Dr. Carrighar's classes? That spell"—he picked up Niall's hat and looked at it, shaking his head—"I didn't think you had it in you."

"I know you didn't. Now take a drink of that brandy and let me treat you. The sooner you're healed, the sooner you can leave my odious presence."

"That's not what I—"

Pen snatched the bottle from his hand and shoved it toward his mouth. He reached up quickly and took it from her before she could break his teeth with it, tipping it up and downing a good mouthful.

"Good. Now, for the last time, hold still." She held his chin in her left hand and leaned forward till they were nearly nose to nose. She very gently ran her right index finger over the bridge of his nose until a muddy brown feeling of not-rightness told her where his injury was. Ah, there. Definitely broken. So what now? Ally had said that most healing spells were simple in form but required an immense amount of concentration: "You must exert your will on the injury and undo it. Not all that hard to do on yourself, but on someone else's injuries, it can be difficult, indeed. Many witches never learn to do healing magic, though some excel at it."

Hah. Doherty would just *love* it if she tried to heal him and couldn't. So failure was not an option. Straightening her shoulders and doing her best to ignore his eyes, fixed on hers, she told the bone to heal.

An enormous pressure seemed to build inside her head as she concentrated, along with a buzzing sound in her ears and, oddly, a burning sensation over her scalp. Then all awareness of her body abruptly ceased. All she knew was that there was a broken place in front of her, and that when she willed it to, it would heal.

The thin seepage of blood from Doherty's nose stopped.

"All right," she murmured, exhaling. When had she held her breath? But she'd done it! The muddy, not-right feeling was gone when she touched the bridge of his nose again. She swallowed a triumphant "so there!" and said instead, "I can't promise you won't have a bump there, but it should stop hurting."

He stared at her.

"Is that all right, Mr. Doherty? Shall I continue?"

"D'ye think ye ought to, *cailin?*" Corkwobble interjected. "He doesn't seem as appreciative as he ought, I'm thinkin'."

"Hush, Corkwobble." She flexed her hands, then brushed her fingertips several times under first one of his eyes, then the other, willing the lurid bruising to undo itself. The purple streaks faded to green, then yellow, then disappeared completely. As when she had healed the bone, all sense of self disappeared. Only when she let her hands fall to her sides was she aware of a peculiar throbbing, half tickle, half pain, running through them.

Doherty's stiff posture relaxed slightly. "My head's almost stopped aching," he said, sounding surprised.

"How amazing," she muttered. His head may have stopped aching, but hers had begun to feel like an anvil under a blacksmith's hammer, and a deep weariness had settled on her shoulders. Ally hadn't exaggerated when she said healing spells were difficult ones, and Pen had never tried to do more than one at a time before. But there was still that gash above his left eye to take care of. She sighed and blinked, willing her eyes to stay open and focus properly.

This time she stroked the skin all around the cut, murmuring softly, asking it to close and be whole. This spell felt a little easier. The gash was where she could see it, which made focusing easier. The edges of the torn flesh slowly pulled together, like a flower closing at sunset. She leaned forward and breathed gently on his brow, barely an inch above it, and the skin once more was white and unbroken. She felt a tremor run through him as she did, and had to smother an exclamation of annoyance. Good God, she was helping him. He didn't have to shudder with dislike quite so openly.

"I'm sorry if my closeness was distasteful, Mr. Doherty," she said, pulling away and dropping her hand from his face as the last of the power ebbed from her fingertips. "But I think you will find that your injuries are mostly gone."

Her head was pounding so hard that it was difficult to see clearly, and her entire right hand had gone icy and numb, but an excited elation filled her. She'd done it. The power she'd felt coursing through her in those seconds was stronger and more pure than anything she'd felt before. *This* was what true magic felt like. All her work of the last months had begun to bear fruit. Persy might have been able to do what she'd done without missing a beat, but Persy wasn't here. She, Pen, had done it!

Doherty raised tentative hands to his brow, then stared, wide-eyed, at his clean, unbloodied fingers. Now if only he would leave, so that she could go lie down with a cold cloth on her head and savor the triumph of the magic she'd just performed.

"There's a door out the back of the cellar, which is probably the easiest way to leave without anyone seeing you," she said pointedly. "Wear the hat. No one will stop you if you look like Mr. Keating. But don't dawdle. I can keep the spell going another half hour, but I'm a little tired." She gestured to the light that still hovered above them and closed her eyes, feeling herself sway slightly. "And take that to see by. I can find my way up without it."

"Here, *bean draoi*." She felt a tug on her skirt at knee level. "Hold on to the table and get some o' that brandy on yer insides. Ye've fair done yerself up." Corkwobble's tone was quietly respectful. "I've not seen such a neat bit o' healing magic in many a day."

"I hate brandy," she muttered, but took the bottle that someone pressed into her hand and drank anyway. The dry, pungent heat of it made her want to sneeze, but it also made the pain in her head recede slightly. She opened her eyes.

Doherty still stood there, running his hands over his face. "You did it," he said hoarsely. "I can't believe it."

That was annoying enough to make her stand up straight and try to ignore her headache. "Do forgive me for succeeding, Mr. Doherty. Would you have preferred it if I hadn't? I promise I won't do it again if we ever find ourselves in a similar situation. Now, please, don't let me detain you any longer."

"But . . ." He stared at her. "You don't understand. *I* couldn't have done this magic. You—you're—" He took a step toward her.

She set the brandy bottle on the table and sighed. "Be careful. You're coming perilously close to admitting that a mere female, and an English one at that, might be competent at magic." The last of the brandy fumes in her head faded, and the fierce ache redoubled. If her head hadn't hurt so badly that she couldn't think straight, she might have tried the teleportation spell she'd been reading about and sent herself to her room. Or maybe dropped Doherty off the nearest bridge into the Lee.

"Miss Leland," he whispered.

A sharp, staccato knock sounded upstairs. Pen started, then remembered. "That will be Mr. Keating. Please excuse me, Mr. Doherty, but I must go." So much for a rest. Hopefully Niall would understand and stay only long enough to make sure she was all right.

"If you will be so kind as to put on the hat and leave, you should be able to make it home safely. Corkwobble, will you show him out?" Without bothering to curtsey or say good-bye, she turned and hurried toward the stairs.

9

The next morning, Pen rose before breakfast. After dressing swiftly, or at least as swiftly as she could without help tying her corset, she sneaked downstairs to Dr. Carrighar's study to get the book she should have read four chapters of in time for today's class.

Her head had finally stopped throbbing, thank heavens, and her right hand tingled only slightly instead of being totally numb. She'd left Doherty yesterday and answered the door herself to an indignant Niall, who'd slumped against the doorframe in relief, then half threatened to ask Dr. Carrighar to lock her in her room to prevent her from doing anything quite so foolish again. But he'd left after assuring himself that she was home safe, and she'd dragged herself gratefully upstairs to her room. Yes, she probably should have gone back down to Corkwobble's cellar to make sure Doherty had gotten safely out, but quite honestly, she no longer cared.

Then Norah had brought her some tea and asked anxiously if she shouldn't bring the doctor up to charm away her headache, but Pen had refused. The last thing she wanted was Dr. Carrighar asking questions. So she'd drunk her tea and gone to sleep almost as soon as dinner was over.

But that meant she hadn't done her reading for today. Well, that could hardly be helped. And at least today she had a better excuse than that she'd been out at a dinner or concert with the Keatings. Not that she wanted anyone to know she hadn't done her reading. Surely she could finish it now, if she hurried.

Norah was in Dr. Carrighar's study lighting the fire and promised to bring breakfast up to her room. "An' I wish you'd visit that scoundrel in the cellar when ye have the time, miss. Cook and I can hear him bangin' about down there, moanin' that he's bein' neglected," she added. "He's become dreadful spoilt, with you visiting him an' all. Not that I'm complainin', mind you. He watches his manners with me now, an' I'm grateful."

"Of course I will," Pen promised. "I'll bring him a treat after class is over." She owed Corkwobble for his help yesterday . . . but neglecting him? Surely she'd just been to see him a day or two ago, hadn't she? She'd meant to, anyway.

She lugged the heavy book up to her room and set it on her bureau, planning on combing her hair while she read. Drat. Another book written in strange, sixteenth-century language, with bizarre spelling and difficult grammar. At least this one was in English, though. Last week one of the readings had been in Latin, and she'd always relied on Persy, who was more fluent, to help her read any Latin texts Ally had set them. If only Persy were here now.

Norah brought her toast and coddled eggs that she ate without noticing, absorbed in her reading. When the clock on the landing bonged its single note marking the three-quarter hour, she jumped and flipped through the book. Still a chapter and a half to go. There was no way she'd be finished by ten, when the other students usually arrived. Oh, why hadn't she just ignored that headache and gotten this done last night? The only thing she could do now was to make sure she participated in the discussion of the first chapters and hope no one noticed if she fell silent on the latter ones. But for now she had to get the book back to Dr. Carrighar's study; there was no reason to make it obvious to everyone that she'd just been doing her reading minutes before the start of class, even if it was the truth.

She slipped down the stairs and paused, listening. Good; Dr. Carrighar was still in the dining room talking to Cook, it sounded like. She dashed down the hall and had reached for the latch on the study door when voices from within the room stayed her hand.

"Nudge me if I fall asleep, won't you?" Quigley's voice drawled. "Late night, you know."

Pen closed her eyes and tried not to groan out loud. Why, of all mornings, had anyone arrived early?

"It's not my problem if you can't pay as much attention to your watch as you do to Mary Connor at the Rose and Nettle of an evening," Doherty replied loftily.

Doherty! Double drat! Why did it have to be those two? If it had been O'Byrne and Patrick Sheehan, she might not have minded slipping in to return the book. But there was no way she'd go in there now and let Quigley and Doherty stare at her and make scornful comments under their breath. Nor was she quite sure she wanted to face Doherty anywhere but in a formal classroom setting, after yesterday's events. What should she do?

"Huh. You're just jealous because she won't give you the time of day." Quigley's tone was smug.

"No, I just have more important things on my mind than pub wenches, thank you." Doherty's was equally contemptuous.

Pen remembered the blood running over Doherty's face yesterday and his angry "I'm a patriot." Of course he preferred politics to female company.

"Oooh, 'more important,' is it?" Quigley mimicked him. "Mary's no pub wench. Her da owns the Rose and Nettle, and she's his only daughter. She stands to inherit a pretty piece of change from her old man someday. Or isn't that good enough for you?" He laughed suddenly. "I know what it is. Only got eyes for English aristocrats, haven't you? Why look at Mary when you can come to old man Carrighar's and ogle Miss Lela—"

Pen nearly dropped the book.

"Shut your gob, you idiot!" Doherty nearly shouted. There was a scraping sound as if he'd risen from his chair and shoved it aside.

"Hold on, man, I'm roasting you. Let go of my coat!" Quigley choked and sputtered.

"Not till you take back what you said!"

There was a pause. "Why, Eamon," Quigley said at last, his voice amused, if a touch breathless, "if I didn't know any better, I'd say I touched a sore spot—ow! You're throttling me!"

"Don't you dare breathe a word of this to anybody!"

"Have you tried to kiss her—oww! Let *go* of me!"

"Swear it," Doherty snarled.

"All right, I swear I won't tell anyone you fancy—argh!"

Clutching the book to her chest, Pen turned and fled upstairs to her room. Almost panting, she sat down on her bed.

Eamon Doherty liked her? It was laughable. Completely ridiculous. He'd made it clear from her first day that he loathed her and resented her presence in their class. Yesterday he'd been incredulous that she'd been able to heal him and said so to her face. He hated her.

Yet if it were ridiculous, why hadn't Doherty just laughed it off? And what had Niall said when they'd bumped into Doherty? *The look he gave you wasn't one you give to someone you find loathsome.*

Good lord, it couldn't be. Could it?

She shuddered, remembering the desperate anger in his voice just now. Could a man despise a woman and still find her attractive? The very notion of such a thing made her feel soiled, somehow. Why, oh *why*, did she have to overhear that horripilatious conversation? How could she ever face any of them now?

A sonorous tone, and another, broke into her thoughts. She listened numbly as the clock finished striking ten, then resumed its thick, steady tick. Time for class.

But she didn't move from her hunched perch on the edge of her bed. If she walked into Dr. Carrighar's office now, she'd either burst into tears or hysterical laughter, and they'd know, Quigley and Doherty, that somehow she knew—

"Miss." Norah was knocking on her door. "Miss, they be wantin' ye downstairs. 'Tis time fer class."

For a few seconds, she thought about having Norah tell them that she was ill. But no, she'd already fled one class in tears. She couldn't avoid class every time something upset her because then Doherty would be right—she wasn't strong and able enough to learn alongside men. And Norah would worry if she went back to bed complaining of illness, and would tell Dr. Carrighar.

"Thank you, Norah. Please tell the doctor that I'll be down directly," she called. After Norah had padded away, she splashed some cold water on her face and, after a moment's hesitation, undid her plaits and went down with her hair falling unbound over her shoulders. It was not proper to appear so before others, especially men, but she would not be leaving the house and it would give her something to hide behind.

As it turned out, she would badly need to hide.

Everyone rose as she came into the study. Dr. Carrighar merely nodded his thanks as she handed his book to him and took the remaining seat—which, unfortunately, was next to Eamon Doherty. She managed not to meet his eyes, but her skirt brushed his knee in passing and he recoiled as if she'd struck him. Quigley sniggered, and Pen shook her hair over her face as she bent to arrange her skirts, lest they all see how red she'd turned. It was his problem, not hers. She would not let them intimidate or embarrass her.

"I thought that today we would do something a little different and attend to our reading at our next class," Dr. Carrighar began when she was seated.

Pen breathed a silent sigh of relief behind her hair. A reprieve! She would be spared at least one embarrassment today. This would give her a chance to finish reading the chapters she hadn't made it through, assuming that she got back from dinner at the Gormans' at some reasonable hour. Oh, goodness, the Gormans' dinner! She'd nearly forgotten. What would she wear? Had Niall seen her in her dark rose corded silk gown with the paler pink underskirt? It was a little grand for just a small dinner, but it did look very well on her—

A quick motion in the corner of her eye made her look up.

"Miss Leland?" Dr. Carrighar beamed as he looked at her expectantly, holding his handkerchief in the air, and she realized the motion she had seen was him whisking it off something on his desk.

"E-excuse me?"

His smile faltered. "I asked if you would care to begin our practicum this morning." He gestured down with the handkerchief at two small piles of broken crockery that lay side by side on the blotter. Pen realized after staring at them blankly for a few seconds that they were shattered teacups.

A practicum! Oh, why *hadn't* she stayed upstairs and pleaded a headache? She vaguely remembered seeing the handkerchief-covered piles on his desk when she handed him the book. One of the cups was from the blue sprigged breakfast china they used every morning. The other cup was boldly patterned in green and gold reminiscent of Lady Keating's tea set. Borrowing the cups must have been what Dr. Carrighar was discussing with Cook when she'd sneaked downstairs to return the book.

"Er, begin? Very well." She leaned forward and stared at the teacups. Why hadn't she been listening to him, instead of thinking about what to wear tonight? What did he want her to do to them?

Two broken teacups. What did she think he wanted her to do to them? She silenced the snide voice in her head and straightened, taking a deep breath. Reassembly spells seemed a little elementary for this class, but she'd not complain.

"*Reficimini,*" she whispered, narrowing her attention on the two piles of shards.

One of the piles—the breakfast china one—shifted, and in a small flurry of motion reformed itself once again into an intact cup.

The other pile of fragments didn't move.

Pen blinked. Had she been showing off, trying to repair both at once? Or hadn't she fully recovered from all her exertions yesterday? "*Reficere,*" she said a little more loudly, staring at the shards. *You are a teacup. You are broken. Be made whole.*

The pile did not even stir.

Someone—she wasn't sure but it might have been O'Byrne—giggled softly. Pen resisted the urge to snap at him and tried again, putting a confidence into her voice that she did not feel. *"Reficere!"*

"Ahem." Dr. Carrighar coughed. "That will do, Miss Leland. Mr. Doherty?"

Pen cringed. Why hadn't she been able to repair the second cup? Now Doherty would do it and make her look incompetent.

"Sir." Eamon Doherty sat up and took a deep breath. But before he could begin his spell, Patrick Sheehan leaned forward.

"But, sir. Eamon can't fix it. It isn't real," he said, sounding puzzled.

Dr. Carrighar sat back in his chair and smiled. "Excellent, Mr. Sheehan. You are quite right. There is no cup, broken or otherwise."

Pen blinked at the pile of fragments. There wasn't? Bright morning light from the window behind Dr. Carrighar's desk shone on the smooth glaze of the larger pieces. Shadows fell where they ought. There was even a faint drift of white powder and tiny fragments on the blotter underneath them.

"I am sure Norah and Cook will appreciate your mending this, Miss Leland." Dr. Carrighar gestured to the whole cup. She could hear the disappointment in his voice. "And your attempt at mending both might be construed as one way to demonstrate that one cup was real and one wasn't. But perhaps a closer examination into the nature of the cups might have been a better place to start." He waved a finger over the broken cup, and it seemed to melt into nothingness.

"I'm sorry, sir." Pen stared hard at where the second cup had been and told herself fiercely not to cry.

"Indeed. Now, Mr. Sheehan, what made you realize that the second cup was false?"

"I don't know," Sheehan admitted, after a pause. "I just knew."

"Ah. Very interesting, my boy. Has this happened before? We might want to see if you have a natural gift for truth-seeing. Any others? Mr. O'Byrne? Mr. Quigley? No?"

Pen was vaguely comforted by the lack of response from the others, but not much. If she'd finished the reading she was supposed to, would she have been able to tell that the cup was not real? Did that mean that Doherty and the others hadn't done their reading either?

Or was it something deeper? Had she not been able to see it because she just wasn't good enough?

You were good enough to put Eamon Doherty back together yesterday, part of her said indignantly. *Don't forget that.*

"Perceiving illusion is one of the skills a user of magic should cultivate. A nonmagic person does not concern himself with such matters; the evidence of his eyes is enough for him. But those of us who know how easily the eye can be deceived by a fair exterior must learn to cultivate a deeper vision."

Was it her imagination, or was Dr. Carrighar looking meaningfully at her? If he was, then what did he mean by it? What—or whose—fair exterior did he think she was unable to see past?

"Similarly, we need to cultivate an inner vision to discern what intent may lie beneath otherwise fair-seeming magic. This perhaps comes more under the heading of studying human nature than studying magic, but remember that we are all human first and magic users second. My cup illusion was harmless, but it could well have concealed an ill intent. As has been frequently noted through the ages, all that glitters is not gold."

An image of Niall's shining hair popped into her mind. Could he be talking about Niall? But Niall wasn't a wizard.

"We must, therefore, be doubly vigilant and watch for too-fair exteriors in both the mundane and magical levels. We must learn to perceive the true intention behind all magic. As humans we do not do a labor—and magic can indeed be difficult and taxing—unless we have a purpose for it. It is simple to perceive the purpose of regular human labor: One digs a hole in the ground if one wants to have a well. But perceiving the purpose behind a particular piece of magic can be another task altogether."

Pen realized with a chill that Doherty was staring at her.

"If you will recall from our reading last month . . ."

Would this class never end? Would any of them notice if she practiced her invisibility spell and slipped out of the room? If only Doherty would stop looking at her with that speculative look in his eyes.

Somehow she managed to sit through the next hour and a half without squirming or turning herself invisible. Thank heavens for Mama's training on how to sit up straight and look attentive when one was mentally miles away. She rose promptly when Dr. Carrighar excused them, wishing that she were in the chair closest to the door. As the four young men filed out of the study ahead of her, Dr. Carrighar cleared his throat.

"Please stay, Miss Leland. I would like to speak with you."

"Yes, sir," she said steadily enough, but her heart sank to somewhere around ankle level. Had he noticed her inattention? Was she about to experience her first tutorial bloodletting at the hands of the doctor? She sat down in Sheehan's chair and hoped some of his imperturbability would rub off on her.

Dr. Carrighar toyed with the teacup still on his desk, not looking at her. His brow furrowed, but he remained silent. Pen took the moment of respite to brace herself for a scolding at her decidedly lackluster performance in class, but it didn't come.

"I'm worried about you," Dr. Carrighar finally said, setting the cup down and meeting her eyes.

"M-me?" She knew that sounded dull-witted in the extreme, but it came out before she could stop it.

"Yes, you. I don't think this visit is working out the way we expected, what with poor Melusine being so ill. I cannot give you the attention she has, and I fear that you need it."

Pen counted to five before she spoke. Ten might have been better, but she just couldn't manage it right now. "I was not aware that I had given anyone cause to worry."

"You haven't. Not quite yet, anyway. But I—" He shook his head. "You see? I can't even say what is troubling me without doing it wrong. I was not the, ahem, the best and most attentive of fathers, and count myself fortunate that only one of my sons went to the bad."

Pen remembered the stories she had heard about Michael's older brother, the one whose improprieties had left Michael open to blackmail by Sir John Conroy in London last year. "I do not think there is any danger of my going bad, sir," she said, trying to temper her annoyance. Dr. Carrighar had been devastated by his older son's behavior and subsequent removal to Canada.

Dr. Carrighar sounded as if he was choosing his words carefully. "I didn't say that you would. It is not your behavior I'm worried about. It is your vulnerability in this time and place, without a proper guardian to keep watch over you. You have no family here, and poor Melusine is too ill. I should be grateful that Nuala Keating has stepped into the breach and taken you under her wing, but something about her troubles me."

Pen sat straighter in her chair. Was this what he had meant by "a fair exterior covering some other purpose"? Not Niall, but Lady Keating? But what could possibly be wrong with Lady Keating? She opened her mouth to speak, but he held up one hand.

"The fact that I can't put my finger on what it is troubles me even more. And so, I have been debating writing to your father and advising that you go home as soon as possible."

"What?" She stared at him. Leave Ireland? A choking sensation came over her at the thought. Leave Ireland . . . and Niall? "No, you mustn't write that to Papa! Oh, please don't send me back. I love it here! I feel as if"—she took a deep breath—"as if I've come home. As if I belong here. The people, the . . . the everything. Even the magic feels different—as if it fits me better. And Lady Keating has been an absolutely correct chaperone, not to mention a kind one."

She thought of the glad, warm light in Lady Keating's eyes whenever Pen arrived at the house, the motherly embraces, the concern for her comfort and happiness. "I think Lady Keating's really become fond of me," she added.

"That may be so, Penelope. But you have a mother and father at home who can take even better care of you. And though you may feel a kinship with the magic, I'm afraid that has not shown up in your studies."

Pen rose and took a few paces back and forth, trying to calm her agitation. "I'm sorry about the work. I meant to finish the reading last night, really I did. I promise that I shall plan my days so that I can get it all done. I've been bad, I know, about accepting all of Lady Keating's invitations to stay for tea or dinner when I should be here studying. Please don't send me back to my parents, not yet. What would Ally say if I left? I am quite sure her feelings would be hurt."

Dr. Carrighar sighed and clasped his hands on the desk in front of him. "I rather doubt she would even notice. That is another thing. I have been trying to determine what is in the elixir Lady Keating gave Melusine, and I cannot."

Pen stopped pacing. "But you said that you didn't think it was harmful."

"I know I did. It—it troubles me, but how can I deny it to poor, dear Melusine when it's the only cure for her illness?"

Pen looked at his bowed head as a new thought struck her. He positively doted on his daughter-in-law. Was that his real problem with Lady Keating? That she'd been able to help Ally and he hadn't?

"Sir," she said gently, "don't worry about Ally—er, Melusine. She's comfortable, and that's the important thing. And don't worry about me, either. I am a grown woman, after all. I shall work harder at my studies. It will all work out in the end, I'm sure." She touched the back of his hand, then picked up the intact teacup. "I'll just bring this back to Norah, shall I?" Without waiting for his reply, she left the room.

Norah and the cook were sufficiently pleased to get the teacup safely back that they immediately agreed to make a plate of toast and honey for Corkwobble. While Cook got out her toasting rack, Pen hurried upstairs to her room. Dr. Carrighar's concern over Lady Keating's elixir had given her an idea. She retrieved the mostly empty bottle that she'd taken from Ally's room the other morning but forgot to give back to Lady Keating and slipped it in her pocket. Then, armed with a lamp and heaping plate of toast and a bowl of clotted cream, she ventured into the cellar.

"Corkwobble?" she called, entering the wine chamber.

"Eh?" Corkwobble's surprised voice came from the corner of the room.

Pen blinked. The clurichaun was standing in the far corner of the room, his back to her and his hands occupied with something in front of him. A faint splash, as of liquid spilling on the ground, could be heard.

"Oh, 'tis you, *bean draoi*. I'll just be a moment," he called over his shoulder.

What was he doing? Then it hit her. Good heavens, he was . . . Pen nearly dropped Corkwobble's snack. Should she laugh or shriek indignantly and run right back up the stairs again?

In a few seconds, however, she regained her composure. After all, she had a younger brother. Nothing should shock her. And Corkwobble was no human, bound by a human sense of propriety. She'd gotten so used to chatting with him that it was easy to forget he was of another kind entirely. She set the plate and bowl on the table and turned away to inspect a rack of bottles on the wall opposite Corkwobble, doing her best not to giggle.

The liquid sound stopped. "Now, *that's* better," he sighed.

Pen counted to ten then turned back. Corkwobble was doing up the last of the buttons on the front of his breeches as he sidled toward the table. He gave her his crooked grin. "'Tis glad to see you I am, *bean draoi,* though ye came at an inconvenient moment. Almost as glad as I am to see what you've brought me."

"Norah would raise the roof if she had come downstairs and seen what you were doing just now." Pen crossed her arms and tried to look stern.

"Well, I don't see her down here emptying chamber pots for

me." Corkwobble pulled a stool from under the table and clambered up on it. "And she should be grateful, she should. Why do you think there isn't a rat or even a wee mouse in this house? Clurichaun pi—er, you know what I mean—'tis a grand remedy against vermin." His eyes gleamed as he pulled a small spoon from the air and began to slather the honeyed toast with cream.

"Are you sure that the cure isn't worse than the disease?" Pen muttered.

"I heard that, missy," Corkwobble said through a mouthful of toast. "But I'll be gracious-like an' pretend I didn't. Now then." He swallowed. "What's so important in yer life that's kept you from visiting poor Corkwobble, apart from when ye need him to set the *Draiodoir*'s sniveling scholars right? That was a neat bit o' magic ye were after doing, I'll say again, but 'tis pining away, I am."

She rolled her eyes. Was Corkwobble going to start scolding her too? "Thank you for your help yesterday. I assume he made it safely out?"

He snorted. "I thought he'd climb through me, trying to get out after ye'd left. It seems the lad hadn't made the acquaintance o' one of the *Sidhe* before and wasn't terrible eager to extend the visit. But ye haven't answered my question, *cailin*. What's kept ye from visiting poor Corkwobble?"

"I'm sorry. I've been neglecting a lot of things lately, it seems."

He stopped chewing and looked at her shrewdly. "There's something on your mind, or my name's not Corkwobble . . . which it isn't, but you'll be taking my meaning just the same."

Pen felt a twinge of shame at her peevishness. But only a twinge. Now that she was away from his study, she'd begun to feel angry with Dr. Carrighar. How would he feel in her place, away from home and everything? Why couldn't he be a little more understanding? "I'm sorry. Dr. Carrighar just gave me the lecture of the century and I . . ." She shrugged and busied herself with adjusting the lamp.

He licked his spoon then waved it airily. "We-e-ell, I suppose I'll forgive ye this one time. After all, you're only young and thoughtless once."

"If all you can do is insult me, I can go back upstairs and—"

"Smooth yer feathers, *cailin*! I was just teasing ye. Now what's troubling ye?"

Pen sighed. "I have a favor to ask you."

"Another favor, is it? Well, that'll cost you, it will. The fairy folk don't go about giving something for nothing. 'Tisn't good for business and gives us a bad name. How big a favor is it, then? I'm no great hand at sniffing out bags o' gold, mind ye."

Pen slipped the almost-empty bottle of Lady Keating's elixir from her pocket and held it out to him. "Not too big a favor, I don't think. I wondered if you could tell me what this is."

He squinted at it for a long moment then looked at her, nodding wisely. "'Tis a bottle, as far as I can see."

"Corkwobble!" Pen resisted the urge to snatch his plate of toast away. He caught her expression and crammed the last bit in his already-full mouth.

"Sorry. Couldn't help funning you just a bit. Here, let me see it." He dusted his hands off on his coat. "Now, what'll it be worth to ye if I can tell what's inside this bottle—as I'm guessin' that's what you're wanting to know?"

"Um. . . ." Was she going to have to promise him her firstborn, or an eye, or something equally outrageous?

He snorted. "Oh, for Dagda's sake. You're asking for my professional opinion, not for a golden throne and lordship of the land. 'Tis a matter of scale, ye know. Bring me a plate o' toast like you just did for the next three days, and the deal's done."

"Very well." Relieved, she handed him the bottle.

He held it up to the light and shook it gently, then eased out the cork in one smooth motion and held it to his long nose. An expression of surprise crossed his face. "Where did ye say you were after getting this?"

"I didn't. But it came from my friend Lady Keating. She brought it for my former governess, who's been under the weather. It seems to make her sleep all the time, and we just wondered if it was safe."

"Sleep all the time? I should say so—and with the sweetest dreams to match. 'Tis *uisce beatha, bean draoi*. Fairy whiskey, as ye once called it." He upended the bottle and tasted a few drops, smacking his lips. "From up-country, I'll be saying. Doesn't taste like the brew of anyone I'm knowing in town here."

Pen wished she could sit down. "Fairy whiskey? Are you sure?"

Corkwobble crammed the cork back in the bottle and sent it spinning through the air toward her. "Well, o' course I'm sure. You asked me, and I'm telling ye," he replied with an affronted sniff.

Pen caught the bottle. "I'm sorry, Corkwobble. You're the expert. I would never doubt your word on this."

"But maybe on something else?" Corkwobble cackled. "No, no, I'm only teasing ye again, *cailin*. Don't look so moithered."

Pen stayed another few minutes to chat with the clurichaun. But all the while, her mind was churning in confused surprise. Fairy whiskey! Where had Lady Keating gotten it, and did she know what it was?

10

Niall stared moodily out the window of the carriage as it jolted up St. Patrick's Hill. Opposite him, Mother was fussing over Miss Leland, as usual.

"I *do* like your hair dressed in that fashion, my dear," she was saying, turning sideways in her seat as the carriage passed a gaslight. "We should always have Griffin do it before we go out. What do you think, Niall?"

Niall glanced up. "It's very lovely. But I rather doubt it's all Griffin's doing," he said.

Mother beamed at him as Miss Leland smiled down at her gloved hands. He was sure she was blushing, though there was not enough light in the carriage at this moment to tell. Niall smiled too, but only outwardly. There. He'd made Mother happy for a half hour or so.

Life had been deucedly difficult over the last few weeks. Ever since their walk together, when he resolved he'd honestly fall in love with Pen, he'd been courting her twice over, for both his mother and for himself. When Mother was with them, he would play the ardent beau, all bold glances and caressing remarks. Only when she'd left them strategically alone for short periods or they went out for a walk could he put off his aggressive suitor act and just be himself. Then they could discuss the politics and current events that he had studied for so long, or she would listen, wide-eyed, as he told her about growing up in the green, enchanted countryside of his parents' estates at Loughglass and Bandry Court. It wasn't that he disliked the quick, stolen squeezes of her hand or the smoldering glances. But what he loved most was the thoughtful, interested look in her eyes during their more serious conversations, the sense that he could say anything to her and she would understand and sympathize.

Not that Mother wasn't doing her own wooing. She hovered over Pen, flattering and occasionally admonishing her affectionately, for all the world like a doting mother with her favorite child. Not only did she take Pen everywhere with her—visiting as well as shopping—but she'd taken over the direction of Pen's wardrobe, Pen's social life. . . .

Nor did Pen seem to mind. "Your mother is so kind!" she'd said to him only a few days ago after Mother had made her a present of a bottle of her own perfume. "I've never had anyone . . . I mean, she really seems to care about me."

"What about your own mother?"

She'd smiled, a little ruefully. "Mama loves me dearly, I know. But she is such a self-sufficient person that I don't think it occurs to her that others might like . . . well, to be fussed over a little bit. And Papa's a dear, but he gets lost in his books sometimes and . . . oh, I don't know. Ally was the person who did the little things for me, but she's got her own concerns now, and I *am* a grown woman, after all." She'd sighed and fallen silent.

Niall knew he wasn't the only one watching Mother's behavior toward Pen. Doireann too watched them—sometimes with amusement lurking in the corners of her mouth, but sometimes with a brooding, resentful regard that sent a shiver of foreboding through him. Doir bore grudges, he knew. As to whether she was developing one against their mother or against Pen . . . neither prospect was pleasant to contemplate.

"I declare!" Mother's voice interrupted his thoughts. "Still light in the sky at this hour of the evening. Spring is coming at last, isn't it? After this dreadfully cold winter"—she shuddered delicately—"it makes me quite long to see the country again. Perhaps a visit to Bandry Court is in order sometime soon." She leaned toward Pen. "Bandry Court is my home, dear. It's where I grew up. It is the most beautiful place in Ireland in the spring, but I am biased, of course."

"I'm sure it is very lovely, Lady Keating," Pen politely agreed.

"Well, I wish you could see it and judge for yourself—oh!" Mother sat up straighter on the maroon leather of the seat. "But you could see it, couldn't you? Why don't you come with us for a visit, Penelope?" She took Pen's hand. "We don't need to go for very long, just a week or two. I'm sure that the Carrighars could spare you that long, couldn't they? Surely you've earned a brief holiday from your studies."

Niall saw Pen's smile fade just a little. She hadn't mentioned her studies at all lately—not that she had frequently before. But any mention of her academic work seemed to make her uncomfortable these days.

"Well," she said slowly, "I would love to go, thank you. But I'm not sure that Dr. Carrighar would approve of me missing—"

"Nonsense, Penelope. Surely seeing more of Ireland while you are here is part of your education? Leave it to me, darling. I shall take care of the doctor. Ah, here we are. What do you know? For once the Whelans remembered to hire a policeman to keep the carriages from getting completely jammed in this narrow street."

Niall helped Mother and Pen—Doir had elected to stay home, claiming that she felt a head cold coming on—out of the carriage. "I get the first dance, mind you," he murmured into Pen's ear as he handed her out.

She was wearing Mother's perfume, but on her it smelled different—less smoky and musky, sweeter, like spiced peaches. He resisted the urge to push her back into the carriage and spend the rest of the evening driving around Cork, seeing if she tasted as luscious as she smelled—even Mother would think that was going too far—and returned her smiling assent with a gentle squeeze of her hand. Mother preceded them up the stairs into the brightly lit hall where Sir John stood, beaming, to greet the guests and direct them upstairs to the small ballroom.

When Mother and Pen came back from leaving their mantles and changing into their dancing slippers in their hostess's boudoir, the quintet of musicians were already warming up, ready to open the dance on Lady Whelan's nod. Niall was waiting for them, to claim the dance Pen had promised him. But to his surprise Edward Enniskean leapt in front of him and practically snatched Pen's dance card from her to pencil in his name for the opening set of a quadrille and waltz. Mother frowned ferociously at him, but he didn't notice as he bore Pen off in triumph. Pen did glance back at him, looking nettled, just as a feminine voice spoke behind him.

"Why, good evening, Mr. Keating," it purred. "I'm so happy to see y—er, that is . . . I'm . . ."

Niall stifled a sigh and turned to bow to Charlotte Enniskean, who held her fan over her mouth as she gazed at him with bright eyes.

"Good evening," he said politely. "I trust you are well? And your family?"

"Very well, thank you, Mr. Keating. In fact we are here in force tonight. My cousins are in town on a visit from the country." She curtsied and reached for his arm, more or less forcing him into offering it to her, and steered them into a slow promenade around the perimeter of the room. Niall just caught sight of Pen gravely going through the figures of the opening quadrille on Edward's arm before Charlotte cleared her throat pointedly.

"I hope you will forgive my, ah, forwardness, Mr. Keating, but I wonder if I might ask a great favor of you."

Favor? Oh, lord, now what? Still, a gentleman could not refuse to help a lady, no matter how irritating he found her. "I would be most happy to oblige an old family friend."

She winced slightly at the last three words, but her bright smile never wavered. "Oh, thank you. You see, it's my cousins." She gestured delicately with her head toward a group of young women clustered against the wall, whispering to one another behind their fans. "They've not been to Cork in many years and know so few people here, and I know they're dreading being wallflowers all evening, unless—"

Niall's heart sank further. Dancing with strangers all night—probably gauche, giggling country girls—was not how he'd envisioned himself spending his evening. "I should be most happy to prevent their taking root in their seats," he forced himself to say, with a small bow.

Charlotte's narrow face blossomed in an even broader smile. "Oh, you *are* a lamb," she crooned, and held his arm a little tighter.

"This was not how I'd planned on spending my evening," Pen muttered under her breath as Edward Enniskean led her after their fourth dance back to where Lady Keating sat scowling at the dancers. Lady K. was in a frightful mood, though she'd been all kindness in the carriage earlier; Pen wasn't sure she'd ever seen her in such bad temper, apart from the first moment or two when they'd met. Well, she wasn't feeling any happier than Lady Keating looked. It was nearly time for the supper break, and she had not danced with Niall once. Not once. It was enough to make anyone cross.

As he relinquished her hand and bowed, Edward suddenly chortled and made a grab for her dance card, yanking it hard enough that it tore loose from the silk ribbon that tied at her waist. "It's mine!" he crowed, waving it in the air over her head. "All mine!"

Pen closed her eyes and didn't bother disguising her groan. She'd wondered if she'd caught the smell of spirits on his breath once or twice that evening, and now she was sure she had. He'd had three cups of punch to her one when they paused after a set, and whatever was in the Whelans' punch bowl would have brought tears of joy to Corkwobble's eyes. Only that could have turned the usually quiet, gangling boy into this—this boor. "Mr. Enniskean, if you please," she began.

"Want it back?" he asked, flapping it at her. "Gotta gimme another dance, then. Two dances. Waltzes."

"Mr. Enniskean—" Oh, what fun it would be to snatch her card away from him by magic and stuff it up his nose.

"Edward. You promised you'd call me Edward." He shook the card at her like a reproving finger.

"I did not! You asked me to and I said that I never—"

"Mr. Enniskean." Lady Keating sat up straighter in her chair and fixed him with a disapproving stare.

"Yes?" The young man swiveled his attention to her, swaying slightly. *Oh, yes,* Pen thought. Far too many trips to the punch bowl.

"Go away." She did not raise her voice in the least, but the coldness of it seemed to cut through Edward's alcoholic fog.

He caught himself and stared at her for a few seconds, looking confused. "Oh, I, er—"

"Do I need to ask a second time?" The temperature dropped another few degrees.

"Er . . . no . . . good evening, ma'am . . . Miss Leland." He shoved Pen's dance card at her, jerked his head by way of a bow, and fled.

Pen sat down with a sigh next to Lady Keating. She'd almost forgotten just how chilly Lady Keating could be when she wanted to. Edward had looked as though his heart had frozen in his throat.

"Thank you," she murmured, settling her gown in graceful folds around her. She'd worn a jaunty striped silk evening frock that had seemed perfect back in Madame Gendreau's very exclusive shop in London but was just enough ahead of the fashion here to make her feel conspicuous. That wasn't helping her mood, either.

Lady Keating made a slight disgusted noise. "He was drunk. It was positively shameful. You should have refused to dance with him after the second time he asked you."

"I tried. He somehow didn't hear me. I didn't want to create a scene, so . . ." She shrugged and hunched her shoulders. Putting up with it had been bad enough; now why did she have to explain herself to Lady Keating?

"There, child. I'm not scolding you." The frown vanished as Lady Keating patted her hand, but it quickly reappeared. "Where the devil is Niall?" she murmured to herself, scanning the room.

Pen sighed again and began to fold her dance card into pleats. She'd been asking herself the same question. Nothing had gone the way she'd hoped it would this evening.

First, there had been Doireann. She had helped Pen dress earlier that evening before Lady Keating's maid had come to do her hair. At first it had almost seemed like the old days, when she and Persy would get ready for balls together during their season. Sometimes Doireann was like this, friendly and girlish and funny in an acerbic way. But as she did up the long row of tiny hooks that fastened the back of Pen's dress, she'd sighed. "Maybe I'm glad I'm not feeling well and won't go to the Whelans' party tonight."

Pen held her breath while Doireann finished the last hooks, then exhaled. "Why?"

"So that I won't have to watch my dear brother make an utter fool of himself over the girls. I don't know what it is—the music, maybe? The dancing? It just seems that whenever we go to a ball, Niall is just, well, incorrigible." She wrinkled her nose and shook her head. "Sometimes it's downright embarrassing, the way he goes on. I hope you won't find it too off-putting. Maybe he'll try to behave himself tonight, in front of you. I should hope so."

Pen had shrugged and assumed that it was Doireann being Doireann. But could she be right? Pen knew from personal experience that Niall was more than capable of flirting, and accompanying the Keatings to so many social events lately, she'd seen how women looked at him, as if he were a dish of particularly luscious sweets they were aching to devour. Surely Niall must be aware of the effect he had on them as well?

The evening had gone downhill from there. They had arrived at the Whelans', and Edward Enniskean had been practically lying in wait for her to claim the first dance. She'd danced with him politely enough. Delayed gratification was supposedly sweeter, after all, and she'd been looking forward to dancing with Niall for *ages*. Another fifteen minutes wouldn't kill her.

But when she'd finished dancing with Mr. Enniskean, Niall had been nowhere to be found. She'd sat out the next dance trying to look nonchalant while searching the room for him, which should have been easy—after all, how many men were there tonight who were as tall and fair-haired as Niall? But she did not see him until her gaze fell by chance on a group of young women on the far side of the room, clustered around a man. It was Niall.

He was smiling and chatting, and appeared quite relaxed and at his ease. She'd turned away and pretended to be suddenly fascinated by one of the carved ivory sticks of her fan. Surely he'd escape in a moment and come to claim her for their promised dance. From the look in his eyes, he'd wanted it just as much as she had.

But barely two minutes later, she saw him once again . . . and he was leading a young lady Pen had never seen before out into the room as the musicians played the opening notes of a waltz. Then Edward Enniskean had reappeared beside her, and before she knew what had happened, she too was dancing.

For a while she fumed in silence. So had Niall's fervent little "I want the first dance" been just another of the flirtation games he still seemed to feel the need to play with her? Then she'd contemplated what she could do to relieve her feelings. Changing the color of his cravat very slowly from snowy white to bright purple was a possibility. After all, she and Persy had worked on color-changing spells last year when the London draper's shop had sent the wrong shade of tussah silk for the curtains in Persy's bedroom.

Then he waltzed by her again—with Charlotte Enniskean.

With some effort, she restrained herself from bypassing the color spell and just setting his shoes on fire. Satisfying as that might be, she knew she couldn't actually harm him. Well, not physically, anyway. But Doireann's soft voice seemed to be murmuring in her ears. *I'm glad I won't have to watch it . . . sometimes it's downright embarrassing.*

So she'd danced with Edward and several other young men, outwardly smiling and inwardly seething as she watched Niall dance with others from the little group of women . . . and with Charlotte again. And again.

Now sitting next to Lady Keating, she watched as he danced by with Charlotte once more. His cravat was a faint shade of lavender, but no one had seemed to notice yet. For a moment Pen wanted to laugh—neither she nor Niall seemed to be able to escape the Enniskeans tonight. Honestly, if she didn't see another one again, male or female, it wouldn't be too soon. Too bad Niall didn't seem to feel the same way.

Next to her, Lady Keating muttered something under her breath and rose. "Will you excuse me a moment, my dear? I just saw someone I must speak to."

"Of course." Pen watched Lady Keating sweep away, looking determined. Drat. There went her insurance against Edward Enniskean taking it into his addled brain to come ask her to dance again.

"M-miss Leland?"

Pen looked up and tried to smile. "Why, Johnny."

Sir John Whelan's young nephew stood before her, looking terrified at his own daring in speaking to her. She'd danced with him
once, earlier, after Sir John had brought him over and introduced
him. He was Sir John's heir as well as namesake, and this dance was
partly in honor of his sixteenth birthday. He was as shy as Sir John
was bluff and hearty. Remembering her own sister's shyness, Pen
had tried to be nice to him.

"W-would you do me the honor of giv—" His voice broke in a
comical squeak. Pen kept her expression perfectly sober and waited
as he cleared his throat and began again, but her heart sank. He was
asking her to dance. This was the last dance before the supper
break, and she would have to let him take her down to the dining
room and spend the next three quarters of an hour with him. She
wasn't sure her kindness could hold out that long, not after the way
the evening had turned out. On the other hand, he wasn't an
Enniskean. That counted for a lot just now.

"Would you—"

"I say, Whelan, there you are." Niall had materialized behind
Johnny. He put a hand on the boy's shoulder. "Your aunt has been
looking all over for you. I believe she's in the supper room. Better
run along and see what she wants."

Pen stole a glance at him from under her lashes. His voice was
cheerful, but his countenance was anything but. Well, what was he
so cross about? He was the one who'd just spent practically the
entire evening glued to Charlotte Enniskean and every other female
in the room but her . . . or at least it felt that way.

Johnny cast her an agonized look but bobbed his head. "Yes, sir.

'Scuse me, Miss Leland." He twisted from under Niall's hand and scurried away.

Pen watched him go, pointedly not looking at Niall.

"Since your young swain had to run along, would you give me this dance instead, Miss Leland?" he asked after a moment of silence.

It was on the tip of her tongue to say no, but she didn't. That would be childish, and she was not a child. But it certainly would have been gratifying.

"Thank you, Mr. Keating," she replied, permitting herself to sound faintly bored and reluctant instead as she took his proffered hand. He practically yanked her out of her chair and out into the room.

That was it. She was going to step on his toes every chance she got.

But as the grace and movement of the dance wove its spell, Pen remembered that for days she'd been looking forward to her first waltz with Niall. They'd spent hours together in conversation, but dancing was different: It was conversation with the body, not with words. She'd wondered just what it would be like—the touch of his hand at her waist, leading her through the steps, the subtleties of posture and stance communicating what words could not . . . oh, why did it have to happen when they were both in such bad moods?

Well, she'd done nothing to merit his annoyance. Being civil and gracious would not only be morally correct but also a sneaky form of revenge.

"Miss Enniskean looked very well this evening," she observed politely after a few moments of getting the rhythm of Niall's dancing.

"I hadn't noticed." His voice was neutral, but clouds had begun to gather on his brow.

"I had thought you were dancing with her just now—"

"I was, *thank you*"—venom edged his words—"but she had a slight mishap with her, um, attire, and had to leave. Something to do with petticoats, I believe."

"Oh." Bother, why hadn't she thought of that? She could have done a spell to dissolve all the ties and hooks on Charlotte's underclothes and got rid of her *hours* ago.

They danced in silence. "Is Lady Whelan all right?" she inquired a few moments later.

"The devil if I know."

"But you told Johnny—"

"*Johnny?*" he mimicked. "Since when are you on a first-name basis with that puppy?"

"Since he told me he had just turned sixteen last week and this was his first dance and it frightened him to pieces to be called Mr. Whelan," she shot back.

Niall snorted. "It's time his nanny brought little Johnny back up to the nursery. Lady Whelan is quite well. I just said the first thing that popped into my head that seemed believable enough to get him away from you."

Pen nearly lost her footing. "What?"

"Damn it, I've been watching him and Enniskean monopolize you all evening, and I—"

"Monopolize me? Pardon me, but you were free to claim a dance with me if you wished. But you seemed quite occupied with Charlotte Enniskean, or should I say preoccupied?"

"Do you think I wanted to be?" Niall glowered at her from under ferociously furrowed brows.

"It certainly looked that way."

"Look. Charlotte fell upon me and claimed she'd brought half a dozen cousins and would I have mercy on them and give them each a dance. I wanted to ask why the hell wasn't their cousin Edward doing his duty by them instead of me, but I couldn't. So I signed all their damned dance cards, but half the time when I went to find any of them to dance with, they'd disappeared. Then Charlotte would get flustered and say it would be a shame for me to miss the dance so she'd fill in and scold her cousins later. There was nothing I could do about it without seeming monstrously rude." He shook his head. "And it gave her brother a clear shot at you as well. I suppose I ought to be impressed at her grasp of tactics."

"I somehow never suspected Miss Enniskean had quite the, er, mental capacity for such a stratagem." Pen stared fixedly at his jaw above his spotless—and once again white—cravat. When had she told it to stop being purple?

"You're saying that you don't believe me." Niall's voice was flat.

She couldn't help it. The little imp of jealousy that had been murmuring in her ear all evening prodded her, sounding exactly like Doireann. "Yes," she said, equally flatly.

He was silent for several seconds as they danced, though she thought she saw his jaw tighten and felt his hand at her waist grip her more tightly than was seemly. Suddenly he reversed his steps— she just managed not to trip over her own feet as he did—and backed them into a corner behind a tall Chinese screen and a pair of slightly bedraggled potted palms. "Will you believe this, then?" he demanded.

Before she could even reply, he pulled her against him and kissed her.

Maybe she should have shrieked and jumped away. Or pulled

back deliberately and withered him with a cold, cutting, well-chosen word or two. But she was so surprised, in so many ways—by his audacity, first and foremost, but also by the amazing feeling of his mouth on hers, warm and intimate . . . and his arms tight around her . . . and his sheer closeness, pressed against her—that she didn't—*couldn't*—move.

Niall broke the kiss after a few seconds but did not release her. "There," he whispered after dropping more kisses across her cheekbone. "Now do you know who it is I wanted to spend the night dancing with?"

His lips brushed against her ear, and all at once she was glad he held her in so close an embrace, because everything below her shoulders felt as if it had turned to jelly. "Niall" was all she could say.

In one part of her brain she knew she should put a stop to this now. They were in a room with twenty other dancing couples. If anyone were to peek around the screen, there would be an uproar. But only a part of her brain was saying so, and right now it didn't seem to have much authority over the rest of her.

Niall trailed kisses down to the side of her neck. She breathed in suddenly and shivered. Dear God, was this why Persy and Lochinvar could hardly bear to leave each other's sight? No wonder she'd constantly found them kissing when she'd stayed with them last fall, if this was what it felt like.

"Who is it that's kept me from getting to sleep six nights out of seven, because I can't stop thinking about her, and who ends up haunting my dreams after that? Who is the only woman I've ever been able to talk to and know she understands? It's you, Pen. I'm sick to death of the Charlotte Enniskeans of this world. You're the only one I want." His voice was soft but fierce in her ear.

"Niall," she said again, and realized that at some point her arms had closed around him so that she was holding him as tightly as he held her. "Oh, Niall."

"My dearest, sweetest, tell me that you feel the same way."

He kissed her again, and all at once she wanted to laugh, not from embarrassment or shyness, but from happiness. She returned his kiss as well as she could—there seemed to be an element of practice and technique to it that she hadn't suspected before—then broke away. "I—I do feel the same way. About you. I think I love you," she said, a little breathlessly.

He stared down at her, and she saw the same happiness in his eyes. She pressed her hand against his chest before he could kiss her again. "No, wait. Before you say anything, there's something I need to tell you. About me. It wouldn't be fair if I didn't."

He raised an eyebrow and pretended to think. "Hmm, let me guess. . . . You love me, but you've already accepted a post as Johnny Whelan's nanny?"

"Stop that, you goose. I'm serious." She glanced behind her. Good; a couple of extra chairs were set against the wall. "Might we sit down? This may take a few moments."

"Yes . . . if we must." Niall stole one more kiss, then released her with a reluctance that made her heart sing. When they were seated, he leaned forward and took her hand. "What is it, sweetheart?"

Pen looked at his eager expression and more-than-slightly mussed hair—goodness, had she done that to him? She'd always wanted to touch it, and it had felt so wonderful under her fingers, thick and soft. . . . She tore her attention away from it and took a deep breath.

She had made the resolution last summer, after Persy and Lochinvar's engagement, that she would not find herself caught in the same situation that Persy had: being afraid to admit her powers. It meant breaking the rule of secrecy Ally had taught her so many years ago, but sometimes rules had to be broken.

But drat it, how should she say this? Why hadn't she spent any time rehearsing this speech, once she'd decided it was a necessity? She cleared her throat. "Um . . ."

"Please go on. I'll listen to anything you have to tell me," he prompted.

"Oh. Good. Well, then." She paused, then took another deep breath. The only way to get this done was to do it. "Well, it's just that . . . I'm a witch."

He blinked and looked at her, his expression blank. "Oh."

Oh? Was that all? Was that his only reaction? "No, really I am. I do magic. That's why I came to Ireland—so I could keep studying with Ally. She's a witch, too. She taught Persy and me, only Persy was better than I was, and now I have to play catch-up. Fortunately, the Carrighars—" She stopped. Oh, drat again, she'd have to tell everything, wouldn't she? "Fortunately, Dr. Carrighar has been able to continue to teach me during Ally's illness—he tutors in magic as well, but you mustn't *ever* tell anyone."

Niall didn't say anything, but stared down at their clasped hands. A muscle over his right eyebrow twitched. How should she interpret that? Was he angry? Repulsed? Or just struggling to understand? But she couldn't stop now to puzzle it out.

"And I decided that I had to tell you now, even though as a rule witches never tell anyone, because last year my sister and her husband—well, before he was her husband—she was afraid he wouldn't love her if he knew she was a witch, and I didn't want to ever have the same problem. So I'm telling you now, because I—because I do love you." She took a deep breath and met his eyes. Had that made any sense? "Can you still love me, knowing this?"

"Pen." At last his face came alive . . . with a smile.

She felt almost dizzy with relief. "It's all right? You don't mind?"

"No, I don't mind. I don't mind at all. It's—it's amazing, and wonderful, and . . . and *you*. And"—he hesitated—"and maybe not as shocking as you think it might be. Ireland is not like the rest of the world. I learned that much from my travels." He reached up with one hand and caressed her cheek. "I always thought you were bewitching. I was right, wasn't I?"

"Oh, Niall." Another burst of happiness threatened to overwhelm her, this time with tears. "I was worried that it wouldn't be all right." She turned her face and kissed his hand. He was taking it so calmly, so well. She was the luckiest girl in the world. "You don't know what a relief this is, in all sorts of ways. I don't have Persy to talk to anymore about it, but now I'll have you."

"To talk to about what?"

She looked down at their clasped hands. "Do you know what it's like to be so different from everyone else and to have to always conceal that difference? Can you guess how lonely a feeling that can be?"

"I—no, I never thought about it that way," he said slowly.

Should she show him? Why not? She looked up and met his eyes, took a breath and willed herself to rise until she hovered, still seated and holding his hand, a foot above the parquet floor.

He stared at her, and though he looked a little pale did not otherwise seem alarmed.

"Do you see?" she asked, coming down with a slight bump. "It's like being the only lark in a room full of chickens. The thing is, Persy's been able to do that since we were ten. I just finally mastered doing it without having to hold my breath and scrunch my face up last year. Ask Ally." Dear heaven, it felt so good to talk about all this at last! "When we arrived in London for our coming out last year, Ally disappeared and we had to rescue her. Only Persy ended up doing all the real work keeping the princess safe—"

"The princess?" His voice sharpened with interest. "Which princess?"

Well, she *would* have to tell all, wouldn't she? "Victoria, of course. Oh, Niall, it was dreadful. Someone was trying to gain control of her and needed to use other people's magic in order to do it. Ally was one of those people, and Persy and me too, except that Persy rescued us all. After Victoria became queen, she invited us to tea—do you know what that was like? Persy and I have loved her all our lives—we have the same birthday as she does, even—and to know that we, well, Persy, kept her safe. . . ." She realized that she was probably beginning to sound slightly incoherent, but he didn't seem to mind. "Anyway, she invited us to tea to tell us that she had created a secret order for people who worked on her behalf using magic. We decided to call it DASH—Dames at Service to Her Majesty—and Persy and I received the first awards, only it was really Persy who deserved it, not me. If I had learned what I should have, I wouldn't have gotten caught in a magical trap and Persy wouldn't have had to save us all by herself. So when Ally got married and moved to Ireland, I decided to skip the season and come with her so that I could concentrate on becoming a better witch. It's why I was cross with you sometimes—I knew I was falling in love with you, and I didn't want it to distract me from working if you weren't going to . . . to love me too." There. She'd said it all.

He raised one of her hands to his lips. "I'm sorry, Pen. I wasn't sure if I should, because you seemed so serious about your studies. And as far as being a witch goes, I don't care if you turn into a giant green parrot at the full moon and spend your nights perched on the dome of St. Paul's gossiping with the pigeons, if that makes you happy. You're perfect just the way you are. Perfect for *me*."

She laughed. The sound suddenly seemed unnaturally loud, and after a second she realized why. While they had been behind this screen, totally absorbed in each other, the dancers had left for the supper break. From the quality of the silence, it sounded as though even the musicians had left.

"We should probably go before we're missed," she said, rising reluctantly. "This isn't a large enough party for us to disappear completely."

"More's the pity, but you're right." Niall rose too, but took her hand. "One more?" he asked, almost shyly.

She would have promised him a thousand more, but well-brought-up girls didn't say such things. Well-brought-up girls didn't usually kiss men they weren't related to, either, but right now she didn't care. She nodded and raised her face to his. He kissed her gently this time, with a careful respect that spoke more than words. Then he held out his arm to her, and they left the shelter of the screen.

The room was deserted, and the musicians' instruments lay silent on their chairs in the far corner. A lively hum of laughter and conversation drifted up the stairs from the dining room below, filling the empty room with a ghost of gaiety.

No, not entirely empty. There was sudden movement near the door. As Pen blinked, Lady Keating rose from a chair behind one of the half-closed doors, gave them a radiant smile, and disappeared into the hall ahead of them.

Back at home later that night, Niall strode purposefully down the carpeted corridor to his mother's room. He hadn't bothered changing out of his evening clothes. The memory of Pen pressed against the waistcoat he still wore was like a good luck talisman. He couldn't help suspecting he'd need all the luck and moral support he could get when he confronted Mother.

What would she say when he told her that he'd succeeded in making Pen love him, but that he loved her too? She'd have to give up her dreams of marrying him off to a German princess or whomever, because if he was going to ask Pen to marry him, then he was going to keep that pledge. And if he didn't ask Pen to marry him, then Mother wouldn't be able to do her magic to bring him and the duke together. It would be Pen or no one.

Not that he'd had a chance to ask Pen tonight if she would marry him—it had been enough for tonight to admit their feelings for each other. Tomorrow, as soon as it was a decent hour to pay a call, he'd go to the Carrighars' and ask Pen if he could write to her father to state his intentions. He'd have to write to Papa, too, and maybe go to see him at Loughglass. Surely Papa would approve of Pen. Besides, if Papa gave his blessing to him and Pen, then there was little Mother could do to stop them.

Publicly, anyway.

Niall put that thought resolutely aside.

What about Pen's friendship with the queen? Couldn't they use that, somehow, to introduce him to the duke? The duke was the queen's uncle, after all, and her heir until she married and had children. Surely a quiet word or two in the right ears could accomplish the same thing as Mother's spells and rituals. It would be amusing to explain to Mother that she had indeed chosen Pen well—just not for the reason she'd originally thought. Oh, it would all work out after all. He'd have Pen, and Mother would see her dream realized without any subterfuge or trickery. He grinned to himself and nearly skipped the last few feet to Mother's room.

Outside her door, he paused to collect himself. Cool and calm, that was the best way to face Mother. And maybe she wouldn't be against him marrying Pen after all. She and Pen had become close; he'd seen her look at Pen sometimes with something in her eyes that wasn't entirely scheming and predatory. Had his sweet Pen charmed her too?

He smiled and brushed his hand across his waistcoat again, then raised his hand to knock. A low laugh startled him.

"Mother?" he said, turning.

But the hall behind him was empty.

Then the laugh sounded again, and he realized it came from inside Mother's room.

"I wish I'd seen Charlotte's face when you made her petticoats fall," he heard someone say, giggling. It was Doireann. "Jolly good way to get her off poor Niall. I'll bet she doesn't show her face in public for a month."

"It was the only way I could pry the hussy off him, since he was being too polite to shake her and do what he was supposed to be doing with Miss Leland. Once she left, though, he seemed to make up for lost time. They emerged from behind a screen after everyone had gone into supper, and she looked downright starry-eyed. I tried to get a report from him on the drive home, but he was being unwontedly quiet." Mother's voice was briskly pleased, as if she'd just crossed several items off a long list of tasks.

"Hah. Was Niall looking starry-eyed too?"

"Don't be ridiculous. He knows better than that. Now, I've already invited her to Bandry Court and she seemed willing to come. It's time we finished up our preparations for the *draiocht*. We need to have it down perfectly so that we can do our parts and still manage her. Have you been studying your incantations?"

He smiled to himself and reached for the latch handle. This seemed like a good time to interrupt. He'd throw open the door and say, "Don't bother. I've got a better way to get to the duke."

"Yes, yes," Doireann said crossly. "Really, Mother, killing the queen isn't going to be any harder than any other long-distance spell we've done."

Niall froze.

"As if you've had any experience in magic of this magnitude." Mother had begun to pace; her voice grew clearer, then more distant, then clear again. "Even I've done it only once, and it wasn't easy. I didn't mean to remove both of your father's brothers—only Valentine, who was threatening to tell your grandfather about my relationship with the duke. The last thing I wanted was for both of them to die, because that forced us to return to Ireland."

"So that's what it was! Poor Mother," Doireann murmured. "Forced to come back and learn how to run Loughglass and be with her young daughter who'd been left to the care of nannies and governesses while she herself was gadding about London society and entrancing the Duke of Cumberland—"

"You were quite well taken care of at your grandparents', and your father and I could not afford the house and staff needed to bring you to England with us. Now stop this chatter and pay attention," Mother snapped. "You need to be perfect to the smallest gesture and syllable. As the Mother you are the anchor of the magic. I will be managing both the Crone's part and keeping our Maidenly Miss Leland in line. Fortunately this spell isn't reliant on a time factor as much as it is on will, so it can take all night if necessary. All we'll have to do is make sure that the circle we raise is large enough and that Miss Leland gives her power willingly. I don't think that will be a problem, thanks to Niall. I must say, I had my misgivings about him. I was afraid we'd cut too close to the queen's coronation, which would have a protective effect and make our job a lot more difficult, but he's played his role very well."

Niall realized that he was clutching the doorframe to keep from sliding to the ground in a shocked heap.

"Are you quite sure of that? Don't you worry that he might have been too convincing?"

"Doireann, I am simply too tired to spar with you on this. Niall knows better than to have taken too many liberties with Miss Leland. I made it quite clear that she had to be a virgin. Stop being so contentious, though I suppose I might as well ask the clouds not to rain. Just think, this time next year we'll all be in London! Niall will be the son of the king of England—unofficially, true, but no one with eyes in his head will be able to ignore the truth. Especially not his father."

"So, what's next?" Doireann drawled. "Will you be changing English inheritance law so that he can become the Prince of Wales?"

"Don't be ridiculous. All I want is for him to be acknowledged as who he is and to be given a place as befits his birth and qualities."

"Hmm. Sorry, Mother, but the position of God has already been filled. Oh, stop gritting your teeth at me. I'll be happy enough with my London season and a big enough dowry to let me marry whom I choose," Doireann said pleasantly, but with an underlying edge to her tone. "Not to mention that pretty ring of yours and Bandry Court someday."

"Yes, yes, you'll have what you wish. *I* keep my bargains."

"And so do I, Mother dear. Just not in ways you'd always expect. Lord, I'm tired. I think I'll go to bed—"

"Not till you show me you've been practicing. Come on, I want to hear your invocation," Mother commanded.

Doireann groaned but began to chant softly. Somehow—he wasn't quite sure how—Niall made it back to his room without anyone's seeing him. He staggered to the chair by the fire and slumped into it.

Mother was planning on killing the queen.

A memory from last June returned to him. Mother had greeted him that morning with luminous eyes and held out a broadside to him as he entered the sunny breakfast room at Bandry Court. He took it from her and glanced at it carelessly.

"So? They've been waiting for the old king to die for weeks, and now he's done it. God rest his soul, and all that." He tossed it on the table with a shrug and went to the sideboard for breakfast.

Behind him Doireann had snickered unpleasantly.

"Quiet!" Mother commanded. "Don't you understand, Niall?"

"The king is dead. Long live the king," he muttered, scooping eggs and kedgeree onto his plate. What did it matter to him, wasting his life at his mother's beck and call, waiting for something that might never happen?

"Long live the *queen*," Doireann corrected him, and tittered again. "It's Victoria, dunderhead."

"Be silent!"

At the tone in his mother's voice, Niall turned around. She was glaring daggers at Doireann. He considered abandoning his breakfast and wheedling some toast from the housekeeper in her room, so that he wouldn't have to witness yet another row between his mother and sister.

"With William gone, the duke is one step closer to the throne. Don't you see?" Mother hissed.

There wasn't any need to ask which duke she meant. "But the Duke of Cumberland is only next in line until Victoria marries and has an heir of her own," Niall said. He cautiously set his filled plate on the table and reached for the teapot. "And that will happen soon. There are at least half a dozen princes in Europe ready to parade themselves in front of her for a chance to become husband of the queen of England, if Leopold of Belgium hasn't already arranged a match for her with his nephew Albert."

"But she hasn't married yet, has she?" Mother's eyes flashed angrily, but her voice was a low purr. "And until she marries and drops a brat, it is only her life between the duke and the throne."

Niall swallowed a mouthful of eggs that had suddenly gone as dry as sand. "What do you mean, Mother?"

Lady Keating shrugged. "Or even if she marries, look at her cousin Charlotte, bearing a stillborn son and then dying herself. Life is full of perils for young women. Even royal ones." She leaned back in her seat and took a sip of tea. "What I mean, my son, is that our time may be at hand. His time. *Your* time."

Niall put down his fork. Mother's eyes had taken on a cold, glassy cast that made him uneasy. "Mother—"

But then she had laughed. "Well, one can hope, can't one?"

Now it sounded as though she was going far past mere hoping. That was how she was going to unite him with his father—to make the duke king of England as well as Hanover so that he would have to come back to London and then drag Niall there and establish him conspicuously in society, where it would be impossible to miss the resemblance between them. It was ridiculous, and horrifying and outrageous. And Mother was more than capable of accomplishing it, it seemed. Good God, if she'd killed Papa's own brothers, why should she hesitate to bring about the death of a young woman off in London?

A young woman whom Pen Leland just happened to worship.

Mother wanted Pen's help in assassinating her heroine, the person whom she'd already helped save once, for his benefit. She had so charmed Pen that the poor thing would be putty in her hands. And when Mother brought Pen to Bandry Court and invited her to practice magic with her . . . he remembered Pen's wistful expression when she said, "You don't know what a relief it is to have someone to talk to about this." Pen would be thrilled to find out Mother was a witch, and would eagerly consent to work with her, and then it would be too late. But if Pen were to find out what Mother was plotting, if she were to find out that *he* knew about it . . . he gripped the arms of his chair. She'd hate him, and rightly so. If she even believed him.

No, the only thing was to stop Mother from doing this. But how? Niall rose from his chair and began to pace. Should he confront her with what he knew and refuse to be a part of it? Should he threaten to tell Papa or someone like Dr. Carrighar, who was versed in magic? That would be difficult, and it would create a breach between them that would never heal. And though he hated what his mother wanted to do, he did not want to make it public knowledge.

Could he beg Pen to return to England? No. There wasn't time for that. Mrs. Carrighar was in no condition to accompany her, and it would be at least a couple of weeks before someone from her family could arrive to escort her home. Nor could he take her; he would never be able to convince her to run away with him, either, even if he proposed to her first.

If only they were in England! He would storm the archbishop of Canterbury's offices at daybreak to obtain a special license and would have fetched Pen before a minister by noon. Or even Dublin, where the archbishop of Armagh did the same. But there was no other way to obtain a marriage license secretly or swiftly. Besides, he could not know that Pen would consent to marry him without her father's permission.

So what else could he do? If he could stop Mother in some other way. . . . If he could do something to make it so that she couldn't even attempt her spell. . . . He stopped pacing.

If Pen were no longer a virgin, she would be useless to Mother.

A nervous laugh rose to his throat. He loved Pen. He wanted to marry her, and he wanted to protect her from Mother's plans. If he were to ask her to marry him . . . and then to take her to bed. . . .

It would be very wrong of him. But to save Pen from his mother, wouldn't it be justified? After all, he would be marrying her in the end. It wasn't as if he were going to ruin and then abandon her. Betrothed couples frequently got carried away before the actual marriage ceremony, didn't they?

He sat down again because his legs had suddenly grown shaky. Good God; he was sitting here coldheartedly contemplating seducing a young woman.

No, said a part of him. *Not coldheartedly. Not ever. And not just any young woman. You love Pen. You'll be saving her. She would thank you, if she knew.*

That made him smile, but only for a second. So did the thought that most men would be delighted to be in the position of rescuing a beautiful young woman by taking her virtue. Was there any other way?

He paced his room for another hour despite the fact that it was nearly three. When a dark gray, not quite light began to replace the blackness of night in his uncurtained windows, he sat down at his desk and wrote two letters, one to Papa and one to Lord Atherston, explaining his intent to marry Pen. As soon as it was light, he himself would see that they were posted. No matter what else he decided to do, wedding Pen was his ultimate goal. If he could think of some other possible way to stop Mother in the next day or two, fine. If not . . . well, if not, he would know that he was seducing Pen with the most honorable intent in the world.

11

It was two days before Pen returned to the Keatings' house. The morning after the Whelans' party, she awoke with a dull pain low in her stomach and blood on her nightgown.

Drat. Of all mornings, why did she have to wake up with her monthly inconvenience? All she wanted to do was run to the Keatings' and see Niall . . . *her* Niall, her sweet, beautiful boy. But on the first day of her courses, it was safest to stay at home so she could change the absorbent towels made of old folded linen as frequently as was necessary. Norah, bless her, brought her a warm brick wrapped in flannel to hold against her aching stomach and cups of chamomile tea, just as Ally always had. It was all the fault of this soft city living; when she was home at Mage's Tutterow and could walk and ride as much as she liked in the fresh air, she never felt much discomfort at these times.

After breakfast she tried to settle down to do some reading for Dr. Carrighar, but her attention would not stay fixed on her book. Instead of the words on the page, she saw Niall's burning eyes just before he kissed her and his smile after she told him about being a witch. Should she write to Papa and Mama and tell them about Niall, or would that worry them? Or maybe she should write to Persy and let her begin to drop hints to them about her feelings for Niall. After what had passed between them last night, Niall would surely be thinking about writing to her parents himself soon. And she should write to her brother Charles, too. Would Charles come to worship Niall the way he did Persy's husband Lochinvar?

A soft tap at the door made her sit up straighter against her pillows and fix her eyes studiously on her book again. "Come in," she called.

"Well, child, I've not seen ye for a while," said a soft voice.

"Mrs. C—er, Mary Margaret!" Pen closed her book and folded back the quilt that covered her legs. "It *has* been a while. How nice to see you."

The little lady—today in a lavender dress but still with her old-fashioned mobcap and fichu—edged around the door and shut it behind her. "No need to get up," she said as Pen began to swing her legs over the edge of the bed. "I know why you're there. A woman's courses may be one of her connections with the Goddess, but they're also a blasted nuisance at times and aren't anything *I* miss at all. Is that chamomile tea in that cup? Good. I suppose that Norah isn't a total fool, then."

"Oh, don't say that about Norah. She is really very kind." Pen pulled the quilt back up and settled her hot brick more comfortably against her stomach. "I had never thought about—about this business as having anything to do with the Goddess, though."

"From what ye've told me, child, you weren't knowing much about her at all before you came here, so that shouldn't be any surprise. 'Tis a mortal shame your education was so neglected." The old lady softened her tart words with a smile as she walked around to the far side of Pen's bed and pulled up a chair.

"It wasn't neglected. Ally was a wonderful teacher—you should meet my sister if you want to see how good she was. It's just me. At home I never seemed to learn magic as easily or as well as I do here."

"Hmmph. Doesn't that tell ye something?"

Pen tried not to sound too hopeful. "I don't know. Should it?"

"Don't be dense, child. The Goddess chooses you—ye don't choose her. If she thinks you belong to her, there's not much ye can do to avoid her. If you find that magic comes more easily to you here in the Goddess's land, could it be because it's her magic you're doing, and should have been all along?"

"I never thought about it that way." She'd always thought about the Goddess—any of the old deities, really—as abstract concepts, cloudy and insubstantial. But if Mary Margaret was right, they were living presences. A mental picture of three women wrapped in shimmering robes and wearing the latest fashion in hats while sipping tea in the Carrighars' drawing room made her smile. "I suppose that means I'll have to stay in Ireland to study longer, then."

"And maybe even find an Irishman to marry and make it permanent?" Mary Margaret's eyes twinkled behind her glasses. "Oh ho! That's a guilty expression if I do say so meself! So have ye got an Irishman in mind already that ye're not owning up to?"

"Well, er, sort of. Last night at a party . . . Mr. Keating and I, we . . . well, his mother has invited me to her house for a visit—Bandry Court—and I can't help wondering. . . ." She fell silent at the odd expression that crossed the old lady's face.

"Bandry Court, did you say?" Mary Margaret said slowly.

"Yes. Do you know—"

A knock on the door interrupted her. "Penelope? Are you all

right? Norah said you're not feeling well." Dr. Carrighar's rumbling voice held an anxious note.

"Come in, sir," she called, then turned back to Mary Margaret. "I'm going to run out of chairs if I get any more visit—"

Mary Margaret wasn't there.

Dr. Carrighar poked his head around the door. "I trust I'm not disturbing you. I thought I heard—"

Pen peered around the edge of her bed curtains. "Where did she go?"

He advanced a few steps into the room. Pen saw that he carried a flask. Oh, dear, he wasn't going to try to dose her the way he had Ally, was he? Ally had made his remedies sound worse than the illness they were supposed to cure.

"Where did who go?" he asked. "I thought I heard you speaking to someone just before I knocked."

"Mary Margaret, of course. She was sitting right here just a second ago—" She stopped, because Dr. Carrighar's round face had taken on a peculiar expression.

"Mary Margaret? Is that what you said?" he asked, carefully setting the flask on her nightstand.

She realized that his peculiar expression was one of shock. Was he upset because she called the venerable old lady by her first name? "Er, I mean, Mrs. Carrighar. That's what she told me to call her, sir."

He stumbled around the edge of her bed and fell into the chair Mary Margaret had just been sitting on, then pulled out a large handkerchief and mopped his brow.

"Is there anything wrong?" This was getting alarming.

"No—that is, quite the contrary." Dr. Carrighar straightened in his chair and called out in a loud voice, "Gran!"

"Ye don't have to shout, Seamus. I'm not deaf, ye know." Suddenly Mary Margaret was there, perched on the end of Pen's bed.

"How—" Pen felt her jaw drop.

Dr. Carrighar's face broke into a broad grin. "Gran, what are you doing, slinking about without telling anyone? Have you been around all this time? Why didn't you visit me?"

"It's good to see you, too, grandson." Mary Margaret sniffed. "Ye never did have a gift for social niceties, though, did you? And those clothes! At least I have an excuse for not following the latest mode. That's what they were wearing about the time I died, young man. Haven't ye noticed that fashions have changed in fifty years?"

"About the time you *died*?" Pen nearly choked.

"Gran, you didn't tell her." Dr. Carrighar looked reproachfully at Mary Margaret, who suddenly appeared to be uncomfortable.

"I didn't see as how it mattered much. I just wanted to talk to the girl. She's the most interesting thing that's happened in this house for a good thirty years—her and the babe that's coming, though young Michael's wife is being vaporish about the whole thing, a pity, because I would have liked to talk with her as well."

"You're a ghost!" Pen felt foolish blurting that out, but she couldn't help it. Mary Margaret Carrighar, for all her daintiness, looked about as ghostly and insubstantial as the wardrobe in the corner.

"Ye don't have to take that tone with me, young lady." Mary Margaret frowned, but her hunched shoulders looked defensive. "So what if I'm dead? It doesn't mean I've lost interest in things, though interesting isn't how I'd be describing this household till you arrived. I'd just about given up and was planning to retire for good when ye moved in, and I thought to meself, 'Well, she'll stir things up for a change,' and decided to stay put. And if ye were wanting to have a word with me, Seamus, ye might have said so."

Dr. Carrighar shook his head, but his eyes were suspiciously bright. "I'd forgotten what an outspoken old battle-ax you were, Gran, and if it weren't impossible I'd come over there and give you an almighty hug."

"Hmmph. Sentimental boy. You may have gone soft with age, but I certainly haven't." But Mary Margaret looked pleased. "Now, about our Penelope here. What have ye been teaching the girl? Books are fine up to a point, but they're no substitute for life. Unless I'm mistaken—and I rarely am—"

Dr. Carrighar cleared his throat.

She paused and gave him a hard look. "Wipe that doubting expression off your face, Seamus, and stop interrupting me. Now, if I'm not mistaken, the Goddess has business with her, and it's not going to get done if she's always got her nose buried in books. That may be fine for your other students—most of them should be librarians, not wizards—but it won't do for this girl. Why, when I was her age—"

"When you were her age, Queen Anne was on the throne," Dr. Carrighar interrupted.

Pen gulped. Queen Anne had died in 1714.

"And has magic changed since then? Do ye think the Goddess has even noticed that the time has passed?" Mary Margaret crossed her arms.

"What makes you so sure she's the Goddess's, Gran?"

"What makes ye so sure she isn't? Who taught you about the Goddess all these long years ago? Why else is her magic thriving here, when over the water in England it didn't? Ye may like to take credit for that, Seamus, but you'd be wrong. Has she come to ye in dreams yet, child? Hmm? And what about this invitation to Bandry Court? She's circling you, ever closer. Ye must be ready to meet her."

Pen opened her mouth, but Dr. Carrighar was quicker. "What invitation to Bandry Court? And what does it have to do with the Goddess?"

"Lady Keating invited me last night. I was going to ask you today if it would be all right for me to go with her." Pen strategically did not mention Niall's name.

The old lady shook her head. "Of course she can go, Seamus. This is Penelope's path we're discussing, and it's not up to us to interfere. You should go, young woman. Be watchful, but don't be fearful. Ye may be tested—that's just her way. Be who ye are. The Goddess already knows ye anyway, but she likes to see what choices we make before she decides."

"Decides what?" Pen's head was starting to ache as much as her stomach. This morning was getting to be too strange.

"Penelope's needing her rest." Mary Margaret ignored her question and rose, shooing Dr. Carrighar toward the door. It opened obediently. "Let's leave her be. Now *you*, ye great stick-in-the-mud. What have ye been doing with yourself since Katherine died? Nothing, as far as I can see. And ye wonder why I've had nothing to say—" The door closed behind them.

Pen lay back against her pillows. Mary Margaret, the *late* Mary Margaret, had given her a great deal to think about. Was what she'd said true? Was the Goddess really watching her? What did she have to do with Bandry Court?

Well, at least she'd gotten permission—more or less—to go to Bandry Court with the Keatings. And Niall.

It was going to be wonderful.

The morning after the Whelans' party, Niall went to post the letters to his father and to Lord Atherston as soon as he was decently shaved and dressed. After a moment's hesitation, he decided to splurge on an express; it was some relief to his feelings to have *something* happen quickly.

Then he waited in a fever of impatience to see Pen that afternoon. But she sent a note shortly after breakfast claiming an indisposition, and another the day after that. Two days, during which his imagination swung between worrying that she'd changed her mind about him and thinking about what he would do with her when she got over her ailment and came back to the house. He tried to relieve his feelings by walking past the Carrighars' house twice a day, but he never caught a glimpse of her—only their maid Norah, shaking out dusting cloths in the area.

Pen finally came on the third day, and what was more, came unexpectedly early. This was an unhoped-for turn of events, for Mother was not at home; indeed, she and Doireann had gone out on a round of errands and had planned on stopping at the Carrighars' for Pen when they were through. As Healy showed her into the library, Niall realized that they could probably expect to be undisturbed for at least an hour and a half. A tremor of excitement mixed with indecision ran through him. If he was going to "save" Pen, now would be the time. He rose from his chair by the window and tugged slightly at his cravat, which had grown uncomfortably snug for some reason, as Healy bowed himself out.

"I've missed you," he said as soon as the door had closed behind the butler. Pen looked pale, and though she smiled at him as she took off her bonnet and gloves, there was a hint—no, more than a hint—of agitation in her attitude and face.

"I've missed you too. I . . . it's . . ." she trailed into silence and looked down, blinking.

"Pen?" he said, approaching her and holding out one hand. "Is there something wrong?"

"No. Everything's fine. I'm quite well, thank you," she said brightly, then looked away and sniffed.

He bent and tried to look into her face. She dodged him and turned away, but not before he caught a glimpse of her eyes, bright with tears. "All right, Pen. You're quite well. You're also terrible at lying. What is it?"

She sniffed again. "I'd rather not say. It's over and it won't happen again if I can help it."

For a second, Niall was alarmed. She wasn't talking about the other night, was she? When he'd kissed her at the Whelans' ball?

"Pen?" he said, more quietly, and reached for her hand. She didn't snatch it away, so he drew her to the sofa by the fire and sat, pulling her down next to him. "What happened? What has upset you so? Was it"—he swallowed—"was it something I've done or said? You've stayed away two days, and I was worried that—"

"No!" She looked up at him then. "It's nothing to do with you. I haven't come for—for personal reasons. And I shouldn't have come today until I was better able to control myself. It's just . . . I needed to see someone that I . . . that I could trust. I'm sorry, Niall. I'll be better in a few minutes, now that I'm here with you."

Someone she could trust. He tried to ignore the irony in that. "Whom can't you trust, sweetheart? Has someone tried to hurt you?"

"No, not really. . . ."

"Not really?" Righteous anger suddenly flared up, making his throat tight. "Who is it? What happened? Did Edward Enniskean come bothering you again?"

She laughed, but it half sounded like a sob. "No."

"Then who was it, damn it?"

"Niall—"

He slipped his arm around her waist and pulled her toward him, so that her head rested on his shoulder. "Tell me."

"It—it was Eamon Doherty," she whispered.

"Doherty?"

"One of Dr. Carrighar's students, the one we rescued that day in the street. He—he just tried to—to *kiss* me."

For a moment, Niall was sure he'd choke on his anger. Someone had dared to touch Pen—his Pen. And not just touch her. "Tell me what happened, so I know just how hard I'll have to hit him next time I see him."

Miraculously, she laughed. "I already took care of that. I stomped on his foot so hard that I'm sure I broke something. Oh!" She shuddered. "How can I face him again after what he said . . . after what he tried to do? After the horrid way he's behaved toward me, insulting my intelligence and ability in practically every class. I should have turned him into an ant and stepped on him!"

"Why didn't you?"

"Believe me, I wanted to." She nestled closer, as if she'd been doing it for years. "It was after our tutorial with Dr. Carrighar just now. Mr. Doherty left as soon as it was over, before the rest of us could even rise from our chairs. I left the room last and was about to go upstairs when I heard someone call my name. He had hidden himself in the drawing room. He asked if he could speak with me. I assumed it was about the other day—you know, when he was hurt during that political rally?"

"I remember. Go on."

"Well," she paused and moved slightly against him, as if she were suddenly uncomfortable. "I asked you to leave us that day because I wanted to use magic to conceal him and get him back to the Carrighars'. I did so, and then I healed him. I began to get a hint that maybe you were right about him . . . about him maybe not hating me . . . but I had no idea. . . . I went into the drawing room, and he closed the doors. He had a strange look on his face, as if he weren't sure whether to be pleased or angry. He started to thank me for saving him that day, and I brushed it off because I'd . . . well, I'd been a little rude to him after I healed him—"

"I'm willing to wager he was rude first."

"He was." She laughed again, then sighed. "He was very stilted and obviously hated having to say what he was saying, but something didn't feel right. And then he began to speak of one of Dr. Carrighar's recent lectures on perceiving the purpose behind any given piece of magic, and that he thought he knew why I had helped him. I wasn't really paying attention because I was trying to think of a polite way to end the conversation and leave, and had turned toward the doors again, and then he . . ." She swallowed. "He caught at my hand. I tried to yank it away, but he wouldn't let go, and then he started spouting the most horrendous nonsense—how he'd tried to fight his feelings because he'd considered me unworthy of him, and even though he'd had to admit that he was wrong, he still fought his feelings, but couldn't overcome them. It was like a ghastly parody of Darcy and Elizabeth in *Pride and Prejudice*. And then he grabbed my waist and tried to kiss me."

Niall felt like baring his teeth and growling as he pictured it. "What did you do?"

"Stomped on his foot—fortunately with my heel, so it had some effect—and gave him a shove. And then I ran. It would have been so satisfying to give him a thorough dressing-down, but all I wanted to do was escape. I ran upstairs and locked myself in my room, but I could not calm myself. I couldn't face eating dinner with Dr. Carrighar and pretending nothing had happened, so I left a note for Norah and came here. It was quite dreadful, worrying that he might be lying in wait around every corner." She shivered. "It sounds a little comical, now that I tell it, but it was anything but at the time. He looked so angry and desperate, and so determined, that I was quite frightened."

"I'm not surprised. He's an utter blackguard." Blackguard didn't begin to cover it; if he were to ever meet this Doherty in the street, he would knock him down. "You were very brave."

"I didn't feel brave at the time." Her voice broke. "Oh, how am I going to face him at our next tutorial? I shall have to give them up. I just can't be in the same room with him again, even if others are there."

"I'll cheerfully make it so that he can't attend your next tutorial, much less walk."

"I'd be delighted if you did, but you can't. It just . . . oh, it makes me furious!"

Niall felt the heat of her skin and how her breathing came quick and hard, and his own anger shifted subtly. She was in a high, fine passion. Could he change it from anger to something else? Should he? Now would be the perfect time, if he was determined to save her.

"Poor darling," he murmured, tightening his arm around her. "Of course you're furious. You should be furious."

"I hated it, the implication that he was attracted to me against his will, that it was his baser side that had taken over. Instead of respecting my power, he resented it. It was almost as if he were trying to put me in my place—"

"Reprehensible," he agreed, and pulled her onto his lap.

"Niall!" She froze for a second.

"Shhh. I only want to comfort you." He pressed her head against his chest and began to stroke her arm and shoulder. "You need it."

She slowly relaxed against him. "Yes," she said, on a sigh. "I suppose I do."

"You do," he whispered, and gently kissed her temple.

"Why did it have to happen this way?" she asked after a few minutes of silence. "I was ready to respect Dr. Carrighar's students as fellow magic users. I just assumed they'd be like Ally's husband and be able to respect me in turn."

"I don't know." He let his hand drop down slightly and brush across her breast. She shivered again but did not pull away.

"I suppose it isn't all of them. Mr. Sheehan and Mr. O'Byrne seem to be able to endure me, though Mr. Sheehan sometimes goes a little too far in the other direction and thinks my sensibilities are too fine to permit me to study magic."

"Nonsense." He bent his head and placed a soft kiss on the side of her neck while letting his hand wander to her breast again. She made a soft sound deep in her throat and arched her back slightly.

Damn it, he was enjoying this too much. He should be feeling much guiltier right now, should be having to force himself to touch her like this, but all he was conscious of was how good she felt.

Was he doing it right? She seemed to be enjoying it too, so maybe he was. Whenever his friends at Oxford or Göttingen had tried to cajole him into visiting brothels with them, he'd always claimed a headache or too much work or not enough money. He had been taught to be gallant to women, but to touch and be intimate with one he did not love seemed like a crime.

How different it was to touch and kiss his Pen. He moved slightly under her weight on his lap; could she feel just how much he was enjoying this?

"You don't mind that I'm a witch, do you?" Her voice was lower and huskier than he'd heard it before, and her hand had strayed under his coat and was pressed against his chest, on the silk of his waistcoat.

"Not at all," he murmured. "I love everything about you. I love your face and your laugh. I love to talk to you and dance with you and look at you and touch you—" He slid his hand over her breast and down her waist to her thigh. Her breath caught, then released with a faint "ohh" as he caught a handful of her skirt and petticoats and pulled them up her leg, and then another.

"I love to kiss you." He caught her mouth and kissed her hard and deep, then drew back and looked at her. "I want to wrap myself around you like a cloak and feel every inch of you under me."

Her eyes were half closed, as if he'd mesmerized her, so he kissed her again and felt her lips open under his. "Niall," she whispered into his mouth.

He'd finished rucking up the hem of her skirt and felt the fine linen of her drawers under his fingers. Only a thin veil of cloth lay between his trembling hand and the warm skin of her thigh. "Pen," he moaned. "Please, let me touch you. Let me love you—"

"Niall, no." She stiffened as he caressed her, and though her voice was still low and throaty, there was a distinct note of finality in it. "We can't do this. It's not right." She gently lifted his hand from her thigh and pushed her skirts back down.

"But you don't understand. I have to. . . ." He kissed her again, hard and desperate. Dear God, how could he explain to her that it was for her own good to let him ruin her?

She returned the kiss for a moment, long enough for him to regain hope. Then she turned her head.

"I want you too, Niall—oh, so much! But I can't let you do this," she said quietly.

"I should think not!" said a shocked voice from the doorway.

Pen nearly bolted off Niall's lap, but he saved her the trouble by leaping to his feet. Fortunately, she slid sideways onto the sofa rather than straight down to the floor and looked up to see Lady Keating, wide-eyed and pale, her gloved hand clutching the polished latch of the door for support. She still wore her maroon shot-silk mantelet and bonnet as well as gloves; evidently she had just come in.

"Mother!" Niall said, giving her a short, abrupt bow. His face had gone very white.

She straightened and let go of the door but did not respond as she crossed the room and held out her hands to Pen. Pen rose, still feeling breathless, and tried to read Lady Keating's expression. She saw anger there, but it did not seem to be directed at her. Indeed,

Lady Keating pulled her closer and put a protective arm about her shoulders.

"Are you all right?" she murmured, looking into Pen's face.

"Yes, I'm—I'm quite well. Just a little overset—" She was about to explain about Eamon Doherty and how Niall had been trying to comfort her and perhaps got somewhat carried away, but Lady Keating interrupted her.

"Of course you are, my dear child." She smiled and gave her shoulder a gentle squeeze, then turned back to Niall. Her expression turned glacial. "I am utterly appalled at your behavior. Not to mention disappointed. Have you so forgotten yourself? Have you forgotten what we—" She pressed her lips together then, as if to prevent any more words escaping them, but her blazing eyes spoke for her.

To Pen's surprise, Niall's shock slowly changed to something else. The color returned to his face as he squared his shoulders and met his mother's angry stare. A silent, electric conversation seemed to pass between them. "I haven't forgotten, madam," he replied quietly.

His words seemed to strike Lady Keating harder than a physical blow. "You . . . you . . . ," she spluttered. "You're just like any other man, thinking with the wrong part of your body. After all that I've—"

This time she pressed the knuckles of her hand against her mouth to stop her words, shaking with repressed emotion. "Out of my sight," she hissed. "Go!"

Niall looked at his mother, then met Pen's eyes. She wasn't sure what she saw in them: Was it apology? Regret? Longing?

"Niall," she mouthed soundlessly, not sure what she wanted to say. He dropped his eyes, bowed again, and stalked from the room.

Lady Keating let out a slow, shuddering sigh. Pen glanced at her and saw that her eyes were closed. Oh, lord. What did one say to a woman who had just walked in on you dallying with her son, even though it had been his idea . . . ?

No, that wasn't fair. She'd enjoyed Niall's kisses and caresses. Was *enjoyed* a strong enough word? She'd been almost as swept away by sheer physical sensation as he . . . almost.

Two things had stopped her from letting him go any farther. One was the fact that she still wore a linen towel pinned into her drawers to catch the last of her monthly flow; if he had found it there she would have died of embarrassment on the spot.

Even if that hadn't been the case, though, she still would have stopped him: After all, they weren't married or even engaged. Heavens, they'd just acknowledged their feelings for each other a scant two days ago. If he were to ask for her hand, she knew she would say yes. But she would not become intimate with him until they were married. Her body belonged to her, and her alone, until she shared it with her chosen husband.

After what they had just experienced together, Niall would surely ask her to marry him. Maybe she could ask Lady Keating to chaperone her home, and then Niall could ask Papa for her. In another two or three months, they could be walking down the aisle of the church at Mage's Tutterow, starry-eyed and glowing—

"Are you sure you're all right?" The fury had left Lady Keating's voice, but she still sounded agitated and anxious.

"Yes, I—I'm fine."

"You're *sure*?"

There was a peculiar intensity to the question. Ah. Was Lady Keating concerned that something more than kissing had taken place before she walked in? "*Quite* sure," she replied firmly.

"Thank God for that." Lady Keating dropped to the sofa as if her legs would no longer hold her. She pulled Pen down to sit beside her, took her hands, and gazed at her with an earnest expression. "My dear, I must apologize for Niall's behavior."

"Oh, no, you don't have to." This was *so* embarrassing. She couldn't very well say, "But I liked it, thank you," could she?

"I must. Niall is . . . well, how were you to know he wasn't to be trusted alone with you? True, I've let him take you walking, but I assumed that a public street was a safe venue for you to be together without my chaperonage. I've been so delighted by what I thought was the growing regard between you two. I thought perhaps that the affection of a good and virtuous girl would change him and make him put aside those *habits* he had acquired." Lady Keating looked away with a little sigh.

"Habits?" What was Lady Keating talking about?

"I blame myself entirely. I should never have let him wander the Continent without a proper guardian to keep rein on him. It was a disastrous decision."

Now she was totally mystified. "I don't understand. I thought that . . . his studies abroad . . . he always mentioned companions—"

"Oh, yes. His studies." Lady Keating gave a bitter little laugh and half turned away from Pen. "Indeed, he had companions. Companions of the worst possible sort for a wealthy, impressionable, lonely young man. Oh, how can I explain to an innocent, gently bred girl like you? I'm afraid that when Niall left Ireland, he also left behind his restraint and judgment and became . . ." She shook her head. "I can't say it. It cost a great deal of money to hush up the worst of it, though. Thank God the police closed down that hideous club in Paris. That was a near thing, keeping his name out of the papers. The young women in Rome and Berlin were safely confined, I heard, but I hope the payments will be enough to keep them safely in their own countries . . . and that no other women show up on my doorstep with unexpected grandchildren. And then his health—the doctors assured me after his last examination that the disease had been caught in time and that his need for the absinthe was finally under control, but I still worry."

Pen stared at her averted profile. Women. Payments. Disease. "Are you saying that Niall—"

"I had hoped never to have to admit any of this to another soul, least of all to you, my dear girl. You two seemed so fond of each other. I thought, 'Ah, now he has seen what true love is, not just lust and depraved sensation.' I had hoped that he had seen the errors of his ways, that he would treat you with the honor and respect that you deserve. . . . That in falling in love with you, he would reform." A tear fell on the tan kid glove in her lap, spotting the leather. She dabbed at her eyes with a handkerchief. "I am so sorry. So very, very sorry."

Pen sat still as a peculiar numbness crept over her. This was impossible. Could she have heard Lady Keating correctly? Had Niall spent his years on the Continent in a drunken round of debauchery?

"He is still my son—my only son—and I love him. I had so hoped you would be his salvation. There is no one I would rather have for a daughter-in-law." Lady Keating squeezed her hand, and another tear trickled down her cheek.

Niall, a profligate? A rake? A drunk and a lecher? How could it be? She'd never had the least hint that he was anything but what he appeared to be: a handsome, educated, charming young man.

But she knew how Lady Keating adored her son. She could never say any of those things about him—those horrid things—if they weren't true.

Now everything began to make sense: Lady Keating's eagerness to promote their friendship and her anxious hovering over them. Then, in a rush of words and pictures, memories of Niall assailed her . . . memories that now seemed two-sided: the compliments, the hand holding the night of the dinner party, Doireann's hints about Niall's past, his dancing the entire evening with Charlotte Enniskean . . . had it all been just a game? A more subtle continuation of his sordid past?

"It—it can't be," she whispered.

Lady Keating finally met her eyes. "My poor darling, I'm afraid it is."

"But . . . he loves me! I know he does." As she looked at Lady Keating's pale face, it blurred in a haze of unshed tears.

She sighed and shook her head. "Not in the way that he should. You are very attractive, my dear. I fear that his attentions to you were inspired more by the thought of a challenge than any finer emotion."

"A challenge? To what?"

"Your virtue, of course."

Her virtue. Pen buried her face in her hands, hardly noticing Lady Keating's arm around her shoulders or her murmured words of comfort. Was that all it had been? An elaborate attempt to seduce her? Why her? Why not Charlotte Enniskean or any other woman in town? Why did it have to be her?

"I loved him," she muttered. "I actually told him I loved him."

"It is very hard not to love him. He is worthy in so many ways—handsome, knowledgeable, polished. I have not yet given up hope that he might be reformed someday. It is so sad. I had hoped you would be the one to help reform him—"

Pen interrupted her with a laugh, a short, harsh sound that she did not know she was capable of making. "Yes, well. It doesn't appear as if he wants to be reformed by me."

Lady Keating reached up and took Pen's chin in her hand. Her fingers were cold and trembled slightly. "My dear, you don't know how much your pain hurts me. But there is another way you could help him, if you don't despise him utterly."

Pen dropped her eyes from Lady Keating's intense gaze. Did she despise him? Of course she did; she'd hoped to marry him, but all he had been interested in with her was a game, to make her another notch in his bedpost. But despise him beyond all recall?

She remembered their talks and spirited discussions of history and politics, interspersed with companionable silence. There had been real friendship between them at first; no other young man of her acquaintance had been so intelligent, so stimulating a conversationalist, so much fun. Could she forget that side of him so completely as to loathe him?

"N-no," she said at last. "I—I don't wish to see him, but I can't wish him ill." Well, not too much ill. Nothing that would leave scars. At least, not deep ones. "I hope that he can overcome this . . . defect someday and live a happy, upright life."

"Oh, my dear, that is all I wish for him as well. It is all I think about, all I work for." She took a deep breath. "Perhaps the time has come for me to share some other information with you. It is not . . . it is not something that I have told anyone else, ever. Too many people could be hurt by it, and so I have kept it to myself all these years." She looked at Pen with an expression half proud, half ashamed, in her green eyes. "Niall is not Lord Keating's son."

Oh, dear. What should she say to that? Wasn't Lady Keating aware of the gossip that even she, a newcomer to Cork, had heard? "I—" she began.

"No, my dear, you don't have to say anything. What can you say to such a statement? Nevertheless, it is true. Before my husband inherited the title, he was a soldier, an officer in the Duke of Cumberland's Fifteenth Dragoons. I came to London when they were there—we had been married only a few years, you know. And then I met the duke." She sighed, and her eyes grew dreamy and distant. "I tried, but I could not deny my feelings for him when he indicated his interest in me. My marriage had been an arranged one. *This* was love. We had a brief time of heaven together, but I was already married, and he was the king's son—there was no future for us. I have his son as a living reminder of that love.

"Niall has always been a restless boy. He has his father's brilliance and boundless energy as well as his handsome face and figure. His poor father—Lord Keating, that is—is a good man, but he has been ill so long that he has never been able to be a father to him, and so Niall fell by the wayside. But I have dreamed . . . if Niall could be united with his father—his real father—perhaps it would give him the strength and purpose to turn his life around and prove himself worthy of such a parent. It would give him his proper place in the world. Do you see? Do you understand what I hope for?" She took Pen's hands and gripped them.

Pen remembered all the unpleasant things she wanted to inflict on Niall when he spent the evening glued to Charlotte Enniskean at the Whelans' dance. Funny that it never occurred to her to do anything to Charlotte. Was it because, deep inside her, she knew it had been his fault?

Men! First Doherty and now Niall. Was this all they cared about? Getting under a girl's skirts? Their education, their future, their very honor were forgotten or ignored at the sight of a pretty girl. Or else they coldheartedly pursued women who they thought could be helpful in their careers, like that awful Lord Carharrick who'd chased Persy last year. No wonder it had taken Ally so long to find a man she could respect enough to marry.

Lady Keating cleared her throat. There was an odd note in her voice as she spoke. "Niall attempted a great wrong on you, and he will be made to pay. I cannot let what he tried to do go unpunished. But we can ensure that it never happens again, if you will help me."

Oh, it certainly never would happen again. At least not to her. "I think so, but how can I be of help in this? What can I do?"

"Ah, a great deal." She fixed Pen's eyes with hers once more. "Listen."

Pen waited, unable to tear her eyes away from Lady Keating's. Then she heard it: a soft sighing sound, as of wind blowing through long grass, and a thin, silvery thread of tune.

"Music," she whispered. "I hear music." Or was it music? Was it just the wind playing those sweet, flutelike notes?

"Yes." Lady Keating's eyes narrowed in concentration.

The musical sighing grew louder, and now Pen could feel it, a warm, gentle breeze that blew across the back of her neck, lifting the fine hairs that had escaped from her coiffure after Niall's passionate embraces. Or was it something else that sent shivers down her spine—an otherworldliness, a sense of something that was not from the here and now?

"What is it?" she whispered. Now a scent of greenness and moisture surrounded them, like a spring meadow just after a rain.

"Can't you guess?" Lady Keating smiled, then leaned forward and gently blew into Pen's eyes. She blinked, and in that instant the library, with its comfortable sofa and shelves of books and curios, vanished. Instead, she and Lady Keating were standing on the crest of a great grass-covered hill under a lavender-blue sky. All around them, rolling plains of grass stretched away, dotted with lower hills and clumps of tall trees. On the horizon, the dark line of a forest met the grass, but how far away it was Pen couldn't judge because the air, though clear and invigorating, seemed to shimmer slightly as the wind blew through it.

"What . . ." She tried to form a question, but the words bubbled and seethed in her mind and would not come together. Had she fallen asleep in the middle of talking to Lady Keating? Or was her mind playing tricks on her?

Lady Keating laughed, and the sound of it seemed to ripple and blend with the music of the wind. "I'm sorry to have startled you, my dear. But it just seemed easier to show you than to try to explain. Welcome to *An Saol Eile*—or at least to the part of it I know. It doesn't do to explore too far into these lands unless one is prepared for a very long and perhaps strange journey."

"*An Saol Eile*," Pen repeated. She had heard those words before. Hadn't Corkwobble once used them, to talk about—

"It means 'the other life.' So much more poetic than 'the land of fairy,' don't you think? And more apt. Have you ever seen a place that is more alive?" She looked up into the sky, a small smile just touching her mouth. In the soft light, her lips looked very red and her skin glowing and translucent, like alabaster. In fact, all of her suddenly seemed . . . *more*. It was as if she'd been magnified—no, intensified, like wine distilled into brandy.

And it wasn't just her. The grass blowing around them was so green that Pen could practically taste it, and the air felt like champagne as she breathed it in, going straight to her head and making her feel almost tipsy. Fairy. How did Lady Keating know about the world of fairy? How could she—

"It is very simple, my dear." She reached up and brushed a loose strand of hair out of Pen's eyes. The ring she always wore, the silver one with a green stone, positively glowed. "I know about it for the same reason you do."

"I don't understand." She had fallen asleep somewhere along the way and was dreaming it all—these colors and scents and feelings could exist only in a dream.

"It's not a dream, my dear." Lady Keating bent and ran her hand through the grass at their feet, then brushed her dew-soaked fingers across Pen's cheek. A rivulet of it rolled down to the corner of her mouth, and she could taste it, like a rare liqueur.

"Can you taste a dream? Oh, Penelope—I will not call you Miss Leland, for it is not a name that matters here—I think you do understand. This place is real, and you are not dreaming. As soon as I saw you that day in the street, I knew who, or perhaps I should say what, you are. Or at least I strongly suspected and soon realized that I was right. You're a *bean draoi*—a witch, though I hate that English word. And so am I. It was why I was so drawn to you from the very start. What a coincidence for us to have met, though perhaps not so coincidental. When magic-wielding people meet, it is usually for a reason, though that reason may not always be evident at first."

"You're a . . . a *bean draoi*? Really?" Pen stared at her, then looked away. The slightly drunk feeling that she was getting seemed to intensify. "I mean—yes, of course you must be, or else we wouldn't be . . ." She gestured, indicating the green plains around them. "I'm sorry, I'm just—"

"A little overwhelmed? Is that so surprising? Come, my dear, of course you are. Though there are more of us in Ireland than in your home, it should still be a surprise to meet a fellow *bean draoi*." Still holding Pen's hands tightly in hers, she raised them, arms outstretched. "You know me as Lady Keating of Loughglass. That is my husband's name and title. But I have a name and title and lands of my own that I inherited in my own right. What you see here is part of my land. The rest of it is in the mortal world, around my home at Bandry Court."

Bandry . . . ban dree . . . *bean draoi* . . . she had never paid much attention to the name before, but now it made sense. Was that why the name had startled Mary Margaret Carrighar? Did she know it too? "You hold a fairy title? But how, unless you're—"

Lady Keating laughed again. "No, I'm not a fairy. I am as human as you are. And it isn't a fairy title. It was given to my family by Danu, the Triple Goddess, so many years ago that no one now remembers when. I am one of her—not priestesses, for she doesn't have a hierarchy. Perhaps the term 'lady-in-waiting' best describes it. I serve her, keep her word and bear witness for her in whatever way she requires. It's a position that can be held only by a *bean draoi* of my family. Your family has a history of the powers, am I right?"

Pen nodded.

"So has mine. One woman in each generation has the power. She inherits the title of *Banmhaor Bande*—Steward of the Goddess—and all that comes with it, the privileges as well as the responsibilities. Look behind you." She let go of Pen's hands and turned her to face the opposite direction.

Not far away was another hill, higher than the one they stood on. Was Pen imagining things, or was the grass even greener and more lush on its flanks, and the light shining on it clearer than anywhere else?

On the summit of the hill were three standing stones arranged in a triangle, silver-gray and exuding an air of deep timelessness, and yet they stood straight and firm, as if raised only recently. Three other stones rested on their tops, linking them.

"That is the Goddess's place, where I come to speak with her when she summons me," Lady Keating explained. She dropped a slow curtsey toward them.

Pen copied her, feeling awkward. "Does she . . . summon you often?"

A small line appeared and disappeared between Lady Keating's brows so quickly that Pen was not sure it had been there. "Not as often of late. But her ways are mysterious and not for us to comprehend." She waved her hand, and two chairs of carved wood appeared behind them. She gestured for Pen to sit; after a few seconds, Pen realized that her chair was just slightly lower than Lady Keating's. Well, that was only appropriate; this was Lady Keating's place, not hers.

Pen looked at the trilithon on the hill in silence. Either sitting down had helped or she was getting used to the intoxicating air of this place, for now she could think more clearly. Lady Keating was telling the truth. She could feel the presence of the Goddess in this place, wherever it was. Lady Keating—a witch and one of the

Goddess's ladies! It would explain so much, except for one thing. She took a deep breath. "Lady Keating, why are you showing this to me?"

"Ah, my dear. Can you not guess?" Lady Keating smiled at her fondly.

"Er, no, not really."

"My dear, I sought your friendship because I saw at once you were exactly the type of young woman I wanted Niall to marry: lovely, intelligent, wellborn, wholesome of mind . . . and as a *bean draoi,* worthy of his blood. And also as a *bean draoi,* I hoped that if you came to love Niall, you would be willing to help us with a little piece of magic, one that would serve to remove the barriers between him and his father."

So that was what Lady Keating had meant by helping Niall. "Us?"

"Doireann and myself. Doireann is a *bean draoi* as well, though sometimes . . ." She shook her head. "But the Triple Goddess's magic is best worked by groups of three. With three of us working together, united by our love for my poor, dear, flawed boy—I know that he has behaved reprehensibly toward you and destroyed what regard you had for him, but if any shred of it remains, any pity, even, it could be the saving of him."

Pen sat in her chair and looked down at her hands. She could feel Lady Keating's eyes on her, pleading. Could she find it in her to want to help Niall now, after he'd just tried to seduce her? Was this the test Mary Margaret had mentioned?

"I must confess . . . ," Lady Keating began, then stopped.

"Yes?"

"Well, it is just that I . . . it would be a great honor and delight for me if we could . . . that is, if you wanted to . . . to become my pupil for a while. No, not pupil—I can feel your power, and it is very great.

But if we could work together, you and I, and I could share with you what little knowledge I have that you do not already possess. I know you've had your excellent Miss Allardyce—Mrs. Carrighar, I should say—to teach you all these years, not to mention Dr. Carrighar himself more recently. But I do not think that they and I necessarily know the same things. Working this spell for Niall's sake would necessitate some amount of preparation. . . ."

A little thrill coursed through Pen. No more reading long sections of old books written in antique language on dusty, brown-spotted pages, or having to discuss magical theory with the likes of Eamon Doherty and Quigley. No, working with Lady Keating would mean active, practical magic, and it would be *Irish* magic, the warm, wonderful, slightly wild magic she'd had only sips of, the Goddess's magic. She'd be able to drink it down to the lees, immerse herself in it. . . .

"Could I? R-really? You'd want to teach me?" she stammered.

Lady Keating laughed. And all at once they were standing once again, the chairs vanished, and the sweet, musical wind blew in their faces like the breath of the Goddess herself, and Lady Keating put her hands on Pen's shoulders and kissed her forehead. *"M'inion,"* she murmured. "My daughter you will be, from this moment on. You will come to Bandry Court, and we will work together, you and I."

12

Two days later, Pen watched the spires and hills of the city of Cork give way to green countryside as she, Doireann, and Lady Keating began their journey to Bandry Court.

It had been easier than she'd expected to manipulate Dr. Carrighar into giving her permission to go on such short notice. The memory of their talk still made her a little ashamed of herself, but she'd done what she'd had to do . . . and it had worked, hadn't it? It wasn't Dr. Carrighar's fault that Doherty had been an idiot and decided that he was in love with her. But it had been easy enough to burst into tears in the doctor's study and say she couldn't face another tutorial with Doherty, or even feel at ease knowing he was in the house . . . and just as easy to make him feel as if Doherty's advances were the result of his lack of vigilance. He'd turned pale and been quite speechless, then agreed readily enough to her leaving with Lady Keating for a visit to Bandry Court. Doireann had suggested using that approach to asking his permission, and Pen had to admit that it worked well. She'd comforted herself with the fact that Mary Margaret had already said she should go. Having her backing had surely helped.

And with Dr. Carrighar's permission given, she hadn't needed to trouble poor Ally. Pen now understood why she slept nearly around the clock. Surely Lady Keating's motive in giving Ally the fairy whiskey had been kindness. After all, it had saved her from a great deal of discomfort. Pen hadn't asked her about it yet—there had hardly been time what with packing yesterday, and she hadn't wanted to visit the Keatings in case she saw Niall. . . .

Niall. When Lady Keating had picked her up just now, she'd been almost afraid to enter the carriage for fear that he would be accompanying them. Several hours in close proximity to him, even with his mother and sister present, would have been dreadful. But Lady Keating had seen her hesitation as she put her foot on the step and glanced inside.

"He's not here. How could I do that to you, my dear? No, he left early this morning for a visit at a friend's house near Kinsale. I understand Charlotte Enniskean was to be there as well." She pursed her lips.

Kinsale was in the opposite direction to where they were going. Pen had been relieved, then . . . well, surely it couldn't be jealousy she felt. Not now. No, Charlotte was welcome to charming, debauched Niall. Would *she* let Niall have his way with her if they happened to find themselves alone in a quiet sitting room?

The thought that she might be doing just that in the near future made Pen want to shudder. His caresses that day in the library, his words had all felt so genuine, as if he truly had been swept away by his feelings for her. But she couldn't think about that anymore or it would drive her mad. Heaven knew it nearly had over the last two days. Thank goodness that Lady Keating was taking her away.

The sky was a steely gray as they rattled over the road north to

Bandry Court. The winter had been a hard one, and the roads were bad as a result, still rutted and very muddy. Even in Lady Keating's well-sprung carriage, they were being jounced about quite unmercifully. Pen hoped that the gray clouds wouldn't decide to rain and make their journey even more uncomfortable.

In the seat facing her, Doireann sat with closed eyes and nodding head. It was difficult to believe that anyone could nap while being shaken and bumped like this, but Pen was grateful: It meant she didn't have to make conversation with her.

Doireann had been more like the lions than ever lately. Even with her eyes shut and her breathing in the slow regular rhythm of sleep, Pen got the unsettling feeling that Doireann was watching her. Why? What had she ever done to make her so watchful and distrustful? Did it have anything to do with Niall? He had said that he never knew where he stood with her, either—

She had to stop thinking about Niall.

"Tell me about Bandry Court," she said quietly, turning to Lady Keating beside her. "Is it quite old?"

"Parts of it are. There is a great deal left of the medieval keep and walls, and some sign that those were built around even older structures. It is set on a hill, which is where the ancient Irish preferred building their fortifications, so I should not be surprised if there had been a dwelling there since, well, forever." Her pride in her house was evident. "It grew over the years, and my great-grandmother added on and modernized a great deal in the 1780s but worked around anything that was already there rather than tearing it down. She added several bedrooms, a gallery and drawing rooms, and a library as well as better quarters for the servants. It is a bit of a hodgepodge, but a lovely one. I always resent the time I must spend in town or elsewhere, because it takes me away from Bandry Court."

Pen remembered that Lord Keating lived in seclusion at Loughglass. Was that what Lady Keating meant by "elsewhere"? Would she ever meet him, now that Niall—

Drat. There she went again. She stared out the window, hoping for distraction. There was an intensity to the colors in Ireland—the greens more verdant, the browns richer, even the gray of the sky more forbidding—that was deeply satisfying. The greening land was cut haphazardly into fields, some brown and plowed, some left rough and untouched, here and there dotted with tumbledown hovels. It was not remotely as tidy and orderly as the land around her home in Hampshire, and signs of poverty were frequent. Despite the relative peace that prevailed right now, Ireland was a deeply wounded place, divided in religion and politics. Heartbreaking beauty, side by side with heartbreaking pain, and both called out to her. As much as she loved Mage's Tutterow, *this* somehow felt like where she belonged. If only there were some way that she could stay here and truly make it her home. She'd thought she had, but Niall . . .

Pen was awakened by the ride's not becoming bumpier, but smoother. She opened her eyes and sat up straight, easing the tension in her shoulders. Why had she let herself fall asleep? She hated dozing off in a carriage; it always gave her a ferocious crick in her neck.

"Awake, my dear?" Next to her Lady Keating was still sitting upright, hands folded in her lap, as if she had not moved a muscle since their brief stop at an inn for a cup of tea and a quick snack. "Very good, as we're nearly there." She gestured toward the window.

They were just passing a small stone cottage. Two young girls in brown linen dresses stood beside it, mouths agape as their heads turned to follow the carriage's passage, and a stout woman pegging laundry to a clothesline dropped a deep curtsey.

"My gatekeeper, Mrs. Coffey," Lady Keating commented, returning the woman's greeting with a nod and wave. "She was widowed a year and a half ago, so I gave her the cottage and the position. My Mistress requires that her daughters in need be looked after."

Pen nodded in reply, but her attention was fixed by the view in either of the side windows: Two immense pillars of stone, easily twelve feet high and half that in girth, stood sentinel on either side of the road. They were an uncompromising gray, speckled with lichen, and looked as if they'd been there since the dawn of time.

"And that is my gate," Lady Keating added. "I don't think that any smith's work in iron or brass, no matter how fine, could outdo these."

"No, indeed," Pen agreed fervently. They brooded over the road, almost seeming to watch the carriage as it rolled past them and up the lane. She could well imagine that the two silent, almost menacing stones could keep unwelcome intruders out as effectively as any iron gate.

A short distance past the cottage and gate, the road dipped down and over a stone slab bridge that spanned a tiny brook, then climbed again into a copse of trees, mostly yews and holly and young oaks. When they emerged from the trees, Pen could see that they'd entered a rolling upland. It was much like the down country near Newmarket back in England, but impossibly, richly green, even under the lowering sky. Here and there, indeterminate gray shapes dotted the grass; she was not sure from this distance if they were more mysterious stones or merely sheep.

Crowning one of the hills was a great stone pile of a house, looking to Pen a little like another ancient druidic monument, apart from the smoke rising from its chimneys and the neat gardens and outbuildings surrounding it. Beyond it was an even higher hill, and this one was topped by standing stones. It looked almost exactly like the vision of *An Saol Eile* Lady Keating had shown her.

Just then Doireann yawned so theatrically that Pen guessed she'd been awake all along, or at least for a while. "Home, are we?" she asked, stretching.

Lady Keating glanced at Pen, one eyebrow sardonically raised, and she knew then that Doireann had been indeed feigning sleep. "Did you have a nice rest, my dear? Yes, we're home."

"That's good. If I don't get to a water closet shortly, it'll be—"

Lady Keating closed her eyes and looked pained. "Thank you, Doireann, that will be enough."

Doireann grinned and winked at Pen.

In a few moments they drew up to the front door of the house. The building was made up of several parts, some obviously very old, some modern. It was saved from too much architectural chaos by being built of the same gray stone in all its parts, and in the end looked like what it was: a place that had been occupied for a very long time.

The front façade where they had stopped was probably medieval, a massive, blocky, square tower, though it appeared that the windows had been enlarged and glazed. To its left was a long wing that looked Elizabethan in age, and to the right was another tower, more recent still, and another long wing set perpendicularly to the rest of the house. It was a little jumbled, but Pen decided that she thought it was charming.

The carriage door opened. Lady Keating climbed out, then

nodded to Pen to follow. Pen accepted the hand of the footman who held the door and alighted from the carriage onto the gravel drive, then nearly froze in astonishment. The footman was a foot*woman*. She wore a footman's livery coat over a narrow skirt of the same material and trimming, and a powdered footman's wig. Pen murmured her thanks, trying not to stare.

At the massive planked front door, a tall woman, stately in black silk and crisp white cap, with a bunch of keys at her waist, stood waiting to greet them. "Good afternoon, your ladyship," she said, curtseying as they approached. "Welcome home."

Doireann pushed past them without a word and disappeared into the house.

"Thank you. Penelope, my dear, Mrs. Tohill is housekeeper at Bandry Court." Lady Keating was already untying her bonnet as she crossed the threshold into the hall. Pen followed, smiling a greeting to Mrs. Tohill.

The entrance hall was high-ceilinged and square. Stone floors and walls revealed the age of this part of the house, but deep, gem-colored Turkish rugs and modern furniture warmed and softened the effect. Pen took it all in appreciatively as she unfastened her cloak. More of Lady Keating's unerring sense of taste.

"Miss Leland is a dear friend," Lady Keating continued to the housekeeper, handing her bonnet over. "I shall expect everyone to take very good care of her, Mrs. Tohill."

"Indeed we will, mum." The housekeeper did not return Pen's smile, but her manner was gravely courteous.

"Tea in the library, I think, while our bags are brought in. Miss Leland did not bring a maid, so Niamh should look after her while we're here."

"Very good, mum." Mrs. Tohill took their cloaks.

Lady Keating led the way to one of several doors that ringed three sides of the room. It led into a secondary hall that looked to be part of the most recent additions, with a fine staircase and elegant detail to the moldings and woodwork. But as Pen followed Lady Keating up the stairs, she was less aware of the handsome details and more aware of a growing excitement inside her. She was here, Niall wasn't, and for the next week or two she could live and *breathe* magic, with Lady Keating's help. It was going to be wonderful.

Niall stared out the drawing room window at the street below. He wished he could open it. After a few days of rain, spring had arrived, and the May afternoon was warm and fragrant, even in town. The carriages clattering past the house had their tops down, and their fashionably dressed neighbors stepped out of the other houses on the street to stroll in the soft air. Just as Pen and he had done, not so very long ago.

Pen. He closed his eyes. Just thinking about her hurt.

Someone knocked on the door.

"Come in," Niall called, not bothering to turn around. It would just be one of the temporary footmen Mother had hired while she was away. Why she'd felt she had to remove all the regular servants he didn't know. It wasn't as if any of them would have helped him. They were too loyal to Mother—or too afraid of her.

The footman backed in, his hands clenched around the handles of a tea tray. He set it down on the sofa table without looking at Niall and left quickly. Good God, what had Mother told them about him? They served him, but treated him like a leper. Perhaps it was just as well, considering his mood.

He was still fed, his hot water brought for his bath and his clothes brushed and put away, even his mail brought to him. Life was comfortable and almost normal, even, except for one thing: If he ventured anywhere near a door or tried to open a window so much as a crack, an invisible hand closed itself around his throat and threatened to choke him, holding him back as surely as iron chains. He was a prisoner.

He should have fled after Mother walked in on him and Pen in the library. He should have just walked out of the house, gone back to the stables, saddled a horse, and ridden to Loughglass to see Papa. Mother couldn't have said a word against that, at least not in front of anyone else. But he hadn't. He'd gone to his room and spent the next hour pacing, trying to decide what to do next. She'd come to see him there, entering without knocking or calling to him.

"May I ask," she said without preamble, leaning against the closed door, "what in the Goddess's name you were doing down there with Miss Leland?" Her face was even paler than usual, and her eyes glinted like a January sea.

He'd hesitated. Should he answer and admit what he knew about her plans? But she wasn't finished.

"No, I probably don't want to know. At any rate, nothing did happen, and I've managed to save the situation quite well. In some ways, we may even be better off than we were before. She has agreed to come to Bandry Court and work with me . . . no thanks to you, however." She glared at him.

"Where is she?" His voice was hoarse.

"I sent her home to begin packing. We leave for Bandry Court the day after tomorrow."

So soon? He resumed his pacing. There wouldn't be much time

to try again, then. Maybe he could slip out this evening to see her. Waiting until they all got to Bandry Court was risky, though it would be much easier to stage a seduction there—

Mother interrupted his fevered thoughts. "At least, your sister and I will be leaving then. You will not be accompanying us."

He froze midstride. "What?"

"Do you take me for a complete fool? If I had not come into the library in time, you would have ruined all my plans. You're no rutting animal, like most men, thinking with your—your—" She gestured and curled her lip in distaste. "You knew I need her untouched and pure. So I am forced to conclude that either you are not as disciplined and controlled as I thought you were or you were intentionally trying to corrupt her. In either case, I do not want you within miles of her. You will stay here in town while we go to Bandry Court, and when the deed is done, you will go directly to London to prepare to meet your father."

Niall's mouth felt dry. "Why London? The duke is in Germany. He's the king of Hanover now, if you recall."

"I recall quite well. I also expect that he will be returning to London . . . very shortly." Her tone was matter-of-fact and brisk, and it chilled Niall to the bone. She meant that the duke would be returning to England after the death of the queen.

"In the meanwhile, you will not be seeing Miss Leland again. No, don't protest. Perhaps I should have said that she will not be seeing you. Why would she want to, after all? Ever since she heard all about your escapades on the Continent—"

"I didn't have any escapades on the Continent." But a horrible suspicion was growing inside him. "What did you tell her?"

"I suppose I must thank your sister for the idea. It seems she's been dripping poison in Miss Leland's ears about your dissolute ways for weeks now, just out of sheer mischief."

"She's been . . . about my *what*?" Dear God, what had Doireann said about him? Was that why Pen had been so cool at the Whelans' dance before he kissed her?

"Precisely. At first I wanted to kill her, but in the end she's done us a great service. Suffice it to say that Miss Leland no longer finds you as attractive as she once did. She is helping with a spell to reunite you with your father as a favor to me. Amusing, isn't it? I think I've even thought of a way to get around the relationship issue, so we'll have the additional power of her being my kin." Her voice hardened. "I have already said I won't ask you what your intentions were in the library. But I also want to make it perfectly clear that I will not brook any more interference with my plans. You will stay here, and then you will go to London. In another few weeks, everything will have fallen into place, and you will have forgotten Miss Leland in your new life."

She turned on her heel and left the room. When he'd recovered from his shock sufficiently to go after her, he'd found that the door was locked . . . from the outside. It had stayed locked until they'd left; his meals had been brought to him on trays, as if he were ill. Only after Mother and Doir had left was he allowed the freedom of the rest of the house.

Not that it mattered, particularly. All he had done for the last few days was wander from his room to the library to here, feeling lost. His emotions traveled their own circular route, cycling through boredom, anger at his mother, and a deep sadness.

He'd lost his lovely, lively Pen. She hated him now, if Mother was to be believed, and there was no way he'd be able to regain her. Even if he were to see her in London sometime after this awful business was finished, she would avoid him . . . and would eventually find someone else to fall in love with and marry. He lay abed at night, not sleeping but remembering her in all her moods, from merry and teasing to shy and unsure to ardent as she had been in his arms. . . .

But it was no good remembering any of it now. Niall rose stiffly from his seat by the window and poured himself a cup of tea from the tray the footman had brought, wishing that he had a bit of the whiskey that the pub keeper had once offered him to put in it. Anything to numb the pain.

A knock on the front door made him nearly drop his cup.

For a second, his heart leapt. Could it be Pen? But no—she was with Mother and Doireann at Bandry Court. And besides, she was lost to him. There was no way she would come to visit him now, even if she were back in town.

He heard one of the footmen cross the hall to the door and jumped up from the sofa. Even if it weren't Pen, it would be nice to see and talk to another human being, even the Enniskeans. Well, maybe not them. But somebody.

As he opened the drawing room door, he heard the footman say to the unseen caller, "I'm sorry, sir, but Mr. Keating is not seeing anyone right now," and begin to shut the door.

"Yes I am," Niall called loudly. The footman at the door paused and glanced back in surprise. Another of the new hires appeared from the dining room and started toward him.

"Devil take it, am I not even allowed a caller to relieve the boredom?" he snapped at the man.

The footman paused and looked at him, forehead furrowed. "But Lady Keating's orders were—"

Niall did some fast thinking. Maybe he could bluff and bully his way through this. "Lady Keating's orders were that I not go out. But why can't someone come to see me?"

"But, sir—"

"Who's there?" he shouted.

"Sir," the footman said anxiously.

"Damn it, who's there?" He pushed past the second footman and strode to the door. The first one stepped in front of him, preventing his leaving, but at least he could see the visitor, a tall, thin, red-haired young man who somehow looked familiar.

"You don't know me . . . that is, we—it's Eamon Doherty, Mr. Keating. We met a week or so ago," the man replied, craning his neck to see over the footman's arm. "I've . . . er, I've come to return your hat." He held up a black beaver hat that Niall recognized as his own.

His hat? How had this man ended up with his hat? Then he remembered. This must be *that* Doherty, the one Pen had rescued from the constables and who had repaid her by trying to kiss her. Niall wasn't sure whether to laugh or let the footman slam the door in his face . . . or step forward and punch him in the nose for daring to touch his Pen. But having someone to talk to who knew Pen—however tenuous, not to mention obnoxious, the link—would be a relief. Besides, he wanted his hat back.

"Let him in," he barked at the footman. "Good God, man! If you want to stand in the doorway and watch us talk, you can. But you know there's no way I can leave."

The first and second footmen exchanged frightened glances. Niall understood; they knew that the house had been enchanted so that he couldn't leave. But they were terrified of Lady Keating.

"Have some pity. Mr. Doherty's harmless," he said, more softly. "You may check his pockets before he leaves if it makes you feel better. I won't try to send out any messages with him. I just want to talk to another human being before I go mad."

The first footman gripped the door and looked stubborn, but the second one met his eyes. "Ye're not fibbing? Ye won't leave?"

"How can I?" Niall spread his hands and shrugged.

"'Tis true enough." The footman looked at him a moment longer then turned to the door. "Let's let him see his caller, then, Jemmy. But, sir, ye must leave the drawin' room door open an' let us watch ye from out here, just in case."

"That's fair enough." Niall nodded his thanks.

"But Lady Keating said . . ." The first footman now looked frightened as well as stubborn.

"She won't be knowin' if we don't tell, will she?" The second footman addressed his question to both Niall and his colleague.

"No, she won't. She's got her mind on more important things right now," Niall promptly replied.

"Well . . ."

"I would, of course, be quite willing to show my appreciation in more material terms," Niall added, raising an eyebrow.

The first footman stared at him a moment longer, obviously calculating what sum he might be able to extract from Niall, then dropped his arm. "All right, then. But we'll be watching ye, sir. Ye can come in," he said to Doherty, stepping aside and bowing slightly.

"You may give my hat to him, Mr. Doherty," Niall said, nodding at the footman. "And might we have another cup and more tea in the drawing room? Or perhaps something stronger?"

Doherty handed the hat to the footman with a suspicious

glance. Niall gestured him into the drawing room and followed him in, leaving the door open, as promised. The second footman stationed himself across the hall from the door, out of earshot but where he could watch both of them, and the first footman disappeared in the direction of the kitchen.

"Thank you for the return of my hat, Mr. Doherty. I trust it proved useful to you?" Niall asked after they'd both sat down.

Doherty glowered at him for a moment, then relented. "You know, then? She told you? You know what she is?" His voice caught slightly on the "she."

So he wasn't the only one losing sleep over Penelope Leland. "She told me about it after the fact, yes," Niall responded, watching him.

"She . . . I had no idea she was capable of that. The sheer, raw power of it! My nose was broken—broken, mind you—and she healed it. Do you know what it takes to heal a broken bone by magic?"

"I can guess."

"You can guess," Doherty mimicked bitterly. "You've no power, so you have no idea. When she healed me, she was like a bonfire burning six inches from my eyes. It took my breath away for hours after. It still . . ."

Niall remembered the feeling of her as he held her in his arms and they kissed on the library sofa. "Yes, she would have been like that."

Doherty glanced up at him and flushed a dull red. The first footman returned with another tray containing both tea and a decanter of amber liquid, and they remained silent while he set it down and retreated from the room to join his colleague on watch in the hall.

Niall ignored the teapot and poured them both a few fingers of whiskey. He handed one glass to Doherty. "Your opinion of Miss Leland seems to have improved of late. She had given me to think that she was not as well respected by you as she might have been," he observed.

Doherty flushed again. "Can't a man make a mistake?"

Niall smiled, but it felt twisted on his face. "They can, and often do."

Doherty stared at the glass in his hand, then took a gulp. "She's gone, you know," he said after a few moments. "She hasn't been in tutorials."

"I know. She went to the country with my mother and sister."

"That's what Dr. Carrighar said." He paused. "So why aren't you there with her?"

None of your damned business. "I wasn't invited."

"No?" Doherty leaned forward and refilled his glass from the decanter. "Well, then. So much the better for me," he said softly, sitting back against the green damask-covered chair.

"Don't be so sure, Mr. Doherty," Niall snapped, resisting the urge to get up and clout him. "When I last saw her after you waylaid her in the drawing room, she seemed about ready to put a death curse on you."

Doherty choked on his whiskey. "She—she told you that too?" he gasped.

Niall watched with secret satisfaction as he groped for his handkerchief and wiped his chin with it. "Yes. And I might add that I would not have blamed her if she had."

Doherty seemed to deflate. "I—I couldn't help myself. She was so damned magnificent when she—"

"Is everything all right, sir?" One of the footmen, the suspicious one, had come to the door. He looked at Doherty curiously.

"Fine, thank you." Niall waved a negligent hand. "He just swallowed the wrong way." He winked at the footman as if to comment on Doherty's ability to hold his liquor. The footman grinned and returned to his spot, nudging his colleague and whispering.

Doherty gave him a sour look as he put his handkerchief away. "So if she came to you, why weren't you invited to the country with them? When do the banns get read?"

There was no way to evade such a direct question. Niall tried not to let his voice shake. "There won't be any banns. My mother has seen to that."

Doherty stared at him. Niall coolly returned his stare, but his mind was working double-speed. Doherty was in love with Pen. He was also a wizard. If he could be convinced that Pen was in danger, then maybe he could at least try to break the enchantment on the house so that Niall could go to Bandry Court. Unless the fool took it into his head to go off and rescue Pen himself. . . . He glanced into the hall. The two footmen still stood there, watching them with interest.

"I'm going to tell you a rather startling story," he said quietly to Doherty. "Don't react strongly to anything I say and, for God's sake, don't go spitting your whiskey all over the place again. In case you hadn't already noticed, I'm not exactly free to come and go as I please."

"I, er, had noticed that."

Niall ignored the hint of sarcasm in his tone. "Miss Leland has gone with my mother and sister to my mother's house in the country. My mother and sister are also witches."

Doherty's eyes widened. "Go on."

"My mother wants Miss Leland's help to perform a spell. Miss Leland is unaware of the exact nature of this spell, but if she performs it and then finds out, she will be devastated. I tried to prevent this from happening, but I failed."

"What is the purpose of the spell, may I ask?"

"To kill the queen."

To Doherty's credit, he kept his countenance better than Niall had expected. "Are you joking, Keating? Your mother wants to assassinate the queen?" he asked. "Why?"

Niall smiled and nodded as if he and Doherty had just shared an amusing bit of gossip. "To put the Duke of Cumberland on the throne."

"But why?"

"Because he's my father."

Doherty whistled quietly. "I think I need another drink." He held his glass out to Niall, his hand shaking. Niall poured him a double, and he downed it without seeming to notice.

"So let me get this straight," he said. "Your mother wants to remove the queen and needs Miss Leland's help. But if Miss Leland knew this, she would not help."

"She's the queen's friend. She and her sister saved the queen last year from a similarly unpleasant plot."

"Mother of God." Doherty sat in silence, as if digesting what he had heard. "So what about you?" he asked at last. "Don't you want to be able to traipse off to London and let them all gossip about your being the king's bastard? What have you got to do with it that you're being kept prisoner in your own house?"

"I tried to make it so that Pen could not be used in my mother's spell."

"What, did you tell her about it?"

"I couldn't. I didn't know if she'd believe me, and I was afraid she'd think I'd been in on the plot all along. But my mother lied to me too. It was an accident I found out about it at all."

"So what did you do then, man?"

Niall steeled himself. "I tried to seduce her. Mother needs a virgin for her ritual. If Pen were not a virgin—"

This time Doherty did react, leaning forward and glaring at Niall. "And you had the nerve to preach to me for just trying to kiss her! Why, you blackguard—"

"Quietly, damn it!" Niall growled. "And I'm not a blackguard. I intend to marry her. I've already written to her father to get permission to propose to her. It's not as if I even want to bed her before I should . . . but I have to."

Doherty subsided against the back of his chair, glowering. "Let me guess the rest. Your mama found you in a compromising position, whisked Miss Leland off to the country, and left you here to cool your heels." He grinned suddenly. "Serves you right, I think."

It was deucedly difficult not to leap up and wipe the grin from the idiot's face. "So Pen gets to help kill the queen she adores without knowing it, and I lose the only woman I've ever loved."

Doherty made a rude noise. "So what am I supposed to feel sorry about, apart from Miss Leland's grief? What good have that fat lot of German kings been for Ireland? Will the death of another one of them be such a loss? And why shouldn't I be glad that you lose Miss Leland? Maybe it gives someone else a chance at her. Like me."

"You fool." This time Niall didn't bother to hide his scorn. "You utter, bloody fool. If Victoria goes, who will be king? The Duke of Cumberland, who hates the Irish and is totally opposed to Irish independence. Your reading room will be closed down so fast it will make you dizzy, and you and all your political friends will find yourselves in gaol or transported inside of a year."

Doherty looked deflated. "I didn't think of that."

"Obviously not. And since when do you think Miss Leland would ever even think about giving you a chance? She's a viscount's daughter and a duke's granddaughter and will be back in London before you could ever begin to try to earn your way back into her good graces."

"You don't know that," Doherty protested, but Niall could see that it was just bluster. Doherty knew well that Pen would never view him with anything but dislike.

"Look," he said, leaning forward slightly and catching Doherty's eye. "You owe her. She got you out of a dangerous situation and healed your not-inconsiderable injuries. If you really want to show gratitude to her, help me figure out a way to get out of this house so that I can stop my mother and save Pen from perverting her own magic and killing her friend."

Doherty stared at him, and Niall could sense the wheels turning in his mind. "I owe her," he echoed quietly, uncertainly.

"You certainly do," Niall replied just as quietly, then fell silent and watched Doherty struggle with himself.

"If I were to help you . . . how are they keeping you here, anyway? Leg shackles at night?"

"Magic, thanks to my mother." Niall nodded with his head toward a window. "If I try to go through a door or open a window, something grabs me around the neck and half chokes me to death. If I even touch the window or try to open it, I feel it. Far more effective than shackles."

"Really?" Doherty looked interested. He stood up quickly and went to the window, running his hand over the frame. "I don't feel anything."

"No?" Niall joined him, and glanced back at the door. The first footman stood there, peering at them suspiciously. "I'm just pointing out a mutual acquaintance's house to my friend here," he said with a casual wave. "If it makes you feel better, you can watch us from there." Still casually, he put a hand on Doherty's shoulder and rested the other on the edge of the window.

Doherty stiffened.

"Feel it now?" Niall muttered. His cravat had already begun to feel too snug.

"Jesus!" Doherty gulped. "That's one hell of a repelling spell she's put on there. It's on every portal, you say?"

"Well, I haven't tried to escape through the chimney yet, but it wouldn't surprise me if she had that covered too." Niall took his hand off the window and the pressure on his neck eased. "My mother doesn't do things by halves."

Doherty was silent, regarding the street below them through narrowed eyes, but Niall could see that his attention was focused inward, not on the passing traffic. "Your watchdogs in the hall," he murmured after a few minutes. "They don't have magic, do they?"

"Not as far as I can tell, though I don't know them. Mother hired them specifically to watch me while she's gone. They know there's a spell on the house, but that's it, I think."

"That helps. Put your hand back on the window." Doherty fell silent again, with that inward, probing look on his face. "Good," he said. "There's no alarm spell on it that I can feel. She won't know if I've broken it."

Niall forced himself to take slow, deep breaths to counteract the choking sensation that crept over him again and nodded wordlessly. He hadn't even considered that possibility. Mother had been in a hurry to prepare to leave for Bandry Court, though, and perhaps the precaution had slipped her mind. Thank God for that. "Can you break it?" he whispered.

"I don't know. It's . . . where the hell are these women getting all this power?" Doherty sounded torn between admiration and annoyance.

Niall let go of the window frame again. *"Can you?"*

Doherty didn't respond, but this time Niall sensed that his silence was one of indecision, not concentration. He waited, not daring to breathe too loudly, and watched Doherty wrestle with himself.

"All right," he finally said, exhaling. "But I'm doing this for Miss Leland, not for you or the queen or anybody else. I repay my debts."

"If I am able to, I'll tell her," Niall promised. He wanted to laugh in triumph and relief, but restrained himself. "In the meanwhile, I thank you."

"If I can do it, that is," Doherty added, running a hand along the window frame again. "Don't be getting your hopes too high yet."

"Is there anything I can do to help?"

"Not really. Just stand here and be quiet. I need to work through you, since the spell affects only you. Again, please?" He nodded at the window, and Niall reluctantly placed his hand on it once more.

Doherty began to murmur, a low, indistinct flow of words. Good; at least it would still appear to the footmen as if they were talking quietly. Niall closed his eyes and caught a few rolling *r*'s and crisp vowels. Latin? But Mother always cast her spells in Irish, for the

Triple Goddess. Would Latin work on her magic? Then the choking sensation started again and he focused on his breathing, letting Doherty's words wash over him.

"I'm not getting it." Doherty broke off his low chant. "I can't break through it. When I push on it, it flows away and re-forms around me like water. It's not any magic I'm familiar with."

"The Goddess," Niall hissed through gritted teeth. "It's her magic. Can't break it. It bends." He'd learned that much from living with his mother and sister all these years.

Doherty groaned. "It figures. I can't get away from her lately, can I?" He resumed his low chant, this time in Irish.

Niall hung grimly on to the window, trying not to show by his face or posture that he was slowly being throttled, lest the footmen come in and stop them. Dark shadows began to edge his field of vision as he stared out at the street.

"Ah!" Doherty exclaimed. "I see now. But it's smooth—can't find an edge to pry it loose." He chanted again, a little faster this time.

Purple dots were dancing in front of Niall's eyes, and his lungs felt as though they were being squeezed shut. If Doherty didn't find a way around the spell soon, he'd—

The pressure vanished. He let his hands fall to his sides and gulped in a great, shuddering breath, and another. Next to him Doherty swayed slightly, his face a peculiar shade of pasty white under his red hair. "Whiskey," he muttered, and turned away from the window.

"Wait a minute," Niall croaked. Deliberately, he placed both hands on the window.

Nothing. He was free.

He managed to walk back to the sofa without staggering as his breathing and heartbeat slowly returned to normal. Doherty sat down opposite him and groped for the decanter once more, breathing hard. The footman eyed them with a faint scowl on his face but moved back to his station in the hall.

"Thank you," Niall said again, after they'd both had another whiskey in silence.

Doherty shrugged and leaned forward to set his glass on the tea tray. "So what will you do now?"

Niall glanced at the footmen. "Wait until night, and then leave for Bandry Court."

Some color came back into Doherty's face. "I could go with you."

"No. Thank you, but I think I need to go there alone."

Doherty looked disappointed. "I suppose." Then he shook his head. "I still can't get over it. First Miss Leland and then your mother. Women's magic . . . I'd never have thought it could be so powerful."

Niall smiled to himself. If only Pen could have heard him say that.

13

Pen stood in the rose garden behind the house, hand in hand with Lady Keating. A gentle breeze played across the back of her neck, drying the beads of perspiration there and on her forehead. The cloudy weather that had accompanied them to Bandry Court had not lingered, and the last four days had been lovely. But it wasn't the day's sunny warmth that made her sweat just now.

They'd stood this way for hours, as they had several times each day since their arrival. Lady Keating had not lied when she said that they would work on the Goddess's magic together, and work hard. Pen had found it necessary to take a post-luncheon nap each day after their daily morning session so that she had the strength for their afternoon and evening work.

But the hard work was exhilarating as well as exhausting. Her stamina was increasing with the practice, and so was a sense that as she improved, even greater heights would be attainable. The feeling of power she'd had when healing Doherty seemed puny now compared with the energy that flowed through her during her work with Lady Keating.

Before her, Lady Keating inhaled and closed her eyes. Pen felt her cradle the power they'd been raising, smoothing its rough places and augmenting it. Eight times they'd passed it back and forth, adding to it with each passage, until Pen thought she could almost see it, a glowing, seething mass of energy inside the circle formed by their joined hands. This was the largest amount they'd raised yet, and her arms and legs trembled at the thought of the weight of it. No, not weight—though it felt like a physical load, sometimes. It was the *intensity* of the magic, its sheer size and concentration, that made her feel as if they were holding up an invisible millstone.

Lady Keating nodded at her. "Penelope," she said quietly, "are you ready?"

"I'm ready." Pen braced herself and took a deep breath as Lady Keating passed her the shimmering mass.

"When we get to this level of power, we must work a little differently. It is no longer a matter of conscious effort, but of surrender, in a way. Hold it gently," she murmured. "It will never be greater than you can bear. In circle rituals, the power we make is limited by the weakest member. The magic is still here, so you must be strong enough to hold it. Do you understand?"

I think so, Pen thought. For some reason her voice didn't seem to want to work.

"Breathe, child." Lady Keating sounded faintly amused. "Holding your breath weakens you. Don't try to fight it."

Pen forced herself to take a shallow breath and let it out.

"Yes, that's right. Think about your breathing. Breathe in. Now breathe out that same amount. Again. When you direct your breathing like that, you create a balance, a stillness. Do you feel it?"

Pen concentrated on her shoulders, relaxing them, letting them regulate the ebb and flow of her breath.

"Now, let the power rest on that stillness in you. Lightly . . . yes. Good. It is not so heavy anymore, is it? When you hold it in balance, it is much easier. Stay there for a little while, and think about how it feels so that next time it comes around, you will be able to find that point again."

The sweat had stopped beading on Pen's forehead. She cautiously opened her eyes and murmured, "It *is* better," careful not to let her breathing falter.

"Yes. Now, think about giving it back to me. As you pass it, think about making it grow. You are a vessel of the Goddess's magic. Let it draw from you . . . oh, yes! Very good." Lady Keating broke into a wide smile. "That is as much as we can safely manage on our own. I think that is enough for this morning. Let's see."

She turned her head and glanced around until her attention fell on one of the roses that was, for some reason, not as large and hale as its neighbors. "There we are," she said. Releasing Pen's hands, she reached toward the small shrub.

The energy rolled off her fingertips and hit the rosebush. Its leaves shivered as if caught in a wind and then began to grow, doubling in size and in number, till it was covered in glossy, dark green foliage. Pale, sickly shoots thickened and lengthened, and multiple buds swelled at their ends. Pen stared, and then laughed. "What will the gardeners think when they see that?"

Lady Keating smiled too. "They won't think. They'll know. My roses are famed over most of Cork for a very good reason. Come, my dear, let's have a stroll. We have a few minutes before luncheon."

Pen stretched, then glanced down at her watch pinned to her dress. They'd been standing in the rose garden for nearly three hours. No wonder she always needed a nap after luncheon.

Lady Keating took her arm and guided her up a short flight of stone steps from the rose garden to an old-fashioned herb garden. White gravel paths and low boxwood hedges trimmed into ribbons of knotwork surrounded the beds of plants, many of them just blooming. Ecstatic bees hummed among the lavender and hyssop, opening in the warmth of the sun.

"You know, Penelope, that you are much like that rosebush," Lady Keating said after a few moments. "Look how you have changed since the Goddess's power touched you."

"Have I changed?" Pen's skirt brushed a shrubby rosemary plant. Its fresh, almost piny scent wafted past her.

"Haven't you? Didn't you tell me that until you came to Ireland, your magic lagged behind your sister's? It was because *this* is the magic that you were meant to do. You have come into your own at last."

Pen stopped and bent to pick a twig of the rosemary. "I—I had been thinking something very like that," she said after a moment. "In fact, I told Dr. Carrighar that I felt as if I'd come home."

"And what did he say to that?"

She allowed herself a small sigh. "I'm not sure he was convinced."

"My dear girl, Dr. Carrighar is a very learned man. But I am not sure that he understands the Triple Goddess or her ways." Lady Keating resumed their slow circuit through the garden's paths.

"No, I don't think he does." Pen thought about telling Lady Keating about Mary Margaret but decided it would be too complicated.

"I believe that you have come to where you ought to be," Lady Keating continued. "We'll know better tomorrow, though. I think it time Doireann joined us in our work, and we see how you fare with the Goddess's magic raised by three, the way it truly should be."

A tremor of excitement ran through Pen. What would it be like? "We had better be careful, or your rosebushes will turn into trees," she said, trying to keep her voice light.

Lady Keating did not smile back. "There is an element of risk, of course. Working the magic through three participants makes it stronger by a factor of three. It will be that much more strenuous, but the rewards are also greater. As one of the Goddess's ladies, I can keep you mostly safe if it proves too much for you. But I don't think it will. You're—" She hesitated, then spoke slowly, without her customary self-assurance. "There's something about you. I've never met anyone who has taken so quickly and naturally to raising the circle."

"Raising the circle?"

"What we were just doing—calling up the Goddess's magic. When Doireann came of age, it took her nearly a year of work to make it to the point that you've reached in just a few days. You remind me . . . you remind me of myself, when I was a girl. My mother was amazed, not to mention gratified, at how quickly I progressed in the Goddess's work. She knew right away that I would be a worthy successor to her as a *Banmhaor Bande*." She squeezed Pen's arm and smiled. "But there are many things we share. Did you know that my given name, Nuala, is short for Fionnuala, the Irish form of Penelope?"

"Really? What an odd coincidence."

"Coincidence? Perhaps. When you told me your name the day we met, I took it for a sign. I've been watching you ever since and can't help wondering if the Goddess made our paths cross for a reason."

A shiver darted up Pen's back, not of fear but of what? Recognition? "What reason could that be?"

"I don't know, my dear. But I sense that we might find out soon. Ah, there's Ellen, probably come to call us to luncheon." She gestured to one of the liveried women servants marching down the gravel path toward them. Pen had almost gotten used to the exclusively female household staff at Bandry Court. A few men worked in the stables and gardens, but even there women predominated.

As they followed the servant past a large clump of rhododendron bushes on the way to the house, a sudden movement caught Pen's eye. She stopped.

"What is it, Penelope?" Lady Keating paused too.

"N-nothing." Pen squinted at the bushes, covered in just-opening clumps of pale rose pink, where overeager bees already hummed looking for nectar. Here and there the long, glossy green leaves swayed gently in the breeze. "I thought I saw something move in the rhododendrons. Or someone."

Lady Keating shrugged. "This is a favorite nesting spot for birds. They're always flitting in and out of them. Come, my dear."

Pen let her lead them on, but glanced back at the bushes before they turned a corner in the path.

The next few days were rainy and chilly. Lady Keating decreed that the three of them would work in the tall and shadowy front hall, which she declared had the best resonance for magic work. It also, unfortunately, meant that the servants had to trudge across the courtyard in the rain in order to attend to their regular duties, but somehow Pen didn't think Lady Keating would be too concerned.

Doireann was frequently late for their sessions, but bore her mother's chiding with a shrug and a smile. "I'm here, Mother dear.

Don't get your stays in a twist," she'd say as she breezed in and plunked down on a bench. "I told you before that I keep my promises—just not always in the way you expect me to."

But once they got underway, she worked just as hard and intently as Pen and Lady Keating herself did. Pen privately did her own shrug and smile. The best way to deal with Doireann was to accept her on her own terms, and after all, she'd been pleasant enough since they'd arrived. In fact, Pen rarely saw her, except at dinner and their work. But since Lady Keating made no comment on Doireann's absences, Pen put them out of mind.

When the warm spring sun returned, Lady Keating decided that they should go out to the small stone circle that capped the hill a short distance from the house, and practice raising the circle there. Pen was unprepared for the result. The stones had a curious effect, amplifying and yet containing the power they raised. They were even able to stop holding hands and let the circle of stones hold their magic for them. It hovered above them like a whirlwind tethered with invisible ropes, much to Pen's fascinated awe.

"I didn't think that was possible. So that is why there are so many stone circles in Great Britain," she said as she paced restlessly around the perimeter. It took a great deal of restraint not to kick off her shoes, yank the pins out of her hair, and dance like a frenzied wood nymph around the stones while their magic crackled and rippled above them. The energy was infectious.

Lady Keating smiled at her. "I can feel your excitement, child. It can have that effect, sometimes."

"I can't help it. I should like to—to fly, just now." Pen threw her arms back and stared up at the sky, turning in a slow circle, and then another. The bright afternoon sun sparkled above her, all alone in the sky with only a few wisps of cloud for company, and their magic drew her like a moth to a candle—

A sudden jerk at the hem of her skirts startled her. She glanced down and saw that she was hovering several feet above the grass. Doireann stared up at her, one hand shading her eyes and the other firmly holding the edge of Pen's dress.

"Going somewhere?" Her expression was difficult to read, half hidden by her hand.

But Lady Keating laughed then, a joyful, exultant sound. "*A thaisce!* You are indeed a treasure, my dear." She held out her arms, and Pen drifted back down toward her. Lady Keating caught her in a fierce hug. "It calls to you, doesn't it?" she whispered in Pen's ear. "The Goddess's power burns bright in you, brighter than I've seen it in anyone else. Oh, my dear, this is . . . well, perhaps not so unexpected."

They stayed in the circle a little longer while Lady Keating gathered the magic they'd raised and sent it down into the stones "so we can use it later." Pen held her hand flat against the surface of one of the gray pillars and felt a tingling warmth on her palm.

"It's there—I can feel it," she exclaimed. "Oh, I can't wait until we come back again and use it."

Doireann gave a short laugh. "Mother did choose you well, didn't she?" She ran off down the hill to the house as if hounds were after her.

Pen sighed as she watched her. "I don't get the feeling that was supposed to be a compliment," she said to Lady Keating, who had come to stand with her.

"Doireann is—well, I expect she is a little jealous. She can't help seeing how advanced you are and how well you and I work together. Don't let it trouble you."

"More advanced than she is?" Pen did not want to comment on the other parts of Lady Keating's speech. She remembered how she had been jealous of Persy and Ally's closeness at times, during magic practice back in the schoolroom.

"In many ways, yes." Lady Keating stood silently for a moment after that, looking at her with a meditative expression. "Come, my dear," she said at last. "It's nearly time to dress for dinner, but there's something in the library I should like you to read, something that Doireann is not ready for and that I'd rather she didn't know about. We'll stop there first."

In the library she went to a paneled wall between two bookcases and pressed delicately on a flat section between two carved swags. It slowly fell outward, like a miniature drawbridge. She reached into the small cavity that was revealed and drew out a small, leather-bound book, flipped through it quickly as if looking for a particular section, and slipped a faded purple ribbon to mark a page.

"Here you are. Remember, not a word to Doireann." She handed the book to Pen and pushed the secret hatch shut.

Pen opened it and looked at the yellowed pages and cramped, dense writing with a sinking feeling. Hadn't she done enough poring over dusty old books with Dr. Carrighar? "Er . . . ," she began.

Lady Keating shook her head solemnly. "Just give it a chance, Penelope. It is my many-times-great-grandmother's grimoire on circle magic. I want you to understand what it was we did today and what we can do with the power we raise. I think that in a few days' time, we will be ready to do the *draiocht*—the spell—that will help bring poor Niall and the duke together. Are you still willing to help me in this?" She looked down at the rug. "I'll understand if you feel you can't."

Pen reached for her hand, feeling contrite. "Of course I'll help you. You've given me so much—what else can I do to thank you?"

"Ah, my dear one." Lady Keating looked up, her eyes bright. "You are a treasure. Now bring that up to your room, and read as much of it as you can tonight. We will discuss it in the morning."

As soon as dinner was over, Pen went to her room, pleading tiredness. After such a day she should have been exhausted. But the afternoon's exhilaration refused to leave her: Raising the circle within the stones was the most stimulating, inspiring magic she'd ever done, and Lady Keating's confidences and giving her the book on circle magic—to *her*, not Doireann—was even more so.

"I'm doing it," she murmured, ringing the bell for the maid to come help her undress for bed. "I'm becoming as good a witch as Ally and Persy. Lady Keating wouldn't be so complimentary if I weren't."

Niamh arrived then to undo the row of hooks down the back of her dress, unlace her corset, and unpin and brush out her hair.

"Anything else I can do for ye, miss?" she asked, arranging Pen's dress over the door of the wardrobe to air until morning. "Shall I close the window an' draw the curtains?"

"No, thank you. It's a beautiful evening—leave them open for now. That will be all for tonight," Pen said, crossing to the window in her nightgown and dressing gown as the maid bowed herself out of the room.

It *was* a beautiful night. The moon, although still four or five days from full, illuminated the lawn under her window and, below it, the edge of the sunken rose garden. A spectacular end to a spectacular day—

Something was moving about in the rose garden.

Pen quickly drew to the side of the window, then peered around the edge, shading her eyes from the moon so that she could see into the dark shadows below. Could it have been an animal? A deer or an escaped sheep looking for tastier fare than meadow grass? She squinted down, waiting for whatever it was to move again.

No, not an animal, but a tall figure, swathed in a cloak and hooded so that she could not even see if it was male or female. It paused in the edge of the shadow cast by the garden wall, then hurried across the garden and out of her sight.

Pen turned away from the window. If anyone was sneaking about the gardens of Bandry Court in the moonlight, she had no particular desire to know why—well, apart from the usual curiosity, of course. Right now she had Lady Keating's book to read. She carried the bedroom candlestick from her dressing table to her nightstand, tossed her dressing gown across the foot of her bed, and climbed under the covers. She glanced toward the window once more and saw that the moon was framed there, beautiful if a bit on the overdramatic side. Just like one of Mrs. Radcliffe's gothic novels. No wonder there were people sneaking about in the rose garden. She smiled and picked up Lady Keating's book.

> Circle Magick, when worked in ye Triple Goddess's Name, is the Most Powerfull of ye Magicks that we do. It differs from the common Raising of the Circle, the Summoning and Adding to of Power, in this Way, a Way that we save for the Most Solemn, Needful, and Direst of Purposes.

Solemn and needful. Well, that would probably describe how Lady Keating felt about doing this spell for Niall and his father. Hopefully dire wouldn't come into it.

The Way that it Best be Accomplished is to take you
the Goddess's Form: three Must take the Position of ye
Virgin, ye Mother, and ye Crone, in Fact and in Form,
so that She can work the Best through Them. So then
Find you One Who is yet a Maid, and One a Woman
that bear a Child, and One that has ceased in her
Lunary Cycles or Soon shall do So. On a Night when
the Moon be at Her Fullest, let Them come together
and raise you the Circle in the Name of the Goddess,
and then will You Of a certainty have great Potency,
even over Life and Death and across the Seas.

Lady Keating's ancestor evidently had difficulties with grammar.
Pen chuckled, then frowned at the book in her hands. What connection did this have to their work together? Surely it couldn't have anything to do with the *draiocht* to bring Niall to the Duke of
Cumberland. The three of them couldn't do this sort of magic. She
would not venture to guess whether Lady Keating qualified as a
Mother or a Crone, but certainly both she and Doireann had to be
counted in the Maiden category—

A stealthy scraping sound from somewhere near the window
made her look up. A tall, hatted figure in a dark coat was peering at
her through the open window. As she stared, openmouthed, it
swung one leg over the edge. It was Eamon Doherty.

Pen gasped, too shocked to make more than a squeaky inhaled
sound, and yanked the covers up to her chin as he finished clamber-
ing over the window frame. The top of a ladder propped against the
side of the house was just visible behind him as he dropped to the
floor and adjusted his clothes.

"Nnnnn . . . wwwwh—" Pen stopped trying to speak and drew in a deep breath. Screaming would be much easier than trying to be coherent just now.

"For God's sake, Pen, don't shout!" he hissed, glaring at her. "I'm not going to hurt you."

"B-b-but, Mr. Doherty!" she whispered, cowering against her pillows. "How did—why are you—" An incongruous indignation seized her. Since when did he think he could address her as Pen?

He looked at her in confusion for a brief instant, then grinned. "Oh. I forgot about that." He reached up and took off his hat.

It was Niall.

Pen very nearly did scream then, but he leapt toward the bed and launched himself at her, falling across her legs and covering her mouth with his hand.

"Don't scream!" he whispered urgently. "It's me! Doherty and I thought we'd borrow your spell so that I could come to Bandry Court and take a room over at the inn in the village without being recognized. It would have been all over the countryside within ten minutes that Mr. Keating was staying at the inn and not with his mother."

Pen squirmed under his restraining hands and jerked her head to one side. "What are you doing here?" she whispered back, just as fiercely. "How dare you come sneaking into my room like this after—"

"Blast it, Pen, keep your voice down. Please don't make me cover your mouth again. You've got to listen to me—"

"Why should I? What could you possibly have to say to me? Oh, why did you have to come here just when I was starting to forget you—" She broke off in a muffled squeak as he covered her mouth again.

"Hush! You were getting too loud—"

"Dratted well right I was!" she mouthed against his hand. What was he doing here? Was he under the illusion that climbing into her room with a ladder was impetuous and romantic, and that she would throw herself at him as a result? Well, if he was, then he didn't know Penelope Leland.

"Please, Pen, hear me out. You don't know what I've been through just to get here." His blond hair was rumpled, and he hadn't shaved today. Why did he still have to be so good-looking even when disheveled? Even worse, why did she still notice?

"I don't really care," she tried to say. Maybe she should bite him. It would relieve her feelings and maybe make him let go—

His eyes pleaded as desperately as his voice. "Can't we talk about this quietly and rationally? Please, darling—"

Darling? Now that was definitely going too far. Her scowl must have been ferocious, for he nearly snatched his hand back.

"Please, just let me talk to you. Please?"

Pen narrowed her eyes as at him as she considered. He'd startled her, climbing in her window like that and looking like Doherty—Doherty, of all people! She jolly well wanted to know what Eamon Doherty had to do with Niall's being here. Very well; she'd let him talk. If he tried anything threatening she could put an immobilizing spell on him and scream for Lady Keating.

She nodded and Niall withdrew his hand. She saw him watch her carefully, in case she changed her mind. When she remained silent, he sighed and rolled off her, moving to sit on the foot of the bed. She drew her legs up and huddled under her blankets.

"All right, Mr. Keating," she said with as much dignity as she could muster. "Perhaps you could begin by explaining what you're doing in my bedchamber, and why you looked like Eamon Doherty, and—" Then it struck her. "The hat! He did borrow my spell! It was the same one I did on your hat that day when we found him."

Niall nodded. There were lines of care and worry in his face that she'd never seen there before. "It was his idea. On the journey up here, I couldn't help wondering what you would do when you saw his face looking in your window, and which you would find more alarming, his or mine."

"It was a toss-up," she retorted. "How did you come to meet with him? I thought you were in Kinsale, working your wiles on Charlotte Enniskean. Or wasn't that challenging enough for you?"

He closed his eyes and looked pained. "I wasn't in Kinsale. I haven't left our house in Cork until a few days ago. Mother made sure that I couldn't leave it, but Doherty happened to call to return my hat. I prevailed on him to remove the enchantments she had put on the house to keep me prisoner—"

Pen snorted. "If—and I repeat *if*—she was keeping you from leaving the house, it was probably for a very good reason. Like preventing you from coming here."

"And he kindly did so," he finished, ignoring her comment.

"So was that you creeping about in the rose garden half an hour ago? Where's your cloak? And what about the rhododendron bushes the other day? Was that you as well? How long have you been skulking around here, waiting to do something as stupid as this?"

Niall frowned. "I have no idea what you're talking about. I told you—I just got here this afternoon. The weather slowed me up until today. Believe me, if I could have gotten here sooner, I would have."

"Why?"

He leaned forward, and she tugged the blankets closer to her chin. He ignored the gesture. "Because I love you, and I'm here to rescue you, one way or another."

That time she laughed out loud.

"Quiet!" he said, glancing anxiously at the door. "What's so funny?"

"Because I cannot think it was anything but a joke—and a feeble one, at that."

"I am not joking, damn it! Pen, no, don't look so angry. I want you to come away with me. We'll ride to Dublin and get a special license from the archbishop and marry as soon as we can."

Pen smothered another urge to laugh. "Oh, shall we? Tell me, how many other young women have you tried that line on? Mr. Keating—"

"You used to call me Niall," he muttered.

"I used to believe that you loved me, too."

"But I do!"

"Is that why you tried to seduce me in the library that afternoon? Because you loved and respected me and wanted to marry me? Usually it is the custom in the civilized world to hold the wedding ceremony before the consummation."

"No, it's not why I tried to do what I did," he said calmly, to her surprise. "And, yes, I do want to marry you. I did it to try to save you, because I love you."

That was the second time he'd said something like that. What could he possibly mean? "Save me? I'm sorry, but that simply is going too far. Did you feel you had to save me from the perilous condition of virtue? Is that why?"

He looked down at his lap for the space of a few breaths, then up at her once more. "I'd rather not say why. All I would say is that while you remain . . . er, untouched, there is danger that you will be forced to do something that would eventually cause you great distress. I wanted—*want*—to save you from that."

Why, the sheer, brazen gall of him! "I . . . oh, really! Am I supposed to believe that?"

"Pen." To her alarm he began to crawl up the bed toward her, pinning her under the blankets. "Pen, please. Let me—let me do this. Let me make love to you. Later tonight, as soon as we're sure everyone is abed, we'll take a horse for you and ride to Mallow. We'll get the coach there and be in Dublin in a couple of days, and I swear we'll be married as soon as we get the license."

"Quite an admirable plan, but I think you've neglected one important point: *What makes you think I want to marry you?*"

He stared at her, and she might have laughed if she hadn't been so angry. "Mr. Keating, your mother told me about your—your *doings* on the Continent. If you think that I have any desire to spend the rest of my life with a man of such vicious, dissolute habits, then you are more lacking in wits than I'd thought."

Niall had grown pale, but his determined expression did not alter. "Those were lies my mother told you, all lies. Pen . . . oh, Pen, you have to believe me. Nothing of what she told you is true. She was angry that I was trying to stop her plans—"

"What plans?"

He fell silent again, then sighed and squared his shoulders. "I wish I didn't have to tell you this. . . . It would be so much easier if you could just let me—"

"If you don't tell me, I *shall* scream." Pen drew in a deep breath and opened her mouth.

"No!" He shook his head frantically. "Don't do that!"

"Well? I'm waiting, then."

"Blast it, Pen, why—"

She opened her mouth again.

"All right, I'll tell you! Mother's been practicing magic with you, hasn't she? She's told you that she has a special magical project she needs your help with. Am I right?"

Pen watched him warily. "So?"

"And she's told you that it has something to do with bringing me and the Duke of Cumberland together, right? But nothing more specific than that? No explanation of the actual magic you'd be doing?"

"As a matter of fact, she said—" What had she said, exactly? Something about bringing them together so that Niall could have a father's guidance and put aside his profligate ways. Had there been anything else?

He shook his head. "Pen, my mother is using you."

"What? Oh, that's just grand, coming from you."

"I'm telling you the truth. She's using you. Yes, she wants to bring me closer to the duke so that maybe he will, at least informally, accept me as his son. Only she doesn't want him to just be the duke, or just the ruler of a little German principality. She wants him to be the king. Of England."

"But that's impossible!" This was making no sense. "Victoria is on the throne."

"It's not impossible, if Victoria were to be . . ." He paused, as if searching for the right word. "To be removed."

"Removed? What do you mean . . . oh!" Pen dropped the blankets she still clutched and stared at him.

Niall nodded. "'Oh!' is right. Until the queen has children, the duke is next in line for the throne. Mother wants him to be king and me to be recognized as the king's son, if an illegitimate one. After all, look at the late king's family of bastards—one of them was made an earl. I heard her, Pen—I heard her discussing it with Doireann."

He inched closer, resting his hands on either side of her hips, and spoke very quickly. "She can do it, but she needs your magic as well—something about the Goddess and the Maiden and the power of the Three. She's been planning this for a while now, and I'm ashamed to say I helped her at first. I agreed to flirt with you and be charming so that you'd love me and want to help Mother help me . . . until I fell in love with you, and until I learned just what it was she planned to do about the duke. When you told me how you'd helped save the queen last year, I knew you'd never want to have anything to do with such a plan. But I was afraid to tell you what I knew because . . . well, because I had deliberately set out to make you fall in love with me."

"On purpose. You did it on purpose," Pen said dully. Her head had begun to ache almost as badly as it had the day she healed Doherty. It had all been a game to him, then.

"I—God help me, I know that. But only at first. After the night of the dinner party, I resolved that I was going to fall right back in love with you. I didn't know then that Mother planned to kill the queen. And once I found that out, all I could think of was to make sure that she couldn't use you—"

Something snapped inside Pen. "Stop it!" she cried. "I don't want to hear any more. Have you been listening to yourself? Do you know how ridiculous this story sounds? Your mother told me about you, you know. All about your drinking and roistering and wenching through Europe. Did you have to tell any of your conquests there such an outrageous story to get them to go to bed with you?"

He drew back. "None of that is true! I never—"

"I saw you! I saw you flirting with Charlotte Enniskean and her cousins. And Doireann told me how you are at parties and balls—"

"Oh, I see. So you'll listen to Doireann and Mother, but not me?" he said in a harsh voice.

"Whose story do you think is more believable?" she retorted. "Your mother is a *Banmhaor Bande*. She could never use the Goddess's magic to kill an innocent girl like the queen—the Goddess would never let her, and she knows it." She took a deep breath and slipped out of the high bed, crossing to the door as she spoke. "I'll give you ten seconds to get down that ladder. If you are not on your way down by the time I reach ten, I will open this door and scream. Very loudly."

"Pen—"

"One." She pointedly put her hand on the doorknob.

He climbed off the bed and turned toward the window. "Fine. That's your choice, then."

"Two."

"Go ahead and help murder your dear friend the queen. Her death can only benefit me."

"Three."

He slid one leg over the window's edge. "Pen, think about what you're doing—"

"Four." She rattled the doorknob menacingly.

"All right!" He swung off the sill and onto the ladder but still stared at her through the window. "Good-bye, Pen Leland. If we meet again, maybe in London next season, you'll pardon me if I don't pursue an acquaintance with you. It's hard to chat about the weather when one's heart is breaking—"

"Five!" To her horror, she had begun to cry.

He gave her one last anguished look and disappeared from sight.

Pen slid to the floor and huddled there against the door, knees drawn to her chest, still staring at the window. After a few moments, the top of the ladder vanished too. But it was nearly an hour before she could bring herself to go to the window and shut it against the night air that now seemed to have grown bitterly cold.

14

The next morning Pen slept late. It had taken her several hours after Niall left to stop crying and calm herself sufficiently before exhaustion could do the rest and send her into a deep but unrefreshing sleep. She finally awoke just past ten and dressed hurriedly, pausing only to bathe her eyes in cool water in an attempt to keep them from looking too red and puffy—an attempt that wasn't entirely successful, as she saw when she looked in the mirror.

She needn't have worried. When she slipped into the breakfast room, where chafing dishes of eggs and oatmeal and the local sausage still simmered gently on the sideboard, it was to see Lady Keating uncharacteristically slumped in her chair at one end of the table, staring at a half-drunk cup of coffee. There was no sign of Doireann.

"Good morning. I'm sorry I slept so late—I suppose our hard work caught up with me," Pen said brightly, sidling toward the food. If she could busy herself with eating, Lady Keating might not notice her swollen eyes and reddened nose.

"Good morning, *cinealta* Penelope. Don't apologize; I didn't get here much before you." Lady Keating did not even glance up.

Pen paused. Lady Keating's words had been spoken in a dull monotone, so different from her usual resonant, slightly theatrical tones. "May I bring you a plate?" she asked. "Eggs? Toast?"

Lady Keating didn't stir. "No food, thank you, though you are a dear to offer."

Something was evidently very wrong. Pen stared down at the dishes. She didn't feel much like eating either, but that might make Lady Keating think that there was something wrong with *her*. She took some scrambled eggs and toast and a sausage and seated herself, not too close to Lady Keating. One of the footwomen appeared from nowhere with a fresh pot of coffee and filled their cups, then vanished once again.

Pen picked up her fork and resolutely attacked her eggs while covertly watching Lady Keating. Should she ask her what was wrong? Might she be ill? That would explain her refusing to eat, though if she were that ill she probably would have stayed abed. Had she received some bad news, then? Or had something upsetting happened during the night, something that—

She nearly dropped her fork. Could Niall have been found on the grounds? Did Lady Keating suspect that he'd tried to see her . . . or maybe even succeeded?

But Lady Keating's mood did not seem to be aimed at her. What could it be, then? "Shall we be going up to the hill this morning?" she asked, pouring milk into her coffee and trying to sound offhand.

Lady Keating stirred. "Yes, we shall, but it will just be the two of us for this morning."

It was on the tip of Pen's tongue to ask why Doireann wouldn't be working with them, but something in the grim edge to Lady

Keating's voice stopped her. Could this bad mood have anything to do with Doireann, then? Had Niall gone to see her as well? Or did Niall even have anything to do with this?

Surely Lady Keating would have said something if it did, though, if only to ask if he'd attempted to see her. So evidently Niall had gotten away from Bandry Court without getting caught. Was he already on his way back to Cork? Or back to Kinsale, where he could forget his sorrows in Charlotte Enniskean's willing arms? Surely he hadn't expected her to believe that his own adoring mother had locked him up in their house.... Pen mentally shook herself. No more thinking about last night.

She stole another look at Lady Keating. Whatever had happened to put her in this mood, she wouldn't add to it by telling her about Niall's clandestine visit. After all, she'd handled him quite well on her own, if she did say so herself.

"Thank you for the loan of your book, ma'am," she said instead. "I found it very interesting."

Lady Keating looked up with a hint of her old smile. "Ah, yes. So you read it?"

"Not the entire book, but all the parts that you had marked. I can finish the rest later if you wish me to."

"No, that won't be necessary. Not unless you wish to." She seemed to be trying to throw off her gloom, at least to some degree. "When you are finished eating, shall we go and get a little work done before luncheon? Nothing too strenuous, I don't think, but I'm not sure that circle raising *is* strenuous for you anymore."

Pen warmed under her praise. Dear Lady Keating. "Oh yes, let's. I'm done." She took a last sip of coffee and rose from the table.

❊   ❊   ❊

It was just her and Lady Keating working on magic alone together not only that morning, but also the afternoon and next day. Pen couldn't help breathing a sigh of relief, though without Doireann they could not raise as potent a circle. Her attitude had been so much more changeable lately, bouncing between friendliness and hostility without any apparent cause, that Pen felt constantly on her guard with her.

Lady Keating seemed pleased with their work, though. Under her tutelage, Pen began to be able to better control the amount of energy she put into a spell or magical command, so that she did not waste it and tire herself out. Raising the circle had become second nature to her, so that she no longer had to watch Lady Keating for cues but could close her eyes and go inward, gathering and strengthening her will to make her augmentations even stronger.

As they returned to the house that afternoon, Lady Keating slipped her arm around Pen's waist and gave her a gentle hug. "Sometimes I—" she began, then trailed into silence.

"What?"

"Oh, sometimes I can't help wishing that you and I had come together sooner, so that I could have taught you more. I feel that we are so alike in so many ways—our strengths and abilities . . . not that I'm disparaging your dear Mrs. Carrighar, of course, but if you'd been born my daughter . . ." Her voice became ever so slightly wistful. "I would have been a very happy woman if you were my—but this is just idle daydreaming. We are not allowed to choose our families in this life, alas."

She shrugged and went on to speak of something else, but Pen hardly heard her. Lady Keating wished she were her daughter. Pen loved her own dear mama and was sure Lady Keating must love Doireann, but Lady Keating would have chosen *her.*

At the house, Pen paused before opening the door. "May I tell you something?" she asked, feeling shy but determined.

"Of course you may."

"I . . . I know it sounds silly and childish, but while I am here with you, you *are* my mother."

"Ah, my dearest girl." Lady Keating's green eyes grew misty. "You are indeed my child." A slightly strange smile touched her lips, but before Pen could decipher it, she drew her into her arms and embraced her tenderly. "You are truly mine."

Doireann did not make an appearance for the next two days, not even for dinner. Only on the third morning was she at the breakfast table when Pen came down. Her mumbled "good morning" was sullen and her manner chilly, as if Pen, not she, had been avoiding everyone for the last few days.

Lady Keating, when she came in, hardly even acknowledged Doireann's presence. She ate her breakfast in wintry indifference, addressing an occasional remark only to Pen, which was uncomfortable in the extreme but seemed to confirm her guess that Lady Keating's bad mood must have had to do with Doireann.

Fortunately, their mutual frostiness didn't extend to their work up on the hill. Doireann slipped into her place in their circle raising as if she'd never been away, her power casual and almost lazy but still measured and strong. She seemed surprised, though, at the advances Pen had made.

"At this rate, she'll be ready for the full ceremony in no time," she said to Lady Keating as they stood on the hilltop.

Pen wished Doireann would stop talking about her as if she weren't there. "A full ceremony?" she asked.

"She was ready several days ago," Lady Keating said coolly, then turned to Pen. "Doireann is referring to a circle raising by the light of the full moon. The moon is, of course, the Goddess's planet. When we work the Goddess's magic under it, it enhances the circle."

Circle raising by the light of the full moon . . . like in the book Lady Keating had given her to read? Pen turned to Lady Keating, who nodded slightly as if she knew what she had been thinking.

"Yes, Penelope. Tomorrow night is the full moon, the perfect time to perform the *draiocht* for Niall. Between the power we have already raised together and what we will summon under the moon's light, we will surely succeed. We shall practice this afternoon, but I shall require all day tomorrow to prepare."

"Jolly good. I can catch up on my sleep, then." Doireann yawned and stretched. "Come on, Pen, let's go for a walk before luncheon. Have you seen the river yet? We crossed over part of it when we got here, down near the gatehouse and the spinney. It's not much of one, but deep and wet enough for me to get thoroughly muddy in when I was small, whenever I felt particularly cross with Nanny."

Pen gave her a quick, measuring look. Evidently Doireann was in a good mood this morning. Did she alternate every quarter hour according to a schedule, or were her mood swings entirely random?

"What a charming idea! Yes, let's do that." Lady Keating linked arms with Pen and gave Doireann a wide smile.

Doireann did not smile back and, without another word, stalked down the hill ahead of them. Pen watched her rigid back as they picked their way down the slope and into the meadow below. Either the quarter hour had passed and it was time to change moods, or she did not want her mother joining them.

Why? Why would Doireann have wanted her alone? She'd seemed to avoid being alone with Pen until this sudden about-face. But being alone with Doireann the sleeping lioness was not what she felt like doing right now. She squeezed Lady Keating's arm in gratitude. "Thank you," she murmured.

"I thought you might prefer that I came," Lady Keating whispered back, and patted her hand.

Dear, dear Lady Keating. Pen swelled with affection. She *was* like a mother to her.

Late that evening Pen was propped in bed, reading Lady Keating's ancestress's book, when there was a knock on her door.

Drat. It couldn't be Doireann, could it? "Come in," she called, hiding the book under the bedclothes and snatching another off the nightstand, just in case.

"Ah, still awake. Very good." Lady Keating came in, holding a candle. She wore a lovely dressing gown of pale green quilted satin, and her black hair hung unbound on her shoulders, like a girl's. It made her look like Doireann, but there was an indefinable authority in her face that Doireann lacked.

"Might we talk for a few moments?" she asked, shutting the door behind her and gliding to the bed.

"Of course." Pen put down the Scott novel she'd grabbed and pulled out the grimoire. "I was reading this, but I put it away in case you were Doireann."

"Clever girl." Lady Keating blew out her candle and set it on Pen's nightstand, then seated herself on the edge of the bed. The folds of her dressing gown shimmered around her. "As a matter of fact, it is of Doireann that I would like to speak."

"Oh?" Pen sat up a little straighter against her pillows.

Lady Keating sighed, then sighed again. "I'm not quite sure how to begin, save by saying she is a great disappointment to me. A very great disappointment. You might have noticed a certain coolness between us over the last few days?"

"Well, now that you mention it . . ."

Lady Keating chuckled. "You are thinking that *coolness* is putting it mildly."

"Um, the word *glacier* had come to mind." Pen grinned but only outwardly. Did she really want to know about the latest quarrel between them?

"I think you will scarcely blame me when you know why. Three nights ago—"

Pen swallowed. Three nights ago had been when Niall appeared at her window.

"Three nights ago, when I went to speak with my daughter, I was shocked to discover . . . well, I won't trouble you with the details . . . but three nights ago I discovered Doireann entertaining a—a friend in her room. A male one. He had followed us from Cork, it seems."

"Oh!" Pen didn't have to pretend to blush. That cloaked figure she'd seen in the rose garden—perhaps Niall hadn't been lying when he denied that it had been him. But who had it been?

"Oh, indeed," Lady Keating agreed grimly. "Furthermore, it seems that this wasn't the first time. When pressed, Doireann confessed that she believes herself to be with child."

"Good God!" Pen knew her mouth was hanging open, but

she couldn't help it. "Will she . . . does she plan on . . . can they be married?"

"I certainly hope so. As soon as we return to the city, I shall be calling on the young man's father, you may be assured of that." Lady Keating closed her eyes.

Pen leaned forward and reached for her hand. "No wonder you've been unhappy. What a dreadful shock for you." It was a miracle that she hadn't been stomping up and down the halls of Bandry Court, screaming in rage. Thank heavens she hadn't come to speak to Pen after seeing Doireann, or she might have found her with Niall—but certainly not in the same position Doireann had been in with her clandestine visitor. She shivered inwardly.

"Unhappy." Lady Keating laughed a short, harsh laugh. "I have rebounded between anger, sadness, disbelief . . . but most of all, disappointment."

"I can see why."

"Thank you, my dear, but until you are a mother yourself you cannot know the full extent of my wretchedness. But it is deeper than even that. Doireann is my daughter, but she is—was—also my heiress as *Banmhaor Bande*. Do you think the Goddess would accept as one of her ladies someone who cannot restrain her own appetites? Who could so casually give herself away for a moment of fleeting pleasure, without thought for the consequences?" She looked away.

Pen looked away too as a thought struck her. Doireann must have known of her mother's position and her own status as heiress, and what jeopardizing it might mean. What if she—well, could she be in love with whoever Lady Keating had found her with? That would make her almost seem human. She took a deep breath. "Perhaps Doireann and this young man—"

"I believe that you loved Niall," Lady Keating interrupted her quietly. "But that does not mean that you were willing to let him seduce you. You rule your passions—they do not rule you."

What could she say to that? But Lady Keating did not seem to require a response.

"Penelope," she said, her face somber, "I have a proposition to lay before you. I have spent almost every waking hour these last few days—and believe me, sleep has been so elusive that those hours are numerous—mulling this over. Please hear me out before you say anything, and remember that I have spent much thought on it."

A vague, nameless feeling of excitement began to tickle the back of Pen's mind. "Yes?"

"I have watched you over these last many weeks and been more impressed with each passing day. But my good opinion of you has changed to awe since we've been at Bandry Court and have worked together in magic. Your dedication, your strength—your sheer, raw talent . . . I have never seen another witch of your capabilities. My own daughter was never your equal. If only Niall had not been such a worthless rogue, for then I could have welcomed you as my daughter too. You don't know how disappointed I was when he— well, it would seem that I was destined to be disappointed in both my children. I shall always love them and do my duty by them, but . . ." She stroked Pen's hand, which still lay in hers, her lips compressed into a thin line.

"I'm so sorry," Pen whispered. She hadn't thought about that. What an awful few weeks it must have been for her—first Niall and now Doireann.

"Yes, I am too." She looked up with a tight, brave smile. "Or at least I was. After our work the other morning, you were kind enough to say that you regarded me as almost a mother. That was balm to my spirits, but it also made me think. Penelope, I should like to make you my daughter by making you my heiress. When I am gone, I want you to take my place as *Banmhaor Bande*."

Pen did not leap out of bed and shriek, or even allow herself to visibly start. But Lady Keating's words took her breath away. Did she really think that highly of her? So highly that she thought the Goddess herself would accept her as her own? Her shock must have shown in her face, for Lady Keating laughed.

"My dear! Is this such a surprise?"

"Well, yes!" Pen blurted out. "You're joking, aren't you?"

Lady Keating's face sobered. "I would never joke about such a matter."

"Then you're speaking hypothetically." Yes, that had to be it. There was no other explanation. "Oh, I agree, it would be amazing if you could—"

"I was neither joking nor speaking hypothetically, my dear. Of anyone I know, you are the most worthy of serving her after me. Now, listen to me before you say yes. You have come far on the Goddess's path, but you will have to continue to work hard as we have done here, which may mean forgoing the pleasures of a social life or indeed the promise of love. You will have to dedicate yourself to her . . . and she can sometimes be a difficult, even demanding mistress. She may ask you to do things that you do not like, or that you fear, and you must do them willingly and trust her—not just a little, but completely.

"But if you do—if you give her your complete trust—she will

reward you beyond imagining. You will be powerful as few have been before you. Even the Carrighars and your governess will only be able to guess at your abilities."

Pen's breath caught in her throat again. To be so powerful a *bean draoi* that even the Carrighars and Ally—even *Persy*—would seem like dabblers compared to her? She would finally feel like she deserved the queen's trust and regard, and could wear her DASH order instead of hiding it away in shame. And she would know the Goddess as few others ever were able to.

"There is a chance," Lady Keating continued, "if the *draiocht* to help Niall is successful, that he might reform enough to—"

"No." Pen was surprised by her own decisiveness. "I won't do this hoping to fix Niall. I want to do this for me, and for the Goddess, and for you. Do you know what it means to me, knowing that you think I'm worthy and capable of being what you are?"

"My dear child, are you sure—"

"My sister is married, and my brother will be too when he is grown. I don't have to take that path if I don't want to. I want to stay here with you and follow the Goddess." She held very tight to Lady Keating's hand. This was it. This was what she wanted, and if she had to give up other dreams to get this one . . . well, life was like that. She would get over her dreams of a perfect, loving marriage with Niall. It wasn't like what Persy had with Lochinvar, because it was just that, a dream. A phantom with no substance. But to be the Goddess's servant and companion—*that* was real.

Lady Keating regarded her in silence for a moment, then smiled. "Then it will be so. Tomorrow night we will do both the *draiocht* and your dedication to the Goddess's service."

Pen's happiness clouded slightly. "What about Doireann? Will you tell her that she no longer—that I—"

Lady Keating rose. "Leave her to me. She will have to accept my decision. Now it is time for sleep. Tomorrow will be a very busy day." She leaned over Pen, adjusting pillows and tucking her in, then kissed her brow. "Sleep well, my daughter."

15

Clad only in a thin, white linen shift, Pen stood in the evening-dim entrance hall of Bandry Court with Lady Keating, waiting for Doireann to come down so they could walk out to the hill together. The stone floor of the hall was chill on Pen's bare feet, but she was past caring. Her excitement seemed to be enough to keep her warm right now.

Lady Keating wore a plain black robe, its hood hanging down her back. Her dark hair also fell unbound over her shoulders, and her pale face and restless green eyes were startling in the midst of all that blackness. The lamp on the sideboard near her, the only light in the room, cast eerie shadows over her narrow features. Tonight she would be the Crone; in this light, it seemed an appropriate role for her.

The door that led to the kitchens opened and Mrs. Tohill, the housekeeper, came in bearing a small tray on which was a pair of goblets. At Lady Keating's nod, she set it down on a sideboard, curtsied, and vanished back to the kitchens as quietly as she had appeared.

"Come, Penelope." Lady Keating had picked up the two goblets.

Now Pen saw that they were different, one made of silver and the other of gilt. She took the silver one that Lady Keating held out to her and peered into it questioningly.

"A little something to fortify you," Lady Keating said. "Drink, my dear." She lifted her own goblet and drank.

Something bracing would be helpful right now—Pen had spent the entire day feeling as if she were going to jump out of her skin with excitement. Not that it had been a particularly busy or bustling one; in fact, Pen had been alone for most of today, barely even seeing any servants about. Lady Keating had made a brief appearance at breakfast and suggested she spend her time before they left for the hill in rest and meditation.

"We will probably be up all night, and it is not at all unlikely that you will meet the Goddess herself this evening," she had explained. "She will want to look over her new acolyte. While it is a wonderful experience, it can also be an exhausting one, in all senses. Use today to prepare yourself however you see fit. I will be completing my preparations for this evening."

For the *draiocht*. Pen shivered and tried not to think of Niall. He was probably back in Cork by now, wreaking havoc among the young ladies of the town. "Is there anything I can do to help?"

"Thank you, but no. Believe me, you are helping more than you can know." Lady Keating had patted her shoulder and glided from the room.

Other things, small but noticeable, had added to the sense of difference and anticipation in the air. Instead of the hearty breakfast and elegant luncheon that Cook usually produced, all meals today had consisted of grains and eggs, prepared simply and washed down with cool water instead of tea and coffee or wine. Dinner was not served that evening; instead, Lady Keating had brought Pen to her own room, where a steaming tub waited, and directed her to bathe and wash herself thoroughly. There had been something in the water—salt and some crushed herbs—that made her skin tingle and glow . . . or was that just excitement again? Lady Keating had also given her a small flagon of scented oil to rub on her skin, and the plain shift that she wore now.

The silver goblet contained something cool and sweet. Pen sipped, then drank more deeply. "Mmm, it's lovely. What is it?"

"Mead, brewed from honey raised on my lands. Do you like it?"

Pen drank again. Cool and sweet, but heady too. Corkwobble would have approved. "From your lands here, or in *An Saol Eile*?"

Lady Keating laughed. "Clever girl! A little of both. I thought it an appropriate drink for tonight, since we will shortly have feet in both lands. To you, my new daughter." She raised her goblet in salute to Pen, then drained it.

"Thank you, Lady . . . Mother." Pen felt herself blush, but she raised her goblet in turn to Lady Keating then drank it down.

"Charming. No goblet for me? Dear, dear. If we're going to stand about all night toasting each other, let me run back to my room for my tooth glass."

Doireann stood halfway down the stairs, hands on hips, wearing an indecipherable expression. She looked like a column of flame in a dress of red silk that clung provocatively to her torso, then flared into deep folds below her hips. She was uncorseted like the rest of them, and Pen thought she could detect the faintest swelling in her abdomen and an unusual fullness in her breasts. She looked away, blushing again.

"How lovely that you could join us." Lady Keating matched

Doireann's ever-so-slightly mocking tone. "As we are all here, then let us go." She took Pen's goblet and set it back on the tray with her own.

Doireann said nothing in reply but continued down the stairs and past them to the door. Lady Keating shrugged and took Pen's arm, and they followed Doireann into the deep dusk.

The moon hung just over the eastern horizon, fat and yellow and already casting shadows. Fortunately, the night air was soft and mild on Pen's bare arms and legs; it almost seemed to caress her skin as they crossed the gravel drive—which in contrast to the air did not caress her bare feet—then waded into the grass of the lawn.

Stars began to wink into view in the sky. Pen marveled at them, holding tight to Lady Keating's arm. Only the brightest stars would be visible tonight as the moon rose; all others would be cast into invisibility by its silvery light. The dew had already begun to fall, and the grass was deliciously cool and wet underfoot, gently brushing her ankles as they walked. When was the last time she had gone barefoot out of doors? It must be years. From now on when she and Lady Keating went to the hill together, she would always leave her shoes behind . . . at least once they'd gotten past the drive. But even the bite of the gravel had its uses—it had made her appreciate the softness of the grass more. A rich scent of green growing things and damp earth drifted up, and she breathed it in, opening her mouth so that she could almost taste it.

"It's so beautiful here," she sighed. "I wish we could do this every night."

Lady Keating chuckled and squeezed her arm.

"No, really I do. I feel like I could just . . . just float up the hill and into the Goddess's arms and give her whatever she wants of me. . . ."

That sounded silly, she vaguely realized, but it was true. Where had this dreamy submissiveness come from? Had that mead been stronger than it tasted? Or was it something else? Somehow it felt right, though. Here she was, barefoot and clad only in the simplest of linen garb, on her way to a moonlit stone circle to summon a goddess. How else should she feel?

The moon was already higher as they ascended the hill to the circle, its yellow tinge fading to cool white. The great stones reflected its light, glittering like pillars of silver. As they stepped between two stones into the circle, Lady Keating released Pen's arm and stepped to one side, where a square of linen lay on the grass. She folded it back, and Pen saw that it covered objects that lay on another cloth below it: a broad silver dish. A decanter of water. A knife with a black handle. A long, slender sword. A coil of silk cord. A low, flat drum.

"No candles? Is there no fire in this spell?" she asked, leaning over the cloth curiously.

Lady Keating took the silver dish and placed it in the center of the circle, then poured the decanter of water into it. "No fire tonight," she said. "This spell uses only dark elements. Penelope, I want you to take the knife and gather up some dew from the grass where the moonlight touches it, then add it to the dish."

Pen nodded solemnly and did as she was asked, scraping the blade along the grass till it was covered in droplets, then swishing it through the bowl. Then Doireann took the knife from her and repeated the action, and lastly Lady Keating did as well. As the last droplets slipped from the blade into the water, Pen gasped. Had the water begun to glow, or was it just reflecting the moon's light?

"Full moon magic," she breathed.

Doireann glanced up at her, a curious expression on her face. "No, it's not. The full moon was last night. Tonight it has already begun to wane, of course."

"Hush, you two," Lady Keating commanded. She had replaced the knife on the cloth and taken up the silk cord and the sword. Doireann ambled over and picked up the drum.

Waning moon? Pen felt a brief surprise rise through her dreamy serenity, then sink back down into slumber. The ritual in the grimoire had specifically called for a full moon, but Lady Keating surely must know what she was doing. She waited by the silver moon-dish until Lady Keating and Doireann had joined her and placed the sword and the drum on the grass behind them.

Lady Keating lifted her hand. The coil of cord dangled from it. She stepped forward and looped it around Pen's waist. "Here is the Maiden," she murmured, then stooped and picked up the sword. "Penelope, give me your hand."

Pen held her hand out. Lady Keating took it firmly in hers and, before Pen could react, ran the heel of it across the sword's blade.

"Oh!" Pen gasped as a thread of pain ran up her arm. A thin line of blood welled up from the sword's cut. Lady Keating set down the sword and pressed Pen's hand to the cord until several inches of it were stained dark with her blood.

"Very good, my child." Lady Keating lifted her hand and blew gently across the cut. It vanished, though the pain lingered a few seconds longer.

She turned to Doireann and repeated the procedure, wrapping the cord around her in the Mother's name and marking it with her blood. When she had completed the same steps on herself, she brought the ends of the cord together and knotted them. "And here the Crone. Now we are complete and triple-bound: bound by our womanhood, bound by your image, and bound by blood." She smiled a small, private smile at Pen.

"Bound by blood?" Doireann's startled reaction could even be felt through the cord that tied them together. "But how—I thought that Niall—"

Lady Keating's lips tightened. She tugged gently on the blood-stained cord. "Bound by this," she said. "Now please stop interrupting."

Doireann stared at her for a moment, and even through her blanket of calm acceptance Pen felt how the air suddenly quivered with tension between them. Lady Keating returned her daughter's stare, her face expressionless, until Doireann looked down.

"Very well," Lady Keating said, exhaling. "May we proceed?"

Still looking at her bare feet, Doireann nodded.

Lady Keating held out her hands. "Tonight we will be raising a very large and very powerful circle, and adding to it the power we have already summoned and put in the stones. It will require your absolute concentration and your absolute obedience to my word if we want to avoid letting this power loose on the countryside. Do you understand me?"

Pen took her hand. "Yes."

"Good." Lady Keating smiled at her. "Tonight we will also begin a little differently." She took Doireann's hand—did Doireann seem to hesitate before letting her grasp it?—closed her eyes, and began a low, rhythmic chant.

"Hear me calling, O my Goddess, your handmaid calls unto you. Join us this night and bless our labors, smile on them and make them fruitful. Lend to us your limitless power so that we may succeed and know truly your gracious might. I, your handmaid, ask this of you.

Triple Goddess, threefold strong, as three we call out to you. Come to us, be in us, fill us with your glorious power."

Pen closed her eyes and relaxed into the slow cadence of her words, letting them hold her up like an invisible scaffold. There must have been something else in that mead, or perhaps it was just that it came from the fairy world, because she felt as if she were slipping into oblivion . . . or at least parts of her were—the outside parts, the mundane parts, the layers of Pen that knew how to make small talk with dowagers in ballrooms and how to order a proper dinner for twenty and how to write polite notes to hostesses after a party. What was left was the Pen who gloried in the night air on her bare arms, the Pen who had levitated with rapture during her visit to the stone circle, the Pen who could now sense the power humming in the stones around them, slumbering but slowly waking at Lady Keating's call—

"Penelope, my dearest child, will you begin the circle?" Lady Keating asked quietly.

Had her words been spoken aloud, or sounded only in Pen's mind?

Did it matter?

Pen took a deep breath, reached inside her as Lady Keating . . . as Mother had taught her, and lifted forth a circle of power, like a golden, glowing, perfect flower. She held it with her mind, stroking it, whispering to it, encouraging it, then released it to Doireann. As she did, she felt Lady Keating's hand tremble in hers and opened her eyes. Lady Keating was staring at her with an expression of fierce, burning joy, and Pen knew she was pleased.

After a while, she lost count of how many times they passed the circle among themselves, adding to it with each passage. More often than they had before, that was all she knew for sure. But somehow the weight and magnitude of it was no longer a burden; she felt as if she could stand here until they'd raised a circle large enough to cover all of county Cork, spitting gold and blue sparks and glowing like an aurora. The stones around them had given up their stored power to it as if it were a magnet, but Pen had begun to feel as if they too were passing and augmenting it, as well as containing it. Was that why it was less burdensome tonight? Did the stones support the circle so that the three of them could dedicate all their energy to increasing it?

"Enough," Lady Keating commanded. Pen felt her release the circle, felt it waver and then settle into the stones, waiting. She sighed and let her shoulders slump. No wonder Lady Keating had suggested she rest today; the stones might support the circle, but they didn't support her.

"Here. We have a moment before the moon is in position." Lady Keating was unstopping a silver flask. She held it out to Doireann, who refused it wordlessly, but Pen nodded and took it.

The flask contained more of the mead she had drunk before, honeyed and cool as she tipped it down her throat, and the tiredness she'd felt receded into calm. She blinked up at the sky as she drank; while she had been lost in the circle raising, the moon had risen until it was nearly overhead. It seemed to waver as she gazed at it, as if she were looking at it through water, and she realized that she was seeing it through the magic energy they had raised. "I can actually *see* our circle," she marveled to Doireann. "It looks like a veil, fluttering on a breeze."

Doireann didn't answer or even look up. Instead she bent and retrieved the drum that lay in the grass behind her and started to beat a rhythm on it with her fingers, two slow beats followed by three slightly more rapid ones: *thump, thump, thump-thump-thump; thump, thump, thump-thump-thump.* A shiver ran down Pen's spine, not of cold but of anticipation. The time had come. They were going to begin the *draiocht.*

Lady Keating handed her the silver sword. Pen held it tightly, tip pointing toward the moon as Lady Keating had directed her earlier that day.

"Your strength is the newest and freshest," she had said, holding Pen's hands and gazing into her eyes. "I will need you to bear the sword and focus into it the circle magic we have raised as I say the words of the *draiocht.* You will *become* the sword, my tool to carry out the *draiocht.* It will require your complete surrender to my will . . . no, to our will. Do you understand? It will be hard work, harder by far than raising the circle. When it is done, you will be empty and weak. But you will also be ready to accept and be accepted by the Goddess, who will be pleased by the offering of your power in the *draiocht* and will return it to you threefold. Then you will be hers."

Hers. Pen took a breath and relaxed into the beat of Doireann's drum just as she had relaxed into Lady Keating's chant. *Thump. Thump. Thump-thump-thump.* What a somber sound. It sounded more like a funeral march than a magical invocation. She felt a tugging on the cord that still bound them as Lady Keating shifted, spreading her feet slightly as if she prepared for some physical task. Then she raised her hands to the moon and spoke in a loud, commanding voice.

"Twice three years, and twice three years, and twice three years again, but no more will you have in the light of the sun. For now the gateway between the worlds is opening, and it opens for thee."

Twice three years again . . . that added up to eighteen. Eighteen years only in the light of the sun. What did that mean? But now was not the time to stop Lady Keating to ask questions.

"Go you quiet into the dark, where a gray hand will close your eyes and muffle your ears, so that you no longer hear and see the world of the living."

Pen stirred, even while carefully keeping the sword pointed properly at the moon. Lady Keating's words sounded as funereal as the drum did. How was this going to bring Niall and the Duke of Cumberland together?

"Penelope." It was quietly spoken, but Pen understood. She had given her word to obey Lady Keating. It was time to stop woolgathering and concentrate on bringing the power of their circle into the sword. She would pretend it was a sponge, thirsty for magic. The sword began to throb slightly in her hands, in time to Doireann's drumming.

Lady Keating was swaying, her hands delineating odd patterns in the air before her. "Now your steps falter, and your shoulders bow, and your face is turned toward the dark at the end of your journey. The Goddess awaits thee, and will take up your soul from your body so that you will sleep the dreamless sleep of death."

Death? A chill ran over Pen, this time born of cold. It felt as if the temperature around them had dropped twenty degrees. Even the sword suddenly felt icy in her hands as their circle power flowed into it, was sucked into it at a pace so rapid that she could hardly hold it. Lady Keating was shaping the magic with her words, shaping it into something cold and black and deadly. For the first time, Pen felt afraid. Something was happening here that she did not understand. Swords and darkness and death—

"It comes closer, ever closer, the silver sword that will cut the thread of your life, and you will bow to it, for it will not be turned aside."

Had Doireann begun to play more loudly, to match the growing volume of Lady Keating's voice? Or was it to compete with the rushing wind that had sprung up within the stones, born of the swirling power overhead? Pen's arms were shaking, but now it felt as if the sword had turned to ice and welded itself to her hands. The circle power still flowed into it, and now it felt as though a whirlwind hovered at the sword's point. The length of the blade glowed with a cold silver light.

"So I say this unto you: take Death's hand, and go with Death into the dark land. Leave you now this mortal coil and your earthly throne—"

Pen gaped at her. Your earthly throne? Had she heard Lady Keating correctly? "I don't think—" she tried to say through a mouth grown dry with shock. Her feeble protest was drowned out by a shout from somewhere outside the stone circle.

It hadn't been Doireann's drum that she had heard. It was the frantic beat of a horse's hooves as it pounded up the hill toward them.

"Pen!" Niall's voice shouted.

16

Lady Keating's hands fell to her sides. "Niall!"

Pen nearly cried out as well. Hadn't he gone back to Cork after their disastrous conversation the other night in her room? What was he doing, barging into a ritual like this?

Niall flung himself off his horse and darted between the stones toward them. The sight of the glowing sword in her hands stopped him for a second; she saw him look up at it in consternation, then shake himself and press forward, fists clenched.

"That's enough, Mother. Pen's not going to do any more of your work," he said in a low, steady voice. "I won't let her. She's coming with me back to—"

"No, she's not." Lady Keating's face looked pinched and angry. "Why didn't I just put you on a boat to London before I left Cork? I don't need you interfering right now, you foolish boy. You'll take your proper place as son of the king, like it or not!"

She swung one hand in a sweeping gesture. Niall staggered back as if blown by a wind, then toppled, striking the ground with a painfully loud thud. Beyond the circle she heard his horse whinny in terror and gallop off down the hill.

"Niall," Pen whispered as she stared at his unmoving form. Good God, was he all right? But the sword in her hands seemed to have pinned her to the ground so that she could not go to him.

Lady Keating turned back to them. "He'll be all right," she said quickly. "I just stunned him. The *draiocht* is nearly completed. Doireann, the drum! Penelope, my dearest one, when I say the word, point the sword to the east, and then we will be done."

Doireann resumed the somber *thump, thump, thump-thump-thump,* her mouth a thin line under hooded eyes. Pen looked from her to the glowing sword she still held aloft in aching arms, and then at Lady Keating.

"Take Death's hand. Leave your earthly throne. You'll take your place as son of the king . . . son of the king . . . the king."

Lady Keating's voice echoed in her head, then mixed with Niall's: *She needs your magic. . . . She's using you. . . .*

Niall hadn't been lying to her.

"Penelope?" Lady Keating called. "Are you ready?"

Pen took a deep breath. "No," she said.

"What is wrong? Was it Niall? I'm sorry he interrupted us. Do you need a moment to collect yourse—"

"I said no. I can't do this. I'm sorry."

Lady Keating looked at her. "My child," she said kindly. "We have come this far in the *draiocht,* and it must be completed. If Niall had not been stupid enough to interrupt us, we would have been done by now. We are all tired, but I know you are strong enough to finish. Now, then—*Hear me, O*—"

"You don't understand. I just can't do this. I didn't realize before how you'd planned to help Niall." She looked up at the sword again and shook her head. "I cannot harm the queen."

Lady Keating considered her. "Don't be foolish, Penelope. What could the queen's death matter to you? She's just a girl, as likely as not to die in childbirth in another few years once she marries, just as her cousin did. The Duke of Cumberland is a strong, healthy man, far more suited to wearing the crown. And might I also remind you, child, that you have given me your obedience? I offered to teach you the ways of the Goddess, and you consented. I asked for your help, and you said you would give it. I told you that tonight I required your complete surrender to my will, and you willingly surrendered it to me. Willingly."

Her voice was quiet and reasonable. Pen almost wished she would shout and rave at her instead. "I know I did. But I can't do this. The queen is my friend. My sister saved her from a magic attack last year, and I helped her. I helped save her once . . . and now I am bound to save her again."

Lady Keating had gone still. "Why didn't you tell me before?"

"Because . . . oh, because I was ashamed that I hadn't done more to help last year because I wasn't good enough. I don't like to remember when I was . . . when I was weak and ignorant. I didn't want you to know." The silver light of the sword grew hazy and indistinct for a moment, but she couldn't put it down to rub the tears from her eyes. Oh, this was hard, far worse than last year when she had refused to give Michael Carrighar her power. It had been easy to refuse the man who'd kidnapped Ally . . . but this was the woman she'd come to love and admire over the last months, the woman who had brought her to the Goddess and called her daughter.

Lady Keating was silent for a moment. "Penelope," she finally said, "that was another girl in London last year. It isn't who you are now. You, weak and ignorant? Not anymore. Look at yourself—

you're like the moon, fading all the stars around her into oblivion. Nor are you bound to that queen anymore—you've pledged your-self to the Goddess. She expects your service."

"What?" Doireann dropped her drum.

"I know I have." Pen stared up at the sword she still gripped. Her arms had mercifully gone numb, and it felt as if it were the sword that was holding her up and not the other way around. "I love the Goddess. But I love the queen too. Can I not serve both?"

"You, serve a mere mortal?" Lady Keating laughed and shook her head. "Penelope, my dearest Penelope, you are more queen than that chit on the throne could ever be. As a *Banmhaor Bande*, you will be a queen amongst witches—and, like me, the most pow-erful one."

"Mother, what are you saying?" Doireann asked in a low, danger-ous voice.

Lady Keating ignored her. "Ever since we met, I have marveled at how alike you and I are, even down to our names. Down to our very names, my dear! Could there have possibly been a clearer sign that we were meant to find each other? I look at you and I can see myself so clearly. I had that same hunger for power and mastery, to be the strongest and the best above all. When I look at you, it is like look-ing in a mirror."

Pen fought to close her eyes. Just what was it that Lady Keating saw inside her? Was that what she truly wanted, in her inmost heart? Absolute power? To be a queen among witches?

No, no! said a small, shocked voice inside her. She wasn't ambi-tious or power-hungry. Not at all.

Not ambitious? said another voice from even deeper within. So why had she come to Ireland to study magic, then? Why hadn't she been content to study with Persy back in England?

Because doing that would have been acknowledging that her sister was and always would be the better witch . . . and she couldn't do that. It had taken Persy saving them all last year to make her realize that she envied Persy's strength and wanted to prove her own magic to be as good . . . or better.

"I have watched you work hard here with me, and it has been like my past has come back to me." Lady Keating's voice was low and passionate. "Only now I can help make this new me even stronger and better. Can you imagine what we could accomplish together, you and I? With power like ours combined, we could own Ireland if we wanted to. If you stay here with me, you will become as great as I, perhaps greater someday. Don't you see that it's almost in your grasp? Help me now—give me your power for this *draiocht*."

Over by the edge of the circle, Niall groaned and stirred. Pen looked at him, and remembered their last encounter with a pang. "Niall," she half whispered.

A faint note of impatience crept into Lady Keating's voice. "You yourself said you don't need Niall. He belongs in London with his father. I suppose that if you wish to take him as a lover someday you could, but your fates lie on different paths. You shall be too busy learning how to be *Banmhaor Bande* after me to—"

"What!" Doireann shrieked and jerked against the cord that still bound them. "Mother, what have you done?"

"What do you think I did? Did you really believe that you were worthy to be the Goddess's lady after me? As a witch you are nothing compared to Penelope," Lady Keating said dismissively.

Doireann's eyes bulged as she sputtered, too angry to speak.

"Don't worry. Once Niall's established as the king's son, you'll still have your season in London and whatever husband you want . . . next year, after you've rid yourself of Lenehan's little bastard, of course. I will keep that promise to you. But as for being my heir—no. Penelope will wear my ring after me, not you. The Goddess will not accept an inferior servant." She turned her attention back to Pen.

Pen felt almost as shocked as Doireann obviously did. "But—"

"My daughter, it is time. When I say 'so be it,' you must complete the *draiocht*."

"Lady Keating—"

"I am your mother now, Penelope. Do as I say, and then you will have your reward." She stared hard at Pen, who found herself unable to look away.

Reward. All she had to do was keep her word and do Lady Keating's bidding. How hard would it be to bring down this sword, laden with dark power, and point it to the east, toward London, where a girl her own age probably lay asleep in her bed in Buckingham Palace? Victoria would never know what had happened. No pain, and no blood. One little sigh, and her breath would cease. It wasn't as if Pen would have to see it. So easy just to give in . . . and it wasn't even really her doing at all . . . and then she would join with her new mother, Lady Keating, and learn at her side until she took her place as *Banmhaor Bande* and became just like her. . . .

"No!" she cried in a loud voice, and brought her arms down. The glowing sword swept toward the ground. Its blade sliced through the cord between Doireann and Lady Keating, and the whole length of it vanished in a puff of gray smoke. Pen staggered back and, with the last of her strength, drove the blade straight into the ground.

"NO!" Lady Keating screamed as the silver light plunged deep into the damp earth. Through her bare feet, Pen could feel the circle magic roiling and surging through the soil, seeking outlet. The ground trembled, then shuddered like a horse shrugging off a stinging fly—a shudder that knocked them all to the ground. The water in the silver dish trembled, refracting the moonlight, then slopped over the sides. A low, growling, angry roar sounded from beneath their feet, growing louder as it rolled through the circle, and the entire hillside seemed to jerk and twist so sharply that Pen was sure the stones of the circle would come tumbling down on top of them or go rolling down the hillside. A scorched, sulfurous smell permeated the air.

Then all was still.

Pen lay where she had fallen, half on her side, one arm thrown across her face, and listened to the breeze that had sprung up whisper through the stones of the circle. It wasn't a very comfortable position to lie in, and the dew-laden grass had quickly saturated her short linen shift so that she had begun to shiver. Or was she shivering for some other reason?

But uncomfortable or not, soaked and shivering or not, lying here seemed the best thing to do . . . perhaps the only thing she was capable of doing right now. In a few minutes, when she felt less stunned and shaken, she'd drag herself down the hill to the house, get dressed, and pack her trunk. She had intentionally broken the circle and released a vast amount of unfocused magic. Presumably

Lady Keating would want her out of the house as soon as possible. She'd go back to Cork and keep studying with Dr. Carrighar, enduring Eamon Doherty's disdainful sneers. She'd made her choice, and this was the result. She'd kept her word to serve the queen and broken her word to Lady Keating.

And to the Goddess.

That thought made her groan and struggle to her hands and knees. She needed to get out of this circle and off the hillside, for surely the Goddess would be angry with her and find her presence here abhorrent.

"I'm sorry," she whispered, sitting back on her haunches in order to rub the tears from her eyes. "I'm so sorry."

"Are you? Perhaps so, but not half as sorry as I am." A voice came from somewhere above her. It was quiet and deadly cold.

Pen looked up. Doireann still lay sprawled on the grass to her right, but Lady Keating had regained her feet and stood over her. Her dark robe and hair were shadowed and indistinct; only her white face was clearly visible in the moonlight. That, and the sword she held in both hands, its point aimed at Pen's breast.

"You betrayed us," she said, still quietly. "You betrayed *me*, daughter. Or should I say, daughter-no-more? It seems I'm doomed to be betrayed by all my children."

"I'm sorry, Lady Keating. You were wrong about me. I just couldn't do it. I—I'll go now." Pen pressed her lips together to keep from sobbing aloud. The least she could do was hang on to her dignity. She clambered awkwardly to her feet, wincing. Everything, from her feet to her scalp, felt battered and sore.

"Yes, you'll go," Lady Keating agreed in that soft, dangerous voice.

She let go of the sword with one hand and made a gesture, and Pen felt herself freeze in place, stiff and statuelike. But unlike a statue, she could feel the point of the sword press against the hollow of her throat, just hard enough to pierce the delicate skin there. A small trickle of warmth ran down her chest.

Lady Keating watched it dispassionately. "The Goddess's vengeance is swift. Some might call it merciful, even, but you'll not have much time to ponder that. You brought it upon yourself, though, you stupid girl. How I wish I had been right about you. Now all I can do is mourn the waste."

Pen's thoughts seemed to move at both lightning speed and at a snail's pace. She was about to die, and there was nothing she could do to save herself. All she could do was stand unmoving and be executed like a criminal. She searched frantically through her mind for some release spell, but nothing would come—only useless fragments, like shards of sparkling broken glass.

Lady Keating adjusted her stance and changed her grip on the sword, and Pen knew she was about to shove it deep into her throat. Would death come quickly, or would she have time to crumple to the ground and stare up at the moon with glazing eyes, thinking her good-byes to everyone she loved as her life's blood spurted from her throat into the cool, wet grass? Good-bye to Mama and Papa, and Charles and Ally . . . she'd never see Ally's baby now . . . good-bye to Lochinvar and Persy, her dearest, dearest other self . . . and to Niall—

"No!"

A sharp pain at her throat brought her back, along with another trickle of warmth, and she opened her eyes.

Doireann, her red dress dark maroon in the moonlight, was

grappling with Lady Keating, trying to wrest the sword from her. "No, Mother," she panted. "You're not going to kill anyone. There's been enough of that for one night."

Lady Keating bared her teeth as she struggled to wrest her arm from Doireann's grasp. "Get away from me, traitor!"

Doireann laughed, a strange, high thin sound. "Traitor? Me? I don't think so. You're the one who went back on your promises to me. If I can't have what I want, neither can you." She braced herself and yanked her mother by the arm, swinging her in a half circle, then let go. The momentum carried Lady Keating sideways toward the edge of the circle before she lost her balance altogether. There was a sickening thump as her head struck one of the stones and she lay without moving.

Pen was not sure how long she and Doireann stood there, breathing hard and staring at Lady Keating's inert form. Nor was she even sure if she could move, though she had felt Lady Keating's immobilizing spell disperse seconds after she fell. In the end, it was Doireann who broke the silence.

"Are you all right?" she asked.

Pen swallowed hard, trying not to think of what her throat might have looked like just now if Doireann hadn't saved her. "Yes, I . . . mostly. Doireann . . ." She took a few tottering steps toward her.

But Doireann backed away from her, shaking her head. "Get away from me. I didn't do it for you, so don't thank me." She walked over to her mother and bent over her. "Still alive. I suggest we both get the hell out of here before she wakes up."

Pen stared at her and felt as if the immobilizing spell were back on her. "I . . . but . . ."

Doireann shook back her dark hair, so like Lady Keating's, muttered something under her breath, then gave a piercing whistle. "Mother took away what I wanted. You took away what she wanted. I owed you for it." She whistled again, then stood, head cocked, as if listening. "But mostly I did it because of Niall. He's the only one who's ever cared about what *I* want. You were quite ready to step into my shoes as the next *Banmhaor Bande,* and for that I should have let Mother kill you. But Niall loves you."

A thudding sound below the hillside could now be heard, and a faint, inquiring whinny. Niall's horse, Pen guessed.

Doireann smiled sardonically. "Well, I'll never be *Banmhaor Bande* now, but I can still do a damned good summoning spell. Good-bye, Miss Leland. Goddess willing, we'll never meet again."

Pen found her voice. "Where are you going?" she rasped through a throat thickened with tears.

"I don't know. Brian and I hadn't decided that yet, but it seems our running-away plans will be unexpectedly moving up. Nowhere in Ireland, that's for sure. There's nothing here for a dispossessed daughter and a second son." She turned away from Pen then paused, her back to her. "Say good-bye to Niall for me. Remind him I promised that everything would work out in the end. Oh, and enjoy the rest of your stay at Bandry Court." She laughed as she ran past the stones and down the hillside. A moment later, the steady *thud-a-thud* of cantering hoofbeats retreated into the night.

17

Another eternity seemed to go by while Pen stood with bowed head in the center of the circle, feeling drained of everything—emotion, strength, the will to even sit down until her shaking stopped. The moon still shone overhead but it had begun its descent to the west. When the sun finally crept over the horizon, she would probably still be here, unsure of what to do next.

It was the breeze that had sprung up earlier that finally roused her from her apathy, or rather the scent it carried—that of burning pitch, like a torch. She raised her head and sniffed the air. Was someone out there?

Then she saw them. Two figures were slowly ascending the hill in a circle of golden light. The taller one wore a red dress, much like the one Doireann had worn tonight. It clung to her lush breasts and swaying hips. In one hand she held a burning torch, and with the other she was solicitously helping her smaller, black-robed companion climb the hillside.

A faint hint of something—recognition?—stirred Pen's numbness. She watched the pair finish their climb and slip between two stones, watched as they glanced at the still form of Niall in the grass, then bent for a moment over Lady Keating. Pen thought they did something to her, for there was a flash of white light over her that quickly faded away. But it could just as easily have been a flicker of the torch.

They finally came to a halt a few feet from her.

"Hail to you, daughter," said the smaller figure. She put back the hood of her robe so that Pen could see her beautiful, lined face and silver hair.

"Hail, indeed," said the tall, red-clad woman. Her mouth curved in a smile, and her face was strong and young and handsome.

Pen stared at them, and the numbness that shrouded her receded just a little bit. She wasn't sure she wanted it to, because then she would start to feel again—guilt, and loss, and shame. "Are you who I think you are?" she finally said, and immediately wished she hadn't. It had sounded beyond idiotic.

But the women only laughed gently. "You know who we are," said the younger one. "And we know who you are. We've been watching you with considerable interest, Penelope."

It would have been nice, about then, if the earth had kindly opened up and swallowed Pen on the spot, but to her dismay it didn't. "I . . . I was just going," she said. "I know I don't belong here on your hill—"

"Not belong here?" said the Crone, looking mildly perplexed but still smiling. "What gives you that idea?"

No. She couldn't explain it all. Not so soon. It hurt too much. "Because I . . . don't."

"Oh, my child, if anyone belongs on this hill with us just now, it's you." The Mother's voice was warm and gentle, like a soft blanket on her shivering heart.

Pen looked at her and the numbness slipped again, enough to allow the frozen tears inside her to flow—but this time, her tears were cleansing, not bitter.

"But I failed you. I don't understand," she whispered.

"Listen to me, my daughter. You did not fail. Your power is very great, and Nuala Keating was tempted by it to do evil to get her own desires. She in turn tempted you—but she failed. You knew what she wanted was wrong, and you refused to use your power to bring untimely death to an innocent girl. You did not break your word to your queen, or to yourself, or to us," said the Mother.

"Instead, by your choice you kept your word and proved yourself worthy of us." The Crone nodded as she spoke. "Give me your hand, my child."

Pen held out her right hand, trembling slightly, and the Crone took it in both of hers. She felt something cool and heavy slide over her ring finger.

"Nuala Keating is no longer acceptable to us as *Banmhaor Bande*," the Mother said, and there was sorrow in her voice. "She served us long, and because of that we took her memory and her authority, but not her life. She will spend the rest of her allotted days as a child would, living in the moment and unable to harm anyone, including herself."

"Which means someone else must take her place as *Banmhaor Bande*," the Crone said. "We thought, perhaps, since you're here . . ." Her eyes twinkled mischievously at Pen.

"And since you are full worthy," the Mother added, smiling.

Pen looked down at her hand, resting in the Crone's. Lady Keating's green and silver ring glittered on it in the torchlight. A huge bubble of surprised joy threatened to choke her. "You're choosing me? To be *Banmhaor Bande?*"

"Whom better might we choose?" inquired the Crone, that mischievous twinkle brighter than ever.

"It's just that I thought . . . are you sure? I'm not really of Lady Keating's family, for one thing."

"You can't convince us out of it, child, so don't try. She made you her heir, did she not? We are pleased to accept you as such. And you may find that you'll soon be more closely related to her than you are now." The Mother leaned forward and took her left hand. "Welcome, Penelope. We take you as our own."

The Crone still held fast to her right hand. "Come, Maiden, our *Banmhaor Bande.* Join with us. Let us be complete." She glanced at the Mother and held out her hand.

Where had the torch gone? Just a second ago, the Mother had still been holding it high to illuminate them, but now it had vanished as she reached out and took the Crone's gnarled hand in her own. But the torch was no longer necessary. As the two joined hands, completing their circle, a brilliant light seemed to be everywhere around them.

No, it *was* them.

Pen looked at the two women who stood with her and felt the connection between them all, a circle that was ever unbroken. *As I am now, they once were. As they are now, so will I be. As I am now, so will they be again.* Changing and unchanging. Different and the same. Eternal and complete. Strength and wisdom and power flowed among them like a circular river, and Pen both laughed and ached with the perfect beauty of it. She had thought earlier that the circle she'd raised with Doireann and Lady Keating could have illuminated all of Cork. This circle could have lit all Ireland.

How long did they stand there, the Goddess, full and complete? Afterward Pen was never sure; what was a measure of time in the face of forever? But all at once she realized that they were separate once more, the Mother and the Crone and her, for a few eternal seconds, the Maiden that completed Them.

"Oh," she said, looking down sorrowfully at her empty hands, resting by her sides.

"Do you think you will ever be apart from us, in your heart?" The Mother smiled, again holding the torch above her head.

"No, I don't think I will," Pen replied slowly. "But that was . . . well . . . perfect. Complete. What magic will I know that could ever be greater than that?"

"Daughter." The Crone's eyes still twinkled, but her voice was gentle and serious. "We are but one part of magic, one part of life. Remember that magic is male and female, and that life is a cycle. Would you restrict yourself to be the Maiden forever and not move on to the rest of magic and life?" She took Pen's arm and, pulling her down, kissed her. "We will always be near. Don't forget that you serve us now. We shall expect to see you very shortly. Very shortly."

The Mother bent and kissed Pen as well. "Fare you well, daughter, until we meet again." She turned away and held her arm out to the Crone, who took it with a nod. Then, slowly, without looking back, they crossed the circle close to where Niall still lay. The Mother paused and held the torch while the Crone leaned over and touched his forehead, and then they slipped past the stones. Pen watched as they descended the hill, the torch in the Mother's hand flickering in the wind. She blinked, and they were gone.

Was it the throbbing pain in his head or the pins-and-needles ache in the arm pinned beneath him that woke him? Niall groaned and shifted off his arm, then groaned again as the blood started to flow painfully back into it. Damn it, the landlord at the Three Ladies needed to do something about the accursed mattresses in his rooms—

"Don't move till I've had a chance to look at your head," commanded a soft voice. It was accompanied by a pressure on his chest, as if someone were holding him down. "I don't think you hit it on the stones. Not like . . ." The voice trailed into silence.

He opened his eyes and tried to focus on the source of the voice, but they weren't working right. All he could see was a blaze of silver light crowning a figure bent over him . . . or did the light shine from the figure itself?

"Can you hear me?" He felt gentle fingers stroke his forehead, brushing back his hair, then trace the contours of one cheek. "Thank goodness you aren't wearing that horripilatious hat again tonight or I would have stomped on it."

That horripilatious . . . "Pen?" he whispered, and blinked furiously.

Her face finally swam into focus, but it didn't help. For some reason, her face, her hair, her bare shoulders—good lord, what was she wearing?—all seemed too bright for him to look upon. He tried squinting, which helped a little.

"Oh, good, you are awake." She sat back, sounding relieved. Niall wished she'd start stroking his face again. It had felt almost as if she cared about him again.

"Do you think you can make it back to the house on foot in a little while?" she asked him. "I'm afraid Doireann took your horse. If not, I could do a carry spell to get you home. It might be tricky since you're awake, but it worked on Lady Keating."

"Pen?" he said again. What was she talking about—his horse, and Doireann, and Mother—

Memory came crashing over him then like a storm wave. Mother's ritual to kill the queen, and Pen standing there looking like a *Sidhe* princess, bare-armed and -legged, holding a glowing sword over her head. "What happened?" he said, trying to sit up.

She pushed him back down again. "Nothing did. Well, not nothing. But the queen is safe."

There was something in her voice, both great sorrow and great joy. "And?" he asked. "Why are you glowing, anyway? Did you paint yourself with phosphor?"

Pen held up a hand and surveyed it. "Am I glowing? Oh, dear. So that's why Mrs. Tohill and the footwomen looked so startled. Odd that it doesn't look any different to me."

The physical ache in his head was rapidly being replaced by a mental one. "Pen, what the devil happened?"

She sighed. "I owe you an apology, Mr. Keating. You were right about the danger to the queen, but fortunately it was averted."

"That sword you were holding, was that it? How did you—"

Pen didn't seem to hear him. "And I'm afraid your sister has run away with someone named Brian, and your mother—" Her voice caught. "Your mother has sustained a serious head injury. She will survive, but her memory has been . . . altered. She won't remember anything about the queen and the duke and what she'd tried to do. And I fear she'll require care from now on."

Niall tried to absorb all this information, but instead found himself mostly preoccupied with wondering what the fact that she had called him Mr. Keating meant. Then the rest of her words sank in. "Mother's memory—how do you know that?" he asked. Did this mean she wouldn't remember any of this—the plots, the lies—

"I know," Pen replied quietly, and he saw her glance down at her right hand. Mother's ring was on it. For a moment he stared at it too.

"Mother's no longer *Banmhaor Bande,* and you are," he said slowly. "That's why she's lost her memory. You saw the Goddess, didn't you? That's why you look so . . . so . . ." What did she look like? It was hard to see her expression by the waning moonlight and by her own mysterious glow, but there was something different in the set of her shoulders, in the way she held herself. Something more assured, more confident, but at the same time more quiet and self-contained.

Well, that would explain the Mr. Keating business. If she was now *Banmhaor Bande* in Mother's place, she was one of the most powerful witches in Ireland. What did she need him for, tagging along after her?

He struggled to sit up. Right now all he wanted to do was find a quiet dark room to hide in till he could come to terms with everything that had happened. If he was lucky, he would have sorted it out by, oh, Michaelmas perhaps. Michaelmas of next year. Except for losing Pen. He wasn't sure he'd ever recover from that.

"What are you doing, Mr. Keating?" Pen pushed him back down. "You've gone quite pale again. I don't think we'd better risk your trying to walk back to the house, after all."

"I'll be fine," he muttered.

She leaned over him and ran her fingertips over his forehead, a small frown of concentration on her face. He wasn't sure whether to beg her to stop or to do it again and again.

"I could try to do something about your head before I bring you back to the house, if you'd like," she said. "It's hurting you, isn't it? Stunning spells can do that."

"You mean, heal it? Like you did for Doherty?"

She smiled but would not meet his eyes. "If it wouldn't bother you too much. After all, Eamon Doherty survived my ministrations and he disliked me, too. Perhaps it's my fate in life to heal people who'd rather I didn't. Here, let's turn you a little so that I can see—"

"It's not my head that's hurting the most right now," he said, struggling to keep his voice steady as hope suddenly flared up. She thought he disliked her? Was *that* why she was calling him Mr. Keating?

"No? That's very odd." Her fingers fluttered over his forehead again. "I can feel it here, and here—"

He reached up and gently clasped her hand, then guided it down to rest against the left side of his chest. "*This* is what's hurting me the most right now. And if there's anyone on earth with the power to mend it, it's you."

Still as one of the stones, she knelt there, staring at her hand pressed against his heart.

"Pen?" he inquired.

"I said horrible, horrible things to you the other night," she whispered. "I believed all those dreadful lies Lady Keating told me about you. How can you still—"

"I'm not going to get into a 'who was worse to whom' contest with you. All that's in the past now. The only horrible thing I can imagine is a future without you in it. I love you, Pen. I know you're the Goddess's lady now and you probably don't need me."

"Not need you?" she interrupted. "But—"

"But I had already written to both our fathers about asking you

to marry me the night after the Whelans' ball, and it might be difficult to explain why that might not happen—"

He never got to finish the sentence. Suddenly an armful of Pen
was upon him, pressing the air out of his lungs with the force of her
embrace, not to mention preventing any further words by the
simple expedient of covering his mouth with hers. Cooperation
seemed inevitable, and then vital.

"Well, that was quite effective." He grinned up at her when she
finally came up for air. "The heartache's definitely cured, and after
that kiss, I'm not even noticing the headache. A few more of those
and I'll be ready to take on the world."

Pen laughed and shook her head, then pressed her fingertips
against his forehead again. The pain vanished. "You'll have to take
on the world, headache or not, and so will I," she said, climbing to
her feet and holding out her hand to help him up. "Beginning right
now. You must make at least a token attempt to find Doireann, and
decide how your mother will be cared for."

He accepted her hand and scrambled to his feet. "I know I must.
But first I need to find out if you'll be willing to do all that taking on
of the world with me beside you."

She looked up at him and then away, her unbound hair blowing
over her bare shoulders, and he realized she was wearing little more
than a shift. But she didn't seem at all cold. Maybe that glow that still
lingered around her kept her warm.

Then suddenly she laughed. "I suppose *that* is our answer." She
held up her right hand, the one bearing his mother's ring. The stone
in it was glowing bright green. "If the Goddess approves of my
marrying you, who am I to say no?"

18

"A special courier has just arrived with letters for you, sir . . . er . . . madam. . . ." Moylan, Lord Keating's butler, standing in the doorway of the library, turned a violent shade of red and averted his eyes.

Pen tried not to giggle as she straightened her dress and slid off Niall's lap and onto the sofa beside him. Poor Moylan. This was the third time he'd walked in on them kissing since they'd arrived at Loughglass to visit Lord Keating on Sunday, and today was only Tuesday. Well, goodness, she and Niall had been married a mere six months, after all. Maybe in another five or ten years they'd be able to behave decorously when alone in a room together. Until then . . .

"Special courier?" Niall raised an eyebrow and held out his hand. Moylan shuffled reluctantly into the room and proffered a silver tray with two cream-colored envelopes on it. Pen caught a glimpse of a large crest on the topmost one as Niall took them. "Thank you, Moylan."

"Sir. Madam." The butler, still blushing bowed and fled.

Pen patted her hair to see how badly Niall had disarranged it.

"Perhaps we need to be a little more careful. I should be mortified if he complained to your father about us."

"If he did, Father wouldn't care. You've bewitched him quite as thoroughly as you have me." Niall put the letters down and gathered her into his arms. "And both of us are delighted."

"Hmmph." But Pen couldn't help being pleased—not to mention relieved—at how life had resolved itself since the spring. Well, *mostly* pleased.

She had left Bandry Court almost immediately after breakfast the morning after the *draiocht*. Niall had to reassure the staff and arrange for Lady Keating's care, as well as attempt to find out where Doireann had gone, and it was not possible for her to stay at the house with him without a chaperone. A grim-faced though polite Padraic drove her back to the city, and she spent the long drive dozing after her mostly sleepless night and drifting into snatches of nightmare. Fortunately, the roads were still in poor repair after the rain, and she was frequently jarred awake.

Another carriage was just pulling up to the Carrighars' house as she arrived in Cork. To her surprise, a very familiar-looking slender woman with exquisite posture alighted from it, followed by a plump, sour-faced woman who looked about her fearfully as if expecting an attack. Pen didn't wait for anyone to open the door for her, but jumped out of the Keatings' carriage as soon as it had come to a stop.

"Grandmama?" she called. "Is that you?"

The slender woman turned. "Penelope, my dear! What perfect timing! Have you been making calls?"

Pen hugged her right there in the street, which made the other woman sniff disapprovingly. Pen ignored her; Lady Harrow, Grandmama's constant companion, didn't approve of much. "Grandmama, I'm delighted to see you," she said, slightly breathlessly, "but . . . well, what are you doing here?"

The dowager Lady Atherston looked past Pen at the Keatings' carriage, from which Padraic was unloading her trunk. "Hmm, I see you've been away. Well, child, I'm here because I've been sent by your parents to vet a certain young man of this city who sent them an earnest if slightly incoherent letter requesting formal permission to pay his addresses to you," she announced.

"I'm not sure I would have called it *slightly* incoherent," Lady Harrow put in.

"Nobody asked your opinion, Jane dear. *I* thought it was charming. Your sister thought it was serious enough to warrant investigation, but your father is caught up in the queen's coronation. So I volunteered to come and investigate, since I've always wanted to visit Ireland. Now, some tea would be welcome just now—"

"They *do* have tea in Ireland, don't they?" Lady Harrow asked suspiciously.

"The crossing didn't agree with her," Grandmama murmured, taking Pen's arm. "Just ignore her. My goodness." She examined Pen's face. "You've grown up a great deal since you came here. You're quite the lady now, aren't you?"

"Yes, Gran." Pen smiled to herself. "Yes, I am."

Lady Atherston set about examining both Niall's credentials and the city of Cork with her customary energy. When Niall returned to Cork a few days later, she subjected him to a thorough examination over a two-and-a-half-hour-long tea, and even managed to arrange an invitation to Loughglass to meet Lord Keating. But what delighted Pen most of all was the fact that Grandmama's constant companion on her jaunts around the city was Dr. Carrighar. Pen and Ally frequently wished they could have been stowaways in the Carrighars' carriage in order to eavesdrop on the unlikely combination of the lively if acerbic Lady Atherston, the gloomy Lady Harrow, and Dr. Carrighar, who defied easy description. Indeed, Dr. Carrighar went so far as to order a new coat and trousers in the current style. Pen wondered if Mary Margaret was watching and enjoying the sight of everyone "getting stirred up."

Corkwobble had been supplying Ally with a concoction to help assuage her nausea, and it made her far less sleepy than Lady Keating's fairy whiskey had. He had also set Pen's mind to rest: Neither Ally nor her baby had been harmed, thank goodness. "Though I wouldn't be surprised if the babe doesn't find herself more easy with the fairy world than a *bean draoi* usually is as a result—present company excluded, o' course," he added, winking.

Ally was equally relieved. "I should hope that Lady Keating merely wanted me so sleepy and lethargic that I could no longer watch over you," she observed to Pen. "It quite neatly prevented me from noticing how she was drawing you away from us and into her power. My poor girl, I let you down, didn't I?"

Pen took her hand. "Not at all. I let myself be drawn away. And anyway, I'm going to be replaced shortly, aren't I?" She gestured toward Ally's growing bulk.

"And so am I." Ally smiled and turned Pen's left hand over, where a gold band set with sapphires sparkled. "You have two new allegiances now," she said, taking Pen's other hand, with the Goddess's ring. "I hope you won't forget your old ones in the excitement of the new."

"No danger of that. I've got a goddaughter coming soon to remind me of the dear old ones." Pen leaned over and gently hugged her.

Pen returned home in early June, just in time for the queen's splendid coronation in London, then concentrated on preparing for her August wedding, which Niall came for alone, as neither of his parents were able to travel and Doireann was still unfound. Lady Keating remained at Bandry Court, still imperious but childlike and docile, with no memory of the duke or of the plot to kill the queen or even of her past role as the Goddess's lady, though she still never touched the teapot when pouring her tea. Fortunately, Mrs. Tohill had a sister who had previously cared for a feeble, elderly lady, and she had accepted the position as Lady Keating's nurse.

It was wonderful to have Persy and the rest of her family meet her dearest Niall. Charles seemed slightly dubious about him when he learned that Niall had earned a first in history, his current bane at Eton, but forgave him when Niall asked him to stand as his grooms-man at the wedding.

"Of course I will. I did for Lochinvar last year, so I know all about it," Charles told him proudly, then deflated. "Except I'll have to go to the tailor and get measured for s'more swell togs because I've grown four inches since last fall. Horripilatious, isn't it?"

Persy groaned. "If you don't stop using that word, Chuckles, I'll cast a forgetting spell on you and make you stop."

After the wedding, Pen and Niall honeymooned at Loughglass, then were back in Cork in time for the birth of Ally's daughter on October 7—precisely when Corkwobble had said she would be born—and then to Bandry Court for Samhain, for it was time for Pen to see the Goddess. It wasn't easy at first to return there. But it was while they were there that they received a letter from Doireann. She and Brian Lenehan had fled to Dublin and married there, then taken ship for India. Niall sent her dowry and an offer to return home, but she refused. Brian had already arranged to take a position with the East India Company before their elopement, and they had settled happily in Calcutta—or as happily as Doireann could ever do anything.

Niall and Pen had decided to spend some months at Lough-glass so that Niall could get to know his father better and begin to take over management of the estate, with occasional visits to Bandry Court to check on Lady Keating and into Cork to visit Ally and the Carrighars and Corkwobble. Pen was happy enough; she liked Lord Keating, who enjoyed nothing so much as having her nearby while he read or tended the orchids and orange trees in his glass conservatory. But she sensed a restlessness in Niall that riding around the estate with the steward and inspecting fields and live-stock couldn't satisfy. When she asked him about it, he denied it, then sighed.

"I'd be happy to be lord of the manor for part of the time, or later, when we have a family," he said, staring up at the brocade canopy of their bed. "But right now Loughglass is still Papa's house, and despite Mother's condition, Bandry Court is still hers. I'd like to have something that's my own—"

"And what am I?" Pen demanded, indignantly bouncing onto his stomach.

The rest of the conversation degenerated into a mock wrestling match, but it had made Pen think. Perhaps they might travel for a few months. Niall could show her the places he'd visited on his Euro-pean tour, and they could be silly and romantic in Paris, or Venice . . . and maybe visit Hanover while they were there? She wondered if a part of Niall's restlessness wasn't over the one bit of unresolved business in his life: meeting the duke. After all, Lady

Keating had held the image of his real father over him for the last ten years. Surely he couldn't put it out of his mind now without wondering what the man was like . . . well, maybe in the spring. But she should really broach the topic now so that they could prepare.

In the meanwhile, she leaned over Niall's arm to peer at the forgotten letters on the sofa beside them. "Heavens, are those what I think they are?"

"Do you find the mail more interesting than me?" Niall's face was muffled in her neck.

"No. I just don't want to give Moylan apoplexy if he comes back in." She picked up the letters and looked at them more closely. "Of course, if you'd rather not read a letter from Her Majesty—"

"What?" That got Niall's attention.

"One for you and one for me." She handed him his envelope, then turned hers over. "Oh, mine's marked 'Private and Personal.'" She slid off his lap and unsealed the letter.

31 January 1839

To the Hon. Mrs. Niall Keating
Loughglass House
Cty. Cork, Ireland

My dear Pen,
You must forgive me for not having written sooner. So many
necessary but alas <u>trying</u> duties and obligations clamor for my
attention that my personal correspondence must needs be
attended to last, but I was quite determined to write you once
and for all! I must wish you a very happy New Year, the first

full one of your married life. Such a strange and wonderful thing it must be to be a married woman—I confess I wonder what it will be like to be so myself someday, and I hope and pray I shall find myself a husband I love and respect as well as you do your dear Mr. Keating.

It is of Mr. Keating, in fact, that I would like to devote a portion of this letter. When she visited me just before Christmas, your dear sister (we had such a lovely afternoon together—*dear* Lehzen made sure we were quite undisturbed while we had an "official" meeting of that most high and puissant order of , DASH accompanied by much mirth—though we sorely missed your presence there!) in between our bouts of laughter told me in great detail just what happened to you in Ireland last spring, and how you once more rescued me unaware from a most hideous peril. I assure you, I was appalled to hear what danger you endured to guard my life, and what danger too Mr. Keating faced. I am now doubly indebted to my dear Leland sisters, and can only thank our Heavenly Father for such dear, loyal friends as yourselves. Powerful friends, too, it would seem—for Persy made it clear that your own most extraordinary magical abilities have drawn the attention and approbation of very high powers. She was impressed, indeed, as am I.

Pen looked up from the letter and blinked back tears. She had never expected that the queen would know of what she had done—certainly telling her about it herself had never entered her mind. And Persy had called her magic most extraordinary—*Persy*. She went back to her letter, trying not to sniffle.

However, in your case I understand that I may address you not only as friend, but as <u>cousin</u>. Dear Persy acquainted me too with the fascinating (if shocking) story of your dear husband's birth. I am most sorry that I cannot, of course, publicly acknowledge our connection, but I will always <u>think</u> warmly of you as family and look forward to meeting my cousin Mr. Keating someday soon.

It has puzzled me, since then, to think of something I might do for the both of you to demonstrate my deepest gratitude without, of course, drawing the attention of the world at large. But I flatter myself that I have thought of a possible gift, if Mr. Keating chooses to accept it, and my good Lord Melbourne has approved it and made all the necessary arrangements with the Foreign Office. If he does not, I shall understand perfectly. If he does, however, I will wish you now a fair and safe journey, and enjoin you to write me often and tell me <u>everything</u>, as both a friend and cousin and as one of my stalwart ladies of DASH.

Yr. <u>most</u> affectionate cousin and friend,
VICTORIA R

Pen read her letter twice, then turned to Niall. He was staring at the letter in his hands as if he could not quite believe what it contained.

"Well? What is it?" But she had already guessed.

"I don't know what to say," he murmured.

Pen extracted the letter from his unresisting fingers. "*Six-month position, with option to extend on your or the ambassador's request . . . ,*" she read aloud, skimming, "*special attaché to Her Majesty's embassy to the court of Hanover . . . to aid in maintaining the strong bond between the two countries, based as they are on long association and family ties. . . .*" She looked up at him. "The duke," she said softly.

"The duke," he echoed. "This means . . . I could meet him on *my* terms."

"Your terms?"

Niall's eyes were shining, either with happiness or unshed tears, or perhaps both. "I'd have my own position and purpose and reason for being there. I won't have to meet him as a supplicant, the way I would have under Mother's scheme. We can both decide if we want to acknowledge each other, if only in private—"

He dropped the letter and buried his face in her shoulder. Pen held him tightly and stroked his thick, gold hair. It would be exciting to travel and see more of the world, and to meet the duke—or king, as he was in Hanover—and see how much of him there was in Niall. She would miss Ireland, but they would return home soon.

She kissed Niall's head and then smiled to herself as she looked hard at the door into the room. The door, slightly ajar, shut itself, and the bolt slid home with a sharp snap. Niall raised his head and looked around, then at her.

"Just a precaution," she explained, taking his face in her hands. "We don't want to shock poor Moylan again, do we?"